Annie watched her husband covertly as he shivered and huddled down next to her under the rug. In the icy church he had gone quite pale, his lips almost bloodless, so that he seemed a man carved from stone, like the marble crusader she had once seen in a church in Brighton. She held his hand under the rug and nestled against him, hoping the warmth of her body would help. But he still looked white and chilled when they reached Darrington Hall, which was a short distance out of Bilsden on the edge of the moors, beyond their own house, which itself lay nearly at the top of Ridge Hill.

Also by Anna Jacobs

Salem Street
High Street
Ridge Hill

Hallam Square

Anna Jacobs

CORONET BOOKS
Hodder and Stoughton

First published in Great Britain in 1996 by Hodder and Stoughton
First published in paperback in 1996 by Hodder & Stoughton
A division of Hodder Headline PLC

A Coronet Paperback

10 9 8 7 6 5 4 3 2

A CIP catalogue record for this title is available from the British Library

ISBN 0 340 65377 9

Typeset by Avon Dataset Ltd, Bidford-on-Avon, Warks

Printed and bound in Great Britain by
Cox & Wyman, Reading, Berks

Hodder and Stoughton
A division of Hodder Headline PLC
338 Euston Road
London NW1 3BH

To my agent, Bob Tanner
who has represented me effectively
and guided me with patient good humour.

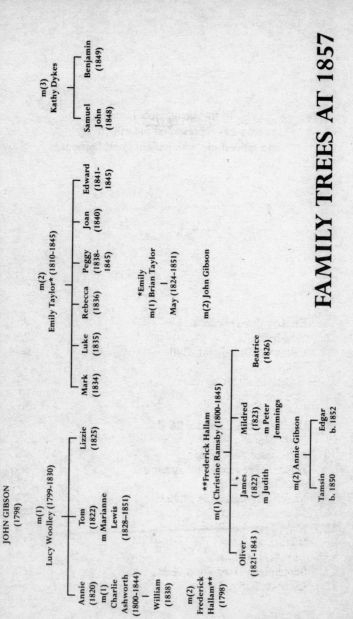

FAMILY TREES AT 1857

JOHN GIBSON
(1798)

m(1)
Lucy Woolley (1799–1830)

Annie (1820)
m(1)
Charlie Ashworth (1800–1844)
|
William (1838)

Tom (1822)
m Marianne Lewis (1828–1851)

Lizzie (1825)

m(2)
Frederick Hallam** (1798)

m(2)
Emily Taylor* (1810–1845)

Mark (1834)

Luke (1835)

Rebecca (1836)

Peggy (1838–1845)

Joan (1840)

Edward (1841–1845)

*Emily
m(1) Brian Taylor
|
May (1824–1851)

m(2) John Gibson

m(3)
Kathy Dykes

Samuel John (1848)

Benjamin (1849)

**Frederick Hallam

m(1) Christine Ramsby (1800–1845)

Oliver (1821–1843)

James (1822)
m Judith

Mildred (1823)
m Peter Jemmings

Beatrice (1826)

m(2) Annie Gibson

Tamsin b. 1850

Edgar b. 1852

Contents

1857

1858

1859

1857

Prologue

*I*n September 1857, Beatrice Barrence returned to London from a visit to Brighton with her maid, Mabel. She paid off the cab driver and left Mabel to carry the suitcases up the short flight of steps to the front door. Frowning, she waited for the maid to answer her knock; the frown deepened when there was no sound from inside the house. A second knock produced the same lack of result, so she muttered angrily and fumbled in her purse for the key.

When she pushed open the door, Beatrice gave a little screech of shock. The hallway was bare of furniture: no carpet, no hall stand, no pictures on the walls.

Behind her, there was a gasp and Mabel whispered, 'Whatever's happened, Miss Beatrice?' They had neither of them been looking forward to coming home, but they had not expected to find anything like this.

Beatrice forced her stiff legs to move forward. What had he done now? 'Reginald?' she called, her voice high with nervousness. 'Reginald, I'm home!' But there was no answer. Dread sat heavily on her stomach, and for a moment she wanted to run away. Her husband had many ways of making her life miserable, some of them very ingenious. What had he thought of now?

She turned to hiss at Mabel: 'Bring in the luggage and

shut the door, you fool! We don't want the whole street to see this.'

Mabel did as she was told, puffing as she carried the two heavy suitcases and the smaller portmanteau into the hall, and banging the door closed with one foot.

Only then did Beatrice move again. She took a deep breath, clasped Mabel's hand for comfort and together they pushed open the door of the front parlour. They had done many difficult things together, these two.

Both women stopped dead as they looked inside and Beatrice moaned aloud. The parlour was as bare as the hall. Not a stick of furniture was left, only bare dusty boards and a window gaping without curtains. Dust motes floated in the sunbeams that cut the room in half. Ash lay cold and grey in the hearth.

'What's happened, Miss Beatrice?' Mabel whispered, not daring to speak loudly.

Without a word, Beatrice let go of her maid's hand and moved out of the parlour, walking slowly, like a very old woman. Suspicion chilled her. If what she guessed was true, this was the worst thing he had done to her yet, the very worst.

Without a word, Mabel followed her mistress. From room to room they trod, their shoes thumping on the bare floorboards, their hushed voices echoing in the empty rooms.

'Why?' Beatrice whispered once, but Mabel didn't know how to answer her. She never could understand why Mr Barrence behaved as he did.

Only in Beatrice's bedroom was there anything to be found. A lingering scent and some shards of glass in the fireplace showed where the perfume bottles she had left behind had been smashed. Around the fireplace there was a broad semi-circle of splinters, as if the bottles had been thrown very forcefully into the grate.

In the middle of the floor was a pile of Beatrice's clothing and personal effects, tumbled one on top of the other as if someone had just dragged them from the wardrobe, pulled them from the drawers and tossed them there. A few books and ornaments. A sketch of a house, torn into shreds. Beatrice picked up a piece of it and sniffed back a tear. She would *not* cry! She had sworn long ago not to weep at the things he did to her.

On the mantelpiece was propped a white envelope, with her name on it in flourishing script. Reginald's handwriting. She swallowed hard as she stood and looked at it. She did not want to touch it even. She knew it would contain hurtful news.

It was a moment before she could gather together enough strength to move forward and pick it up. Her fingers trembled as she tore it open, then she sobbed, just once, and passed the letter to Mabel, who read it through slowly, her thick lips mouthing the words and tears falling down her plump cheeks. 'Oh, Miss Beatrice! Oh, he's a wicked man, he is! Whatever are we going to do now?'

Beatrice shook her head, and for a few moments the only sounds to be heard were the clop of a horse's hooves and the rumble of wheels passing in the street. It was a very quiet and respectable place. There were no hawkers, no children playing, nothing but quiet houses whose inmates minded their own business and privacy quite ferociously. All she knew of her neighbours was their faces. They would merely nod to her in the street and pass on.

'We'll have to go to Mrs Jemmings,' Mabel said, when her mistress did not speak. 'She'll help us.'

Beatrice drew in a long hoarse breath and shook her head, her fingers digging into her maid's arm. 'No. No, I won't! You're not to let my sister know.'

'But we can't stay here, miss.'

Beatrice gave a croak of laughter. 'Why not? The rent's paid until the end of the month.'

'But there's no furniture. And – and we haven't much money left.'

5

Beatrice looked down at her hand and gave a mirthless chuckle. She pulled off the diamond engagement ring and closed the other woman's fingers around it. 'Go and pawn this, Mabel. It meant nothing, anyway. You should get quite a bit of money for it. Then you can buy us a couple of blankets for tonight.' She brushed her hair impatiently out of her eyes and blinked at her maid. 'If you still want to stay with me, that is?'

Mabel immediately hugged her mistress. 'Of course I want to stay with you, lovie! You know I'd never leave you.'

Beatrice reached up one hand and patted her maid's cheek. 'Yes. You're a faithful creature. And I do need you.' She lowered her voice and glanced around before she spoke, as if to check that no one was listening. 'I know who did it. I know who gave him the idea.'

'Pardon, miss?'

'*She* did it.'

Mabel knew exactly who *she* was, and she had no more love for the woman than her mistress did, but this accusation made no sense. 'No, miss. How could she have? She's still in Bilsden.' She cast an anxious glance sideways. Whenever poor Miss Beatrice got to talking about her father's second wife, she came over funny. The rest of the time she was as nice a mistress as you could hope to find anywhere. But just occasionally she had these funny turns. It wasn't her fault, poor thing. She'd been badly treated. Badly. But you had to tread a bit carefully when she had one of her turns.

Beatrice shook her head, hatred twisting her face, making it even uglier. 'I know she did it, Mabel. She's always hated me. But now I'm going to make her pay. I've waited too long already, let her get away with it. Now the time has come to get my revenge.' She crossed to the window and stared blindly out, swaying to and fro and muttering to herself.

After a few moments, she started, as if something had surprised her, and turned to her maid. 'Haven't you gone yet? Go and pawn that ring. Buy us some blankets. And get yourself some food. I'm not hungry. Tomorrow we'll go and look for lodgings.' Then she turned back to the window and resumed her muttering and swaying.

Mabel shook her head, clicked her tongue softly and went to obey her instructions. They'd had to pawn things before, when Mr Barrence ran out of money, and she was well enough known at the shop. There would be no trouble, no accusations of theft. And they'd always redeemed the things before, so Mr Blithe wouldn't sell the ring.

She sighed as she walked along the street. When her mistress got one of these funny turns, there was no doing anything with her. All you could do was humour her and wait for the mood to pass.

But even though Mabel also hated Annie Gibson, if truth be told, this wasn't anyone's fault but Mr Barrence's. *She* hadn't done this. He was a wicked man, Reginald Barrence was, and should never have been allowed to marry her poor mistress, Beatrice Hallam as was. But Mabel was still there to look after her, though how they were to manage without money or home, she didn't know.

But Miss Beatrice was clever. She'd think of something.

1858

1

Bilsden: January 1858

*W*innie knocked on the door of the small parlour. 'Excuse me, ma'am, but Miss Hibley says to tell you she can't find Miss Tamsin or Master Edgar anywhere. They're not in the garden and no one has seen them.'

Annie looked up, her thoughts still miles away. 'What? Oh, Tamsin's probably hiding somewhere. It's very naughty of her.' Winnie always made such a drama of things.

Winnie drew herself up. She knew when someone wasn't taking her seriously. 'Well, they're *not* in the house, ma'am. And their outdoor clothes are missing.' Now she had her mistress's full attention. 'We've looked everywhere. Miss Hibley is that worried. She's sitting crying her eyes out in the schoolroom.' And Miss Tamsin was more than naughty, thought Winnie. She was a wilful young madam and that silly fool of a governess couldn't control her at all!

Annie sighed and stood up. 'Does Mr Hallam know?'

'He's still at the mill, ma'am.'

Annie led the way downstairs. 'Call Mr Jervis in, will you, please, Winnie? We'll get the outdoor staff to search the grounds.' Then she went to see Miss Hibley, who promptly tendered her resignation.

'I'm too old for someone as . . .' the governess hesitated,

11

seeking a word that would not prejudice her chances of getting a reference '. . . as *lively* as Tamsin.'

Annie sighed. Miss Hibley had been a disaster from the start. 'Very well. I accept your resignation. I'll make sure you have good references to help you to your next position.'

Miss Hibley shed some more tears. 'Thank you! Thank you so much. So kind. So very kind.'

Annie left her to it.

While the search was taking place, the two children were walking across the moors. Tamsin kept breathing in deeply, enjoying the wind and the bracing air. She loved it out here, but Miss Hibley would never go anywhere except into town when they went out for walks. A sunny day was so rare in the middle of winter that she easily persuaded Edgar to come 'just a little further' and just to 'walk to the top of one more hill'.

When five-year-old Edgar eventually started to complain about feeling tired, Tamsin heaved a sigh. 'I suppose we'd better go back, then. Honestly, you are a baby!' At seven, she enjoyed feeling superior to him.

'Which way is back, Tamsin?'

It was then that she realised she had gone further than ever before. 'Oh. Well, I'm not quite sure. Don't *you* have any idea?'

He shook his head.

'Well, we'll try this way, then. It looks like the right direction.'

By that time, the short winter afternoon was drawing in and the wind was starting to turn chilly.

Edgar clung to his sister's hand. After a while, seeing her look round, seeing the worry on her face, he said, 'We're lost, aren't we?'

'Shut up!'

'But we are, aren't we?'

'Yes.'

He began to cry, so she relented and gave him a rare cuddle. 'It's all right. We'll find a farm and ask them to send for Robert. He'll come for us in the carriage with hot bricks for our feet and take us home, you'll see.'

That thought kept them both cheerful for another five minutes, then Edgar said, 'Mother will be very cross with us, though.'

Tamsin shrugged. Her mother was often cross with her. A sniff made her look round. Edgar was trying hard not to cry. She was supposed to look after her little brother, so she put an arm round him and began to sing one of his favourite songs. That helped a little. Singing at the tops of their thin childish voices, they walked on for another ten minutes.

When it began to rain, Edgar's voice faltered to a halt and he began to cry in earnest. 'I'm frightened. And I'm c-cold.'

'Let's just sit down for a minute behind this rock. It'll keep the wind and rain off us a bit.'

Half an hour later, every inch of Ridge House and its gardens had been searched and no one had found the slightest sign of the two children. When the carriage turned into the driveway, Annie rushed to the door. Perhaps the children had gone down the hill to waylay their father. But Frederick got out on his own.

'Don't put the carriage away yet, Robert!' she called. 'Frederick, have you seen the children anywhere?'

'No. Is something wrong?' He came and put his arm round her.

'They're missing. And Miss Hibley has given notice.' Her voice faltered as she explained the situation. When you lived so close to the moors, you knew better than to go wandering across them, especially near dusk. Or at least, adults knew better.

Frederick turned back to the coachman. 'Robert, go and check that the children are not at their grandfather's

or their Uncle Tom's. As quickly as you can, if you please.'
When he went inside, Frederick himself helped search all
the rooms and cupboards again. In vain.

Robert returned to say that no one in the Gibson family
had seen the children, but Mr Mark and Mr Luke wanted
to know if they should come and help search for them. Mr
Hallam had only to send word.

Annie turned and clutched Frederick. 'Do we need
them?'

'No. We have enough people here.' He tried to speak
soothingly, for he could see the fear in her eyes, but in fact
he was more worried than he cared to show. 'It's fully dark
now. Let's hope they've found shelter somewhere.'

'It gets so cold at night,' she whispered.

'I'll go with them,' Frederick decided. 'With Nat. No one
knows the moors better than he does.'

'I'll come too,' Annie said at once.

Frederick shook his head. 'No, love, you stay here.
Someone has to be here, just in case . . .' No need to put it
into words.

The outdoor servants were provided with lanterns and
made ready to go out and search the moors along the three
tracks that passed Ridge House. 'But keep to the paths!'
Nat Jervis told them. 'You can't go a-wandering 'cross the
moors in the dark, or we'll be losing you, too. Keep to the
paths and shout them children's names every now and
then.' With nods and murmurs the gardeners and stable
staff set off.

Annie watched the lanterns bob away into the vast
darkness of the moors. It was hard to stay behind and wait.
She would, she decided grimly, deal very firmly with
Tamsin if – *when* – the children came back. For she knew
that Edgar would never have left the grounds on his own.
It was always Tamsin who led the two of them into
mischief. And she would make sure that Miss Hibley left
as soon as possible. She would be glad to see the back of
that lachrymose and ineffectual woman.

Nat Jervis stopped as soon as they reached the moors and looked at his master. 'Children allus take the easiest path, sir. That's why I said we'd come this way.' He led his master across the moors on a rambling route, stopping every now and then to think where he was and what there was nearby to appeal to a child. Even in the darkness, he knew every path, every hump of ground.

'I've found folks as was lost afore, sir,' he said once, when he saw by the flickering lantern light how worried Mr Hallam was. 'Don't you fret. I know these moors like the back of my hand and I've got a gift for finding folk. It's a matter of thinking as they would, you see.'

Once, when the wet tussocky grass made walking difficult, Nat stopped, shook his head and retraced his footsteps until he found an easier path. Once, when his master stumbled and fell, Nat set down the lantern and pulled him upright. He'd noticed how breathless Mr Hallam was getting. 'Let's rest a little, sir, eh?'

Frederick Hallam was ashamed that he had so little stamina, but he did need a rest. He watched his head gardener walk round him in careful circles, holding the lantern high and calling to the children through the rain and darkness.

'What's that?' Frederick asked suddenly. 'Nat! Can you hear something?'

They both stood still and listened. Far away, there was a thin shrill sound.

Nat handed the lantern to Frederick, cupped his hands to his mouth and yelled loudly.

When they listened, the faint cry was repeated.

'That way, sir!' said Nat. 'I think we've found them.' He set off again, lantern held high, leaving his master slipping and sliding behind him on the muddy path. 'They're here!' he called suddenly.

'Thank God!' Worried as he was, Frederick had to stop again to catch his breath before he could join Nat.

Tamsin and Edgar were huddled in the lea of some

15

rocks. Both children were soaked and shivering with cold. They burst into tears at the sight of their father. 'We saw the light,' Tamsin sobbed. 'So we shouted as loudly as we could.'

Edgar clung to his father, shivering. 'I thought you hadn't heard us.'

Angry as he was, Frederick hugged them both. 'We heard you. Let's get you back home again.' He swung Edgar into his arms and let Nat give Tamsin a piggy-back.

But to all of them it seemed a very long way back to Ridge House, and Frederick could not remember when he'd last felt so tired.

Annie took one look at their white chilled faces and bit back the angry words that were boiling up. She took Tamsin's clammy hand in hers and jerked her rain-soaked daughter towards the stairs, looking up at Tess, who was leaning over the banisters. 'Run a bath for the children. At once.' Then she turned back to the hero of the hour. 'We're all extremely grateful to you, Mr Jervis. I'm sure you could do with a brandy?'

Nat nodded.

'Please get Mr Jervis a brandy, Winnie.'

'I'll just let the others know we've found them, first, ma'am.' Nat went outside and a minute later there came the sound of two pistol shots. When he returned, Winnie was waiting for him, eager to hear what had happened.

'They'll have caught their death of cold, Mr Jervis,' she muttered as she led the way across the hall to get some brandy, with her peculiar flat-footed gait. 'Death of cold. And did you see how the master was shivering?'

Up in the nursery, Annie looked down at her daughter. For once, Tamsin had lost her air of defiance and bravado.

'Whose idea was this, Tamsin?'

'M-mine. I'm s-sorry. I didn't mean to go so far.'

'You shouldn't have gone on the moors at all! I'm very angry with you both.'

Edgar started sobbing again, so Annie stopped scolding.

'Come over to the fire and take your wet clothes off. We'll deal with your naughtiness tomorrow.' She turned to look at her husband, who was standing in the doorway, and was horrified to see how white Frederick was looking. 'Are you all right, love?'

'Just soaked, chilled through and tired.' He managed a wry smile. 'Not so young as I was and it's a raw night out there.' He turned to Tamsin. 'I am *very* displeased with you, young woman!' Rarely was his voice so cutting when he spoke to this beloved child.

Tamsin, who had stopped crying, began to sob again.

Annie gave her husband a little push. 'You'd better go and change out of your wet clothes. And get Jimson to bring you up a brandy. We'll deal with all this tomorrow.'

She turned back to her shivering daughter. 'Let Miss Hibley help you get your clothes off, Tamsin, then come to the bathroom as quickly as you can.' She finished pulling Edgar's things off, wrapped him in a blanket and carried him along to the children's bathroom, where Tess was waiting beside a steaming tub. Annie waited to make sure Tamsin joined her brother in the hot water, then left them in the governess's charge. She wanted to see how Frederick was.

A frown creased her brow as she walked along the landing. She doubted that the children would take much harm from their adventure, but she could not get the memory of Frederick's white face out of her mind. In fact, he had not been looking well for a while now. A feeling of apprehension rippled through her. When you married an older man, you could not help being more concerned for his health than you would with a younger husband.

A week or so later, Annie's father, John Gibson, strolled back from chapel with his family on a bright but chilly day, and sat down to enjoy his Sunday dinner with appetite. He loved to have his whole family gathered around the table. Afterwards, the two girls helped their step-mother to clear up. 'Let's go for a walk this afternoon.' Joanie stared out of the window, automatically pushing back the fine soft hair that was forever falling in front of her pale blue eyes. 'It might be cold, but it looks like it's going to stay fine.'

Rebecca shook her sleek dark head. 'No, I've got things to do.'

'You never want to come out with me!'

Kathy Gibson stepped in, as she often did, to prevent a quarrel. 'You should go out sometimes of a weekend, Rebecca. You work far too hard. Your father and I have been worried about you lately.'

Rebecca stared at her in surprise. 'But I enjoy working at the salon, Kathy, and dealing with the clients.' Well, most of the time, anyway. She was very proud that her half-sister, Annie, trusted her with such an important part of the business. 'And besides, I have some designs I want to work on today.' The dress designing didn't come as easily to her as it did to Annie, who often changed some of the details of Rebecca's sketches when she was checking things over.

Kathy laid one warm damp hand on Rebecca's slender shapely one. 'But you're only twenty-one, love. You should be out enjoying yourself, meeting folk, not working every hour of the day and night.'

'You mean out meeting young men, I suppose?'

'What's wrong with meeting young men, our Becky?' Joanie smiled as she used the nickname Rebecca hated. 'It's fun.' At nineteen, Joanie's thoughts ran mainly on young men: the ones she met at chapel, the ones she saw in the street, the sort of man she'd like to wed. She never stopped babbling about them when she and her sister were alone.

Rebecca smothered a sigh. 'I'm not interested in men.'

Joanie's smile faded. 'Well, you needn't pull your high and mighty face at me, Rebecca Gibson! You're turning into a right snob lately, since you started dealing with the clients at the salon.' She scowled. She worked in the sewing room above the salon, and was sick to death of it. It wasn't fair, the way Annie kept her upstairs and let Rebecca deal with the customers downstairs. She looked down at her roughened fingertips and the scowl deepened. She didn't intend to spend the rest of her life sewing rich women's clothes. She wanted to get married and have children and a house of her own. And to do that, she needed to meet young men.

For a moment, Joanie continued to scowl at Rebecca, then she remembered that she needed her sister's company or else her father wouldn't let her go out, so she banished the frown. 'Do come out for a walk with me, Rebecca,' she coaxed. 'There aren't many days as fine as this in winter.'

'Yes, do go, love!' Kathy chimed in.

'Go where?' said a man's voice.

They all turned round.

'Out walking, Dad,' said Joanie, rushing across to give him a hug and to hang on his arm, her face raised to coax. 'Tell Rebecca to come out with me. She's so mean.'

Rebecca watched Kathy's face light up, as it always did at the sight of her husband and felt a pang of jealousy. Her father might be thirty years older than his third wife, but he was the centre of Kathy's universe. Would anyone ever love Rebecca like that?

John looked out of the window and nodded. 'Good idea. You spend too much time shut up inside, Rebecca love.'

'But, Dad—'

John just looked at her.

Rebecca sighed. 'Oh, very well! But only for an hour.'

Joanie seized hold of her sister's hand and dragged her upstairs to collect their mantles and bonnets. 'Come on!'

'What's the rush?'

Joanie did not reply, just opened her top drawer, hunting through the jumble of oddments for her gloves and not bothering to pick up the articles that fell out. 'I want to get outside before the sun goes in! There! I'm ready.' She waved her hands covered in the thick woollen gloves that Kathy had knitted for her.

Rebecca took out the fine kid gloves she had saved for and pulled them on carefully. They would have to last a long time, because her father only allowed her three shillings a week to spend from her wages. He gave the rest of the money to Kathy, who put some away for each girl's 'bottom drawer' or used it to buy them larger items like clothes and shoes. The Gibsons weren't short of money, with four grown children working. They had enough to keep a maid. But John had seen hard times and was not one to throw his money around. Nor did he allow his daughters as much financial freedom as his sons. After all, the girls had only to ask if they needed to buy something extra.

Within minutes the sisters were walking briskly out of Moor Close and down Market Street.

'You didn't ask me where I wanted to go,' Rebecca commented.

Joanie pulled a face and skipped a few steps for the sheer joy of being outside. 'There's only one place to go on a Sunday afternoon – down High Street and along to the park. Don't you sometimes wish we lived in a bigger town than Bilsden?'

Rebecca nodded. 'Sometimes.'

As they approached High Street, Joanie slowed down to walk more sedately at Rebecca's side. 'Where would you like to live if you had the chance?'

'In a house like Annie's.'

Joanie pulled a face. 'Ridge House is too big. Nor I wouldn't like to have so many servants watching what I was doing all the time. It's better just having one, like our Lally.'

'Lally doesn't seem like a maid. She's part of the family now,' Rebecca protested.

'Oh, Lally can't do owt wrong with you and Kathy!' Joanie snapped. Fortunately they reached High Street just then and her sulky expression brightened, for quite a few

groups of people were taking advantage of the fine day to
stroll around the town centre. Joanie's eyes darted from
one group to another and her smile faded.

'Who are you looking for?'

She shrugged. 'Just seeing if there's anyone I know.'

Rebecca stared at her suspiciously. 'You haven't agreed
to meet that Maddie again, have you?'

Joanie crossed her fingers behind her back. 'I was just
hoping we might see someone we know. Oh, come *on*!' She
tugged at her sister's hand when Rebecca slowed down.
'You spend all week in the salon. What do you want to look
in its window for now?'

'I was just seeing how the new display looked.' Rebecca
sighed and allowed her sister to lead her on again. 'It's not
a very pretty town centre, is it?' She stared along the street
towards the railway station. 'Tom's hotel looks nice, but
everything else,' she pulled a face, 'seems tired and a bit
shabby. It's more fun to walk around the shops in
Manchester, and of course London is best of all.'

But that was another source of grievance to Joanie and
brought back the frown. 'It's not fair. Our Annie ought to
take me with her to London sometimes. You're her
favourite, you are.'

Rebecca bit off a reply. No use telling Joanie that she
would stick out like a sore thumb in the elegant London
hotels and shops Annie frequented on their little trips.
Joanie could not be bothered to learn to speak more
genteelly, refused to take advice about her clothes and was
turning into a real hoyden ever since she'd met Maddie
Pickering.

With a sudden shriek of 'Maddie!' Joanie ran across the
street and threw herself into her friend's arms. Reluctantly
Rebecca followed, realising now that this had all been
arranged. She stopped dead in the middle of the street when
she saw that Maddie was accompanied by her brother
Harry. Oh, no! Harry Pickering was the last person she
wanted to meet.

He beamed and swept off his cap. 'Miss Gibson!' Then he offered her his arm.

Joanie and Maddie were already walking along towards the park, chattering like two parrots, and making about as much sense, Rebecca thought sourly. She looked sideways at Harry Pickering's admiring smile and the arm he was offering her. 'I'd rather walk on my own, thank you.' He was shorter than her anyway, and she'd feel a fool on his arm. She wished sometimes she wasn't so tall. But out of common politeness, she had to walk beside him and that didn't please her at all.

Harry Pickering was a heavy-featured young man who worked in the office at the Bilsden Gas Company and who had sought Rebecca out before. She didn't know why she detested him so much, but she did. And when they got back home again, she would kill Joanie for arranging this meeting. It was the last, absolutely the *last* time she was going for a walk with her sister on a Sunday, whatever her dad said. She winced as Maddie shrieked with laughter so loudly that passers-by turned round to stare.

'Our Maddie does enjoy life.' Mr Pickering sounded approving. 'She and I were thinking of going to spend a few days in Blackpool next summer. Perhaps you and your sister might also enjoy some sea air? We could all stay at your auntie's boarding house. Joanie tells me that it's a very comfortable place.'

'I hate Blackpool.' That was a downright lie but at least it shut him up. Not for long, though.

'And how are things at the Bilsden Ladies' Salon?' Harry's voice was every bit as loud as his sister's, but his heavy features rarely showed any signs of animation and a few minutes of his conversation always made Rebecca want to scream with boredom.

'Fine.'

'And how is your dear sister, Mrs Hallam?'

'Fine.'

'And her husband?'

'Fine.'

'I saw Mr Hallam in town the other day. He's a splendid figure of a man, considering.'

Rebecca bristled. 'Considering what?'

'Considering his age.'

'You speak as if he's in his dotage. He's not turned sixty yet.' In fact, Frederick's sixtieth birthday was at the end of February and Annie was planning a big family party, but that was none of Harry Pickering's business.

After another pause, he said, 'There's a dance at the Methodist chapel next month. Maddie and I were hoping your family would be attending.' This was on the initiative of the new minister, who believed in offering rational entertainment to respectable families. The dancing was frowned on by the stricter members of the chapel, but John and Kathy approved and had spoken of taking part.

Rebecca said immediately, 'I'm afraid I shan't be going.' And if anyone tried to force her, she would plead a last-minute headache. She knew exactly why Harry Pickering had started attending chapel and dragging his irreverent sister along with him. And it wasn't because he had turned Methodist! He had an eye to the main chance, Harry Pickering did, and as Frederick Hallam's sister-in-law, Rebecca had a lot to offer a man like him. Only she didn't intend to offer it. She'd met men before who judged her by her sister's wealth, and she wasn't going to be taken in by this one.

He frowned. 'But Joanie said—'

'Joanie can go if she wants. I dislike dancing.' Which was another lie. Rebecca would have loved to go dancing. But not with this man hovering possessively nearby. And not with any other young man from chapel, either.

As they walked along Rebecca burned with embarrassment at the stares she received from people she knew. If anyone so much as hinted that they thought her to be walking out with Mr Pickering, she'd curl up and die. She stole a sideways glance and encountered such a fond

23

smile from her escort that she quickened her pace to catch up with her sister.

After walking around the park once, so briskly that Joanie protested, Rebecca broke up the party by insisting they return home. She refused Mr Pickering's offer of an escort quite sharply and then had to endure Joanie's complaints about her snobbish attitude as patiently as she could. For Joanie was right – Rebecca knew in her heart that she was a snob. The salon and the people she met at Annie's house had spoiled her for local men with no thoughts in their heads beyond a bit of pleasure at the weekend, or a week in the summer at Blackpool.

And if Harry Pickering, who was as slow and ponderous as a cow in a field, and about as interesting, tried to attach himself to her again, she would tell him straight out that she wasn't interested in him. Straight out!

2

Elizabeth

*I*n a small village in the Pennines north of Bilsden,
Elizabeth MacNaughton went to bed early, locking the
door of her room with a shudder of relief. When her father
died a month ago, she had come across the border to
Yorkshire to stay with her father's sister, the only family
Elizabeth now had.

She set the candle down near the bed and went over to
stand by the window and stare bleakly out at the darkness.
She had thought to stay here for a while to recover from
the long hard months spent nursing her father in his final
illness, but had decided today that she would have to leave
as soon as she could.

She had never liked her cousin Lewis, never! But now
she was afraid of him. He had been pressing his attentions
upon her ever since her arrival. Not offering her marriage,
no, never that with a woman who had nothing to bring a
man but a few rare books and a paltry annuity of twenty
pounds per annum. Lewis Melby would never marry a
poor woman, he had made that plain enough. But he had
an eye for an attractive one. And hands, too. When
Elizabeth threatened to tell his mother about the way he
kept touching her and the things he kept saying, things
that made her blush, he just laughed. 'She wouldn't believe
you, Lizzy.'

And Elizabeth knew he was right. 'I'm a respectable woman and you're supposed to be a gentleman,' she cried once, when he cornered her on the stairs. 'How can you treat me like this?'

He had just laughed. His loud confident laugh was one of the things she detested most about him. 'Oh, come on, Lizzy!' he breathed hotly in her ear. 'You'll enjoy it. And you won't need to worry about anything going wrong. I'll protect you. There are ways to stop the babies coming, you know. This is 1858, not 1758. We fellows know a thing or two nowadays.'

'*No!* I'm not that sort of girl!' She pushed desperately against his broad chest.

He moved backwards, fondling her breast as he did so. 'You will be.' Another of those laughs. 'I'll make sure of that.'

When she had said her prayers that night, a desperate plea to the Lord to turn Lewis's attention away from her, Elizabeth lay awake for a long time thinking things over. In the newspaper, she had found the address of an employment bureau in Manchester and had decided to apply to it for a position as a governess. She could get references from a minister friend of her father's who lived in nearby Todmorden and she had always liked children. She was well enough educated. Her father might have been impractical, but he had undoubtedly been a scholar of note. Her aunt would be upset at her leaving, of course. Poor trusting Aunt Janet! But there was no helping that.

It was a long time before Elizabeth fell asleep.

Some time later she awoke with a start to find a heavy body lying half on top of her and a hand across her mouth. She tried to scream, but a voice whispered in her ear: 'If you scream, I'll throttle you. Don't think I won't, Lizzy.' The hand uncovered her mouth but hovered over it.

Elizabeth began to tremble. 'How did you get in?'

A quiet chuckle. 'Do you really think we don't have spare keys to each room?'

'Go away! *Please* go away, Lewis!'

'Why should I? I'm feeding and housing you, aren't I? I want some return for my money. And you're pretty enough, if a trifle tall. Now, are you going to be sensible or must I take steps to keep you quiet?'

She opened her mouth to scream and the hand came back, turning the scream into a choking gurgle in her throat. With his other hand Lewis squeezed her neck until the blood started pounding in her temples and she thought she would die. When he let go, she could only lie there, gasping for breath, too terrified now to shout for help. This was a nightmare, it was, it must be.

But the voice sounded all too real in her ear. 'I meant what I said, Lizzy. I always do.'

'But why? Lewis, why? I'm your cousin!'

'Ah, but a reluctant virgin is such fun. How could I resist you?' There was silence for a moment, and when she opened her mouth to plead with him again, Lewis stuffed a piece of material into it and tied her hands above her head. She struggled against him, but he was a big man, powerfully built. When he had her helpless, he proceeded to enjoy himself at leisure, ignoring his victim's muffled whimpers of pain and distress, and doing things to her she had never realised possible.

The degradation seemed to Elizabeth to go on for a very long time.

Afterwards, Lewis stretched and made a contented noise, then dressed himself. When he bent over her again, it was to whisper, 'I'm going to untie you now, Lizzy. Let me remind you that if you try to complain, I'm fully dressed and you're naked. Whom do you think my dear mother will believe?' He waited a minute, then chuckled softly. 'And even if she did believe you, you're no longer a virgin.' He reached out to tweak one nipple painfully. 'You'd lose your good name, whatever you did.'

She lay there with a sour taste in her mouth, aching all over her bruised body. When the bonds had been removed,

Lewis's big dark shadow crossed the room and he left without a word of regret for what he had done. The door opened and closed silently, and no footstep sounded on the thick runner of the landing.

After a few minutes had passed, Elizabeth dragged herself up, pulled on her torn nightgown with hands that trembled and stumbled across to the door to set a chair beneath the handle. Then she leaned against the wall, shuddering. A tear trickled slowly down her face, but she would not let herself weep for her loss. Slowly she sank to the ground, shaking with the sobs that she did not dare release. No one must know. No one. If her face showed signs of tears in the morning, her aunt would want to know why.

Slowly Elizabeth's brain began to function again. If she wore a high-necked gown, the bruises wouldn't show. Lewis was right about one thing. If people found out what had happened, innocent as she was, she would lose her good name – and with it, all hope of making a respectable future for herself. That would leave her dependent upon his charity. The mere thought of that sickened her. She would not give in to him. She would not! So she must go away, must make sure that she never went near Lewis Melby again, never!

It was half an hour before she got back into bed, and that was not to sleep, but to lie there, thinking furiously, working out a plan and checking through the details again and again. Nothing must go wrong. She would have only one chance, she was sure of that. Her father had always said she was intelligent. Now she must prove it.

In the morning, Elizabeth did not go downstairs to breakfast until Lewis had gone whistling along the frosty path to his work as estate manager. When she entered the breakfast parlour, her aunt looked round with a smile that faded instantly. 'Oh, there you – my dear, you look dreadful. Are you feeling ill?'

'It's just a headache, but it kept me awake.'

'You should have stayed in bed. You look as white as a sheet.'

'I think some fresh air will help. Shall I go for the post?' Elizabeth already had her bags packed and her plans laid, for if she stayed, she was sure Lewis would attack her again, but this outing was an essential precursor to action.

'Well, if you're sure. But there's no hurry. Have some breakfast first.' Plump, comfortable Aunt Janet could not start her day without a pot of tea and several rounds of hot buttered toast.

'No, thank you. When I get one of these sick headaches, food makes me feel nauseous. It's fresh air that I really need.'

When Elizabeth came back half an hour later, she rushed into the house, waving a letter she herself had written that morning. 'Oh, Aunt Janet, I've heard such bad news from my friend Harriet. I'll have to go to her immediately. Her husband has just died. Only thirty, too.'

Her aunt blinked. 'We must send for Lewis immediately. He'll know how to arrange things.'

Elizabeth shook her head. It was the last thing she wanted. 'I've already seen to everything. I can catch the morning stage to Todmorden, then the train to Leeds.'

'You modern girls are so independent!'

'I must go and pack.'

'Very well, dear.'

Elizabeth stayed in her bedroom for fifteen minutes, keeping a careful watch through the window to check that her aunt did not send the garden lad with a message to her cousin Lewis. After that, she could stand it no longer and started carrying her bags downstairs.

Her aunt came and stood in the hall. 'Isn't that rather a lot? I mean, you'll only be gone for a few days, surely?'

'Oh, I dare say Harriet will want me to stay with her for a few weeks. We're very close friends. You wouldn't mind that, would you?'

'Well, no, but Lewis might want to—'

Elizabeth went outside and found the boy she had hired earlier already waiting with his handcart, as arranged. She kept up a bright flow of conversation to her aunt as she helped him load the luggage, then told him to carry it to the inn ready for the stage coach. She did not want her cousin to see her with the luggage and guess that she was leaving.

'So annoying not to have the railway to the village,' her aunt murmured. 'The jolting of the stage will make your headache worse. Are you sure you'll be all right, dear?'

Elizabeth nodded. 'Yes.' She hesitated, then hugged her aunt, who had made a penniless niece more than welcome and who was not to blame for her son's behaviour. 'Thank you for taking me in.' Then she was off, forcing herself to walk at a moderate pace, though she longed to run. For every step of that short walk she kept a careful watch, hoping desperately that she would not meet her cousin in the village.

But halfway along the street, a hand grasped her arm and swung her round.

'Lewis!'

'Who else is likely to grab you?' he asked, smiling. Then his smile faded. 'You look dreadful. What did you tell my mother?'

'That I had a headache, and needed some fresh air.' She did not shake his hand off, though she longed to. 'I'm going to fetch the mail,' she added, hoping her voice sounded normal.

'I'm going that way. I'll walk along with you.'

He let go of her arm and they walked along the single muddy street together. Elizabeth made no attempt to talk to him and he whistled cheerfully, as if pleased with himself. She could understand now why people committed murder.

When they got to the village store, which also acted as post office, Lewis tipped his hat to her and walked off. 'Busy day,' he said cheerfully. She stood in the doorway to

watch him go, then went inside and asked to see some
ribbons, but declined to make a purchase.

'Your aunt's mail is here. Came on the early stage today,'
Mrs Loughby said, turning to pick up a couple of letters.

For a moment, Elizabeth's mind went blank, then she
pulled herself together. 'I think I'll leave it until I'm on my
way back, then. It's so nice a day that I've decided to go for
a little stroll first. We don't often get days like this in winter,
do we?'

When she went outside there was no sign of Lewis, so
she walked quickly across to the inn, and checked that the
boy had left her luggage there. Then she stood in the
doorway, behind the other stage coach passengers, praying
that the stage would not be late. All the time, she kept
glancing down the street, hoping desperately that Lewis
would not come back yet.

When the coach arrived, she saw her luggage loaded on
and stood fretting in line while the other passengers got in.
When it was her turn, she wedged herself in the middle,
letting the others take the favoured window seats. As it set
off, she pressed her head back against the dusty
upholstery, terrified that Lewis would see her and stop the
coach.

At the end of the street, where the coach slowed down
to turn right to get on to the Todmorden road, Elizabeth
saw a figure on horseback and as they overtook it, realised
that it was her cousin. Terror iced her veins. She could not
move, could not breathe, could not think of anything to do.
He would see her. She had failed!

But Lewis continued to trot along without turning his
head and as the coach drew level, he moved on to the grass
at the side of the road. He waved to the coachman, but just
at that moment, his horse started pulling at the reins, not
liking to be so close to the lumbering vehicle, so he had to
turn his attention to quietening the animal.

The coach overtook him and trundled along down the
road. There was no cry from behind them, no sound of

galloping hooves trying to overtake them. Elizabeth let out a slow cautious breath, drew in another, and another. The other passengers grumbled about the state of the roads, the weather, the high prices. She could not say a word, so she closed her eyes and they left her alone.

Elizabeth didn't breathe easily until the Manchester train started huffing its way out of Todmorden station. Safe! She was alone in her compartment, so did not try to hold back the tears of relief. She had done it! She had got away! Now she must make sure that he never found her again.

After a while, she pulled out the crumpled page she had torn from the newspaper, studying again the advertisement which offered to find positions for ladylike governesses with good references. She knew it by heart, but read every word again. She had enough money to find cheap lodgings and live for a little while as she waited for a position. But not for long.

'Dear Lord,' she whispered as the train drew into Manchester, 'let me find a position quickly!'

3

February: Darrington Hall

Tom stormed into Ridge House without knocking and marched across the hallway, leaving the front door gaping wide and an icy wind whistling in.

Winnie pattered after him, torn between a parlour maid's duty to announce a visitor to her employers and a strong desire to close the dratted door. That wind was getting stronger by the minute. 'Mr Gibson! Mr Gibson, wait! Please let me announce you, sir.'

He did not slow down, nor did he attempt to remove his overcoat, just swept his hat off and tossed it on a small table as he passed. 'I'll announce myself, thank you, Winnie.' He crashed open the door of the library, his sister and brother-in-law's favourite room, and sure enough, there they were, sitting cosily together in front of a roaring fire.

'I've heard about Darrington's funeral. Is it true?' Tom demanded, not attempting to shut the door behind him. 'Is it?'

Annie and Frederick exchanged startled glances.

'Do come and sit down, Tom.' Frederick nodded to the hovering maid. 'Thank you, Winnie. Just shut the door as you go.' But he knew it would be too late to stop the servants gossiping about why Tom had come bursting in, and he was not looking pleased as he turned back to his brother-in-law.

'Well?' Tom stared at his sister. 'Is it true, Annie? Are you really going to that man's funeral?'

'Come and sit down near the fire, Tom.' When he didn't move, she got up and linked her arm in his, trying to pull him across to the sofa, but for once he was not to be cajoled. She sighed and let go, taking a step backwards and looking at him with loving concern

He was not much taller than she was, but stocky against her slenderness, with crinkly brown hair very unlike her auburn curls. She had only a few silver threads, but the brown of his hair was threaded with grey now, for all that he was younger than she was, and there was a weather-beaten look to his skin. A stranger would not even have taken the two of them for relatives, since he resembled their father and she their long-dead mother. Tom continued to glare at her, something that she was not used to from the brother who was the closest to her of all their father's nine children, and who, in addition, had been her business partner for years.

'Oh, Tom—'

'Just answer my question!' He snapped the words out as if he were cracking a whip.

Annie sighed and reached up to smooth his hair back from his damp forehead. How cold he was! It had just started to rain and his overcoat was soaked. The hand was brushed aside like an annoying insect, so she took another step backwards and said quietly, 'Yes, it's true that we're going.' She pulled a face, trying to jolly her brother out of his anger. 'It's actually a rare honour for a mill-owner to be invited to a Darrington funeral. It's never happened before.'

Tom's expression was stony with barely controlled rage. 'Honour or not, I can't believe that you'd accept.'

Frederick came up and slipped a glass of brandy into Tom's hand before his brother-in-law had realised what he was doing. 'We can hardly refuse.'

Tom stared down at the glass, blinked and took a

34

careless gulp, choking on the brandy. When he had caught his breath again, he said bitterly, 'That man's son killed my wife. You *can't* be serious about going to his funeral!'

'It's nearly seven years since that happened, Tom.' Annie spoke gently.

Her brother's face was bleak and suddenly he looked much older than his thirty-five years. 'It still seems like yesterday to me. I still get sick with fury every time I think of it. I still—' He broke off. He still lay awake and hungered for his lovely young wife, but that was no one else's business. At the moment, anger was his dominant emotion, and it had been throbbing through him since this morning, when his half-brother Mark had told him about the invitation. Casually. As if it didn't matter. As if the Darringtons hadn't ruined Tom's whole life.

The anger had been building up since then and in the end he had not been able to contain it, so had come here to confront his sister.

Annie's heart twisted at his bleak unhappy expression. Tom had not been the same since Marianne's death. He was so stern and serious nowadays. Sometimes, when she remembered what fun he used to be, how his eyes used to twinkle with mischief, she felt like weeping. He had not even looked at another woman since Marianne died, though most men widowed so young would have re-married by now.

Frederick squeezed her hand and tried to deflect Tom's anger. 'Well, Jonathon Darrington killed himself seven years ago when he realised what he'd done. Surely that more than atoned for the arrogant stupidity that caused Marianne's death? Tom lad, you can't continue to bear a grudge against the whole family for what one person did. It's Lord Darrington's funeral, not his son's. His lordship wasn't even in Bilsden at the time.'

'The Darringtons never are here in Bilsden. They just use the bloody Hall to house their indigent relatives and the sons who can't behave themselves in *polite society*. And when one son causes someone's death, they're a little embarrassed by it and send their regrets – *regrets!* – but they don't really care.' The glass trembled in Tom's hand with the vehemence of his speech. Without thinking, he took another gulp of brandy.

'The other son seems to behave himself well enough,' Frederick said quietly. 'We've heard no scandal about him.'

'Well, as Master Simon never comes to Bilsden, either, that's neither here nor there. And he's still a Darrington, isn't he?'

'He's *Lord* Darrington now, so he'll have to come here occasionally – unless he decides to sell the place.' Frederick looked at the younger man seriously, but with compassion. 'Let it go, Tom. You can't change the past. Nursing grudges pays no dividends.'

Tom gulped the rest of the brandy and set the glass down on the nearest surface with a thump. 'Marianne was only twenty-three when she died. The same age as our brother Mark is now. And the children don't even remember her.' He looked at Annie pleadingly. 'Don't go to the funeral! For my sake.'

Frederick's voice was as firm as Tom's was anguished. 'We must. It would be the height of rudeness to refuse an invitation which, if I read it aright, is an attempt to atone for Jonathon Darrington's behaviour.'

Tom laughed harshly. 'Atone with a funeral invitation! What good do they think that will do? It won't bring my Marianne back. It won't give my children a mother.'

'I think it's their idea of atonement – well, a first step anyway. And it's *not* the rest of the Darrington family's fault, Tom.' But Frederick was talking to empty space, for Tom had swung on his heel and left.

Annie sucked in a deep breath and blinked away sudden tears. 'Oh, Frederick! I didn't think it would hurt Tom so much, our accepting.'

'It's more than time he faced facts, love. The Darringtons have a house in Bilsden, and the new Lord Darrington is

36

bound to come here every now and then. Anyway, Tom's a grown man and he's chosen his own path. How he feels is not your responsibility.' But he knew she would pay no heed to that. Where her family was concerned, Annie still felt as responsible for their welfare as she had been in the past, when she had brought them all out of the poverty of the Rows.

Frederick went to the doorway of the library and looked across the hall to the front door, swinging open again to let in the damp chill of the February wind, and shivered. Rain was sleeting across the gardens now, giving a blurred look to the small lake in the light streaming from the windows, and the bare branches of the trees were lashing around as if they were as tormented as poor Tom.

Winnie came scurrying along from the servants' quarters, tutting to herself, and shut the front door again with a long-suffering sigh. She looked at her master questioningly to see if he wanted anything, but when he shook his head, she vanished through the servants' door again.

Frederick sighed and went back into the library where his wife was slumped on the sofa, staring blindly into the fire. He sat down beside her and took her into his arms. 'I'm sorry, Annie, but I can't let Tom's unreasonable fixation on his dead wife influence my dealings with the Darringtons, and I hope you won't, either, though I will understand if you don't wish to go to the funeral tomorrow.'

'No. I agree with you. I think they are offering us an olive branch, and it would be wrong to reject it.'

'Apart from anything else, judging by the little I've seen of him, Simon Darrington seems a decent enough sort – for a member of the aristocracy.'

She nodded. But the thought of the funeral was disturbing her, if truth be told. The last funeral she had attended had been Marianne's. Strange how nobody she knew had died since then. Well, nobody who mattered to her, anyway. Nobody in the family. They were a very close bunch, the Gibsons. She hoped her own three children would be close, too, when they grew up, even though William was twelve years older than Tamsin. Suddenly she reached out to touch the wooden arm of the sofa. 'Touch wood,' she said automatically.

'What on earth for?'

'Because I was just thinking that we Gibsons haven't had anyone die since Marianne. That was tempting providence.'

He raised his eyebrows in surprise. 'It's not like you to be superstitious.'

'I'm not risking anything where my family is concerned. And life's been too easy lately. It makes you worry sometimes when things are easy, makes you wonder what lies ahead.'

'You're a Hallam now, not a Gibson.' He ignored her other remark. Who could foretell or influence the future? There was only the present, and it was a good present for him, with a wife like her.

She smiled at him, her green eyes glinting in the light from the gasolier. 'I feel like both a Gibson and a Hallam – I never did feel like an Ashworth, even when I was married to poor Charlie.'

She stood up and went across to draw the green velvet curtains. 'You know, in weather like this I'm not surprised that some people worship the sun. The world seems to have been cold and grey for ever. And although it was a clear day, the weather has set in wet again.' She rejoined him on the sofa and they sat there in silence for a while, in perfect accord, beyond the need for words, as they often were.

But Annie couldn't get Tom's bleak tortured face out of her mind. She would do anything to make her brother happy again, more like the old Tom had been. Over the past year or two, she'd introduced him to several young women who would have made very acceptable second wives, kindly women who would have loved and cared for little Lucy, David and Richard, not women who thought only of Tom's increasing fortune. But he hadn't noticed them or even realised what she was doing. He lived only for his many businesses and his children now, with a cooler regard for the rest of the Gibson family. It was as if he couldn't see them all as clearly as he used to; as if Marianne's death had cast him into limbo, just a few steps away from everyone else.

Shaking her head at such fanciful thoughts, Annie realised that Frederick was speaking again and tried to concentrate on what he was saying about the state of the cotton markets. It was unusual for him to talk about such things nowadays. He had so many other interests, including his second family, that he left the running of the mill mainly to his manager, Matt Peters.

She grimaced as the thought of Matt brought with it a train of memories. Like the Gibsons, Matt had grown up in Salem Street and, also like the Gibsons, he had made something of himself. Indeed, his life had run parallel with the Gibson family's for years. She had been engaged to him once, though not for long, when they were both very young. She was glad now that she hadn't married him. He had become too – she sought for the right words – too rigid and conformist. He would not have made an easy husband, especially for a woman like her, who was of an independent turn of mind. Matt's job was the most important thing in his life, not his family. He was a loyal deputy to Frederick, but not the sort to carve out an empire for himself. And he was a pillar of the Established Church, though that upset his father who was a staunch Methodist, like Annie's own father.

Matt was a good husband to Jane, though. Dear Jane was a poor relative of Frederick's first wife, who had had the thankless task of acting as companion to his younger daughter Beatrice when her mother died. Matt and Jane had been married for six years now. Annie was well aware that it wasn't love that had made Matt propose, but a need to be married, and a hard-headed business acumen that said it would not hurt to be married to a relative of his employer. She didn't think he could fall madly in love with anyone. Jane seemed very happy, though, with the husband, home and family she had never expected to gain for herself.

Annie became suddenly aware that while she had been wool-gathering, Frederick had turned the conversation to his growing desire to create a really fine new square in the centre of their bustling little town. He felt that Bilsden had no real town centre, just a straggle of streets and terraces, of which the main focus was High Street, with its jumble of shops and business premises and the station which lay at one end of it.

She made soothing noises and let him wonder aloud exactly what to do about it. She did not care much what happened to the centre of Bilsden. What she cared about was her husband, her family, and to a lesser extent, her businesses. For she had still maintained her own business interests, even when she married the richest man in town. She could never have borne to sit idle at home.

The next morning Annie twitched her full black silk twill skirt into place over its cage crinoline, buttoned up the separate bodice, then reached for the cashmere jacket with the matching moiré silk trims and began to do up the tiny jet buttons down its front. She smoothed the jacket's basques over her hips and nodded her approval at her reflection in the mirror. 'Mary did a good job on this, didn't she?'

Frederick grinned. 'She always does. The Bilsden Ladies' Salon bears your imprint, even though you haven't worked there since we married.'

'I still design clothes for the salon.'

'Yes. Though you have one or two other little activities to keep you busy.'

'Like Tamsin,' she agreed ruefully. 'We should have got a new governess for them straight away when Miss Hibley left, but I've been enjoying having them to myself for a while.'

'We've had three governesses in the past two years – they don't seem to stay. Though Tamsin has behaved herself since that escapade on the moors. For a seven-year-old, that daughter of yours has a powerful personality.'

'She's your daughter, too.'

'She looks like a reincarnation of you, Annie, and well you know it. Red hair, green eyes, small and mischievous.'

'Is that how you think of me? Small and mischievous?' But she was smiling as she spoke. She knew Tamsin took after her, though Annie had had some hard times as a child and her daughter hadn't. And since Annie had gone into service at the age of twelve, she'd not had much energy or time left for getting into mischief. Maybe she should find something to keep Tamsin occupied, something to use up that energy and also to teach the child that money must be earned, was not a divine right. Annie glanced at her little fob watch and stored the thought for later consideration.

Frederick watched her walk across the dressing room towards him, her bell-shaped skirts swaying gracefully. 'If skirts get any fuller, my love, we'll all have to widen our doorways.' He moved across to plant a kiss on her cheek. 'But you look lovely whatever you wear, even in that ridiculous contraption. I don't think I've ever seen a fashion as preposterous as the crinoline.'

'At least I can wear several layers of petticoats under it.' She grinned at him mischievously. 'Not to mention my new flannel knickerbockers.'

'Another ridiculous fashion! The most unromantic of garments.'

'But they keep the legs nice and warm.'

He reached for her fur-trimmed mantle and draped it around her shoulders. '*Voilà, Madame.*'

She adjusted the small bonnet that was now fashionable,

using hatpins to fix it to the back of her auburn curls, then twirled round in front of him. 'There, what do you think?'

'I think it's disgraceful that you don't look anything like thirty-seven.' And galling that he was feeling all of his fifty-nine years lately. Heavens, he'd be sixty later this month! What a ghastly thought!

He pulled out his pocket watch and held it at arm's length to peer at the numerals, squinting in vain, then clicking his tongue softly with annoyance. Moving out of the dressing room, with its single narrow window shaded by nets, he squinted at the watch again in the brightness of the big window of their bedroom. Even in the full light, it was the position of the hands, rather than the blurred figures, which told him what he needed to know. He sighed. He hated to use his spectacles. When you had a wife so much younger than yourself, you didn't want to do anything that added years to your appearance. But he couldn't put off wearing them any longer.

He turned back towards the dressing room. 'Are you ready?'

'Nearly.'

'You'll have to get a new maid for yourself, love, as well as a governess for Tamsin. If we don't hurry up, we'll be late for the funeral.'

'I'm ready.' She tucked an errant curl back into the mass of auburn hair that absolutely refused to lie over her brow in the smooth curves that current fashion dictated, and then picked up her fur muff. 'I'm going to need this today as well as my gloves. It's bitterly cold outside. Nat thinks we'll have snow before the week is over.' And their head gardener was usually right about the weather. 'Are you going to be warm enough, love?'

He shrugged. 'As warm as clothes can make me. Jimson has provided me with every item of clothing that it's possible to wear underneath. And my drawers and vest are of purest merino wool.' But he still felt cold. It was bitter weather.

Coming out of their bedroom, they saw two small figures sitting on the top stair, waiting for them. Tamsin bounced to her feet, dragging Edgar with her. 'I wanted to see you in your special mourning clothes,' she announced. 'Turn round, Mother.'

Annie chuckled and obliged.

Tamsin studied them both, head on one side. 'I don't think I like you wearing only black.' She pulled a face. 'It looks so miserable. Dead people won't know whether you're in mourning or not. Can't you wear your dark green instead, Mother?' It was Tamsin's very favourite colour. If she had her way, everything she owned would be green. 'After all, you didn't know Lord Darrington, did you?'

'I did meet him once.' Annie pulled a face at the memory.

'That's a horrid dress,' Edgar announced, screwing up his face in an even worse grimace than his sister's. 'I don't like you in it, Mother.'

'It's a mark of respect to wear black,' Frederick informed his children for the umpteenth time, indulgent as always with this lively red-haired imp of a daughter and with his youngest son, the child he had not wanted Annie to bear. How glad he was now that chance had intervened and taken the decision for him. Edgar was a delightful child, with huge solemn eyes. He was nearly as tall as his sister already, for he resembled the Hallam side of the family.

It was Edgar who would inherit the mill, Frederick had already decided that, Edgar who would learn how to run it as he worked by his father's side. Frederick's younger son, from his first marriage, was a lawyer in Leeds and had no interest whatsoever in the cotton industry. James would just sell the mill if it were left to him.

Tamsin grabbed her brother's hand and the two of them followed their parents down the stairs into the big oblong hall that was larger than most of the houses in the Rows down in Bilsden. 'Grandad says when you're dead you go

43

to heaven and you can still see what's happening here on earth, but I don't believe that,' Tamsin announced. She had been fascinated by the idea of death ever since the news came about Lord Darrington's sudden demise. 'What do you think about it, Father?'

'I think that I don't know what happens after you die, as I've told you twenty times already, young lady.' He moved on across the hall.

'But Father . . .' Tamsin's voice trailed away and her bottom lip stuck out mutinously.

At the door, Annie turned. 'Look after Edgar for me today, will you, Tamsin love? And you are not to leave the house.'

The child nodded. 'I won't. Anyway, we're going to play funerals today.' She dug Edgar in the ribs. 'Aren't we?'

He nodded, but looked dubious at the thought of this treat.

As Annie and Frederick sat in the carriage with their feet on hot bricks, jolting down the hill into Bilsden, she slipped her gloved hand into his. 'I can't believe how furious Tom is that we're going today. I knew he wouldn't be pleased but not so – so wild with anger.'

'Well, he'll just have to be furious, love.'

She grimaced. 'I hate funerals, and this one is bound to drag on as they all tell lies about how wonderful the late lord of our manor was. Why, the people on his estate have to live with leaky roofs and without a proper water supply!' She cuddled up against Frederick. 'I met him once, that time I made his wife a ball gown in a hurry after hers was destroyed, and he didn't even look at me, just the dress. Do you remember?'

He nodded. 'Yes. Someone broke into the salon and destroyed the new gown you were making for her ladyship. I took you into Manchester in my carriage to buy some more material.' He grinned reminiscently. 'I was glad of the excuse to spend some time alone with you.'

'We weren't alone. Rebecca came too.' It had been the

first time Annie's half-sister had visited Manchester, for ordinary people travelled much less before the coming of the railways.

'Mmm. But I wasn't interested in Rebecca. Only you.'

They exchanged smiles, then Annie pursued her train of thought. 'And now anyone can get to Manchester quite easily by train in forty minutes. And from there to the rest of the country. Haven't things changed, Frederick? And so quickly.'

'Yes. But I like to see progress.' He sighed, a weary sound.

Annie stared out of the carriage window, frowning. She had noticed how shivery he seemed today and how he'd hugged the fire all morning, but had said nothing. He didn't like being fussed over.

Frederick stared blindly at the passing scenery. He was feeling rather down today. George Darrington had only been fifty-four, five years younger than Frederick himself, and that made him feel insecure. In fact, his father, Owd Tom, as the mill folk still called him, had also been younger than Frederick when he died. It made you think. And wonder about your own future – in particular how much of it there was left.

The carriage slowed down as they approached St Mark's Parish Church and joined a line of other vehicles. The horses' breath was misting the chill air as their hooves clopped slowly along the cobbled street. The Hallam carriage stopped in its turn at the lych-gate to disgorge its passengers into the icy wind and flurries of rain. Lord Darrington's funeral was clearly being attended by everyone of note in that part of south-east Lancashire.

'I hear The Prince of Wales didn't have a single room vacant last night,' Frederick commented. He had a minor share in that hotel, with Tom and another partner, Seth Holden. 'I bet your brother didn't turn custom away because it came from the Darringtons.'

Annie just pulled a face at him.

When they were at last sitting in their pew, a harassed church warden came along and whispered in Frederick's ear. He nodded and leaned over to whisper in his turn to Annie: 'I've just agreed to let some cousins of his lordship sit in our pew. Amazing crush, isn't it?'

Two very elderly ladies and a slightly younger gentleman walked down the aisle and slipped into the end of the Hallam family pew, nodding their thanks as they did so. The ladies' full black skirts nearly filled the rest of the pew and the gentleman was squashed uncomfortably into the last foot or so of space.

Annie inclined her head graciously in return, suppressing a sudden urge to chuckle at the gentleman's obvious discomfort in the unyielding corner of the hard pew. Those carved bosses on the pew ends were most inappropriately placed. She herself was sitting on a soft cushion a short distance away from the end panel. But she soon lost the inclination to smile. The air in the church seemed raw, in spite of the charcoal braziers which she knew would have been burning there all night. The eulogies to his lordship by the parson, who had rarely met his benefactor and who certainly had not seen him do any good in the town, made Annie snort in disgust.

Frederick nudged her to be quiet, grinning as he did so. His Annie was not known for her tact and diplomacy, but rather for her forthright utterances and clear gaze. And also, he had to admit, for her obsession with making money. Her business acumen would shame most men. Even he did not know exactly how much she was worth, with her various concerns and her careful saving for her son William's future. He would have been quite happy to provide for his stepson. Most men would have taken charge of all the family finances, but he was not most men, just as his wife was not most women.

Annie felt only relief as the service ended and she saw the pall bearers walk forward to pick up the coffin and carry it outside, where his lordship was to be laid to rest in the square mausoleum of grimy stone that dominated the churchyard. Darringtons were always buried here and had been for more than a hundred years – regardless of where they spent the rest of their lives, which was not usually in Bilsden.

By the time Annie and Frederick were standing respectfully with the others around the mausoleum, she was shivering and her toes were numb, in spite of her warmly lined ankle boots, whose fashionable patent leather trimmings also served the practical purpose of keeping out the damp. She tried to stamp up and down unobtrusively beneath her crinoline, but that made the skirt sway so much that she had to desist.

The widow, very upright and slender in her black veiling, was escorted from the graveside on her stepson's arm and helped into her crested carriage, then everyone was able to move around. There was a general noise of stamping feet and hands being clapped together as people tried to get the blood flowing again. Another wait in the icy wind and then both Annie and Frederick sighed with relief as they were able to get back into their own luxurious carriage.

'Ah!' Frederick pulled the fur rug up and wriggled his numbed feet on the hot brick in its quilted flannel cover. 'Remind me to thank Robert Coachman. He's found us some new hot bricks from somewhere. The man's a marvel.'

'I expect there were lads selling them.' Poor children often found little ways of earning a few pence, as Annie knew from experience.

She watched her husband covertly as he shivered and huddled down next to her under the rug. In the icy church he had gone quite pale, his lips almost bloodless, so that he seemed a man carved from stone, like the marble crusader she had once seen in a church in Brighton. She held his hand under the rug and nestled against him, hoping the warmth of her body would help. But he still

looked white and chilled when they reached Darrington
Hall, which was a short distance out of Bilsden on the edge
of the moors, beyond their own house, which itself lay
nearly at the top of Ridge Hill.

Again the carriages had to wait in a queue until those in
front of them had disgorged their black-clad passengers
under the stone porte cochère of the Hall. The guests
were then welcomed into its shabby precincts by a
reception party consisting of Simon, the new Lord
Darrington, and his step-mother, Lady Lavinia, with her
veil lifted now so that the black silk flowers edging the
bonnet formed a pretty frame for her face.

Although Frederick was the leading cotton master in
Bilsden, he and his wife came far behind the old county
families in status and their welcome by the widow was
accordingly brief and cool. A flicker of surprise showed
when she recognised Annie, but she said nothing.

With the quick eye of one who had once been a modiste,
Annie noted that even her ladyship's mourning was in the
height of fashion. She's not grieving all that much, Annie
thought, if she can turn herself out like that. As she shook
hands with her hostess and murmured her condolences,
the inner voice continued its commentary. Her ladyship's
eyes weren't at all puffy. In fact, she showed no outward
signs of grief, apart from the mourning garb.

Annie looked sideways at her own husband. If I lost
Frederick . . . She pushed that thought away, as she always
did. Her Frederick was in excellent health and did not look
anything like his age – well, not usually. He was probably
sickening for a cold today, poor thing.

Annie moved on from her ladyship to shake hands with
the new Lord Darrington, leaving her hand in his for the
briefest time possible and letting Frederick speak for them
both. Simon Darrington looked too much like his dead
brother for her to feel comfortable with him, though at
least his face was not dissolute. He looked bored, rather
than sad, today.

They followed the other guests through into the Great Hall, an icy expanse of stone-flagged floor enclosed by stone walls embellished with dark dusty paintings and pieces of antique weaponry. Well, the housekeeper's no good, Annie thought scornfully as she stood among a crowd of strangers, trying not to betray how cold she was feeling. There's dust everywhere. And cobwebs. And surely they could have warmed the place up better than this!

Some of the gentlemen nodded to Frederick, but no one approached him, and the only people to nod to Annie were the two ladies who had sat in her pew.

'We're neither flesh nor fowl here,' she whispered, and smiled up at Frederick mischievously. 'I wonder what these people would say if I told them I once made a gown for her ladyship.'

'They'd be horrified, but would say nothing, just move further away from you, as if you were diseased.' He smiled, then the smile faded and he gritted his teeth to prevent himself from shivering visibly. 'Let's see if we can get nearer to the fire. This place is almost as cold as the church was.'

But before they left, Simon Darrington made a point of coming up to them and thanking them for attending. 'I hope we can all forget the past,' he added, 'difficult as that must be for your family.'

Frederick responded for them both. 'We'd be very happy to forget the past – for which you personally bear no blame, Your Lordship.'

'Good, because I shall be coming to live here as soon as I've sorted things out in London, so I expect – I *hope* – we'll be seeing something of one another.'

They were both surprised by that. Darringtons had not lived permanently at the Hall within living memory, except for an old aunt who had spent her declining years in this square windswept edifice when Annie was a child.

'I told you it was an olive branch,' Frederick said as they got into their carriage.

'He'll have forgotten our very existence by tomorrow,' retorted Annie. 'Seeing something of one another, indeed!'

4

Ridge House

*T*he next morning, after a restless night, Frederick woke up with a croaky voice and a hectic flush on his cheeks.

'You're staying in bed,' Annie declared, laying one hand on his forehead and finding it far too hot. 'And I'm sending for Jeremy Lewis.'

She knew Frederick was feeling bad when he didn't argue with her, just closed his eyes and scraped out a weary breath. She rang for his manservant Jimson and sent him to fetch tea for his master, then whisked into her own dressing room to pull on the nearest bodice and one of her skirts that didn't need a crinoline cage. Frederick was right, she thought ruefully, as she looked at the mess she had made. She did need to hire another maid. She had grown used to Laura's services, even though she had not at first wanted a maid. But when Laura left to be married she had been reluctant to entrust her intimate affairs to a stranger, and had tried to manage with Tess's help. It would not do.

Leaving Jimson to wash his master's face and prop him up on a pile of pillows, Annie went downstairs into the icy chill of a library whose banked fire had not yet been brought to life. She had always been an early riser, but did not demand that her servants get up even earlier than her to warm up areas of the house that were not normally used at this time of day. She poked up the fire and quickly wrote a note for the garden lad to take into town to the doctor's.

Later, she refused to let Tamsin into the bedroom to see her father, because she could see how the slightest noise made Frederick wince, and anyway, she didn't want him passing this cold on to the children. Tamsin was the worst patient on earth – which was the reason why the second governess had left. The first had been delighted when an uncle's death gave her an excuse to go and care for her widowed aunt. But she would have gone anyway. How on earth were they to find someone who could control Tamsin?

Jeremy Lewis was at Ridge House within the hour. He spent more time nowadays attending to his duties as the town's Medical Officer, the first to be appointed by Bilsden's new Town Council, than he did visiting patients. But there were a few people whom he still attended in person, instead of leaving them to his partner. The Hallams were among the most important of these, and not because of their wealth, but rather because Jeremy respected Frederick and had known Annie since she was a small child. He still thought of her as Annie Gibson. He had been helpless to prevent her mother dying in childbirth when Annie was only ten, and had admired the way the child coped with running the house and looking after her brother Tom and sister Lizzie thereafter.

He had not expected his own beloved daughter to want to marry Tom Gibson years later, not expected her to *have* to marry him or anyone, but when he had seen how happy Marianne was with her new husband, he had relented and forgiven his son-in-law for getting her with child. Then his daughter had been killed when Jonathon Darrington's rearing horse made her fall backwards and break her neck. Somehow, after that, the world had seemed to stop turning for a time for all of them, especially Tom.

Jeremy had rarely seen grief like Tom's before and had

not known how to help his son-in-law while he was fathoms
deep in his own sorrow for his beloved daughter. Later, he
had continued to be a frequent visitor to the house, one of
the few people whom Tom allowed inside during that first
year. Jeremy had played with his grandchildren and
answered their questions about their mother as Tom never
could. Then, when Tom had got over his first wild grief,
Jeremy had started having his grandchildren over to play
with his own children by his second wife, Ellie, for they
were of a similar age.

It was a funny world, he thought, as he knocked at the
door of Ridge House. You never knew what was waiting for
you around the next corner. For good or for ill, you just
had to continue, to do your best, to cope.

It was Annie herself who opened the door to him. 'Oh,
Jeremy, I'm so glad to see you!'

'Is Frederick that bad?' He was startled, for he'd seen
Frederick only a couple of days previously.

'No – well, he is bad, but not exactly at death's door. He
seems to have a bad bout of the influenza. It's just – I've
been worried about him for a while now and wanting to
talk to you.' She linked her arm through his and drew him
into her own small parlour at the rear of the spacious
hallway. Although the weather was inclement outside, it
was warm and comfortable inside Ridge House now that
the fires were all blazing away. It was one of the garden
lad's secondary duties to bring coal inside for the many
fires throughout the winter, as well as tending the furnace
that warmed the fine new glasshouse.

When they were sitting down, Annie clasped her hands
together and stared down at them, unsure how to begin.

'Tell me, Annie,' Jeremy prompted softly.

'Frederick's been looking tired for a while now.
Unusually tired.'

She was looking at him pleadingly, as he'd seen so many
others look when they were afraid for their loved ones. He
steeled himself to be frank with her. She would be better

knowing the truth. If anyone could cope, it was Annie. She had had to cope with so many things during a life which had not been easy. Well, she'd more than coped. She'd made a great success of everything she touched. He hoped she would be able to handle this next trial of her strength.

'I've noticed that something was wrong myself,' Jeremy admitted. 'When a person gets that grey drawn look on his face, as Frederick has lately, well, you can't help wondering what's causing it. You can tell a great deal from someone's general appearance and demeanour.'

Annie tried to swallow the great lump of fear in her throat, but it stayed there, as solid as a piece of lead and twice as heavy.

Jeremy took her hand. 'I don't think we should come to any conclusions until I've examined Frederick. Why don't you show me up to see him now, and then we'll have a cup of tea together afterwards and discuss things?'

As she walked upstairs with Jeremy, Annie couldn't help noticing how well he was looking, his face rosy from his walk up the hill even on a chill day like this, for he was a firm believer in the benefits of exercise and fresh air and preached the doctrine to everyone he attended. He looked a full generation younger than Frederick, although there were only four or five years between the two men.

She squared her shoulders as she opened the bedroom door, managing a smile as she showed the doctor in. 'Jeremy's here, love.'

As she came out of the bedroom, she found an unusually quiet Tamsin waiting for her, with Edgar hovering behind her as usual. 'I thought I told you two to stay in the schoolroom and draw?'

Tamsin ignored that. 'Is Father very ill?' Her eyes were huge with apprehension and today her red hair looked wild and unbrushed.

'He's not well. I think he has the influenza.'

'Is he – is he going to die, like Lord Darrington did?'

Annie gathered her daughter into her arms. She knew how much Tamsin adored her father and could feel the fear in the tense little body. 'I don't think he's that bad, love. But he'll probably be ill for a week or two. Influenza is a nasty thing. But we'll look after him very carefully, I promise you.'

'But it's his birthday soon.'

'Well, we can always have a party later, when he's better, can't we?' It was difficult to keep her voice cheerful as she tried to reassure her daughter. When she was twenty-five, Annie had seen her step-mother, her friend Sally Smith, and a half-sister and brother die of influenza, all within a week or two. But that had been in the Rows, where comforts were few and life was a constant struggle to put bread on the table, not here at the top of Ridge Hill, where every luxury was available to help Frederick Hallam recover.

'Can I go in and see him after the doctor leaves?' Tamsin pleaded. 'Just for a minute. I won't make a noise, I promise.'

'Not today, love. He'll be very tired after the doctor leaves. People with influenza usually sleep a lot – it helps them to get better. Maybe tomorrow you and Edgar can come to the door of the bedroom and wave to him. I don't think you should go down to your grandfather's today, though, just in case you've caught the influenza, too. You don't want to pass it on to anyone else, do you?'

Tamsin pulled away, frowning. 'Can you do that? Pass it on?'

By now Edgar was standing in a corner of the landing, twisting one foot behind the other, looking as if he were on the brink of tears. Annie went over to give him a quick cuddle, then spoke gently to them both. 'Yes. You can definitely pass things on.' She had seen several epidemics spread through the Rows. She didn't understand how illnesses were passed from one person to another, though. Maybe it was by touch. 'So we all have to be careful.' She looked at Tamsin. 'You will be good today?' The girl nodded.

'Maybe Cook will let you and Edgar bake a cake later.'

'Huh! Edgar always spills flour everywhere. And then Mrs Lumbley gets cross. Still ...' Tamsin heaved an aggrieved sigh and trailed away to the kitchen to arrange it, followed by her shadow. At the door she paused. 'I wish William was here. I miss our William. What's he doing in that university place, anyway?'

'He's studying. I told you that before. Learning things. But I miss him, too.' What's more, Annie was beginning to worry about her elder son. As if she didn't have enough on her mind! William didn't seem to have settled down at all well in London and his recent letters had been very guarded as to how his studies were going. In fact, he had sounded depressed.

Annie didn't remember now where the idea of a university education had come from, but it had stuck in her mind ever since William was ten. When he was thirteen, he had gone to Saul Hinchcliffe for a few years as a weekly boarder to learn his Latin and all the other things young gentlemen seemed to need if they were to go to university. She could afford to give William every chance in life, so why not this one? He was her first-born and for years he had been her only child, both the joy and the focus of her life, even if he was the result of a rape. She shuddered at the memory of Fred Coxton and that dreadful night which had nearly ruined her life.

She watched her other two children walk downstairs, then, as they disappeared from sight, heard a shriek of annoyance from Tamsin and Edgar's unhappy pleading. Poor Edgar got shrieked at every time Tamsin was in a bad mood but there was no doubting their love for one another, and if anyone else had tried to shout at him, Tamsin would have been the first to fly to his defence.

Getting another governess seemed suddenly urgent. She should have seen to it before now. If she were going to be busy nursing Frederick herself, as she was determined to do, then the children would need someone other than a servant to look after them. Frederick did not want his children going to the new elementary school that had opened in the town, nor did he wish to send them away to boarding school, so another governess it must be.

To keep from worrying about what was happening upstairs, Annie went off and wrote a note to the bureau in Manchester which supplied them with staff from time to time. One governess. Urgent. No time for an interview, just a month's trial. Almost as an afterthought she added that she also needed a new lady's maid, since her old one had left recently to get married. No one fussy. By the time Annie had given the letter to Winnie and asked for it to be taken into town immediately, Jeremy was coming downstairs again. 'And send tea to my parlour,' she added, squaring her shoulders and going forward to meet him.

'Well?' she demanded, as soon as the door was closed and before Jeremy had even sat down. 'What do you think? Is it the influenza?'

He nodded and moved to sit beside her on the sofa.

When he took her hand, Annie knew that there was more news, bad news. She had seen Jeremy break bad news to people before. And always he tried to touch them, because he believed that helped. 'What else?' she asked in a voice that was suddenly hoarse. 'Don't try to prepare me, Jeremy, just tell me, for heaven's sake!'

'I think it will be a bad bout of influenza and his heart is – is not functioning as well as it should.'

She swallowed hard. 'Are you sure?'

'As sure as one can be. I could hear the irregularity quite clearly with my new stethoscope. This binaural model is a big improvement on the first stethoscope I had.' Jeremy kept in touch with a group of doctors in America and was usually the first in the district to try the innovations they told him about, sometimes to his patients' dismay.

Annie dug her fingernails into the palm of her hand to keep herself from bursting into tears. What did she care about stethoscopes? 'Is he – is Frederick in danger, then?'

'From the heart problem, no, not immediately. If he takes care of himself and lives quietly, he could last a good few years yet. But if he goes on working as hard as he does now, he'll be putting himself in danger.'

'And the influenza?'

'It's too soon to tell how it will affect him.'

There was a knock on the door and Winnie brought in a tray. By the time she had fussed her way out again, as only Winnie could do, Annie was in control of herself enough to pour Jeremy a cup of tea and offer him a cake. 'Then it'll be up to me to nurse Frederick carefully, won't it?'

'You'll do it yourself?'

She managed a half smile. 'It's the only way I'll feel sure that he's getting the best treatment.'

'I'll ask Widow Clegg to find someone to help you at night.'

'I don't need—'

He held up a hand. 'We all need sleep, Annie. You'll be no help to Frederick if you're exhausted.'

'I have Jimson. He's devoted to Frederick.'

'You'll need a nurse as well, if you're to maintain a watch on Frederick day and night. Jimson's not a young man himself, you know.'

'Very well.' She would do whatever was needed for her husband.

'And once he's recovered from the influenza, you'll have to see that Frederick slows down.' Jeremy sipped the tea and nodded in appreciation, before selecting another small cake from the plate. His sweet tooth was proverbial in the town.

'Does Frederick know – about his heart, I mean?'

'Of course he does.'

'How – how did he take it?'

Jeremy shrugged. Frederick had been silent for so long after he had delivered his diagnosis that he had feared for his patient, but then Frederick had given him a wry smile and wheezed out the words with difficulty: 'Then I shall – have to make sure – that the next few years count – shan't I?'

Jeremy finished his cake and set down his empty teacup. 'He took it well, I think. He didn't even seem surprised. If he makes plans, try to go along with them, provided they don't involve him in any extra work. People who are happily occupied often seem to live longer than those who are unhappy – though I've met a few whose anger seems to sustain them just as well.'

When Jeremy left, Annie sat for a long time staring sightlessly into the fire. She had known the risks she was taking when she married a much older man, but she and Frederick had been so happy together for the past – goodness, it was nearly ten years now! – that she had pushed her fears to the back of her mind.

Now those fears would have to be faced. And she would have to help Frederick through the next few years with a cheerful face, whatever it cost her. She loved him so much, so very much.

In a cheap lodging house in Manchester, Elizabeth MacNaughton wept in relief when she discovered that she was not pregnant. She looked around the room that was little more than a cubicle and shivered. She had some money, but if she didn't get a position as a governess soon, she would have to try to find another way of earning some money.

She was hungry and cold, but she had decided that she could manage on one meal a day, so she spread her one and only winter cloak over the two thin blankets and huddled under the covers. She had not tried to contact her aunt again and could only hope that Lewis did not vent his spite on her few remaining possessions, which were stored in their attic. Her father's only riches had been books and she loved them, too. Perhaps one day she would be able to retrieve them.

Before she fell into a fitful sleep, she prayed to the Lord she still believed in that he would help her to a respectable way of earning a living with a decent family. The people at the agency had been quite hopeful of finding her something eventually. But she needed a position now, not eventually.

5

Netherleigh Cottage

John Gibson walked slowly home from the junk yard which he managed for his children, Tom and Annie. He watched how he set his feet down on the treacherous icy road, rubbing his hands together occasionally and beating them against his body to put some warmth into them, because even the thick overcoat, scarf and knitted woollen gloves didn't seem to keep out the cold today. He sighed with relief as he came out of the chill windy darkness of the street into the cosy brightness and warmth of Netherleigh Cottage.

Kathy came running into the hall as soon as she heard the front door open, to help him shrug out of his overcoat and unwind the long knitted muffler from his neck. He took the opportunity to give her a hearty kiss before walking with her through to the kitchen at the rear, his arm lying loosely around her thin shoulders and his head close to hers. 'Eh, did you see the sky this afternoon? Nearly black, it were. If it's not snowing by tomorrow, I'll eat my hat, I will that.'

He beamed at the two boys sitting at one end of the kitchen table. 'Now, then?' he demanded, as he always did. 'How did you go on at school today?'

He listened indulgently to their tales of penmanship and history tests and the unfairness of the schoolmaster in stopping them from engaging in a game of football in the school yard, just because the ground was frozen hard. But it was his own thoughts that were at the forefront of his mind as he looked around the large cheerful room, which had once been a farm kitchen.

'I love this room,' he declared, as though this would be a surprise to the others. Kathy hid a smile and the boys rolled their eyes at one another.

'You always say that, Dad,' Samuel John complained.

'Do I?'

'Yes, an' you always say "Do I?", too, when we tell you,' Ben chimed in.

John winked at Kathy. 'Just fancy.' But he did love this room. He and his family spent more of their time in it than anywhere else in the house, though the front parlour was always used on special family occasions. In fact, although Netherleigh Cottage belonged to Annie and John paid her rent for it, somehow it felt like his own place and he knew she would never turn him out of it, not even when he grew too old to work. Though that wouldn't happen for a long time yet, he was sure. The men in his family either died young or lived to a ripe old age. And he had survived to nearly fifty-nine, so he reckoned he'd make old bones.

The Lord had been good to him, that he had. John never forgot to acknowledge that in his nightly prayers. He had a wonderful family. Nine children living, the last two these little lads of his and Kathy's. And his two eldest, Annie and Tom, had done so well for themselves that they'd been able to take him from the hard work in Hallam's Mill, which had been sapping all his strength and energy, and set him up to run the junk yard for them. It was a fine healthy place to work after the fluff-laden atmosphere of a spinning mill, and there was always something interesting happening. He'd not felt as well in his whole life as he had in the past ten years.

He'd more than repaid Annie and Tom for their help, though. He knew he had and it was a source of pride to him. They'd not find anyone to run that yard who had their interests so much at heart as he did. Look how the place had continued to bring in a nice profit, even when Mark left it. John admitted to himself that he'd been a bit nervous of taking over completely, more than a bit, but it had all turned out for the best.

Lizzie, his other child by his first wife, lived in Blackpool, where she ran a boarding house. She'd been a surly lass, but had turned out all right in the end and was doing well there, though he wished she lived closer.

And now Mark, John's son by his second wife, Emily, was doing all right for himself as well. At twenty-three, Mark was a fine young man, tall and handsome with steady dark eyes. John had seen the way the lasses looked at him. Oh, yes. Emily's children had grown tall – well, Luke, Mark and Rebecca had, but Joanie was a bare five feet, even shorter than Annie.

Luke, the second son by Emily, was more like John in character than any of the others. John saw himself in Luke, couldn't help it, though Luke, too, was tall, if not as good-looking as his brother. At twenty-two he was a quiet young fellow, not bothered about being rich, just working to earn an honest living and enjoying his gardening of a weekend. Yes, he had green thumbs, that lad did, and loved his flowers. He could coax any plant to bloom for him.

'Where's our Rebecca and Joanie?' John demanded, coming out of his reverie to realise that the girls were missing from the kitchen. 'They should be home by now on a night like this.'

'Rebecca's in the dining room, drawing. She'll come in when I serve up.' Rebecca often worked on designs for the salon in the evenings, and had made the dining room her special province.

John went over to Kathy and asked quietly, 'Has she changed her mind?'

His wife shook her head. 'No. She still refuses point blank to come with us to the chapel dance.' She hesitated, looked across at the two lads, then lowered her voice to add, 'I think there's some fellow going that she doesn't like.'

Samuel John looked up. 'I expect it's that Harry Pickering. He stopped me in the street the other day to ask whether our Rebecca was going on Saturday.'

'Why didn't you say anything about it?'

The lad shrugged. 'I didn't think it were important.'

'I shall have to have a word with that young man,' John said. 'I'm not having him pestering our Rebecca.'

'No! Better not, love.' Kathy knew that Rebecca would hate them interfering, and she suspected that the girl wouldn't have gone to the dance anyway. Rebecca didn't fit in with the young men from chapel. She had a fancy way of talking and looked so elegant that they tended to steer clear of her. Joanie would have no trouble at all finding partners, but Kathy couldn't see the young men braving Rebecca's cool self-control.

'What about our Joanie?' John asked. 'Is she not back yet?' He was very watchful of his girls.

'Joanie's been and gone. She's helping our Mark out tonight at the chop house. He's had to sack one of the girls as was helping the cook, so Joanie's gone to lend a hand. She's a good little cook, that lass.' Kathy took John's cup and refilled it, then turned to check the stew. 'How did it go at the yard today, then, love?'

'Well enough. Mind you, there was a fellow came in this morning as was trying to cheat us, but I soon sorted him out. "What do you think I am, blind?" I said.' John still felt pleased with the way he'd handled that. He might not have the sharpness of Tom and Mark, but he could spot a cheat a mile off and strike a fair bargain with the men who collected junk for the yard, for no one knew the prices better than he did.

'Things are all right at Mark's place, aren't they?' he asked Kathy, a frown furrowing his brow.

'Oh, yes. Doing real well, Joanie says. Full most of the time.'

Last year Mark had opened a snug little eating place just off the High Street. It sold mainly chops and roast lamb and pies to working-class people. The lad had taken them all by surprise when he announced that he wanted to go into business on his own account. He'd saved his pennies carefully and done his sums before starting anything, and then rented the premises before he even told his family.

'Get your things off the table now! And one of you go and fetch Rebecca,' Kathy ordered, and Samuel John hurried to obey. 'Didn't our Luke come home with you tonight, John love?'

'No.' He frowned. Luke had been very quiet and thoughtful lately. You could never guess what was going through that lad's mind, but he'd no doubt tell them what was worriting him when he was ready. John set his empty cup down with an appreciative noise. 'You make the best cup of tea there is, lass, the very best.'

'You always say that, too,' observed Samuel John from the doorway, but this time his parents ignored him.

'Well, where's Luke gone, then?' Kathy prompted. 'I hope he gets himself something to eat. You need good food in your belly in cold weather like this.'

'He said he had to meet someone. I think they're arranging a special lecture down at the Institute. Something to do with those microscope things.'

Kathy pulled a face. 'I don't like looking down them, myself, but our Luke's fair taken with them.'

'He's fair taken with a lot of things. When he's not wandering the moors collecting plants, he's working in the garden, or reading one of those naturalist books of his.'

'I'd rather he was out seeing a girl,' Kathy said wistfully. 'At his age it isn't natural not to be courting. Not a nice-looking lad like Luke. And it'd be good to have some more grandchildren.'

'Nay, he's never shown much interest in the lasses. He's not like our Mark, who never leaves them alone.' John grinned at her. 'Not like me, either.'

She grinned back at him. She had been well pregnant when they married and at first Tom had been furious with his father for starting a third family at the age of fifty. If Dr Lewis hadn't told John she was not to have any more children, Kathy would have liked another babe or two. But John's first wife had died in childbed, so he was very careful to take the proper precautions now, the sort of precautions that might have saved Lucy Gibson if he had known about them then.

Rebecca came in. 'Hello, Dad. Did you have a good day?'

'Aye. There's allus something happenin' at the yard.'

'She always asks him that, too,' Samuel John whispered to Ben and the two boys giggled together until their mother caught sight of their grubby hands and sent them into the scullery to get washed.

'I've missed our Lally this week,' Kathy said as she served the meal after John had said grace. 'I'll be glad when she comes back from burying her mam.' Lally was the maid whom Annie insisted they employ to help Kathy, but so far as they were concerned, Lally was part of the family. Well, she had no parents of her own now, did she? And she was a nice lass, willing to turn her hand to anything.

At nine o'clock Joanie came home, yawning, but full of the happenings at the chop house. 'Our Mark's that fussy. He's taken on a new girl to wait on, but he won't tell her she can keep the job till he's seen how she shapes up.' Joanie giggled. 'Her brother brought her along. And he says her wages have to be paid to her father every week, not to her.'

'Oh? Who is she?' Kathy liked to keep in touch with what was happening.

'Nelly Burns. Her cousin works for Mark as well, in the kitchen, and he says she's a good worker, so he's agreed to give this one a try.'

'Burns?' Kathy wrinkled her brow. 'Do I know the

family?' In the old days, she would have known most families in Bilsden, but times were changing, with the town growing bigger and all sorts of people moving there. 'Burns,' she repeated, annoyed that she felt she could not place the name.

'You know, the one with the mad father.'

'Now, our Joanie, you know I don't like to hear idle gossip that blackens folk's names,' John scolded, but fondly. The only time he ever spoke sharply to his children was on a moral issue. He had a very rigid idea of what was right and what was wrong.

'Well, Mr Burns *is* funny, Dad. He carries a Bible with him everywhere, so they call him Bible Burns. And the brother seems nearly as bad. You should have heard how he talked to Nelly, scolding her in front of everyone, as if she were a child. I wouldn't have stood for it. Mind you,' Joanie grinned, 'once he'd gone it was a different story. She likes a bit of fun, Nelly Burns does, and she says she won't tell her father how much in tips she gets – well, the waitresses don't get much, but it's something anyway. She's to walk home with her cousin every night. Her brother announced that, too.'

'It's safer,' Kathy nodded. 'I don't like you being out on your own after dark.'

Joanie tossed her head. 'Our Luke walked me to the gate, but there was no need. I can look after myself.' And so, if she was any judge of the matter, could Nelly Burns. She had not really taken to the girl, though she couldn't have said why.

The two eldest boys didn't come home till after ten, by which time everyone else was in bed and John was banking up the kitchen fire for the night. Mark called a cheery good night and went straight to bed, but Luke came into the kitchen and started fiddling with the carving on John's rocking chair.

John sat back on his heels. 'Eh, lad, you're going to be boggy-eyed in the morning, staying out so late.'

'Me an' Mark decided to have a bit of a natter after he'd closed up.'

John could sense a confidence coming, so he kept poking at the fire. When folk had something important to tell you, they got nervous if you stared at their faces. He'd learned that a long time ago.

Luke sat down on the nearest chair. 'Dad, I've been wanting to have a talk with you for a while now.'

'Oh, aye?' John murmured, to show he was listening.

'Dad, I don't want to spend my whole life in the junk yard.'

'Oh?' John set the poker down and sat on his rocking chair, risking a quick sideways glance at his son. If Luke had something else in mind for himself, then he must have been considering it for a long time, because he was not one to make rash decisions. 'What do you want to do with yersen, then, lad?'

'I want to work with gardens.'

There was silence for a minute or two, broken only by the soft sound of the ash John had piled on the coals as it sifted down into the glowing cracks.

'I doubt you'd make much brass as a gardener, son. Nor it wouldn't look good for Mester Hallam's brother-in-law to be doing that sort of work, not if you didn't need to.'

'I don't want to be that sort of gardener. I want to grow things in a market garden of my own, things I can sell to folk. Vegetables and flowers and pot plants, as well. Folk like to have plants for their parlours. Ferns and things. And bunches of flowers. I want to grow some of the fancy new plants, too, the ones they're bringing back from overseas. But I'd need a hothouse for that.' Luke's voice was full of longing. 'They're finding all sorts of interesting plants nowadays. Some folk travel the world, just to seek 'em out. If I were rich I'd be goin' off to find some myself before I settled down.'

'That sounds more like farming nor gardening.' John

frowned. He still didn't like this idea of Luke's. It sounded too chancy.

'Well, I think folk would be happy to be able to buy really good fresh vegetables, fancy stuff, not just cabbage and taties, and not only on market day. I'd sell at the market, too, of course, and at my gate the rest of the time. Our Mark said he'd buy from me, if the quality and price were right, but he wants mainly potatoes an' I can't see much interest in growing them.'

'It'd need a fair bit of money to set you up in something like that.'

Luke nodded. 'Aye. I've been saving up for years, but I can't see as I'll ever be able to save enough this way. So I thought I'd go and talk to our Annie about it. Once it's set up, I'm sure I'll be able to make more money than I can now at the yard. I reckon she might help me buy somewhere. She knows I'd pay her back. It'd be a business agreement between us.' He hesitated, then added, 'And I need to see Frederick, too. I'd want to go and work with Nat Jervis for a bit before I did anything on my own, you see. He knows more about growing stuff than anyone I've ever met, Nat does. Only I didn't want to do owt without telling you first, Dad.'

John nodded. 'I take that kindly, lad.' Then he snapped his fingers as he remembered the bad news that Kathy had passed on to him over tea. 'But you'll not be able to talk to Frederick or Annie for a bit. He's come down sick with the influenza and she's nursing him. She sent down word today.'

'How bad is he?'

'He's right poorly, it seems. They had Dr Lewis up to see him this morning.'

'Well, my plan will keep till he's better, won't it?' Luke said in his slow careful voice. 'It never does to rush at things.'

Father and son were both silent, remembering how members of their own family had died in one outbreak of influenza. Eventually Luke broke the silence. 'I hope Frederick will be all right. He's getting on a bit.'

'Oh, yes?' John grinned. 'Well, I'm the same age as he is, an' I don't feel old, I can tell you.'

Luke stared at him, then frowned and shook his head. 'He looks older than you lately.'

John blinked at him in surprise, then went back to the previous topic of conversation again, trying to understand Luke's feelings. 'An' so you were discussing this with our Mark?'

Luke nodded.

'What did he think about it? He's a sharp one, Mark is.'

'He thinks there are better ways to make money than gardening.'

'Well, he'd know about that. Maybe you should—'

Luke looked squarely at his father. 'I need to make a living, I know that. But I don't hanker after a fortune, like Mark does. I just want to earn enough to live decent and work with plants. I'm never as happy as when I'm in the garden. And I'll manage it, too, one day. I'm determined on that.' He got up and went along to the room off the kitchen which he shared with Mark, the room that had once been a dairy when this place was a farm, and had then been John's bedroom when they all lived here with Annie.

He stared after his son in amazement. He'd never seen the gentle, easy-going Luke look so much like Annie and Mark, never seen such passion in his quiet son's face. 'Eh, an' he might just do it, too,' he said. But John couldn't see how. He had a bit of money put by himself, but that was for Kathy, for when he died. He knew Annie would take care of her, but wanted her to have some money of her own. A man his age didn't outlive a wife so much younger. He just hoped he'd last till the two youngest boys were earning their own living and could look after their mother. But that was all in the Lord's hands.

6

The Emporium

That same evening, Tom Gibson was sitting in his office on the third floor of the Bilsden Emporium, taking stock of his life. He smiled as he caught sight of the shelf full of old accounts books, including the tattered notebook from when he and Annie had first started their joint business with a stall in the market place. She had always insisted on their doing things properly, so that they could see how much profit they were making and keep track of their money, and she was right.

After a few years in the market, Annie had gone on to open the Bilsden Ladies' Salon and he had taken over the junk rounds when her first husband, Charlie Ashworth, died. From there they had bought the junk yard from old Mr Thomas's widow, then moved into other areas as well, making a bit here and a bit there.

You should never despise small profits. They built up over the weeks and months into respectable sums. Tom still had a lot of little things on the go. Hawkers who bought their stocks of pins, thread and needles from him, and then sold them round the farms and hamlets. Another fellow who collected fresh eggs, milk and cheeses from the farmers' wives on Tom's cart and sold it at market on Tom's stall. Street hawkers who sold food and drink. A cottage in a useful position that brought in a bit of rent. Oh, yes, it all mounted up.

But Tom's mind did not linger on his business interests. All day he'd been thinking about himself. His anger about the funeral the other day had been a catalyst, somehow, as if it had drained off the last dregs of the fierce feelings of rage and grief that had been slowly ebbing away over the years since his wife's death. The night he had talked to Frederick and Annie, he had wept himself to sleep and woken up feeling scoured of grief, somehow. She was dead, his lovely girl, long dead. Nothing would bring her back. And life had to go on.

It had taken him a long time to get to this point but his visit to Ridge House had been the last flare-up of a fire that had smouldered on for too long. He raised the lukewarm cup of tea he'd been cradling in his hands for a while in a final toast. 'Marianne, I'll never forget you, love. Never.' But Frederick had been right. You couldn't nurse your grief or your grudges for ever – though Tom still couldn't see himself wanting to associate with the Darringtons, not under any circumstances.

The staff had long gone home and the Emporium was quiet, except for the occasional shuffling footsteps of Bill, the night watchman, as he prowled through the darkened premises below. Ever since someone had broken into the junk yard several years previously, Tom had employed night watchmen for his larger premises: old chaps usually, who couldn't hold down a proper job any more, but who could keep watch during the long hours of the night and ring an emergency bell if needed, one that was loud enough to wake half the town. They and their fellows were always glad of an extra shilling or two and cheap produce from the market stalls thrown in.

Even as he was listening, Bill's footsteps stopped and he quavered, 'Who's there?'

Tom was up out of his chair and at the door in time to hear Bill cry out. There was a thud that sounded like a body falling. Tom's eyes lit up, with both anger and relish.

He was just in the mood for a bit of a scuffle tonight. He crept down the stairs and by the light of the street lamps saw something on the floor at the far end of the central shop. His lips tightened with anger. If the intruder had hurt old Bill, he'd see the fellow suffered in his turn.

In the central office, someone was fumbling through the drawers. Tom crept up to the door and listened. Two of them. Then he slipped soundlessly to the rope that rang the alarm bell. He tugged on it and sent a raucous noise clanging across the quiet town centre.

In the office someone swore and when the door flew open, Tom was waiting for the burglars, a poker in his hand. He thumped one fellow into oblivion and grappled with the other. The one he'd hit dropped like a stone, but the other one was a big chap and gave Tom an anxious minute or two until someone grabbed him from behind.

Tom grinned at the two constables, who were holding the burglar prisoner. 'What kept you?'

They grinned back at him. They were proud of their reputation for arriving quickly on the scene if there was any trouble in the town centre.

'There's another one over there.' He pointed to a man who was just regaining consciousness, groaning and rolling his head to and fro.

'We'll see to him, Mr Gibson. Are you all right?'

'Fine.'

It was an hour before the fuss had died down, by which time Bill had had his head tended by Dr Spelling, then been sent home in a cab, and the two men had been charged.

'I'll make sure a constable patrols the street tonight. You don't want anyone getting in through that broken window,' the sergeant told Tom.

'I'll board it up before I go home.' He was sporting a split lip and had a bruised arm, but he had enjoyed the action. It had made him feel young again. He'd been a rough lad, and by hell, he could still take care of himself.

When the police finally left, he picked up a lantern and walked through the dark Emporium. This place was mostly his, though Annie held a smaller share. It had started off as a draper's, next door to the Bilsden Ladies' Salon, and had spread gradually over the years along the row of shops in the better part of High Street, sometimes by negotiation with other shopkeepers, who would, for an inducement, change premises, and sometimes through the death of an owner. Frederick owned the whole row and sometimes joked about Tom being a good risk for rent.

The Bilsden Emporium now covered what had been five single shops and sold not only dress and furnishing materials, together with the myriad odds and ends you'd find in any linen draper's, but also ready-made clothing, with mourning wear a good regular seller. Annie's people were in charge of stocking that section and she sent mourning wear out to all sorts of workers to make up at home.

There was good fresh farm food at the far end of the Emporium from the salon, especially cheeses, on which Tom had become something of an expert. He sold ordinary cheese on his market stall, and the best cheeses in his Emporium, some of which he brought in from outside Bilsden. That had surprised people at first, for they were used to buying their fresh stuff only from the market, but they'd soon got used to the convenience of being able to buy from Gibson's any day of the week.

There was an elegant little tea shop in the Emporium, too, next to the food section, a favourite meeting place for the better class of folk in Bilsden. He grinned. It had separate 'retiring rooms' for ladies and gentlemen at the modest charge of a penny a visit. Annie had had a 'retiring room' put in when she first opened her salon – it had been a nine-day wonder in the town – and she had told him all about the public conveniences at the Great Exhibition in 1851, which were the first Tom had heard of to charge a penny a visit.

The retiring rooms made a small profit for him, and they also paid the wages of old Gertie Bridson, whose pride and joy they were and who kept them immaculately clean. They attracted people into the Emporium, which was more important to Tom. People who came in rarely left without buying something. Though if Frederick's plans for the town square came off, Tom would either have to stop charging the pennies or offer extra facilities, because Frederick wanted to build some free public conveniences near the square, next to the park, to stop fellows going round the back corners when they were taken short.

Tom finished the tour of his domain in the household goods section, upstairs. It sold small stuff, anything from trays to occasional tables, from firescreens to wax flowers under glass. There was also a toy section, and some basic cutlery and crockery. On the third floor were some store rooms and his office.

A man could be proud of an achievement like this. Well, it was his sister's achievement, too. Yes, she made a fine business partner, but he wouldn't like to marry someone as independent as Annie. He preferred women of a more domesticated nature. His Marianne had made her husband and children her whole life, and that's what a woman should do, Tom reckoned. For the second time that evening, he cut off his memories there. It was no use picking at old scars; it was time to move on.

He found some planks and roughly boarded up the window the thieves had broken, then went back up to his office, reluctant to go home. He didn't want to return to an empty house yet. Well, it felt empty once the children were in bed and the two maids chatting quietly over a cup of tea at the kitchen table. He could go and see Seth Holden, of course, who managed their mutual investment, The Prince of Wales hotel. Seth never went to bed till late. But somehow Tom wasn't in the mood for chatting with Seth about old times. All day he'd been feeling restless and twitchy. He was in a mood for action.

He picked up the *Bilsden Gazette* and smoothed it out absently, staring at the front page of the newspaper without taking anything in. He knew one thing that was wrong with him, of course he did. If anyone else had even hinted after Marianne's death that he'd one day need a soft willing body to assuage his physical needs, he'd have punched them in the face. His body had been numb for the first year or two, quite numb, no desire for anything. And that was the first time that had happened since he was thirteen.

But then his body had come to life again and he'd started needing a bit of comfort every now and then, going into Manchester to get it. And lately he'd begun to realise that he needed more. Not just a woman's compliant body, no, he needed a woman whose company he could enjoy. He wanted more than an empty parlour to greet him when he came home at night, and more than an earthenware hot water pig to warm up the fine linen sheets on his comfortable feather bed.

He hadn't told Annie, or she'd have been looking for a wife for him. Well, she'd already thrown a few women his way, but he'd pretended not to notice. He preferred to do his own choosing, thank you very much. But how could you find a wife in a small town like Bilsden? He grinned. You couldn't exactly try a woman out, could you? Ferociously respectable, the people in Bilsden were – except for those down in the River Rows, to which the folk from Claters End had migrated when the Town Council pulled down the last sleazy courts and alleys two years ago.

The grin faded and he let out a gusty sigh. He knew one thing from just looking around: he didn't fancy a very young woman. Young women were silly giggly creatures. He sometimes had to bite his tongue when the ones who served in his shop tittered together over nothing. At thirty-five he wanted some adult companionship, dammit. He drew in a shaky breath. Not a mistress. It had taken him nearly six years to come to this point, but what he wanted now was a wife, a second wife.

Guilt shot through him for a moment, but faded quickly. Marianne of all people would have understood. He needed a companion for the occasional evening out in Manchester, someone to discuss his business plans with, someone to cuddle up to on cold nights like this one, and of course someone who'd be a good mother to his three children. Not someone as independent as Annie – heavens, no! – but still, he wanted someone with a bit of sense in her head, someone intelligent enough to become a friend, but young enough to tempt him to bed. Oh, yes, he needed that, too. His body had surged back to life with a vengeance lately. Visits to Manchester weren't nearly enough. Eh, he was as bad as his father. The Gibson curse, Annie called it.

'Oh, hell!' he said aloud, opened up the newspaper and tried to concentrate on reading it. He had flipped past the advertisement before the information sank in. He turned back with hands that trembled suddenly.

ROSA LIDONI
CONCERT RECITAL
The famous soprano,
who has performed in London and Paris,
will give two concerts in Manchester
in the Fiske Street Hall
Tickets – half a guinea

Tom whistled aloud. 'Half a guinea! You're gone up in the world, Rosie love.' He had watched out for her concerts, thinking he might go to one some day, but it had seemed as if she was avoiding Manchester all these years. And he'd not left the north, for he'd buried himself in his business. So he and Rosie had not met since that time she came to comfort him after Marianne's death, like the good friend she'd always been over the years.

He turned the rest of the pages listlessly. There was nothing else worth reading in the paper. The news was a load of fuss about nothing today. It was not till he was walking home through the icy stillness of a world waiting for snow to fall that Tom even admitted it to himself, then he stopped dead in his tracks to face the thought squarely – he was going to go to that concert. He was going to see Rosie again. Beyond that he didn't allow himself to speculate, but he couldn't help thinking about her as he walked on.

He had known Rosie Liddelow since he'd been a lad. He grinned. He had more than known her. Until he met Marianne, Rosie had been his girl. Of course, he'd been too ambitious to marry a girl from Claters End, but they'd been together for a number of years. And he knew Rosie had been faithful to him, which was more than he'd been to her. A sudden blush of shame warmed his cheeks.

She was a cosy armful, Rosie was. And once, when he'd quarrelled with Marianne just before they married, he'd been stupid enough to go back and spend a night in her bed. Hell, what a fool he had been! But thank goodness Marianne had never found out that he and Rosie had had a son as a result of that night, the only child they'd ever made together. He wouldn't have liked to hurt Marianne. He wasn't proud of what he'd done and had never tried to see the child after that first time when Rosie showed him his new-born son, though of course he'd given her money regularly. He wasn't one to back out of his responsibilities.

He frowned as he tried to calculate how old little Albert would be now. Not so little. Just a bit older than the twins, in fact, and David and Lucy had turned eight last year. Where had all those years gone?

'Damned if I won't go and see her,' he muttered as he turned his key in the lock. 'And I'll get Beeching to make me up a new evening suit for the occasion, too. Something really smart. At half a guinea entrance the place will be full of nobs. It'll not be like one of those public concerts at the Free Trade Hall.'

* * *

After the chop house had closed for the night, Mark Gibson sat in the corner of his storeroom, in the area he called his 'office', counting the takings. The whole of the front part of this place was taken up by the eating rooms, and he let out the upstairs to a young couple to bring in a bit of extra money while he was getting on his feet, so this was the only place he could put the new roll-top desk that had been Annie's gift to him when the chop house opened.

After Luke had left, Mark sat on. He heard voices calling to one another as his staff cleared up, then after a while silence. He frowned. The last person to leave usually came to ask him to lock the back door after them.

Sensing someone behind him, he turned around quickly. No one was going to rob him if he could help it. But it was only Nelly Burns, the new girl, hovering in the doorway. He frowned. What was she still hanging around for? He wanted to finish counting the money before he went home, then hide it away. And he never counted his money in front of his employees. Never. It was not only putting temptation in their way, but they might say something about it that would bring others trying to steal it. Not that anyone would easily find his main hiding place. He had a loose floorboard and in it a tin box with a bit of money that was relatively easy to find, but the bulk of his working capital was in a secret compartment in the desk. You'd never know it was there if you didn't know the trick. He ran a cash business, so he needed a good supply on hand.

He stared at the girl appreciatively, for she was a good-looking piece, with dark hair and large sparkling brown eyes, not to mention a voluptuous figure. Amazing that she was Bible Burns's daughter! Even more amazing to see how she changed and adopted a meek air in the presence of her brothers or father. Tonight, however, she returned his gaze boldly. Too boldly.

'What do you want?' he growled, annoyed at himself for noticing her looks.

'You said you'd think about taking me on permanent, Mr Gibson.'

'Oh, yes?' He was taking every step cautiously. No more than Annie and Tom did he intend to do anything risky, so most of his new staff were told at first that they were on trial and would be working casual hours as needed until he saw how high the takings were and how well they worked.

'I've been waiting on here for two weeks now, an' the place is full most nights. So will I do, Mr Gibson?' She smiled at him cheekily as she said that. Her voice was husky and her eyes were warm and inviting.

He ignored the unspoken invitation. Maud, who ran the kitchens, wasn't much taken with Nelly, but the girl did her work all right, which was the most important thing. 'Yes, you can consider yourself hired permanently from next week onwards.' He knew that he'd need another full-time waitress, even before he counted the takings. The place was doing well at lunch-time, too. He felt he lived in two worlds sometimes: the world of his sister and her rich husband where dinner was in the evening, and the ordinary world where folk worked hard for a living and called their evening meal 'tea'. As he did.

Nelly moved a little closer, pulling her shawl so tightly round her that it outlined the rise and fall of her full breasts. 'Thanks. I'm that grateful, Mr Gibson.'

'Just see that you work hard, then.' He gestured dismissal and ignored her look of disappointment. He'd have to watch that one. He wasn't having any of his girls flirting with his customers. Or with himself. He'd made it plain that he wanted his chop house to build up a reputation as a respectable place where families could come and eat. But give Nelly her due, although she bantered with the clients, she did nothing to which anyone could object. Nothing but look. And that mainly at him.

The thought made him frown, because she'd definitely been hinting at things just then. Strange, that, with her background. And he'd been tempted, because he'd

inherited the family curse, the incessant itch of sexual
desire. That's what had driven his father to wed three
wives, and that's what had driven Tom, too, from all
accounts – well, it had until he had married Marianne.

The curse seemed to have missed Luke, who was more
interested in plants than women, but Mark had inherited
it in full. He had more sense than to spill his seed unwisely,
though. The last thing he needed at the moment was a
bastard child to drag him down, or worse still, the family
of a respectable working girl insisting on marriage.

One day he intended to marry – but it'd be someone
useful, someone from a good family, not someone from the
Rows, and certainly not someone who'd been with other
men. But that wouldn't be for a long time yet. Not until he'd
something to offer such a woman.

A couple of years ago, Tom had shown him where to get
satisfaction without much risk of catching some nasty
disease. But that was in Manchester. Pity there weren't
any of the better places like that in Bilsden. He wouldn't
trust the local street whores, and anyway, he didn't want
to get a reputation in the town as that sort of man. It was a
family business he was running, with everything plain but
respectable, and as owner he had to set a good example.
The very poorest people couldn't afford to eat at his chop
house, but those working folk with a penny or two to spare
could. Young couples courting. Married folk with several
children working. The chop house was warm and bright,
an attractive place to spend an hour or two, and so much
more respectable than The Shepherd's Rest.

He sighed. It was a long time between visits to
Manchester, though, too long. Especially now that his
business was taking up so much of his time. He could do
without the temptation offered by Nelly Burns. But it'd
upset her cousin Jean if he sacked Nelly, and it'd get the
lass into trouble with her strict father, too. No, he couldn't
do that to her.

Mark had not taken to Mr Burns, who came to collect

Nelly's wages every Saturday, spouting the Bible at everyone and acting like he was a judge over the rest of the world. When she'd begged Mark not to tell her father how much she got in tips, he'd agreed to that. He shook his head in irritation. No, he couldn't sack the lass for no reason. Her father would probably beat her if that happened. But Mark wished, he really did wish, that she'd stop looking at him like that! He was not made of stone.

7

London: William

*I*n London, William Ashworth sat in a pub with some fellow students and sighed as the noise of raucous voices singing out of tune beat at his skull. He didn't feel like getting drunk. He had done it once, when he first came to London the previous year, and that was enough to last him a lifetime. He loathed the feeling of not being in charge of his own body, not to mention the thumping headache the day after.

When the song was over, someone nudged him. 'Drink up, Will! You've been nursing that glass for an hour now. Has somebody spat in it?'

There was a chorus of volunteers for the job.

William summoned up a smile. 'I'm just not in a drinking mood tonight, Murden, old chap. I think I'll go back to Mrs Dale's and do some studying.' He stood up.

All the young men at his table made rude noises and protested loudly at this, trying to drag him back into his chair again, but since they were only fooling around, William was sturdy enough to hold his own. In fact, he was the tallest chap in his year, and as strong as an ox. His well-developed muscles were partly the result of the many menial jobs he had done in the family businesses while he was growing up. His mother had insisted that he earn his spending money, even after she married Frederick

Hallam. He hadn't minded that, for mostly he'd been working with his grandfather.

He hoped his mother would do the same thing with Tamsin. He loved the child dearly, but she was a wilful minx and he didn't want her growing up like her half-sister, Beatrice, born to Frederick's first wife, who had hurt him and his mother badly when he was only ten.

His jaw clenched at that thought. He'd never forgotten the pain of discovering that he owed his existence to a drunken man raping his mother. But he'd never seen Beatrice again after that dreadful day when she arranged for her maid to tell him, because Frederick had disowned her for what she had done. Reginald Barrence was welcome to marry a vicious shrew like her, Frederick had said, but he doubted she'd be happy with him. The fellow had only taken her for the sake of her dowry.

When Annie began to talk about sending William to university, it was Frederick who had suggested University College, London, which was, he said, more modern than Oxford and Cambridge and was not bothered about which religion its students were. 'I tried to tell them this wasn't what I wanted to do,' William whispered to the cold night air as he strolled back towards his lodgings. 'And I was right, too.' But once his mother got an idea into her head, there was no gainsaying her.

In the end, William had agreed to give university a try for a year, just to please his mother. But it wasn't working. It was such a useless way of life, and most of the fellows were just there to have a good time, not caring two hoots about what they could learn. Even the studying wasn't as interesting as it had been with Saul Hinchcliffe, who had a deep and abiding love of scholarship and who had made classical literature come alive for his few privileged students. Saul had no need to run his small school, thanks to his wife's money, but did it out of sheer love of teaching and only accepted those who truly wanted to learn.

Since coming to London, William had inevitably had to

take tea with Frederick's elder daughter by his first wife, Mildred. He was sure his mother had asked her to keep an eye on him and did not at all want to go, but could not find a polite way of refusing. On the first visit no one in the Jemmings family mentioned Beatrice, to his great relief. He didn't think he could even pretend to be polite about her.

He had found Rosemary Jemmings, Mildred's step-daughter, who was the same age as he was, just as exasperating as when she had been a child, only this time she was playing off all the airs and graces of a young lady and treating him like a boy. It was with difficulty that he answered her sly jibes civilly.

On his second visit, Mildred made an opportunity to speak to him alone. 'Do you know whether my father has heard from Beatrice, William?'

'I don't think so, Mrs Jemmings.'

Mildred did not meet his eyes, but started fiddling with the ornaments on a small table. 'She has moved from the house they were renting and I don't know where she's gone. Will you ask your mother about her for me? Ask her if they've heard anything at all from Beatrice? I don't like to write to Father. He was so angry with poor Bea. He won't let me even mention her name now.'

William scowled. If Beatrice had vanished, he was glad. He hoped no one would ever hear from her again, or her languid arty husband, or Mabel, her vicious maid. His grandfather said you should forgive your enemies, but William had never been able to forgive Beatrice and Mabel, and he knew he never would.

Mildred sniffed and sighed. 'Please, William. I know Beatrice was unkind to you, but I'm worried about her. She used to call and take tea with me regularly, but she hasn't been for ages. She wouldn't have gone away without letting me know, I know she wouldn't. I'm afraid – I'm really afraid something's happened to her.'

'What does her husband say?'

'I haven't seen him, either. Well, I only saw him once or twice, anyway. He didn't spend a lot of time with Beatrice.'

Innate good manners made William say reluctantly, 'I'll ask my mother when next I see her. But I'm sure she won't have heard anything.'

Mildred's eyes misted with tears, which she blinked away furiously. 'Thank you.'

Later that day, when Rosemary started to treat him as a hobbledehoy lad again, William grabbed her behind the shrubbery and vented his frustration by giving her a kiss that made her gasp and blush. He wasn't proud of himself afterwards, but it shut her up, at least.

On his next visit to Mildred's, however, Rosemary treated him like a possible suitor, and he found that quite horrifying. If he ever married it would not be to a sharp-tongued and self-opinionated shrew like her! Or to a tame mouse like her younger sister Philippa. He refused the next invitation. And the next.

Why can't I be like the other fellows? he wondered for the hundredth time as he walked along. Life would be so easy if it weren't for this remorseless voice of conscience in his head that kept telling him he was wasting his life, doing no good to his fellow human beings, not even learning anything useful to himself.

He didn't see the girl until she sidled up to him and tugged at his sleeve. 'Give you a good time, sir,' she said in a throaty voice.

He thought at first that the voice was an attempt to sound provocative, but as she sputtered and began to cough, great racking spasms that shook her thin body, he stared at her in pity and tugged her out into the light from a gas lamp. 'How old are you?' he demanded, feeling the bones in her arm as fragile as chicken wings.

'Old enough to know my trade.' She smiled at him, still trying without success to suppress the spluttering cough.

'What made you take up this sinful life?'

'Oh, hell, you're one of them Bible-bangers! Well, I'm

not interested in bein' saved, thank you very much! I've got my bread to earn.'

She tried to pull away, but William kept hold of her. How thin she was! And how scantily clad! 'How old are you?' he repeated and gave her a little shake to emphasise that he wanted an answer.

'I'm fourteen, if it's any of your business,' she spat at him. 'Lemme go, you! If you don't want me, there's others as will.'

He was struck by a sudden idea. 'How much?'

She stopped struggling. 'Ah. I knew you was a gent as fancied a bit of fun.' She looked at him sideways, trying to estimate his worth. 'A shillin' if we nip down the alley, half a crown if we hire a room.'

'If I give you a shilling and buy you something to eat, will you talk to me instead? For an hour?'

She gaped at him, her mouth a dark hole in her narrow pale face under the flickering glow of the street lamp. 'Don't y'want t'do it?'

'No.' Which wasn't quite true. He did want to do it, had been wanting to for a while now, but not with someone like her. He was too innately fastidious for that. Somehow he couldn't face the idea of performing such an intimate act with a complete stranger. What if he made a mess of it? And what if the girl was diseased? The mere thought of that made him shudder. His Uncle Tom had given him some very sage advice about avoiding disease before he left Bilsden, and had offered to take him into Manchester for a night out with some clean 'ladies' as a farewell to his childhood. William had declined the offer firmly. So here he was, nineteen and still a virgin. And he certainly didn't intend to try it for the first time with this scraggy child.

'Where can we get something to eat?' he asked.

'There's a pie stall round the corner.' She licked her lips at the thought.

'Isn't there somewhere we can sit down and get a proper meal? I'm hungry.' He was, too. His landlady did not set the most lavish of tables. It was a good thing his step-father had provided him with a generous allowance. He had used it mostly to buy food so far.

'There's the chop house.' She stared down at herself. Her clothes were little better than rags and the shortness of her skirt gave away her profession. 'But they wouldn't let the likes of me in there.' Then her face brightened. 'But we could go to the boozer next door. There's an eating room at the side an' Alf sends out for food from the chop house. He don't mind what you look like s'long as you can pay. It costs a bit more, though.'

'That's all right. The boozer it is.' William did not let go of her arm, afraid she would run away.

'Don't you like girls?' she asked as she puffed along, trying to keep up with his long strides.

'It's not that. I just don't do it with street girls.'

She scowled at him. 'I'm not dirty, you know. I wash meself every night afore I come out.'

'I'm thinking about the diseases I might catch,' he said bluntly.

'Oh.' She shivered. Clearly she knew what he was talking about. 'Well, I ain't got nuthin',' she muttered.

'Yet.'

She gave a huff of annoyance, not wanting to be reminded of this.

'What's your name?'

'Katy. What do you want me to call you?'

'My name's William. Why not call me that?'

'Orright.'

The pub was bright and noisy, filled with pipe smoke and laughter. Katy guided him into a side room, where there were a few couples sitting already, the women in tawdry finery, their faces crudely tinted with rouge and lip colour. The men seemed full of bonhomie, perhaps in anticipation of a good night to come. Some had empty plates, others were just starting to tuck into piles of meat and potatoes.

The landlord appeared as soon as Katy turned into the side room. 'What are you—' he was beginning, when he saw William and stopped to size him up. He grinned at the girl. 'You're going up in the world, Katy my girl.'

She tossed her head. 'We want a table an' somefink to eat, Alf. My gentleman friend's 'ungry.'

Alf led the way to a small table in the corner, and flourished a dirty dish towel across it in a gesture that did little to remove the grease and gravy spots from the scratched wooden surface. 'What'll it be, sir?'

'Steak or a couple of chops. Potatoes. Whatever. I don't mind.' William looked down at himself ruefully. William the Giant, he thought, remembering a nickname Rosemary Jemmings had given him a couple of years previously.

His half-brother Jim, the son of the man who'd raped his mother, was tall, too. And well-built. An inheritance from their mutual father. Probably the only good thing that man of violence had passed on to them both. But William rarely saw Jim nowadays. Jim helped Aunt Lizzie in her boarding house in Blackpool and worked in the local boozer in the evenings. He was a taciturn fellow and William felt none of the pull to know him better that he had experienced as a child desperate for a brother and sister of his own. He had Tamsin and Edgar now.

'An' a glass of porter each, too,' Katy put in eagerly, with a questioning look at William.

'I'd rather have a cup of tea, if you can supply one,' William said quietly.

'Certainly, sir. We can supply anything you like here.' The landlord's wink made it obvious what he meant. 'I hope we see you again here, sir, now that you know about our little services.'

William made a non-committal murmur and when Alf had gone away, he turned to his companion. 'All right. I'm paying you to talk to me, Katy. And what I want to talk about is you. First of all, why do you do it?' He could not remember a time when he had not been interested in people and why they did things, even when he was a little lad.

She pulled a face. 'Why not? It's the best way to make meself some money. A girl 'as to look after 'erself.'

'There are other jobs besides this. What about going into service or working in a shop?'

She hooted with laughter. 'They wouldn't take a girl like me into service! They'd kick me out the door soon as look at me. Nor I wouldn't want to do it, neither. Think they own you, they do, if you're in service. Even tell you what to wear. We laugh at them maids, when they come to the market, all prim an' proper with them silly white caps on. An' as for shops, they want people as can talk nice to work in them.'

'You could work in a bar, then?'

She shook her head. 'You don't get much money for that. An' they still expect you to oblige the customers. If I'm obliging anyone, it'll be to earn money for meself. This is the best way for me, b'lieve me, sir.' She was losing her nervousness, sitting grinning around as if to be here was a rare treat.

The food arrived within ten minutes, and it was good – if you ignored the greasy thumbprints on the edges of the plates. They both abandoned conversation to address the lamb chops and mashed potatoes.

'You look like a feller as eats a lot,' Katy said when her plate was empty. She put down her knife and fork with a sigh of satisfaction. 'You're certainly a big bloke.'

William nodded. 'I do eat rather a lot. I seem to need it.'

'My Jack's big. But fat with it. You should see him eat.'

'Jack?'

'The feller as looks after me.'

'Oh.'

'You 'ave to 'ave a feller to watch out for you, or it can get dangerous.' She watched William's frowning face for a moment, then asked, 'So why d'you want to talk to me?'

'I want to find out about the real people in London, the poor people, not the nobs.'

'G'arn – yer a nob yerself. Listen to you talk. What do you want to come slummin' it for?' She stiffened. 'Unless you *are* a Bible-banger? An' I already told you that I don't want t'be saved.'

'What do you want, then?'

Her expression became wistful and she hesitated, eyeing him sideways before sharing her dream in a breathless rush of words. 'I want t'get meself some good clothes,' she nodded in the direction of two women at a nearby table, 'like them. An' then I can earn meself some real money from the toffs. Jack won't shell out for new clothes, the mean bugger.'

'And you intend to go on selling yourself like this for the rest of your life?'

She shrugged. 'Nah. It wears you out too quick. I want to save enough money to buy meself a barrow, an' then I'll give this up t'sell whelks an' oysters round the streets. I've got a cousin as'd help me set up.' She sighed longingly. 'That'd be the best way of all to earn money. You could earn a living that way till the day you die.'

'How much?'

'Whaffor?' She took a gulp of porter, burped, then giggled. 'Pardon me, dear William.'

'How much would it cost to get yourself a barrow?'

Her shoulders sagged despondently. 'I'd need five guineas first t'get free of Jack. If he'd let me go. An' another two guineas t'buy the barrow.' She was counting off on her fingers. 'Then I'd need the money for the stock an' for somewhere to live an' keep the barrow. I'd get the good oysters, I would, the real fresh ones. An' whelks, too.' Her eyes were glowing. This was obviously a cherished dream. Then her smile faded and she looked down at herself. 'And I'd need some other clothes, as well. Respectable clothes, dark, an' a white apron. Or none of the nobs'd buy from me.'

She fell silent in contemplation of this dream, then sighed, blinked and stared around, facing reality again. 'Ah, well, maybe I'll get lucky one day. Thanks for the food, but I'll 'ave to get back to work now.' She reached out to pick up the shilling which he had laid on the table when they sat down. 'If I don't bring in enough money tonight, Jack'll beat me black and blue.' She started to stand up.

'I'll give you the money for the barrow.'

She fell back into her chair, gaping. '*What?*'

'I said, I'll give you the money for your barrow.' William felt he owed her a favour, because listening to her explain about her dream had crystallised something in his mind. Here was this child, alone in the world and selling herself in a degrading way that utterly revolted him, and yet still she was managing to dream and to plan. While here was he, dawdling around, wasting his mother's money and giving her false hopes about his becoming a gentleman when it was the last thing he was interested in. And he was doing nothing at all about his own dreams of helping people. Nothing. Katy put him to shame.

'Why would you want to do that?' she demanded.

'For luck.'

She opened and shut her mouth, lost for words. When she did speak, she just said, 'You're 'avin' me on, ain't you? It's not very nice, that.'

'I'm not having you on, Katy. I mean it.' For he felt that if he did something for this waif, then maybe the Lord would help him to find something worthwhile to do with his own life.

'You *reely* mean it?' She was clutching her breast, her whole body quivering like the steel watch-spring hoops that supported his mother's wide crinoline skirts.

'I really mean it. Only I want you to stop selling yourself and promise not to do it again. Stop now. Tonight.'

She stared at him and let out her breath slowly. 'But I'll still 'ave to pay Jack off.'

'I'll do that. Do you want me to come with you to see him?'

She nodded, then changed her mind and shook her head. 'Nah. I'll bring him here to see you. It'll be safer. An' I'll get me things at the same time. You – you won't disappear, will you, big fellow?'

William shook his head. 'No. I'll wait here for you. I promise.'

Katy took a deep breath, then rushed out of the room as if it were on fire.

'You all right, sir?' The landlord's voice was honey-warm in William's ear.

'I'm very much all right, thank you. That was a good meal.'

'Katy left you, has she?'

'She's coming back. While I'm waiting for her, I'd love another pot of tea and maybe a plate of pudding.'

'Certainly, sir.' Alf prided himself on being able to supply anything a customer wanted within reason, though none of his customers had ever asked for tea before and few bothered with puddings.

Katy was back, breathless and sporting a new bruise on her cheek, within the hour. Behind her strode a fat man, wearing a wide-awake hat whose wide brim and shallow crown made his face look even broader, and a dark pea jacket over checked trousers, both garments looking very new. It made William angry to see how warmly he was clad and how Katy shivered in her scanty clothing.

'Oh, sir, I'm that glad you're still 'ere,' she gasped. 'This is Jack. See, Jack, I *told* you 'e meant it!'

Jack grumbled under his breath and cuffed her again. 'Shut up an' let us men do the talking.'

William decided to ignore the gratuitous thump, though he itched to do the same thing to the bully and see how he liked being on the receiving end. He gestured to a chair.

'I want ten guineas for her,' Jack said as he sat down. 'I won't take a penny less. She's a good little worker, my Katy is.'

William hadn't been involved in the junk yard bargaining in Bilsden for nothing. He leaned back and laughed uproariously, radiating confidence. 'You can *want* what you like, Jack. My price is five guineas. And I'm not prepared to bargain. I won't pay a penny, no, not even a farthing, more – and I don't intend to waste all evening arguing over this. Take it or leave it.'

When Jack shook his head, William shrugged regretfully at Katy and made as if to stand up. She yelped in fright and clutched his arm.

Jack also put out one hand to stop him leaving. 'Eight guineas, then, and a real bargain at that price.'

'I don't bargain. Five. Take it or leave it. It's the going rate. What do you think I am, a fool?' William's gaze was level and confident, and he ignored Katy's anxious face next to him.

The pimp grinned. 'Well, y'can't blame me for tryin', can you?'

William forced himself to smile back. 'I can't blame you, but I'm not playing games. Now, we'll all three of us go back to my lodgings and get the money, then you can take yourself off, Jack, and leave me to enjoy Katy's exclusive services.' He winked at her as he said that.

As he walked briskly along the dark streets to his lodgings, William dug his gloved hands into his pockets and shivered at the icy wind, but his heart was lighter than it had been for months. Tonight he had made his decision. He was going to leave university. He wanted to do something to help his fellow human beings, not stuff his head full of useless knowledge. And Katy was an earnest of his intent, his lucky piece, if you like.

He would still have to face his mother and try to explain, though how you explained something when you didn't really understand it yourself, he didn't know. Smiling, he pulled his muffler off and wrapped it twice round Katy's scrawny neck. 'Here you are, shrimp. You'll catch your death of cold in those rags.'

She snuggled it around her. 'You're a funny 'un, you are,' she said, half running to keep up with him.

'He's mad as a ferret in a cage,' Jack said. 'You'll 'ave to watch yourself with 'im, Katy girl.'

'Nah, he's just a Bible-banger,' she retorted. 'Thass all.'

William nodded. 'Well, although I object to being called a Bible-banger, Katy, I do believe in Our Lord and I want very much to do His work here on earth.' He smiled. 'But I shan't try to save anything but your body, if it upsets you to talk about your soul.'

Jack growled something angry under his breath, spat at a passing dog and held his tongue. Five guineas and another girl easy enough to find within the hour. It was a good night's work. Or it would be once he'd seen the colour of this fool's money. He might even get Katy back later. He eyed her and pursed his mouth, considering whether it'd be worth it. Yes. He could dress her up a bit more. If she could pull in this toff, she could pull in others. Give it a day or two and he'd get her back, plus the money this toff was giving her, too. The thought pleased him enormously.

When William stopped at his lodgings, he turned to Jack before he went in to get the money. 'I shall be visiting Katy regularly, so don't get any ideas about forcing her back to work for you. Or about taking her money off her.'

Jack stared at him. He was a big man, but he wasn't as big as this young chap. The sod wasn't as soft and stupid as he looked. Pity. 'I can get a dozen other girls tomorrow,' he said loftily. 'You're more than welcome to this one.'

'Good. Stick to the others. This one is under my protection from now on.'

Katy watched wide-eyed as William came out of the house and handed over five shining guinea pieces.

Jack examined them carefully under the street lamp, nodded and strode off along the street without a backward glance.

She let out her breath in a long whoosh of relief.

'Now, shrimp, how do we find you some decent lodgings at this time of night?' William inquired. 'I'm getting tired, if you're not. And then tomorrow we'll see about this barrow of yours.'

She burst into tears and flung herself into his arms. He patted her shoulder for a while until she had stopped weeping, then took her to find some lodgings. At no time did he feel tempted to use her body.

'I'm a fool,' he said aloud later, as he lay sleepless, weaving his plans. But he didn't feel like a fool. He felt that he had grown up this night.

8

Bilsden: Late February 1858

*A*nnie was crossing the landing to check on Frederick before she went down to eat her evening meal with the children, when she heard Tamsin in the hall shrieking with delight and yelling, 'William! William, you're back!'

Annie ran down the stairs and stared at the tall snow-covered figure of her son in shock. 'What on earth are you doing here, William Ashworth?' Her voice came out sharper than she had intended. The last thing she needed at the moment was more trouble, with Frederick so ill and not showing any signs of improvement.

William turned round to greet her, smiling, but when he saw her expression, his face fell and he began to brush some of the snow from his clothes. 'I decided to come home to talk to you. You and Father both.'

'Your father isn't well enough to talk to anyone at the moment.' Frederick could not frame more than a word or two without coughing, and that exhausted him, leaving him white and gasping. He spent most of his time dozing or tossing about feverishly.

William gaped at her. His step-father had never been ill that he knew of. 'What's wrong?'

'Influenza. And why you have to come home just when it's running through the town, I don't know! You'd better

97

have a good reason for all this, William Ashworth, an extremely good reason.'

He didn't reply to that, just let the hovering Winnie help him out of his coat and take it away, tut-tutting under her breath at the little puddles the melting snow was making on the floor. 'You look pretty tired, Mother. Is Father – um, has he got the influenza badly?'

'Yes.' She hid her distress in anger. 'And you'll get ill, too, standing around in wet clothes. Couldn't you have got yourself a cab from the station?'

'They were all taken. Besides, I like walking up Ridge Hill. It always makes me feel I'm home again.'

'*In a snowstorm?*'

'In any kind of weather.' His face was glowing with youthful energy and health, rosy in the bright warmth of the house. 'But I had to leave most of my luggage at the station, so it might be a good idea to send someone down for it before we get snowed in. It's coming down thick and fast out there.'

'*William!*' There was a screech from the top of the stairs and Edgar came clattering down to hurl himself upon his brother. 'William, what are you doing here? You said you wouldn't be back till Easter.'

He laughed and swung the lad round and round in his arms, then did the same to Tamsin, who could get jealous if she thought Edgar was getting more attention than she was. 'You've grown again, young woman!' he declared as he put her down. 'You'll soon be too heavy for me to lift.'

'Silly thing! You've only been away for six weeks. I haven't grown since then.'

'You must have,' he said solemnly, not even smiling as he stared down at her scrawny child's body.

There was the clop of horses' hooves, the sound of wheels and the jingle of harness, followed by another knock on the front door. Annie turned around. 'Ah, that'll be her. Tamsin, calm down and tidy your clothes. You, too, Edgar. We don't want her to think we're a pack of wild creatures.'

William turned to stare at the front door. 'Who on earth are you expecting at this hour?'

'The new governess. We weren't sure which train Miss MacNaughton would be catching, but we knew she'd be coming late today. And who else would be out in this sort of weather except for governesses and lunatics like you? Go and change at once, William – your trouser bottoms are soaked and your boots will need peeling off you if you leave them much longer. Later we'll all have something to eat. I've no need to ask if you're hungry.'

He grinned. 'I'm always hungry.'

'We'll talk then about whatever's brought you back.' She tried to look disapproving, but betrayed her pleasure at seeing him by patting his cheek. 'Mind, I'm not happy about your coming home like this in the middle of term, whatever the excuse.'

William gave her a quick hug and decided it was politic to change the subject. 'What's she like, the new governess?'

'I don't know. I haven't met her yet. She's coming here on a month's trial. She was the only person available, and she had good character references, at least. I've hired a new lady's maid the same way, since I haven't been able to get into Manchester to the agency, but she can't come till next week.' She gave her elder son a shove. 'Now *will* you move!'

He walked slowly towards the stairs, curious to see the new governess. In his mother's house, governesses were treated as part of the family, so he was bound to get to know her.

The young woman Winnie ushered in was tall and thin, with unhooped skirts and hair covered by an extra scarf wound over her plain unfashionable bonnet. Her clothes were shabby, but she was smiling as she shook the snow off her mantle and thanked the cab driver for bringing in the first of her luggage. And the smile, as William didn't fail to notice from the top of the stairs, lit up her whole face, changing it from severe to attractive.

Annie stepped forward. 'Miss MacNaughton?' She held out her hand and found it taken in a firm grasp by a hand that was icy cold. The newcomer towered over her, and must have been at least five feet ten. Annie was not sure she liked that.

'I'm sorry to be so late, Mrs Hallam. I had to wait at the station for the cab to take someone else home and then come back for me.'

'Never mind. You're here now. These are your charges, Tamsin and Edgar.'

Miss MacNaughton gravely shook hands with the children, neither of whom said a word, just stared up at her.

Annie moved across to pick up the purse of small change which was always left on a table near the front door. 'I'll take care of the fare while Winnie shows you up to your room. We'll hold dinner back until you and my son have had time to change out of your wet garments. He's just arrived home, too. You must have caught the same train from Manchester. No, Edgar, let Miss MacNaughton have a minute to herself.' As she grabbed Edgar's arm, she caught sight of William on the landing and made a shooing motion with her other hand. He grinned and disappeared into his room.

Winnie stepped forward to take the newcomer's mantle, her face alight with curiosity, her eyes already assessing the clothes and finding them lacking. No style at all, this one. She'd never last. Worse than the previous one.

Annie gave Tamsin a push. 'You and Edgar go and wait in the small parlour.' Then she went to the front door to pay the driver and ask him to go back for William's luggage. Even under the shelter of the portico, an icy wind howled around her and flurries of snow dusted her gown as she arranged everything. She shivered as she closed the door again. It would be a wild night tonight.

'If you'll come this way, Miss MacNaughton, I'll show

you to your room.' Goodness, the woman looked half starved and frozen to the marrow! 'I'll have a cup of tea sent up.'

'Thank you.' Elizabeth's stomach had been growling since her one meal, which she'd taken at breakfast.

Half an hour later, they were all gathered in the room they called the breakfast parlour, though the family ate all their meals there when they had no visitors.

Annie looked at William, her face tight with suspicion about his motives for returning so suddenly, when he should be in London studying, then turned her attention resolutely to the new governess. This was not the time to pursue matters with her son. 'You'll find us a bit disorganised, Miss MacNaughton. My husband is ill at the moment.'

'I'm sorry. Can I do anything to help?'

Annie tried to smile, but failed. 'It's the influenza. And you can help us best by taking the children off my hands.' She threw a glance towards Tamsin and Edgar, who were listening carefully, no doubt making their own assessments of their new governess.

Tamsin had already decided that Miss MacNaughton was the most dowdy governess they'd ever had, but Edgar had taken a liking to the smile lurking in Miss MacNaughton's eyes and he approved of the hearty meal she was making.

Annie cleared her throat and the two children remembered their manners and stopped staring. 'We'll have a proper chat about your duties in the morning, Miss MacNaughton, but for now welcome to Ridge House. These two scamps certainly need a governess. They've run wild since Miss Hibley left. I don't expect you to stand any nonsense from them.'

Her eyes lingered on Tamsin as she said that, but from the way she smiled afterwards, and the way the two children grinned back at her, Elizabeth realised with relief that this was a loving family.

1858

As they ate, Annie studied her new governess. Miss MacNaughton was very shabbily dressed, but her expression was intelligent and interested as she spoke first to one person, then to the other. Her way with the children met with Annie's instant approval, for she could not abide governesses who were all sugary with their charges when in the presence of their employers. This young woman was very direct in her questions and answers. Maybe not as tactful and genteel as most employers would wish, but then, Annie admitted to herself, she was not like most employers.

After the meal, Annie ordered her children up to bed.

'Oh, but William's just come home, Mother!' Tamsin protested, her mouth taking on that wilful set that irritated Annie more than anything else. 'I want to stay downstairs and talk to him.'

'You heard me, Tamsin!'

The look Tamsin gave her mother was black with resentment.

Miss MacNaughton stepped in. 'Perhaps if I come up with you, you can show me your rooms and the schoolroom quickly before you go to bed?' She looked at Annie for approval and when she received a nod of agreement, held out one hand to Edgar, who smiled widely at her and put his hand in it trustingly.

With his sunny loving nature, Edgar reminded Annie often of what William had been like as a child. She looked across at her elder son, remembering the lad he had been. It still came as a shock to her how tall he had grown. He was a large man already, even at nineteen, not fat, though powerful-looking. But his expression had not changed. William greeted the whole world as his friend.

'I want to go and check on Frederick first, then we'll talk. Wait for me in the library, would you, William?'

'Shan't I come up and say hello to him?'

'No, he's not well enough to receive any visitors.' She did not say that Frederick seemed worse than two days

102

ago, and that she had sent for Jeremy again that morning. He said they were doing all they could, and that only time would tell. Since then, an icy fear had lodged in her heart, though she tried to hide that from the children. She couldn't hide it from William, however.

'You're worried about him. Is he that bad?'

She nodded, not trusting her voice to remain steady.

William put his arm around her shoulders. 'Then I'm glad I came back. Can I do anything to help look after him?'

She shook her head blindly, tears welling involuntarily in her eyes. It was not like her to betray a weakness, but she had not slept well since Frederick fell ill. 'No. Widow Clegg has found a woman willing to keep watch at night for me, so you can't do anything, really. Mrs Houghnell is very sensible.'

She sniffed and found herself turned around by her son, who hugged her close for a moment, then wiped her eyes tenderly with a crumpled and rather grubby handkerchief. 'And you've had all this on your shoulders, and probably Tamsin playing up as well, if I know her.'

Annie shrugged. 'Tamsin never stops playing up. She's an uppity young madam. I'm hoping that Miss MacNaughton will be able to tame her a little. The other governesses had difficulties. In fact, I rather suspect that Tamsin set out to drive them away. She likes to be out doing things, not inside sitting still in the schoolroom.'

He was surprised. 'Has she been that bad?'

'Yes. Lately she has.'

He nodded decisively. 'Well, I can at least make sure the children don't play up, and I can sit with Father for an hour or so in the afternoons, if you like, so that you can get a bit of fresh air – even if you only go and throw a few snowballs at Tamsin on the lawn, or take her sliding on the lake. Is it frozen solid yet?' Sliding on the lake was a favourite occupation of all the family's young folk in icy weather, and their mother had also been known to indulge in it, too, with

Frederick standing laughing at her and servants peering from windows.

Annie nodded again, feeling unaccountably better just to have her large gentle son beside her. 'I don't know why you've come home, but I'm glad you're here,' she admitted. 'If anything happens to Frederick, I'll – I'll—' She took a deep breath, then blew her nose and gave William a wavery smile. 'I'm just being silly. Nothing's going to happen to him. I won't let it.'

And when he gave her another hug, she laid her head against him for a moment with a weary sigh, before straightening herself up and finding something else to scold him about. Only afterwards did she realise that they hadn't really discussed why he had come home.

Upstairs, the large bedroom Annie usually shared with Frederick was quiet, except for the gasps and sighs of the man lying restlessly in the bed. He seemed only half aware of what was happening around him, and his face was hectically flushed. His nightshirt was already damp with sweat, though Jimson had helped him into a clean one before he went off to bed. Jimson was exhausted after the last few days. He was, Annie guessed, older than his master and it was showing at the moment.

Mrs Houghnell stood up and tiptoed across to the door to speak to Annie. 'Mr Hallam's been tossing and turning since you left us. I can't seem to get him quiet and comfortable, whatever I do.' She hesitated, then added, 'I think the crisis will come tonight, Mrs Hallam.'

Annie's heart clenched into a tight hard knot in her chest. 'Then I'd better join you.'

Mrs Houghnell nodded. 'Yes. I think it would be best. He seems to know your touch. Mrs Clegg allus says the night's the worst time. But we'll pull the Mester through, you see if we don't.' She was a plump solid woman with a determined face. She always spoke cheerfully to her patients' families because she believed that being

104

optimistic helped the patients. If they saw relatives with long faces hovering by their bedside, they felt there was no hope and just gave up. She'd seen it time and again.

'You've been a tower of strength to me, Mrs Houghnell. Do you want to go and get something to eat now?'

'Yes, if that's all right with you, Mrs Hallam?' Mrs Houghnell normally called her charges' families 'love', but one of her brothers worked in Hallam's Mill and the owners of Ridge House overawed her.

Annie went and sat by the bed. Frederick looked so hot and uncomfortable that she pulled the covers off him, except for the sheet. Mrs Houghnell would probably have a fit when she came back, but it seemed silly to pile covers on someone who was sweating and feverish. Annie took hold of Frederick's hand, as if by willpower she could help make him better.

After a few minutes without the blankets the hectic colour in Frederick's face died down a little and he opened his eyes. When he saw her, a slight smile twisted his lips for a moment. 'Annie girl,' he whispered. 'Love you.' Then he closed his eyes and slept for a while, his hand still in hers.

By the time Mrs Houghnell came back, he was tossing and turning again, and seemed unaware of anyone, but Annie was still convinced that he was more comfortable without the layers of thick blankets. Mrs Houghnell tut-tutted at this, but Annie said firmly, 'He was too hot before. We must watch to see whether he starts shivering, then we can pull the blankets back on quickly enough. I've noticed before that when people are feverish, they seem to change from burning up to feeling cold within minutes, and then back again.'

'I'll keep my eye on him, don't you worry,' Mrs Houghnell promised, still looking disapproving.

For the next four hours, the two women alternately piled on the bedcovers or removed them.

'Go and get yourself a cup of tea,' Annie said around one

o'clock. 'I gave orders for the things to be left out in the kitchen and for lights to be left burning low so that you could find your way through the house. And if you'd bring me back a cup when you return, I'd be grateful.'

Frederick's condition seemed to worsen the minute Mrs Houghnell left the room, and his fever flared up again worse than before. Nothing helped. He was mumbling incoherently and seemed to think that someone was hurting him deliberately, which made him thrash around and fight the hands that tried to wipe his brow.

When Annie heard the door open, she turned with relief to ask Mrs Houghnell what to do, but found herself instead looking at the new governess.

'I hope you don't mind, but I heard the noise and wondered if I could help in any way? I'm quite experienced in sick rooms.'

And Annie, brave and capable under most circumstances in life, surprised herself by bursting into tears. 'He's getting worse. Nothing I do seems to help him.'

Elizabeth put her arms round her employer, drawn to her by the common bond of humanity. 'It's hard, isn't it? I've just spent three months nursing my father through his last illness and sometimes you feel so helpless.' She let Annie pull herself away and together they turned to stare at the bed. 'Mr Hallam looks so hot. Surely we can do something about that?'

'I've already scandalised the nurse by pulling the blankets off him.'

'I wonder—'

'What?' Annie moved back to the bed to sponge Frederick's sweating face with cool water. She was ready to try anything to help him.

'Well, if we wrung out the cloths you're using to sponge him down in water with snow in it, they'd be really cold, wouldn't they? Do you want me to go out and get some snow, just to try?'

Frederick uttered a long string of incomprehensible

gabble, then groaned and plucked at the sheet which was all that covered him, saying quite distinctly, 'Burning! Burning!' before lapsing into moans and mumblings again.

'It wouldn't hurt to try it.' Annie seized the water jug from the bedside stand and held it out. 'Would you mind?'

'Not at all.'

Elizabeth's return coincided with that of Mrs Houghnell carrying a tea-tray. Once again, the nurse was horrified at what the other women were proposing to do.

But the patient seemed to welcome the chilled cloths on his face, and sighed in relief, so that decided it for Annie.

It was not until dawn was breaking on a still white world that Frederick drifted into an uneasy sleep. Annie sat looking at him, her whole body aching with weariness. For several minutes, the only sound in the bedroom was the ticking of the clock and the coals settling in the grate. Frederick's breathing seemed a little easier, his colour less hectic – or was it just her imagination?

She stood up and walked slowly across the room to where Mrs Houghnell was resting in a chair and Elizabeth MacNaughton was sitting with the jug to hand, ready to go out for some more snow. 'I think he's a little better,' Annie said. Suddenly the whole room began to spin around her and if it hadn't been for Elizabeth's strong arms, she would have fallen.

'I think you need some rest yourself now, Mrs Hallam,' the governess said, helping her to a chair.

Mrs Houghnell nodded. 'The lass is right. You really do need to get some sleep, Mrs Hallam,' she echoed. 'You kept getting up all the night before, as well, though I told you I could manage.'

Annie nodded and gave in. She felt so tired she could not think straight, let alone help Frederick. 'Well, all right. I've got a bed made up in my dressing room. You will promise to call me if he – if I'm needed?' She gestured to the door at one side of the room, then looked back at Frederick and doubt creased her forehead. 'But he's been so bad tonight, I don't know whether I should leave him.'

Elizabeth smiled. 'I'll keep watch with Mrs Houghnell for an hour or two longer, if you like? And I can fetch you in a minute, if you're needed.'

Annie wavered. 'Well – you won't have to watch him for long. Mrs Houghnell leaves at seven o'clock, but Jimson is usually up by then.'

'I have to see to my children before they go to school,' Mrs Houghnell said apologetically. 'Else I'd not leave you, Mrs Hallam. But my youngest is only six, so he can't be left to get ready by hisself. And my eldest doesn't notice things like she ought. She's a real scatterbrain, that one.'

'I'll be here if I'm needed,' Elizabeth said. Her lovely smile suddenly warmed her plain face into near beauty. 'I'm as strong as an ox and I haven't been up for several nights like you have. Has Mr Hallam been ill for long?'

Annie had to stop and think about that. 'It's only a few days,' she said in tones of surprise. 'But it seems more.'

Elizabeth's face shadowed. 'Yes. It always does.'

Annie suddenly hugged the other woman. 'Thank you.' Then she stumbled off into the dressing room, desperate for sleep now she knew that Frederick, too, was sleeping.

When William knocked on the bedroom door just before breakfast, it was to find the governess sitting quietly by his step-father's side, her hair loose about her shoulders and her plain white nightgown showing beneath her shabby dressing gown. Her face was shadowed with weariness. He tiptoed across to the bed and mouthed the words, 'How is he?'

'A little better,' she said in a low voice, then flushed. 'I'm sorry. I'm not – not in a fit state to be seen.' Memories of the last man to see her in her nightgown made her shiver suddenly.

William gave her one of his clear direct looks. 'Mrs Houghnell says you were a tower of strength during the night. How you look is irrelevant after that, don't you think? I'm so glad you were there to help Mother. She always tries to do too much.'

'Oh. Well, thank you.'

'Where's Jimson? I thought he'd be here by now.'

She put a finger on her lips and gestured towards the dressing room, as she whispered, 'He seems to be coming down with the influenza, too. He looked dreadful when he arrived, so I took it upon myself to send him back to bed. If you want to help, you could perhaps look in on him, and if he's awake, get someone to take him up a pot of tea.'

'I'll do that. And I'll keep the brats occupied this morning, if you like? Then maybe you can get a bit of sleep, too.'

'Do you mind keeping an eye on them?'

He grinned. 'Not at all. I've been dying for an excuse to go out and throw snowballs at someone.'

What a nice young man! Elizabeth thought as she watched him go out. Not good-looking, exactly, but with such a clear open face. Wholesome, that was the word. It didn't occur to her that at twenty-two, she was not much older than William. She felt older. Much older.

Three days later, Frederick and Annie were sitting quietly together in the bedroom, he propped up against pillows, she leaning against him with her hand in his.

'I could feel you there, you know,' he said. 'Even when I was delirious, I could recognise your touch.' To speak even a few words still made him splutter and pant.

'Where else should I be but next to you?' Her smile was teasing and filled with love.

'Nowhere else. You're a wonderful wife, Annie. And,' he added, 'you make a wonderful valet, too. I'm thinking of offering you a permanent position.'

'How much are you paying?'

He chuckled. 'That's my Annie.' Then his smile faded a little. 'How is poor Jimson?'

'Getting better. He has the influenza quite lightly and I

had to threaten him to keep him in bed today. I daresay he'll start pottering around tomorrow.'

Frederick lifted his head and listened. 'Are those children playing outside again?'

She got up and went to the window. 'Yes. Nat says that it'll begin to thaw tomorrow, so they're making the most of it. William's there. And Elizabeth.' She smiled as she saw the new governess forget her own dignity and join with Tamsin and Edgar in pelting William with snowballs, until they had him rolling on the ground, helpless with laughter.

'I think we've got a good one in our new governess,' she said thoughtfully, as she came back to the bed. 'I really like her. And she seems able to control Tamsin. She was there helping me that night, you know. When you were so ill—' She broke off, for even to think of losing him upset her.

'It was a close call, wasn't it?' he asked, his expression very serious.

She nodded.

'Then we're going to have to make every day count from now on, Annie love.' He paused to draw breath and then raised her shaking hand to his lips. 'We won't lie to ourselves, will we?'

'What about?' She stared down at her hand, concentrating on not weeping.

'About my health. Jeremy told you that my heart is not functioning properly, I believe?'

She nodded again, hating to put it into words.

'I'll not take his warning lightly, I promise you. I will take care of myself.'

'I'll make sure that you do.' She put her head on his shoulder and just leaned against him for a while. 'I love you, Frederick Hallam.'

'And I love you, Annie girl.' But his expression was serious. He would have a lot of careful planning to do when he got better. He not only intended to take care of himself, but to see that his beloved wife would be taken care of if the worst happened – though Jeremy had said that he could have years of life left if he were careful. It was not a death sentence, he told himself again, just a warning to take things more easily.

9

Early March

The snow had almost disappeared overnight, leaving a cold soggy world of grey skies and drizzling showers. No one was tempted to go outside on such a day. Tamsin and Edgar were prolonging their breakfast, reluctant to go up to the schoolroom. Frederick was sleeping peacefully, and since it seemed to Annie that he was starting to lose the frail white look, she was feeling a little more like dealing with her other main problem, William.

She watched her son eat his way through two huge platefuls of food, more than most poor families got in a day. Did he know that? Probably not. She had made sure that he never went hungry, even when they lived in the Rows. Well, it was time to sort things out with him. She wasn't having him wasting his opportunities like this. Golden opportunities. He must be made to realise that. He must return to London as soon as possible.

She looked across the table at Elizabeth MacNaughton. 'I think the children have finished breakfast now, don't you? Perhaps you could take them up to the schoolroom?'

Elizabeth stood up. 'Of course.'

'But I wanted another piece of toast!' Tamsin protested immediately. 'And William hasn't finished his breakfast yet. It's not polite to leave the table when someone is still eating. You're always telling us that, Mother.'

113

Annie didn't raise her voice. 'Now, if you please, Tamsin!'

Pulling a face, Tamsin shoved her chair back so hard that it fell over. She ignored it and would have stormed out of the room, but a sharp, 'Pick it up!' from her mother made her turn round and with a loud aggrieved sigh, set the chair back in place.

'If you can't behave over meals, perhaps you'd better take breakfast in the schoolroom from now on. We'll see how you go on for the rest of the week before we decide about that.'

Silently, bottom lip jutting mutinously, Tamsin walked out of the room.

Annie rolled her eyes expressively at Elizabeth, who smiled and shepherded Edgar out after his sister. Then Annie's gaze returned to her elder son, who was concentrating single-mindedly on his food. Why was he being so contrary? She would have sold her soul when she was young just for the chance to go to the local dame school, as her brother Tom had. She hadn't even learned to read until she was ten. Her only chance of education had come at Sunday School.

And then, when she'd gone into service at the age of twelve, even that small amount of schooling had stopped. A vivid picture of her old mistress, Annabelle Lewis, floated through Annie's mind. Jeremy's first wife had been a shrew, who counted every potato that entered the house, but Annie had learned so much from her. How to speak properly. How a lady carried herself. Above all, how to dress with taste. She had been Annabelle's personal maid for a time, travelling with her to London and Brighton. What a big adventure it had seemed, and how the rattling of the stage coach had made her head ache! Trains were so much more comfortable, in spite of the smuts.

Annie shook her head to clear it of these memories. She was finding it hard to concentrate today, feeling lethargic and distant. She stared at William across the breakfast table as he ate the last mouthful with as much gusto as the first, then smiled at her.

She could not keep the sharpness from her voice as she asked, 'Well? Isn't it about time you told me exactly why you came home in the middle of the university term?'

He nodded, but his smile vanished and suddenly, for all his size, he looked like a small boy caught out in mischief.

Winnie tapped on the door and poked her head around it. 'Excuse me, ma'am, but if you've finished, could I just clear the table? Cook's in a right old tizzy this morning.'

Annie let out a soft puff of annoyance, but Winnie was only doing her job. She turned to her son. 'We'll go into the library, William.'

In the large book-lined room which she loved so much, Annie sat in Frederick's big leather chair to one side of the cheerful crackling fire and gestured to the velvet-upholstered chair opposite, the one she usually used. 'Right, then. I want to know exactly why you came home like this in the middle of term.'

William leaned back and stretched out his long legs in front of him, digging his hands into his pockets and frowning down at his feet. 'I came because I don't fit in at university, Mother, and I'm wasting my time there. I'm neither fish nor fowl. I speak like a gentleman, thanks to you and the Hinchcliffes, but I don't think like one – and I don't act like one, either.'

'What do you mean by that? You can *learn* to act the gentleman, can't you? Anybody can learn that.'

He sighed, a deep sigh dredged up from the depths of his soul. 'Mother, I can't bear to waste my time on Latin and Greek. It's all meaningless to me.'

'Easy to spurn what drops into your lap like a ripe fruit!'

'I'm sorry to disappoint you, but you knew very well that I didn't want to go to university in the first place. I did tell you that.'

'And you agreed to give it a try.'

'Well, I have done.'

'One term and a few weeks of another! Do you call that giving it a try?'

He was back to studying his feet. 'It's as much of a try as I need to give it to know that it's not for me. More than enough. I'm just wasting my time there, and your money, too.'

Her tone was acid. 'Well, what *do* you want to do, then, William? You had no other ideas when we talked about your future last year. You didn't want to go into the mill and learn how to run it. You said you hated the noise of the machinery and all the fluff floating around made you feel you were choking. You didn't want to work in the Emporium, either, though Tom would have taken you on and trained you till you were old enough to have a shop of your own.' Which she would have been happy to buy for him. 'You said you didn't want to spend your life being polite to silly women who spent an hour choosing a piece of ribbon. You were most eloquent about that, if I remember correctly.'

As he opened his mouth to say something, she raised her voice to add with huge scorn, 'And you didn't want to work in the junk yard, either. Filthy work, you said, and you had no talent for haggling over coppers.' Her voice grew suddenly louder. 'So what *do* you want to do with yourself, William Ashworth?'

He stared into the fire. 'I don't know, Mother, not exactly. But I've found out that I want to – to help people. I know that much.' Then he looked her straight in the eye. 'You don't care about religion, I know, but I do. I care deeply.'

She was amazed. 'You want to become a minister?'

He shook his head. 'No. I couldn't stand up and preach at people. I'm too young and inexperienced. I wouldn't even want to be a lay preacher. It would feel presumptuous for me to try to tell others how to live their lives. What I want at the moment is to do the Lord's work in a secular way.' He smiled in reminiscence. 'I helped a poor girl I met in London, and at first she didn't want me to help her because she thought I was a Bible-banger. I'm not. I don't want to shove religion down people's throats. I want to – to live decently and help those in need. To spread the Lord's message by example, perhaps.'

'You'll still have to earn a living,' she said dryly.

'That's why I came home. To ask you that. Do I have to earn a living? Or at least, do I have to earn a living right away?'

The anger was rising rapidly in her. 'Of course you have to earn a living. Everyone does!'

'*You* don't have to. Oh, I know you still run your businesses. But that's because you enjoy it, not because you need to. Father's got more than enough money to keep you in luxury for the rest of your life. But you like managing things and making money. I don't. I just – I don't have the soul for it.' He hesitated. 'I did wonder . . .' Then his voice trailed away and he shook his head, a small hopeless movement.

She had to struggle to keep her anger buttoned down, because what she really felt like doing was boxing his ears, something she had never done to any of her children. Of all the foolish, impractical things to say! *Help people. Spread the Lord's word by example.* 'What did you wonder, William? You might as well tell me everything.'

'I wondered whether you'd give me the money – even half of it would do – the money that you're spending on sending me to university – and just let me, well, travel around the country? I want to go to the big cities especially, to see how others are helping the poor. I went to one mission in London, but they were so impractical and so smug about what they were doing that I never went back. They made hungry people sit there and sing hymns before they would give them any food. It sickened me. But maybe, if I worked with others for a while, others who're *really* doing good, then I'd be able to see my own way more clearly. I do want to be practical about what I do. I do want

117

to make a real difference.' As he had done to Katy.

Fury boiled over in Annie. Practical, he said! Make a difference. Her son become a do-gooder and give away her hard-earned money! 'That's the most ridiculous thing I've ever heard! I didn't work my fingers to the bone for you to become an idler. And you weren't sent to that university to help poor girls. I know what happens when young men like you start helping poor girls. It runs in the family, helping poor girls does.'

He scowled at her. 'I knew you'd say that.'

'And I'll say a lot more before I'm—'

'Not to me, you won't. You're not *listening*, Mother. You're not thinking about me, only about yourself. And about your money! You always think of that. I sometimes think you care more about money than anything else in the world!'

He jumped up and was out of the room before she could stop him, slamming the door behind him so hard that the glass rattled in the windows. By the time she got the library door open and followed him into the hall, he had crashed the front door back on its hinges and was striding away down the muddy drive, splashing through the puddles of melting snow, hatless and coatless on a raw winter's day.

She opened her mouth to yell at him to come back, then shut it again and leaned against the doorframe, watching him vanish behind the gatehouse. Let him go. Let him feel the cold. She hoped he'd stay out all day and feel the hunger, too, the hunger that came when you didn't earn a decent living for your family. The hunger she'd known when her mother died. The hunger her father and his second family had often experienced, because of her step-mother's incompetence. She'd do no good talking to William while she was so angry, so furiously angry.

She made an inarticulate noise of pain as she turned back to the house. She had never been at outs with her elder son before. Not like this, anyway. Never.

'Did you want something, ma'am?' Winnie asked softly behind her.

Annie took a deep breath. 'No. I just – just wanted to tell William to take a coat. But he's out of earshot now. You know how foolish young men can be.'

Winnie nodded. At nearly fifty, she had no time for young men, just as they'd had no time for her when she was young. Her hair had not been grizzled then, or her body so heavy, but she had never been a looker, never caught anyone's interest. And this rankled, the only black spot in her otherwise comfortable existence. She didn't mind not being married, but she did mind never having been asked. She shivered and shut the door with a thump. 'There's no telling young heads to be sensible, is there?'

'No. There isn't.' Unable to settle to anything, Annie wandered upstairs to the second floor and did not scruple to listen at the door of the schoolroom. Quiet voices inside showed that Elizabeth MacNaughton had her charges under control, which was a big improvement on Miss Hibley, who had had a very shrill voice and had done nothing but scold.

Annie tiptoed away. There was some hope that her problems with Tamsin would be resolved, for a while at least. And Edgar had never given her a minute's trouble. *So far*, a voice in her head added. All children gave their parents trouble at one time or another, whether the trouble was of their own making or not.

What had she done to deserve this from William? she asked herself bitterly.

Tried to turn him into a gentleman, the same inner voice replied.

Well, and what was wrong with that? With Frederick Hallam as his step-father, William would be taking a gentleman's place in the world. And he would have enough money from her to support that status. There was nothing wrong with that, nothing at all.

But the thought didn't comfort her. She had never seen

an expression of hostility on William's face before. He'd always been such a sunny-natured boy, happy to help her, loving his family, especially his young uncles, Mark and Luke, and her father, who was more like William's father than his grandfather. William had been very upset when he'd found out about his real father, of course. And about his half-brother, Jim. But it hadn't made him regard her as an enemy.

It's just a phase. It'll soon pass, she told herself. I'll talk to him later, keep my temper better. It's just a passing phase. It's partly Dad's fault, really, for filling William's head with religion.

Religion had become the foundation of John Gibson's life after his first wife died, but give him his due, he didn't try to shove it down anyone's throat. He just used the name of the Lord and quoted from the Bible as easily as he breathed. He'd even got Kathy doing it now. He was a very popular lay preacher at the Methodist chapel, because he didn't use long words and set impossible standards. He just dispensed sound common sense, in the Lord's name.

As Annie went back along the landing, she heard Frederick's bell ring and her expression brightened. He was awake. She opened the bedroom door and peeped inside, then pushed the door wider and went in. 'How are you feeling now, love?'

He smiled at her from the bed, a real smile this time. He looked pale still, but somehow his face had regained its usual expression. Charm, she decided, looking at him, he had a great deal of charm – as had Tamsin when she bothered to exercise it. And Edgar, too, in a quieter way. They were very like their father. The Hallams had the charm. The Gibsons had the vitality. Put the two together and you got a problem like Tamsin.

Someone behind her cleared her throat and she turned to see the upstairs maid hesitating in the doorway. 'Did you ring for something, sir?'

Frederick spoke from the bed. 'Yes, Peggy, could you

please bring me up some tea and toast? I've recovered now from being shaved and I'm actually feeling hungry.'

When Peggy left, he turned to his wife. 'What's wrong, love?'

'Nothing, now that you're getting better.' She tried to look cheerful, because she didn't want to burden him with her worries.

'You don't usually lie to me, Annie girl.'

She met his eyes and felt tears rise in her own. 'It's William. I've just – oh, Frederick, I've just had a dreadful quarrel with him. And he slammed out of the house.'

Frederick captured her hand and pulled her down on to the edge of the bed. 'What did you quarrel about?'

'About university. Why he came home. He wants to leave. He says – he says it's useless.'

He flicked a tear away from her cheek and said softly, 'It is, if you're not burning to study something, or looking to waste a few years. William didn't really want to go to university in the first place, love. It was your idea.'

'That's what he said.' She moved around the bed and slid down to lie next to Frederick in her usual place, sighing with relief. Her head had been aching a bit this morning, with all the worries she had. 'But he didn't have any other ideas about what he wanted to do instead. Except for foolish fancies about helping people.'

'Well, there's no hurry, is there? He's only nineteen. And it's not as if we don't have enough money to keep him.'

'That's what he said – did he really have to earn his living yet? Imagine a son of mine saying that! It made me so angry.'

'Well, perhaps what he needs is a bit more experience of the world.'

'He said that, too. Then he shouted at me.' She sniffed and brushed away another tear. 'I've never quarrelled with him like that before, never seen him so angry.'

'He's growing up. Young men do get angry at things as

they're growing up. I'm surprised you haven't had problems with him before.'

'Well!' She was so indignant that she sat upright and glared at her husband. 'I didn't think *you* would take his side.'

'I'm not taking anyone's side, love, just telling you about young men. They're bursting with energy and yet the world's ruled by us greybeards and we try to make them conform to our wishes.'

She sagged back on to the wonderful softness of the pillow. 'Were you like that when you were young?'

'No. I was too busy working in the mill. That took all my spare energy. And then my father died when I was quite young, so I was able to do things my own way. In that sense I was lucky.'

Looking at her unhappy expression, he wished he and William were close enough for his step-son to have come to him with his worries, but the one William was closest to was his grandfather. In fact, William was probably down at the junk yard now, pouring out his heart to John Gibson. Oh, Frederick got on well enough with the lad. But it had not really gone beyond that into real closeness. *I've been too obsessed with his mother*, Frederick admitted to himself ruefully. He had not loved his first wife, who had been a weak whining sort of woman, but Annie – ah, his Annie was magnificent!

'I should have made more time for William,' he said aloud. 'Done more things with him. Though he never wanted to come to the mill with me, or to do anything else that I suggested.'

'Unlike Tamsin. That child loves going to the mill. And she knows as much about cotton as I do already. I don't know what I'm going to do with her,' Annie said, rubbing at the pain in her forehead.

'Give her a little job in the mill, make her earn her spending money, as you made William,' he suggested. 'That way she'll realise that it's no fun working there.'

She looked at him and nodded slowly. 'That's a good idea! I've been thinking of doing something like that. Can you find her something to do there? Something real?'

He smiled. 'If I can't, Matt will.'

Annie was pleased. 'Then I'll do that. And Edgar, too, when he's a little older. I don't want them turning into spoilt brats.' She sighed, a desperately tired sigh, and for a while there was silence.

When Frederick turned to speak to her again, he saw that she was asleep. Her breathing was a little ragged and she had a flush on her cheeks which owed nothing to the warmth of the room. My poor little love, he thought. I think you've got the influenza, and oh, you're going to hate it. He couldn't remember Annie being ill, not once, not even a sniffle. Except when she was pregnant and that was not the same thing. She normally had abundant health and energy.

When he flung out of the house William went straight down into town to see his grandfather at the junk yard, as Frederick had guessed he would. He strode down the hill, so angry that he didn't feel the chill of the wind, or the dampness that had other folk huddling their mufflers round their necks and staring at him in amazement.

When he got to the yard, he said simply, 'I need to talk to you, Grandad.'

He looked at his grandfather with such unhappy eyes that John's heart went out to him. 'Well, let's make oursen a cup of tea an' talk things over nice and quiet, eh?'

William nodded, feeling, as he always did, immensely comforted by the warmth and simplicity of John Gibson. He explained at length how he felt, ending up, 'Helping Katy was the only real good that came out of London, so far as I'm concerned.'

John took an experimental draw on the pipe, sucking cold air through it to check that the stem was clear. 'Aye, it were well done.'

123

'Mother just won't *listen* to me, Grandfather. She's got her mind set on – on what she'd like out of life.' He took a few deep breaths, then added succinctly, 'Money.'

'There's no harm to money, if it's honestly earned. She's done a lot of good in our family with her clever ways and her money, our Annie has, and I, for one, shall be grateful to her for what she's done for me an' my childer until the day I draw my last breath and go to join my Maker.'

A flush mantled William's cheeks, clashing badly with the dark auburn of his hair. 'I know that. And – and she's done her best for me, too. I've never forgotten what it was like to live in the Rows, you know, or how people scrabbled to live in Claters End. Or how hungry Mark and Luke were sometimes. I used to sneak pieces of bread out for them when we all lived in Salem Street. Kathy knew. I wasn't stealing it.'

John stared down at his pipe. 'Eh, I were a bad father.'

William stared at him aghast. 'No, you weren't! It was Emily who couldn't cope.'

'She were a weak reed, but I loved her, you know, and I should have found some better way to help her.'

William hastily changed the subject, before he made bad worse. 'I think it's those memories which will always stop me from becoming a *gentleman*.' He put a scornful emphasis on that word. 'And now the River Rows are getting more run-down and children there cry for lack of food, just as they did in Claters End, and old folks die wanting the necessities of life. I walk around sometimes and just – just look, and I hurt inside, Grandfather, hurt badly.'

'It seems to me that you're more cut out to be a minister nor a student,' John said quietly.

William nodded. 'Maybe one day. But not now. I know too little about life at the moment to try to tell others what to do with themselves.' He added quietly and sadly, 'I've prayed every night for months for guidance, Grandfather, for a sign of some sort and – and I think Katy was a sign, a test, if you like. A test of whether I really could help someone. In a practical way. And I did.'

'With your mother's money.'

William flushed again. 'Yes.'

John shook his head. In many ways, William had been slow to grow up. That was Annie's fault. Oh, she had made her son earn his pennies every week, but at the same time she had kept a firm hand on the reins. Too firm, perhaps. The lad had had no chance to make his own mistakes, which was the only way John reckoned most folk ever learned anything worthwhile. Now it was time for Annie to let go of the reins. 'I s'll have to speak to your mother mesen,' he said. 'I won't do owt to help you without her say-so.'

The hope faded from William's face. 'She'll find some way to keep me tied to her apron strings. She always finds some way to get what she wants. She's the most – the most determined woman on this earth.'

'Then we s'll just pray to the Lord to show us a way to untie the strings, an' let you do as you want,' John said sternly. 'But we're not going to go behind her back. And if the Lord doesn't point the way, then mebbe you're not meant to do it.' And from that standpoint, he would not be moved.

When Mark had finished adding up his takings from the chop house that same night, he turned to find Nelly lingering in the doorway, staring at him, half smiling. 'Is something wrong?' he asked sharply.

'That depends.' There was no mistaking the invitation in her wide dark eyes.

He had seen that look before, but on a prostitute's face. He tried not to respond to it, tried to speak coolly. 'You can go home now, Nelly. I don't need anything else. I'll come out and lock the back door after you.'

But before he could get up, she came into the room, moving like a cat in heat. She came right up to him, pressed her body against his and reached out one warm soft hand to stroke his cheek. 'You're working too hard, Mr Gibson, much too hard. All work and no play, you know—'

He stood up and tried to push her away, but she clung to him, raising her face for his kiss, and his body continued to betray him. The Gibson curse. The constant itch. With an inarticulate growl, he grabbed her to him and took the initiative.

Even a few minutes afterwards, as they lay together on the floor of his storeroom, panting and spent, he knew that he had been a fool, a careless fool, too. But he also knew that he would go on being a fool. For Nelly was a woman who enjoyed sex as much as he did. And in spite of her youth and her family background, she had not been a virgin. In fact, she was well-versed in the pleasures of congress. How the hell had she managed that, with a father as strict as hers? What lies had she had to tell?

He looked at her, lying there with her arms behind her head like a sleepy cat who'd just had a bowl of cream.

'We're good together, aren't we?' she asked, her voice slightly husky, her eyes languorous. Then she sighed. 'I'd like to do it again, but if I'm any later than this, my father will want to know why.'

When they were both dressed, he put one hand on her arm. 'Just so that we get one thing straight, Nelly. Whatever happens, I'm not going to marry you.'

She shrugged her shoulders at him. 'Who wants you to? It's no fun being married. I've seen what happens to married women. Housework and babies and a husband who wants you to run round after him. Who wants that?'

He locked the door and watched her hurry down the back lane, then he returned to his office, still wondering if he was being stupid. He wouldn't have to go into Manchester to enjoy Nelly. He wouldn't even have to step out of his office. But he would have to be careful. Extremely careful from now on. For he'd meant what he said. He would never marry a woman like her. In fact, he didn't intend to marry anyone for a long time yet. He wanted to make money first, a lot of money. As much as Annie and Tom had.

10

Manchester: William

*W*hen a shamefaced William returned to Ridge House
ready to apologise, he found his mother in bed and was
told that his step-father would like to see him in the library.

Frederick looked up as his step-son entered, but did not
give his usual smile of greeting. 'Your mother has the
influenza.'

'*Mother?* Is she bad?' William couldn't imagine her ill
enough to stay in bed. She was always so strong.

'No, not bad. But we're taking no chances, so until she's
better, you're to do nothing to upset her. She's spent most
of her life looking after others. Now we're going to look
after her for a change.'

William nodded. It was not until he was getting ready
for dinner that he remembered Mildred's request about
Beatrice. He had not mentioned it to his mother. Guilt
made him sigh out loud. He should have done something
about that before now. He had promised. Well, it would
have to wait until his mother was better. The last thing she
needed at the moment was further worries, and that
included being reminded of Beatrice.

He found himself dining alone with Miss MacNaughton
and the two children. He always enjoyed Tamsin and
Edgar's company, and found the governess an interesting
conversationalist. She was beginning to lose her hesitancy

129

and that gaunt look now, and could have been quite handsome had she dressed her hair becomingly and worn more flattering clothes.

'Mother isn't going to die, is she, William?' Edgar asked, wide-eyed.

Elizabeth looked across at the boy and tsk-tsked under her breath. 'For the hundredth time, Edgar, your mother's just got the influenza, like your father had but not as badly. And he didn't die, did he?'

'No-o-o.' But Edgar still looked worried.

'Honestly, you are a softie!' Tamsin said scornfully. 'You keep on and on asking the same thing.'

Edgar stared down at his soup, tears trembling in his eyes.

'It's not soft to care about those you love,' William said, then as Tamsin still looked mutinous, he changed the subject quickly. 'So, what have you two been learning today, then?'

She shrugged. 'Things.'

William grinned. Tamsin was certainly in one of her moods tonight. 'What things?'

She looked sideways at her governess, then said, 'Silly things!' in a challenging tone.

Elizabeth raised one eyebrow, but did not comment on the rudeness of that remark, merely turned back to William. 'We spoke about history. Not to learn dates of kings and queens,' something which would have bored her to tears, let alone her charges, 'but to see how the world got to be like it is.'

William leaned forward. 'That sounds interesting.'

Tamsin made a low scoffing sound, caught a stern glance from both her governess and her brother, and applied herself to her food with sulky exaggerated movements.

Elizabeth said quietly, 'I think history is extremely interesting. My father was obsessed by it. When he died, he left me a lot of old books and papers, some of them well over a hundred years old.'

'Did you keep them?'

'Oh, yes. They're in my aunt's attic. I've no place of my own for them now. My father's house went with the living.' She just hoped that her cousin Lewis hadn't destroyed them out of spite.

William frowned. It must be terrible not having a home of your own. And he had not failed to notice that Miss MacNaughton's clothes were worn and outmoded. But at least she could earn her own living, unlike some poor souls, and he knew his mother would treat her well. There were so many homeless people. It hurt him to see them huddled in shop doorways and alley corners, especially the children, who should have been rosy and bright-eyed like Edgar and Tamsin. 'You could bring the papers and store them here. We've plenty of room in our attics.'

Elizabeth bowed her head over her plate. 'We'll see.'

'She's only here on a month's approval,' Tamsin jeered. 'So it's not worth her bringing piles of things.'

'Leave the table, Tamsin.' Elizabeth did not raise her voice, but her expression was steely. She already knew that it would be a battle to control this child and she was not one to give way in the face of difficulties. 'That remark was both unkind and unladylike. If you cannot behave properly, then you cannot stay downstairs. Your mother said the same thing to you this morning, yet you've taken no notice of her warning. So you'd better go to your room and stay there.'

'But I haven't finished my—'

'No. What a pity! Now you'll have to go hungry.'

Tamsin stared at her open-mouthed. She had never gone hungry in her life. But something in the governess's expression prevented her from saying anything else. Instead, she flounced out of the room, slamming the door behind her.

Elizabeth immediately got up and rang the bell.

Winnie appeared with a tray, expecting to clear the table.

'Ah, Winnie. Tamsin has just been sent to her room for misbehaving. I'd be grateful if you'd tell the other servants not to let her have any more food tonight. If she cannot behave in a civilised manner at table, she must go without.'

Winnie gaped at her, open-mouthed. So did Edgar.

William leaned forward. 'You're quite right, Miss MacNaughton! That child is getting very cheeky lately.'

'Yes, miss.' Winnie nodded and went out again, full of grim satisfaction. Tamsin had been very impertinent to her only that morning, and though Winnie had said nothing about it – well, the master had had enough troubles lately – the incident had rankled all day. This wasn't the sort of house where the young folk were allowed to cheek the servants, not now, not since Mrs Hallam came to live here. It had been an uncomfortable place to work in before, because the first Mrs Hallam hadn't cared about her servants' feelings and, worse still, had spoiled her youngest daughter to the point where Miss Beatrice was quite unbearable towards everyone. But that had all changed now.

Unable to hide a grin, Winnie bustled into the warm kitchen to tell Cook and the others what had happened, and all the servants nodded in satisfaction. Then she sat down to ease her aching feet.

Tamsin's bedroom bell rang. They all looked at one another and smiled.

Peggy stood up. 'I'm going to enjoy saying no.'

See how you like that, you cheeky young madam! Winnie thought to herself smugly.

Back in the dining room, William looked at Edgar's unhappy face and wobbling lower lip and changed the subject again. 'When did your father die?' he asked the governess.

'Two months ago.'

'So this is your first job since.'

She nodded. 'My first job ever. I did not wish to be dependent upon my aunt.'

'Where does your aunt live?'

'In Yorkshire.'

Edgar blurted out, 'What did your father die of, Miss MacNaughton?'

Relieved to have a change of subject, Elizabeth studied his worried little face. 'Old age, mainly. He was over seventy. He'd had a hard life in a very bleak moorland parish.'

'Oh.' Edgar picked up his spoon again, relief clear upon his face.

'Did your father enjoy being a minister?' William asked, because he had been wondering gloomily whether he should go down the accepted track towards helping people. Nobody worried if a minister wanted to help people, however young and inexperienced he was.

Elizabeth shook her head. 'No, not really. All he cared about was history. The history of Lancashire in particular. This region used to be called Amounderness. Did you know that, Edgar?'

Edgar listened with great interest, now that his fears for his mother had been appeased. *Amounderness.* He mouthed the name once or twice to himself. It had such a grand sound.

William watched Elizabeth with admiration as she caught Edgar's interest and began to tell him about medieval Lancashire, when Earl Tosti had owned estates in the north of the county and the land was divided into 'hundreds' and 'carucates'. Nearby Rochdale had been called *Recedham* then and had belonged to a man called Gamel.

She caught William's interest, too. In more ways than one. Clearly her father had passed on his love of history to his daughter, for her face lit up as she started to explain how life had been then. Why had he ever thought her unattractive? he wondered. Then he realised where such thoughts could lead and cut them off. He might be afflicted with the 'Gibson curse', but he wasn't going to let it rule his behaviour.

* * *

The next morning, news was brought that his mother would be spending the day in bed. Chafing at the mere idea of lounging around the house all day, William decided to take the train into Manchester. It wouldn't hurt to see for himself the poorer areas in the great city that dominated Lancashire. All roads in his part of the world seemed to lead to Manchester – all trains, too.

His eyes were alight with interest as he got into a third-class compartment, sitting on the hard wooden bench dreaming of the future and studying his fellow passengers. The carriage was full and very noisy, but the people seemed cheerful. They were clearly the respectable poor and did not need his help. But there must surely be missions to the needy here in Manchester, as there had been in London?

Standing outside the station, he was tempted first to go for a prowl around the city centre. Manchester seemed to change every time he visited it. He had not spent a lot of time here, but whenever he did come, there was always something new to see.

The shops were growing very grand, the goods in them not suffering by comparison with those in London. He paused outside Kendal Milne's Bazaar on Deansgate to stare into the windows, then he pressed on. The windows at the Emporium looked better than these, because not only had his mother insisted that Tom get some of the new wide windows installed, the first in Bilsden, but she herself had taught some of the assistants how to set out a display which was tasteful, yet caught the eye.

He walked along Peter Street, whistling cheerfully, and there he stopped to frown at the new Free Trade Hall, which was, according to his step-father, one of the most significant buildings in the city, whether you liked the style or not. It had been designed by Edward Walters and – William wrinkled his forehead, trying to remember the exact words – yes, it was 'built in the Lombard-Venetian style of architecture'. He grinned. He had never forgotten that grand phrase, or the interest the building had aroused, even in Bilsden, simply because he hadn't been able to understand the fuss.

Even his grandparents had made one of their rare trips into Manchester to see it when it was completed in 1856, and had been full of its wonders when they returned. But somehow the building did not inspire William. He was more interested in the man selling newspapers outside it, who was shivering in the icy wind, or the two little girls walking meekly along, holding the gloved hands of a woman who looked like their governess.

He moved on slowly. Everywhere in the city centre people were bustling along, bumping into him, pushing past him, swerving to avoid him. It was the very picture of prosperity, with new buildings being erected or old ones refurbished everywhere. On the streets a huge press of traffic snarled and unsnarled, to the sounds of drivers' shouts, the trundling of iron-shod wheels and the clopping of horses' hooves. There was a rather pervasive smell of horsedung, too, though the streets were cleared regularly.

William found a café where he could sit down and eat a mid-morning snack. Around him polite people talked quietly and left food on their plates. He looked down at his own plate and was filled with guilt again. Although he didn't waste food, he ate whenever he pleased, feeding his body well, this big strong body that did no real work and contributed so little to the world.

It wasn't far from the well-kept buildings and warmly dressed people to a huddle of streets every bit as bad as those in the poorer areas of London, streets where puddles of human filth lay unheeded on the ground and thin people stared at William as if he had two heads. Many of the windows were broken and stuffed with rags, and even the brick walls were filthy. The faces of the people huddled in doorways looked pale and hungry, as if they had never ever had enough to eat. How could they live in such places, bring up families, care for the sick? And yet, he noted in disapproval, there were public houses on nearly every street, small shabby places with men sitting drinking inside, even this early in the day, and sometimes women waiting outside for any money that was left.

He suddenly remembered a few years ago, when he had been only sixteen, his grandfather reading aloud from the newspaper a speech Lord Stanley had made in Bolton, a speech in which his lordship had listed the necessary public amenities for modern towns and cities in order of priority. William didn't remember the whole list – indeed, he was surprised that he remembered any of it, because at the time, he had not understood his grandfather's anger – but he did remember that Lord Stanley considered the first priority to be enough accommodation in places of worship.

Looking around him now, William fully understood his grandfather's outrage, staunch Methodist though John Gibson was. Places of worship were all very well, but if people did not have decent houses to live in and food to put in their children's bellies, what use were churches and sermons to them?

William found a man on a corner selling hot drinks and a group of children warming themselves surreptitiously at the glowing charcoal brazier that boiled the water. On a whim William went up to them. 'Are you hungry?'

They just stared at him out of eyes which seemed too large for their thin faces. Then one of them nodded. 'I'm allus hungry, mister.'

'Well,' said William, 'today's your lucky day, then.' He turned to the man. 'I want to buy a hot drink for every child here.'

The man, who had been watching William with sour suspicion, brightened, then hesitated. 'You won't mind if I see your money first, sir – only, I can't afford to give my stuff away.'

'How much,' William stared around, then back at the barrow, 'for tea and a bun for each child?'

The man counted laboriously. 'Ten children – tenpence.'

William pulled a shilling from his pocket and slapped it down. 'And a cup for me, too.'

The children hesitated, then a girl who was taller than the others stepped forward to take the first cup and the stale-looking bun, cramming it into her mouth before she drank the tea, as if she were afraid that someone might take it from her. William had seen dogs gulp down their food like that. It hurt him to see a child do the same.

A man standing on the opposite corner smiled and nodded to William. 'It's nice to see someone as thinks of the childer,' he called.

'How about joining us?' William asked on another impulse.

The man stiffened. 'Nay, I don't need no charity. It's different with the childer, but I can manage for mesen.'

'No charity offered,' said William cheerfully. 'I need some information and then perhaps some help in finding my way around.'

The man hesitated, then stepped forward. 'Well, all right, then.'

'My name's William Ashworth.'

The man stared at William's outstretched hand in amazement, then rubbed his own grimy hand against his threadbare jacket and shook the large warm pink hand. 'Bill Midgely.' He grinned. 'I were christened William, like you, but no one's ever called me that, not even our Mam.'

'Are there many hungry children around here?' William asked, gesturing to the stallkeeper to supply another bun and cup of tea to his companion.

Bill gave a snort of laughter. 'Aye. Hundreds.'

'Is anyone doing anything to help them?'

'There's a group of ladies as hand out Bible tracts. Fat lot of good that does to hungry folk. An' there's a fellow down Little Mistle Street.' He frowned. 'Funny sort of chap, he is, but he helps a bit.'

'Oh?' William waited for his companion to take a swig of

the hot tea and a huge appreciative bite of the bun. 'Who is he?'

'*He* says he used to be a minister,' Bill grinned, 'but he's like no minister I've ever met.'

'What exactly does he do?'

'What he can. He's rented an old warehouse an' he lets the street folk sleep there for nowt. Saves lives in t'winter, that does. He hasn't much brass himself, an' I reckon he goes hungry nearly as often as I do, for he's allus giving his supper to other folk.'

That was more promising. 'He sounds like the sort of person I've come here to meet. I'd be very grateful if you'd take me to see him.'

Bill shrugged. 'Well, I've got nowt else to do since I got turned off from my work.' Indignantly he added, 'After ten year! The Mester had a nephew as was old enough to work, so he told me to find summat else. Only there were nowt going. So I've got plenty of time to help you.'

When he had drained the cup to the last dregs, he wiped his mouth on his sleeve and nodded. 'That were right good. Thanks. *Look out!*' He grabbed a little boy who'd crept up behind them and was trying to slip his hand into William's coat pocket. 'You little devil! What do you think you're doin' when the gentleman's just bought you summat to eat an' drink?' He shook the boy hard. 'What way is that to say thank you? Eh? I should call a constable, I should that!'

William touched his arm. 'Let him go.'

Bill shook the boy again, growling, 'No more thievin', you!' then he pushed him away and watched as the lad ran off bawling. 'Poor little sod. What chance does he have?'

'Not much,' William agreed. But maybe he could save just a few like that. As they walked on through the narrow streets, his face grew animated as he questioned Bill about the man in Little Mistle Street. 'What a good thing I met you!' he said at one point as they waited to let a coal cart go past.

Bill looked sideways and realised in amazement that this well-dressed young fellow really meant it. 'Aye?'

'Tell me what exactly this man is doing with his warehouse.'

'Nowt much. It's a poor sort of place, but at least it keeps folk dry of a night, an' it soon warms up with all the bodies that lie there. Not that I've had to use it mysen, you understand. Since my wife died, my brother's let me sleep downstairs at his place. But his wife don't like me stayin' around the house in the daytime, an' anyway, if I go out, I sometimes pick up little jobs here and there.'

'What did your wife die of?'

'Childbirth. The baby died, too, poor mite.'

'Life can be hard on women,' William agreed.

Bitterness suddenly overflowing, Bill demanded, 'Nay, what does a young fellow like you know about women, or about a hard life, come to that?'

'I grew up in Bilsden, in the Rows there,' William said with quiet dignity. 'It was better than this place, I'll agree, but it wasn't an easy life. My father died when I was seven and my mother sewed for her living.' In spite of himself, pride filled his voice as he added, 'She's a clever woman, my mother. She built up a business of her own, first with a market stall, then with a – a dress shop. Of course, she doesn't need to work now – she's got married again – but she still runs her business. She says she can't abide to be idle.'

'And can she abide for her son to spend his time in places like this?' Bill asked cynically, then sucked in his breath as he realised how rude this sounded.

William's voice was quiet, but firm, and his eyes were steady on Bill's. 'Not really. But like her, I'm not cut out to sit idly at home. I want to help people.' He waited for Bill to jeer at him, and when he didn't, William looked down at the thin man by his side. 'It must seem – well, presumptuous – a young fellow like me who's never hungered or – or really worked for his living – trying to help others. But it's what I want to do,' his voice grew more determined, 'and what I'm *going* to do.'

'Aye, well, there's enough folk needing a bit of help. You won't find any lack of people in trouble.'

'Are you in trouble?'

Bill glared at him. 'I wouldn't be if I could find work an' a mester as didn't try to cheat his workpeople. I had a promise of a place, but I fell ill, an' by the time I were better, another had took it.'

'I could find you a little work, for a few days,' William offered hesitantly.

'*You* could?'

'Yes. I need a – a guide.' William gestured around them. 'Someone who'll show me the poorer parts of the city. Um, what would be a fair wage for that?'

'You're asking me that?'

'Yes.'

Bill hesitated. 'How about half a crown a day?'

William nodded. 'Fine. Two shillings and sixpence daily, and I'll buy you a meal at noon. We'll do it for three days, first of all, then we'll see what happens, see whether I need more help from you.'

Bill eyed him sideways as they walked. He were a funny 'un, this young fellow, but you couldn't help liking him. When he smiled, he made you feel more cheerful, somehow, as if there was some hope in the world.

They arrived at a particularly shabby street, where small warehouses leaned against one another for support and a few scruffy lads stood on street corners, clapping their hands together to keep warm and hoping to earn a coin or two by running messages. Noises of all sorts came from inside some of the warehouses, and dark smoke plumed up from them, but other buildings stood silent, their doors locked and pieces of wood nailed across the windows.

Bill stopped at the far end of the street in front of the smallest and shabbiest warehouse. 'This is where he lives.'

He banged on the door. 'Are you there, Mester Robins? I've got someone as wants to talk to you.'

The man who came to the door was thin, with sparse white hair and age-spotted skin. But his clothing was warm and clean, and his eyes brightened with interest when he saw William. 'Won't you come in? It's very raw outside today.'

William stepped over the threshold immediately, but Bill hesitated.

'You too, my friend.'

Inside it was less cold, for they were protected from the wind, but it was still not warm.

'What can I do for you?'

William stuck out his hand. 'I'm William Ashworth and I'm trying to learn how to help my fellow men,' he said. 'Bill tells me you're doing something in the same line, so I thought perhaps you might spare some time to talk to me, show me what you're doing. I've a lot to learn.'

'That's a worthy ambition.' The man clasped William's hand and looked him in the eyes for a moment. 'I'm Alan Robins. I, too, am trying to help my fellow men. But it isn't easy.' He turned to the third man. 'And you, my friend? Do you have a name to share with us?'

'I'm Bill Midgely.'

Alan shook Bill's hand and smiled at him gently, his manner no different than it had been towards his well-dressed visitor. 'Welcome to my humble home. If you'll follow me, I have a room of my own where we can be somewhat warmer.' He led the way to one of the back corners, where some rough wooden walls and an even rougher ceiling partitioned off a decent-sized space around a rough brick chimney stack. Inside the room were two threadbare armchairs, a small table, three hard upright chairs, and in a corner, a narrow bed, neatly made. A small fire was burning in the grate and a kettle sat singing to itself at the side of the flames.

Alan moved to pick up a teapot. 'I can offer you a cup of

tea, but I'm afraid I have no food until tomorrow, when my grand-daughter comes to visit me.'

'I can buy us some food, if you would go out for it, Bill?' William turned to look at his companion. 'Would you mind?'

'Nay, why should I mind?'

'They sell very tasty pies with peas at the corner of the next street,' Alan said. 'If you tell them it's for me, they'll send a boy round later for the plates and tray.'

William fumbled in his pocket and to his annoyance found only a half guinea. He should have thought to get his money changed into smaller coins. 'I'm afraid this is all I have. Will they be able to change it for you, do you think?'

Bill stared at him, not taking the proffered coin. 'And you'll trust me with it – just like that?'

William was puzzled. 'Of course.'

Bill's voice became suddenly gruff and he swiped his hand across his eyes. 'Well, you *can* trust me, then, an' I shan't let anyone take it from me.' He left quickly.

'That was very well done,' said Alan.

William stared at him in bewilderment.

'Did you not realise how much trust you were putting in him, giving him half a guinea? It's a week's wages for many people.'

'Oh. I never thought of that.'

Alan stared across the scrubbed wooden table at William's ingenuous face and smiled gently. 'No, I'm sure you didn't.'

'I feel so young and ignorant.' He looked humbly across at the older man. 'But I do want to help my fellow men and I'm willing to learn anything you can teach me.'

Alan's gaze was very direct. 'It took me until I was over sixty to realise that I should be doing more to help my fellow human beings. So you're well ahead of me, my friend.'

William blushed.

Alan laid a wrinkled hand on William's young pink one. 'So, tell me about yourself and what you want to do?'

* * *

Although William felt he had crammed a great deal into the day, he was back in Bilsden by half-past three. Already he had all sorts of plans for helping Alan Robins, but could not do much in his good clothes.

He changed his ticket for first-class, wanting to sit quietly on the way back and think over what he had seen. He felt a little guilty about that, but his head was spinning with all he had learned.

Sharing his compartment was a large fleshy gentleman with a high colour and bulbous eyes which reminded William of over-ripe greengage plums. There was a distinct odour of port hanging around him, as if he had dined well.

'Are you from Bilsden, sir?' his travelling companion asked as the train pulled out.

William nodded.

'Then I wonder if you could give me some information?'

'Of course.'

'I'm looking for a place called Ridge House. Is it far from the town?'

Surely this man wasn't an acquaintance of his step-father? William didn't know when he had taken a greater dislike to anyone on mere sight. 'It's not far. A short cab ride.' He hesitated, then added, 'In fact, I live there myself.'

The man raised one eyebrow. 'Name of Hallam?'

'No. That's my step-father.'

'Ah. It'll be your mother I want to see.'

'Oh? What about?'

The man tapped his nose, as if to signify it was confidential, then immediately added, 'The new governess. I'm afraid your mother has been taken in by her.'

'In what way?'

'She's – um – a bit of a lightskirt.'

William could feel himself bristling with indignation. That was the last thing he'd have suspected Elizabeth MacNaughton of. 'Oh? And even supposing it's true, why should that be a concern of yours?'

His companion sighed and pulled out a handkerchief to dab at his tearless eyes. 'She's related to us. Unfortunately. We had her living with us, keeping her out of mischief under our eyes, but she skipped out. Better if we keep her with us, I think. Bring her back to the path of virtue.' He flourished a card. 'Name's Melby. Lewis Melby.'

You could not thump a stranger in the face. 'William Ashworth.'

When they arrived in Bilsden, William hesitated as Melby suggested the two of them share a cab. He would have to get his step-father's help on this. 'Very well.'

At the house, Mr Melby did not offer to pay his share of the cab fare, but told the cab driver to wait. He followed William inside without waiting for an invitation. After a moment's hesitation, William led him into a small sitting room that was rarely used. 'I'll fetch my step-father.'

But Frederick was resting.

William hesitated again, then went along to the schoolroom and tapped on the door. Edgar was sprawled in front of the fire with a story-book and Tamsin was painting on a big piece of white paper, spread out on a corner of the huge table.

Elizabeth MacNaughton looked up from a piece of embroidery. 'Did you want something, Mr Ashworth?'

'Just a word, if you have a moment?' Outside the schoolroom door, he took a deep breath, then said, 'I have some news for you. Bad news, I'm afraid. A Mr Melby is below, asking to see you.'

She turned pale and swayed, as if about to faint. 'How did he find me?' she whispered through lips which had turned almost bloodless.

William put an arm around her. 'Are you all right?'

The breath she drew in was almost a sob. 'I must see your mother before he does. I must tell her – beg her—' Another sob.

'My mother is still ill, and my step-father is resting. Can

you not tell me?' His arm was still around her. There was nothing familiar in this embrace, for she was sagging against him as if she had lost every vestige of strength.

She looked up at him, panic etched on her face.

'I'll promise not to betray your confidence.' He added quietly, 'You should know that I shared a compartment with him and he has already been rather – indiscreet.'

A tear rolled down her cheek and a moan escaped her.

'I'm more likely to believe you, Miss MacNaughton,' William said. 'I'm afraid I took your cousin in great dislike.'

She stared at him, hope warring with the sheer terror in her face.

He took a guess. 'What happened to make you flee your aunt's home?'

A dark flush stained her cheeks and she lowered her eyes, unable to face his scorn as she whispered, 'He came into my bedroom. He – he forced me to—' She was almost swooning at the memory.

William held her close until the trembling had subsided, then stepped back. 'Do you wish to see him?'

She shook her head, shuddering.

'Then I'll see him for you and send him away. I believe you.'

Her voice was faint, hesitant. 'Do you?'

'Yes, of course I do.'

'And will you really see him for me?'

William nodded, his face grim, and turned to go back downstairs. In the small parlour, he found Mr Melby standing stroking his bushy sidewhiskers in front of the mirror. He clearly found the sight of himself very attractive because he was smiling at his reflection. When he saw William, he turned round.

'Miss MacNaughton does not wish to see you. I think you should leave now.' William's voice was curt.

Lewis Melby grinned, not a pleasant expression. 'Go and fetch your mama, lad. It's her I came to see.'

William stepped forward. 'If you don't leave now, I'll

145

take great pleasure in throwing you out.'

'The noise will bring your mama running.'

'My mother is ill. She'll hear nothing. And the servants will do as I say.'

For the first time a flicker of doubt crossed Melby's face, then he shook his head. 'You're bluffing. You're probably enjoying my cousin's services yourself. Don't blame you. She's got a nice body under those dark gowns.'

Enraged, William grabbed him by the lapels, but Melby resisted, kicking him in the shins and shouting for help. William tried to cover that wet pink mouth, to stop the man from disturbing his mother and from further hurting Miss MacNaughton. A small table was sent flying, its ornaments tinkling into pieces against the brass fender.

So engrossed were they in their struggle that neither man heard the door open.

'What the hell's going on?' demanded Frederick.

William pulled back reluctantly. 'I'm trying to get this scoundrel to leave.'

Melby took a step away from William and tried to straighten his clothing. 'Name's Melby. Came to see Mrs Hallam, but this young fellow tried to throw me out. Urgent business, too.' He made a strategic move behind an armchair, panting and sweating like a horse that had just run a race.

'I'm Frederick Hallam, the owner of this house. You can state your business to me.'

Melby eyed him dubiously. 'Came about my cousin. Your new governess. She's—'

'If you repeat any more lies about Miss MacNaughton,' William said loudly, fists clenching at the mere thought, 'then I shall feel obliged to punch you in your lying mouth. Father, please leave this to me. I've spoken to Miss MacNaughton. I believe her side of the tale.'

Frederick eyed him for a moment, then studied Melby and nodded. 'I have every confidence in your judgement. Try not to make too much noise, William.'

As William took a step towards him, Melby snatched up his hat. 'You'll regret this!'

William moved to stand by the door. 'You'll regret it more if you try to come here again. Or if you try to malign Miss MacNaughton.'

When the cab had driven away, William went back to join Frederick in the library, whose open door beckoned invitingly.

'Who was that fellow?'

'He was her cousin. That wasn't a lie, at least.'

'What did he want?'

'To blacken her name.'

Frederick waited, one eyebrow raised.

William stared into the flames. 'She tells me she ran away from her aunt's house to avoid his unwanted attentions.'

'Ah.'

'I believe her.' He looked challengingly at his step-father. 'I'm sure she didn't – encourage him.'

'I believe her, too,' Frederick said mildly. 'But unless I mistake the fellow, he'll not rest at that. His type can be very spiteful. We'd better tell your mother about it all. But not till she's better.' As he stood up, he added, 'Well done, lad.'

William nodded and went back upstairs to tell Miss MacNaughton that he had sent her cousin away. She was not in the schoolroom, so after a moment's hesitation, he knocked on her bedroom door.

She opened it at once, standing white and shaking in front of him.

'I've sent your cousin packing.'

'Thank you. Thank you so much. I'll – leave in the morning.'

He caught her arm. 'Why?'

Her eyes were blind with tears. 'It's better that way. I didn't think Lewis would find me. I'll have to go further away.'

'No. You must stay here.'

She shook her head. 'When she finds out, your mother won't want me to stay.' Her voice faded away and tears ran down her face.

'When she's better, just tell my mother exactly what happened. I promise you she'll not send you away.' He could not betray the secret of his own birth, but he had absolute trust in his mother's generosity and fairness.

She just stared at him.

'What have you got to lose?' he asked gently.

11

Bilsden: Frederick and Annie

*I*t was another three days before Annie came downstairs.
She would have left her bed sooner, but Frederick was
determined to fuss over her and when she saw how it
pleased him to have her to himself in the large comfortable
bedroom, how it made him happy to do little things for her,
she gave in.

When she did leave her room, she walked along first to
the schoolroom, feeling more wobbly than she had
expected, and peeked inside. The two children were
working quietly with Elizabeth and did not see their
mother for a moment. Edgar was absorbed in writing his
letters in a large childish hand, tracing each shape out
laboriously on a slate, with his tongue stuck out of one
corner of his mouth to aid concentration. Tamsin, a sulky
expression on her face, was copying a piece of corrected
work from a piece of paper into a bound notebook.

Both shrieked with pleasure when they saw their
mother, for Annie had allowed them only to stand in her
bedroom doorway every evening and chat to her from
there, not wanting them to catch her influenza.
Tamsin threw down her pen, heedless of the damage to
the new steel nib and the spray of ink drops across the
paper, and pushed her chair back. But it was Edgar
who got to his mother first, seizing her hand and

begging her to come and see his letters.

'She doesn't want to see your baby writing!' Tamsin said scornfully.

'But I do!' Annie insisted, giving her daughter a frown. 'And then I'll look at your work, too, Tamsin.'

'It's not worth it. It's *boring* stuff,' Tamsin muttered, but Annie paid no attention to that, bending over Edgar's primer and slate, and praising his efforts, so that his whole face lit up with pleasure.

Then Annie turned to Tamsin's work and found little to praise. 'I had not thought you so poor at spelling, or so untidy a writer, either,' she said with a look of disapproval. 'In fact, I'm sure your work used to be much better than this.'

Tamsin's face turned scarlet, but she just stared mutinously down at the blotted page.

Annie turned to the governess. 'I hope, Miss MacNaughton, that you will help Tamsin to improve her writing again. I shouldn't like to think my daughter was too *stupid* to spell properly. You must do whatever seems necessary to help her, and I shall support you in any way I can.' There was a hidden message behind her words which everyone except Edgar understood perfectly.

Elizabeth nodded her head in gratitude.

'When I'm fully recovered,' Annie went on, 'I'll have to find you a little Saturday job, Tamsin. William always earned his spending money, and I think you're old enough to do the same now.'

Tamsin gaped at her. '*Earn* my spending money!'

'Yes, indeed.'

'But we're rich. Why do I have to work? No one else that I know has to do that.'

'No one else that you play with is my daughter,' Annie said firmly. 'And being rich is no excuse for being lazy or conceited. William always worked for his pocket money and Edgar will do the same as soon as he turns seven. In our family, we like to remember that money is *earned*.'

Tamsin looked at her mother, apprehension replacing the sulky expression. 'But what shall I have to do?'

'I'll discuss it with your father and with Mr Peters. Perhaps there are some little jobs in the office of the mill. You could go in on Saturday mornings and work for, say, three hours there.'

Relief lit up Tamsin's face. 'Oh, I don't mind that. I love going to the mill.'

'Well, we'll see how much you love *working* there. You'll not be allowed to play around and waste your time. But you're not going anywhere if you're too stupid to do things properly. In business, mistakes can cost you money.' Annie still remembered the days when every farthing counted, still could not abide needless extravagance, still designed her own clothes and had them made up at the salon.

Elizabeth stared after her new employer as Annie nodded pleasantly and left the room. She had never even heard of anyone from such a wealthy family making children earn their spending money, let alone a rich man sending his daughter to work in his mill. A son, perhaps, but not a daughter.

Suddenly, quite fiercely, she wanted to stay here, wanted to be part of this unusual but loving family. No, not part of the family, she corrected herself carefully, you'll never be that. You're a governess and you mustn't forget your place. But Lewis's visit had not only spoiled her sleep, it had left her filled with apprehension of what he might do next and had destroyed the hope that had started to build up in her.

She sighed. She must, she decided, with a shiver of terror at the mere thought, put everything to the test, tell Mrs Hallam. William seemed very hopeful that his mother would understand about what had happened. If he were right, Elizabeth might indeed be able to stay here for a few years, until the children grew too old to need her.

Downstairs, Annie went straight to her own parlour and sank into her comfortable armchair with a sigh of relief.

She was weaker than she had expected. Today Frederick had gone out for the first time to see how things were going in the mill. 'Just for an hour or two,' he had said. She had not told him that she intended to get up today and she wouldn't tell him how wobbly she was feeling, either. He had worried too much about her during the past few days and Jeremy said that worry was not good for him.

Suddenly thirsty, she rang the bell.

'Ah, Winnie, could you bring me a tea-tray – and some scones or cake, if Mrs Lumbley would be so kind. And perhaps you could ask William to join me. He's always hungry.'

'Master William's gone into Manchester again.'

'Oh? Is he meeting some friends there?' Annie frowned. William didn't have any close friends that she knew of outside the family, but perhaps he was meeting one of the young men he'd studied with at Collett House.

'I wouldn't know what Master William is doing, I'm sure.' Winnie sniffed, a sure sign that something was displeasing her.

'Is there something wrong, Winnie?'

'It's not my place to say, ma'am.'

'But if you don't tell me, who will?'

Winnie scowled at the floor, then seemed to make up her mind. The master had forbidden them to mention the damage Master William and that Mr Melby had done to the small sitting room until he told the mistress about the incident, but he hadn't forbidden anything else. 'Well, ma'am, I might not know what Master William gets up to in Manchester, but I do know that he's always filthy by the time he comes home at night. And his hands – well, they look like he's been scrubbing floors with them. He's wearing his older clothes, I'll give him that, but what the washing woman will say when she sees the state of his shirts, I don't know. When Peggy showed them to me, I was fair shocked, I was indeed. Filthy, they were.'

'What's he doing to get so dirty?'

'Whatever it is, he shouldn't be doing it. It's a ruination of his good clothes. *And*,' Winnie hesitated, then leaned closer, 'he's persuaded Cook to pack him a basket of stuff to take with him every day. Stale bread and buns, leftovers and such.' Winnie snapped her lips together and kept them tightly shut as she left the room.

'What's that boy up to now?' Annie wondered aloud. It sounded as if he was pursuing his ambition to help people. But he couldn't just be wandering the streets giving food away, surely? And anyway, that would not get him and his clothes so dirty.

But she was not to find out for several hours, and spent the day worrying intermittently about it and trying not to let her worry show to Frederick when he returned, looking as tired as she felt. They both went upstairs and had a nap during the afternoon, making light of the necessity and joking about their feebleness.

William did not return in time for dinner and the meal was nearly finished when they heard the front door open and his loud cheerful voice calling a greeting to Winnie.

'Ah!' Annie exchanged glances with Frederick. She stood up and hurried out into the hall, catching William as he started to climb the stairs. 'Whatever have you been doing with yourself, William Ashworth?'

The happiness faded from his face at her tone and he stiffened. 'I've been helping a friend.'

'Why don't you wash and change your clothes, then come and tell us about it?' Frederick put his arm around Annie's waist and whispered, 'Shh!' very softly.

'All right.' But William sounded surly, as if expecting to get into trouble, and his expression was disturbingly like Tamsin's when she did not want to do something.

Fifteen minutes later William came down again, by which time Edgar and Tamsin had finished their meal and been sent upstairs with their governess to get ready for bed.

'Have you eaten yet?' Annie asked.

William shook his head.

'Well, we'll keep you company as you eat, then.' She rang the bell and asked Winnie to bring some more food.

'And after that,' Frederick said firmly, 'you'll go up to bed, Annie Hallam.'

'But Miss MacNaughton has asked to see me.'

'You can see her in the morning. You're looking exhausted. You've been up and about for far too long already today.' He turned to his step-son. 'Tell us what you've been doing with yourself, William? Your mother's been worrying about you.'

So much for hiding her anxiety, Annie thought glumly. Heavens, Frederick could read her like an open book.

'Well,' William hesitated, 'I've been working with a new friend to – to help the poor folk in Manchester, the very poorest, the ones who have nowhere to live and who're hungry.' He cast a defiant sideways look at his mother as he spoke, clearly expecting her to take exception to this.

Annie found this hostile glance so upsetting, coming from her beloved William, that she swallowed her anger and reached blindly for Frederick's hand under the table.

'And how does your friend help the poor folk?' Frederick prompted.

At first William spoke haltingly, his eyes going to his mother again and again, expecting her to criticise, surprised when she said nothing. He told them about Alan Robins and what he was doing, waxing enthusiastic about the difference even such a small mission could make to people's lives.

Listening, Annie relaxed a little. Surely, such a man would not harm her son?

In the middle of the explanations, Winnie arrived with a laden tray.

William looked apologetically at his mother and tucked in.

'You look as if you haven't eaten for a week,' she teased.

'I haven't eaten since this morning.'

'Oh?' She frowned. 'Did you run out of money, then?'

He shook his head. 'No. It just – I'd had a large breakfast – and other folk had had nothing at all. I couldn't for shame eat again while they hungered.'

Frederick intervened. 'And your friend, Mr Robins, did he eat luncheon?'

William shook his head. 'No. His grand-daughter brought him a basket of food, but he gave most of it away, just keeping a little for himself for this evening.'

'And is this what you want to do with your life, then?' Annie's voice was tinged with scorn. 'Give food away to the poor?' To her mind, unless people were ill, they should earn their daily bread themselves.

'It's what I want to do for the moment.' William stopped eating to throw her a resentful look. 'I have so much to learn, you see. And I know giving food away won't change things permanently. It's employment these people need, and decent housing. I didn't realise how bad things were in Manchester, far worse than here in Bilsden. You've kept me very protected from life.'

Frederick could see the pain in Annie's eyes at this accusation. 'We all try to protect those we love.' This time it was William to whom he signalled to be quiet with a frown and a flick of his eyes towards his wife.

William remembered that his mother had been ill and did not make any more critical comments.

Nor did she, for she could not think how to talk sense into him, and besides, her head was aching again.

It was left to Frederick to fill the uneasy silence. 'Well, this is clearly important to you, William. But it's important to your mother to know that you're all right. I'd come with you to meet your friend Mr Robins and talk about what you're doing,' he sighed, 'but as you can see, both your mother and I are not yet ourselves.'

'You've no need to check up on him. He's a wonderful man.' William suddenly lost his appetite and pushed the plate away. 'I've met another man, too, with just as much to teach me.'

'Oh?' Frederick's voice was calm and even.

'Yes. Strangely enough, he's also called William, but everyone calls him Bill. He's a working man. He's been ill. His wife died in childbirth and he lost everything. I've been employing him to help me.'

Annie could not keep silent at this. *'Employing him!'*

'Yes. I still have some money left from my allowance and he – he comes with me, shows me around.' William grimaced. 'He's also stopped people from picking my pocket a couple of times now. He says I'm a "babby" in my dealings with people. And he's right.' Suddenly there was dignity in his voice. 'But I'm learning a great deal from him and Alan, Mother. Please don't try to stop me.'

His gaze was so limpid and direct that Annie's hurt angry response died in her throat. 'I won't pretend I'm happy about it all, William, but I don't think any of us should do anything rash – anything we might regret.'

His face lit up and suddenly he was her loving son again. 'Thank you, Mother. I knew you'd understand.'

But that was going too far. 'I don't understand. I most definitely do not. And I'm not promising anything. But you might as well do this as – as laze around the house.' It was the best she could manage.

'When you're better, please come and visit us and you'll see for yourself what we're doing. I've been helping to scrub out the warehouse and to whitewash the walls. And I've been talking to people, learning. Just give me a chance to find my way in life, Mother.'

His face was guileless, a child's innocence shining from it. It would do him no harm to face the realities of life. 'Oh, you always get your own way,' she huffed.

He beamed at her.

'Were you intending to go into Manchester again tomorrow?' Frederick asked.

William nodded. 'They'll be expecting me.'

'Then perhaps you could come home a little earlier, so that we could discuss the matter further before your mother and I fall asleep.'

William suddenly realised that both of them were looking white and tired. 'I'm sorry. I wasn't thinking. Of course I'll come home earlier. I'll try to catch the four o'clock train.'

'Thank you.' Frederick turned to Annie. 'And now, my love, I'm taking you up to bed and joining you there. No arguments, if you please.'

She moved across to William, hesitated, then gave him a kiss and accepted his bear hug in return, before moving towards the door. She could not believe how weak she still felt.

Frederick slipped a guinea into William's hand as he passed. 'It can be expensive, hiring people,' he murmured with a grin.

William frowned at the money, but nodded his thanks. No use standing on his pride when he could use that money to help people.

When they had gone, William sat down on his chair again with a thump and let out a long sigh of relief. They had not tried to stop him going! Then he turned back to his food. It might have gone cold, but he had never been so hungry – or felt so alive and useful.

'Eh,' said Winnie, when she came back to clear the table, 'you've never et it all up! You've got hollow legs you have, Master William, hollow legs.' And wondered why he looked so shamefaced.

The following morning, Elizabeth left the children under Tess's reluctant supervision and went to see her employer. Annie was in her own parlour, looking much better than she had the day before, but still not her usual self. She watched the governess sit down and start twisting her handkerchief, noting the white face and dark-rimmed eyes. Something was very wrong.

'I don't quite know how to start.' Elizabeth faltered. 'But William said – he said you ought to know. And I agree with him – but—'

Annie leaned forward to lay her hand on Elizabeth's. 'Just tell me.'

'The other night, while you were still keeping to your bed, there was a – a visitor.'

Annie watched the younger woman drag in air as if she were finding it hard to breathe and made a soothing sound.

Then the words came out in a rush. 'It was my cousin. His name's Lewis Melby. I – I had left my aunt's house because he . . .' The tears would not be held back and the words came out in tight high bursts of distress. 'He forced his attentions on me. Sh-she didn't know. And she wouldn't have believed me if I'd told her. And if I'd told anyone, I'd have lost my good name. So I ran away, got this job.' She forced herself to look Annie in the eye and was heartened by what she saw. 'The references were perfectly honest. They were from a minister friend of my father's. And I would not – would not ever r-repeat such b-behaviour.'

As she broke down completely, Annie gathered her in her arms and hugged her close. 'Shh. Shh. It's all over now. Don't cry.' But Elizabeth was quite distraught, so Annie let her weep, just continuing to murmur reassurances.

'The only thing I don't understand is why your cousin came here?' Annie said, when the tears had at last stopped.

'To – to blacken my name and take me back. I think he . . .' Elizabeth shuddered. 'I think he wanted to continue using me. William and he had a fight. I'm afraid some of the furniture in the small back sitting room was broken. Mr Hallam knows about that. He – William said your husband told him, told William, to throw my cousin out, but I think,' she hiccupped, 'I think he'll write to you.'

'If he does, I shall return his letter unopened.' Annie studied the girl. 'Is something else bothering you?'

Elizabeth nodded. 'I think he'll destroy my father's things. They're stored in my aunt's attic.' She could not hold back a sob. 'They're all I have left of him.'

Annie felt anger surge through her. She had never forgotten her own similar troubles, only she had been left pregnant. On a sudden thought, she asked, 'There was no – no result of your cousin's actions?'

Elizabeth blushed scarlet and shook her head. 'No.' Her voice was a whisper of shame.

'Then all we have to do is get your things back.'

'*What?*'

Annie smiled warmly. 'I'm very satisfied with your work as a governess. I know Tamsin is not an easy pupil. What happened in the past can stay in the past, so far as I'm concerned. It was certainly not your fault. And I shall consult my husband when he returns about getting your things back.' Her smile faded. 'I was born in the Rows, as you must have heard. I do understand what can happen to young women. And that it's not always their fault.'

Tears were running down Elizabeth's face. 'How can I ever th-thank you?'

'I'm not asking for thanks. There's great satisfaction in helping another woman in distress.'

After which there was nothing that Elizabeth would not have done for Annie Hallam, or any member of her family.

12

Manchester: Tom

*W*hen William arrived back in Bilsden the next
evening, his mind was so full of what he had seen and done
all day that it was not until someone tugged at his sleeve
that he noticed his Uncle Tom standing next to him at the
station entrance.

'What's she like?' Tom demanded.

'Who?'

'The girl you're dreaming of.'

William scowled down at him. 'I'm not dreaming of any
girl!'

'Well, you should be, then, at your age.'

William studied him in puzzlement. 'What are you doing
here, Uncle Tom? You don't usually go into Manchester in
the evening.' In fact, it was not often that his uncle left Bilsden
nowadays. Tom had employees who went out to collect
junk, or to persuade the farmers to sell their cheeses and
hams to Gibson's, rather than at market. He usually stayed
in town, going from one to the other of his various interests,
of which The Prince of Wales hotel and the Emporium
were the main ones.

'Oh, I thought I'd give myself a bit of a treat,' Tom said
nonchalantly.

William eyed his uncle covertly. Surely Tom was looking
a bit perkier than usual? Yes, definitely perkier, more alive,

161

somehow. And that was a new overcoat with a dark evening suit beneath it that William had not seen before. 'You're looking positively elegant, Uncle Tom. What *are* you doing?'

'I'm off to a concert, actually.'

'Since when have *you* been interested enough in music to go off to concerts in Manchester?' William teased. 'I reckon it's you who's going off to meet someone. I haven't seen you so spruced up for years.' He nudged his uncle. 'Who is she?'

'Don't be cheeky! Ah, there's the train now.'

William could hear relief in his uncle's voice and, as he was quick to note, Tom hadn't denied that he was meeting someone. He watched his uncle get into the train, then he looked around for a cab, but mentally chastised himself before he could raise his hand to signal to it. The people he was helping could live all day off what it would cost him for a cab. He would do better saving his money to buy them food. He set off to walk up Ridge Hill, feeling very tired now, and ravenously hungry.

When he arrived home, Winnie bustled across the hall to meet him, looking self-important. 'Your mother and father are waiting for you in the library, Master William. They said there's no hurry. You're to wash and change your clothes first.'

She sounded so like someone scolding a small boy that William, who had comforted a dying old man that day, could not bear it. He picked her up by the waist and held her in the air above him, ignoring her shrieks. 'You're speaking to me as if I'm a child. I'm a man grown, Winnie. When are you going to notice that?'

She gaped at him, feet still dangling.

He shook her gently to emphasise his point and set her down equally gently. 'I'm a man grown,' he repeated. 'I don't need telling to wash my hands and change my clothes before I join my mother. All right?'

She nodded, her eyes still popping out of her head. 'Yes, Mr William.'

It was the first time she had not called him 'Master' William. He nodded in satisfaction at this small victory and went on his way up to his room, taking the stairs two at a time and whistling under his breath.

There was hot water waiting for him, though it had cooled to lukewarm by now, because he had missed the four o'clock train. There was also a glass of creamy farm milk, of which he was very fond, and some buttered scones keeping fresh under a dish. With a grin he gulped down the milk and ate all the scones, then bustled about with a vengeance, not wanting to keep his mother waiting. For it was his mother who would have to be convinced tonight, he was sure of that. His step-father was much more easy-going.

As he strode down the stairs, he heard voices coming from the library. Someone else was there with his mother and step-father. Frowning, he paused to listen, then his face cleared. His grandfather. Now he knew he would get a fair hearing.

He made sure he walked loudly enough to advertise his approach, then squared his shoulders and tapped on the door, not waiting to be asked to enter but going straight in to face his mother's judgement. For it would be his mother who decided things, he knew that. It always was.

'How are you feeling today, Mother?' He strode across to give her a resounding kiss on the cheek. 'You're looking better than yesterday.'

'No thanks to you.' But she pulled his head down and kissed him back.

He looked down at her, his eyes very blue and guileless. He only looked like that when he was plotting mischief, or when he was facing a tricky situation, and for a moment the two of them just stared at each other. Then Annie muttered something and let go of his arm. William went over to shake his grandfather's hand, grinning at him.

John grinned back. 'Eh, lad! You're ripe for mischief, you are that.'

'Eh, Grandfather, I am, too.'

'Won't you sit down, William?' Frederick said. 'We thought it might be a good idea for your grandfather to join us—'

'Since you usually take more notice of him than you do of anyone else!' Annie finished for him tartly. 'Oh, do sit down and stop looking like the prisoner in the dock. If we can't talk about this quietly and sensibly, then I've failed you as a mother.'

He was shocked. 'You haven't done that. Never, ever think that. You've been – I mean, you *are* – a wonderful mother. It's just that I have to – have to find my own way in life. And my way isn't yours.'

Frederick stepped in hastily before Annie said something she would regret. 'What we thought was: your grandfather could stand in for your mother and me. Would you take him into Manchester with you tomorrow, William? Introduce him to your new friends, show him what you're doing?'

His step-son's beaming face was all the answer he needed.

While Frederick was showing John Gibson out, Annie said abruptly: 'I spoke to Elizabeth.'

William tensed.

'I believe her. Your father's sent someone to her aunt's to get her things. I'm glad you were able to help her.'

'I'm glad, too.'

She did not refer to the matter again.

Tom arrived in Manchester to find the ground already sparkling with frost and a chill wind blowing. He called a cab to take him to the hall where the concert was to be held. When he arrived there, he took out his pocket watch and found that he was over half an hour early. Well, it would be warmer inside than out. He bought a ticket, left his overcoat, scarf and hat with the cloakroom attendant and walked inside, rubbing his hands together and looking around him with great interest. He had never been to a grand concert like this one before.

It was a smallish hall, quite new and elegant in both line and dimensions. There was hardly anyone there yet, but the hall was filled with rows of chairs and there was a line of greenery in front of the stage.

'Please take a seat, sir,' said a quiet voice in his ear.

Tom turned to see a gentleman in evening dress standing with one arm outstretched in the direction of the rows of seats.

'Only the front two rows are reserved. Sit anywhere else you like.'

'Thank you.' Tom hesitated. 'Er – is there some way I could send a message to Miss Lidoni? I used to know her when we were both children. We – er – lived near one another. I'd like to talk to her after the concert, if I could.' He fumbled in his pocket for the envelope and the note which it had taken him so long to write the previous evening.

The man frowned and studied Tom more closely, then said slowly, 'I could take it to her for you. But she might not want to see you. She gets very tired after a concert.'

'Oh, I think she'll want to see me, just for a minute or two anyway.' Tom handed the note over, then allowed the man to show him to a seat at the side. He sat there, wondering again whether he had done the right thing coming here tonight and worrying about whether Rosie really would want to see him, for all his brave words. She had been very definite that the two of them had no future together when she came to help him out of the morass of misery into which he had fallen after Marianne's death.

She had left Bilsden the following morning before he awoke and he had not heard a word directly from her since. She might at least have let him know how the boy was going on. Their son. Funny, that. He had only seen the child once, when he was a baby, wouldn't even recognise him if they passed in the street. And that seemed wrong.

The Gibsons didn't usually abandon their own.

And Rosie hadn't sung in Manchester since then. Not in seven years. Frederick had told him how she was going on every now and then, for it was he who had helped Rosie – sent her to singing tutors, got someone to teach her how a lady spoke and dressed – and she apparently wrote to her benefactor occasionally. The change in her had been amazing that one time Tom had seen her. She had seemed as ladylike as his sister, though he'd been too sunk in his own misery then to say how much he admired what she had done with herself. Well, he thought he hadn't said it. His memories of the occasion were a little blurred.

Tom sighed and looked at the quiet-spoken and elegantly dressed people starting to filter into the hall. Suddenly he wanted to be nearer the front, not here at the side, to be where Rosie could see him from the platform and where he could get a really good view of her. On a sudden impulse, he moved further forward, choosing an aisle seat in the third row from the front. Surely Rosie could not help but see him here?

By the time the concert began, most of the seats were taken. Tom calculated how much that would bring in at half a guinea per person, and pursed his lips in a silent whistle. Then someone tapped loudly three times and the audience fell silent. The curtains were drawn back to reveal a grand piano, some more ferns and nothing else.

The gentleman who had taken Tom's note came out to the centre of the stage. 'I'd like first of all to introduce Paul Stepworthy, Miss Lidoni's accompanist.'

Tom applauded half-heartedly and contained his impatience as another sombrely clad gentleman came out on to the stage, bowed and took his seat at the piano. They looked like a pair of stuffed shirts, those two, with their calm cool faces. Look at that fellow flourishing his white-gloved hands. He knew what folk would have thought of such a pretty boy back in the Rows!

'And now, it's my pleasure, my very great pleasure, to

introduce Miss Rosa Lidoni herself.' More flourishes.

Rosie stepped out on to the stage and Tom's breath caught in his throat. This was not his Rosie. This was a supremely elegant lady with a calm and confident bearing. What was he doing here, thinking she'd want to bother with a fool like him again?

He looked down at himself. He was like an organ grinder's monkey, all dressed up in someone else's finery. He wasn't tall and gentlemanly. He had greying crimpy hair, an undistinguished face and work-worn hands. He had never felt so out of place in his whole life as he did at that moment, watching Rosie glide across the stage to her pianist, full silken skirts swaying around her, jewels glittering at wrist and neckline. She turned to face the audience and smiled at them, and suddenly she was his Rosie again. Her smile hadn't changed a bit.

When she started singing, Tom stopped thinking, stopped worrying, simply lost himself in the wonderful music. She'd always had a lovely voice, but not like this. The notes soared effortlessly over the hushed rapt audience, losing themselves in the shadowed ceiling. Sometimes they rippled over him like the Bil did over its stony course up on the moors, before it became a real river. Sometimes they danced through the air, full of fun. Tom didn't know how he understood this, because half of what Rosie sang was in foreign languages, but the way she sang carried a universal message that went beyond words.

Then suddenly, between songs, she looked right at him, her mouth framing the word, 'Tom!' For a moment she stood frozen, then her face became mischievous and she moved back to whisper to the pianist, who looked surprised, but nodded and took his hands off the keys.

'I'd like to sing these songs for an old friend of mine, who's sitting in the audience now. I haven't seen him for years, but when we were young, we used to play street games to songs like these.' And she was off, singing unaccompanied, singing the songs that all the kids in Bilsden knew, the songs to which they skipped and played hopscotch and acted out circle games.

Tears trickled down Tom's cheeks. The songs brought back so many memories: of times when his mother had been alive, of teasing the little lasses, breaking up their playing circles, and sometimes even condescending to join in. He had first met Rosie when she was dancing in a circle, singing this very song. Had she remembered that for all these years? Surely not?

The applause was thunderous and other people were smiling, or wiping tears from their eyes. It seemed he was not the only one for whom those songs had brought back memories.

When Rosie finished her programme, the audience went wild, applauding and standing up and calling out for encores.

So she gave them one of her old favourites, one she had sung in The Shepherd's Rest when she worked there for Tom and Seth: 'I dreamt that I dwelled in marble halls'. And the glorious notes soared up and up until surely, Tom thought, in a rare moment of whimsy, they could be heard in heaven itself.

When it was all over and Rosie had smilingly refused to give them another encore, the audience began to file out. Tom just sat on, lost in his memories. So he didn't see her coming out through a little door at the side of the stage, didn't see anything until she sat down next to him and laid one gloved hand on his.

'Well, Tom, lad, it's been a few years, hasn't it?' she said softly.

To his horror, he felt tears still welling in his eyes. 'Oh, Rosie, can we go somewhere private? Hell, I'm bloody crying all over you again.'

With a laugh, she tugged him to his feet and pulled him through the nodding, smiling crowd to the stage door. And then they were alone in a sudden dimness, where voices and footsteps echoed faintly in the distance, and no one was in sight.

With a growl, he pulled her into his arms and just held her close. 'I didn't know,' he said, again and again, 'I just didn't know.'

Her voice was gentle. 'What didn't you know, Tom, love?'

'That you could sing like that.' He realised he was crushing her beautiful gown and that the corsage was a flattened mess of squashed petals and leaves, so reluctantly he let go of her.

'Well, I didn't know anyone could sing like that, either, till Mr Hallam sent me to those teachers in London. Oh, you should have heard my singing teacher scold me at first! I couldn't do anything right. I was all for giving up several times, but Mr Hallam said I should persevere, said everything worthwhile took some effort. And he was right.'

An expression of jealousy passed fleetingly across Tom's face and she chuckled, guessing what he was thinking. 'There's nothing like that between me and him, you fool. He thinks the sun rises and shines over your Annie, Mr Hallam does. But he's been a good friend to me and a good – what's the word he uses? – yes, a good patron. I'm full of fancy words nowadays.'

'And full of foreign words, too.' He didn't know any foreign words at all.

She nodded. 'Yes. I don't understand half of them, though I know the general sense of them, but somehow the songs sound better in the language they were written for. Mind, it was hell trying to get my tongue round them at first.' She reached up one fingertip to brush away a tear from his cheek. 'You daft great softie. What's got into you tonight?'

'Your music. You. Did you – get my note, then?'

She stilled and frowned. 'What note?'

'I sent one round to you about half an hour before the concert began.'

Her face cleared. 'It'll be waiting for me in my dressing room. I can never think about anything else before a concert. I just need to sit quietly and get myself ready to sing. Come on. We'll go and find it and I'll read it now.'

The dressing room was a mass of flowers, expensive bouquets sent by admirers. They filled the air with a cloying scent that had Tom thinking wistfully of a clean fresh wind blowing across the moors. He had never liked hothouse flowers.

Rosie seemed to read his mind. 'They stink, don't they?' She went across to a small table and fingered through the notes left there. 'Which one is yours, Tom?'

He went to join her. Twice he shuffled the envelopes. 'It's not here.'

'Who did you give it to?'

'The fellow who introduced you on the stage.'

'Stephen.'

'Who is he?'

She gave him a quizzical look. 'My manager, Stephen Harris.'

'Oh.'

She smiled, but then she looked back at the notes and frowned. 'What did you say to him?'

'I said I was an old friend. That we'd grown up together in the same streets.'

'Hmm. Do me a favour, Tom, will you? Go and hide behind the screen.'

'What? Why on earth should I hide?'

Footsteps sounded outside and someone knocked on the door. She gestured urgently to the screen, with a fierce expression on her face, and Tom shook his head in bafflement, but tiptoed across the room obediently. He crouched down behind the screen, feeling an utter fool.

'Come in, Stephen.'

The door opened. 'I know you like to be alone after a concert, but I couldn't wait a moment longer. You were magnificent tonight, Rosa, absolutely magnificent. I don't think I've ever heard you sing so beautifully. But why the change to the programme?' He fingered the pile of notes on her dressing table.

'Oh, a sudden whim.' She grinned. 'We artistes are like that.'

'You aren't usually. Er – did you really see an old friend in the audience?'

'Yes.' She picked up the notes. 'Is this all there is for me tonight?'

'Yes. I'll tell the admirers to clear off, shall I? I know how tired you are after a concert.'

'Tell them in a minute. Tom! Come out, will you?'

He straightened up and came from behind the screen, scowling at the elegant Stephen.

'Tom tells me he gave you a note for me.'

'Did he? I must have mislaid it, then.'

'Or maybe you mislaid it on purpose.'

Stephen looked at her. 'Anything I do, I do to protect you, Rosa, and I wish you'd let me do more. You don't need to—'

She poked him in the chest. 'I'll tell you what I need and what I don't need. And I can protect myself, thank you very much!' Another poke had him taking a step backwards.

Tom hid a grin.

She put her hands on her hips. 'I'll say this just once. If you ever intercept any of my letters again, or try to keep me in the dark about anything – *anything at all* – I'll find myself another manager. I thought I'd made myself clear about your interference last time.'

A flush stained his cheeks and the glance he threw at Tom was vicious.

But Rosie wasn't giving him an inch. 'Now perhaps you'll look through your pockets and see if you can find my letter?'

He pulled a crumpled envelope out of an inside pocket, proffering it silently.

She took it from him without looking at it, and her voice

171

was chill as she added, 'Now, me and Tom have a lot of catching up to do, so I won't need you to escort me back to the hotel tonight.'

He opened his mouth to protest, but she went and held the door open and jerked one thumb at him. He scowled at Tom, then left.

'That's one thing about the gentry, even the impoverished sort like him – they always do things in a dignified way, even when they're seething with fury,' Rosie said, and opened her arms. 'Come and give me another hug, you old rogue, then you can buy me supper. And if you miss your last train back, you can find yourself a room in my hotel. For I want to know what you've been doing with yourself. You look a damn sight better than you did last time I saw you, that's for sure.'

13

March: Annie and Frederick

$\mathcal{A}$nnie lingered over breakfast, but it was an effort to speak pleasantly to Tamsin and Edgar, and to exchange occasional remarks with Elizabeth. Frederick lingered with her, but contributed little to the conversation, just smiling gently at his children from time to time. When they had left for the schoolroom, he looked at Annie, who was staring blindly into space, and snapped his fingers. 'Wake up, love.'

'What? Oh, I was miles away. Sorry.'

'What were you thinking about? As if I can't guess. William was right, you know. You have been over-protective with him.'

'So it seems. I was wondering how he and Dad will get on today. They set off so early. They'll be frozen.'

'Well, whatever happens, they'll enjoy each other's company. They always do.' Frederick hesitated. 'Are you doing anything special or could we have a talk?'

'Of course.'

'I need to ask your opinion on a few things.'

When they were settled in the library, on opposite sides of a cheerfully blazing fire, Annie looked at Frederick and all the love he felt for her seemed to be painted on his face, together with a longing so intense that she knew instinctively what he was thinking. With an inarticulate cry, she slipped from her seat and threw herself down to kneel beside him, her head on his knee. Struggle as she might, she could not prevent herself from bursting into tears.

She wept for only a short time and then, when she looked up, ashamed of herself for burdening him with her own emotions, she saw that his eyes too were wet. 'I'm sorry,' she said huskily.

'What for? Loving me?' His voice was shaky. 'It's been wonderful, hasn't it?'

'Don't talk like that!' Her voice was fierce and tight. 'Don't ever talk like that. It still *is* wonderful. Jeremy said,' she gulped away the lump in her throat, 'he said that you could have years left yet, if you were careful with yourself.'

His eyes were still sad. 'Years of what, love? Years of being an invalid who can't pleasure his wife?'

She pulled herself up to sit on his knee, glad she had not worn a hooped skirt today. They were such a nuisance around the house. And why was she thinking of stupid things like clothes when her whole life was falling apart? She rested her head against his chest, nestling in her favourite position against him. 'It's not surprising we haven't made love, when we've both been ill.'

'I've never been too ill to feel the urge before.' He hugged her fiercely to him. 'I haven't felt the slightest need lately. And Annie, lass, I've felt so – so *old*!'

She could think of nothing to say to that. Easy assurances had never been currency between the two of them. 'Your feelings will come back as you feel better.' She felt him shake his head. 'Has Jeremy – has he said—?'

'He's said I must be as careful about that as about the rest of my life. That I mustn't be too – too energetic.' His arms tightened around her. 'Annie girl, I don't think I can bear to live like an invalid.'

'But – what else can we do?'

He kissed her absent-mindedly on the cheek. 'Well, with your agreement, I would like to continue to live a fairly

174

normal sort of life – as normal as I can, anyway. Shh! Let me finish. I'll be more careful than before, of course I will, but I can't and won't allow myself to be wrapped up in cotton wool. I won't have the rest of you tiptoeing around me as if every minute might be my last. And I won't spend the next few years sitting in this chair doing nothing worthwhile. I couldn't bear that, love. It wouldn't be any sort of life.'

She was silent for a long time and he didn't press her to respond, just held her close and waited for her to think through what he had said. After the clock had ticked away several long minutes, she let out her breath in a gust of anger and determination combined, then she did the bravest thing she'd ever done in her life, by saying quite steadily, 'It must be as you wish, Frederick. I'll accept any decision you make.' She tried to smile, and though it was a poor attempt, she did not let it degenerate into tears. Inside, her heart felt as if it had been pummelled into a big bruised mass. 'But you will – you will be a bit careful, won't you?'

'Oh, yes. I won't do anything rash or foolish or too energetic, I promise you.'

They sat there for a long time and when Winnie knocked on the door, Annie didn't move or even seem to notice.

Frederick raised his head. 'Come!'

Winnie goggled to see her mistress sitting on Mr Hallam's knee like that, but it was not the first time and she was well enough trained not to betray her amazement by more than a quick gasp. 'Mr Luke would like to see you, if it's convenient, ma'am?'

Again, it was Frederick who spoke, because Annie was still staring numbly into the fire. 'Show him in, but not for a minute.' When Winnie had nodded and gone out, he kissed Annie's cheek and gave her a wry grin. 'We can't receive him like this.'

She nodded and stood up, then things fell into place

around her again and she turned a worried gaze on Frederick. 'It's not like Luke to come here during the middle of the day. I do hope nothing's wrong.' She reached out to stroke Frederick's cheek, a quick fond gesture.

By the time Luke came in, they were ready to deal with whatever crisis was about to face them. He hesitated in the doorway, feeling the atmosphere in the room. 'If it's a bad time, I can come back later, Annie. It's not that urgent.'

She felt relief flare through her. Not an emergency, then. Still, Luke's coming to Ridge House in the daytime was unusual enough. His duties at the yard did not normally bring him up Ridge Hill. 'No, do come in, Luke. I hope nothing's wrong at the yard?'

He was still standing near the door, making no attempt to sit down. 'Oh, no. Nowt's wrong, but I've been wanting to discuss something with you for a while, and since it's a quiet time at the yard, and Ron's there to look after things, well, I thought I'd walk up the hill and see if—'

'Come and sit yourself down, then, Luke, before you unburden yourself. Pull up another armchair.' Frederick gestured behind him. 'We never stand on ceremony in the library.' It was not a room in which they normally received guests, rather one where the family liked to sit, one where he and his beloved often sat together chatting quietly once their day's work was over.

Annie leaned back in her chair, hoping her recent bout of weeping did not show.

When Luke was ensconced between them, bolt upright in an armchair, he cleared his throat. 'I – I don't rightly know how to begin.'

'Just tell us simply and clearly what the problem is,' Frederick prompted, seeing that Annie was still not her usual brisk self.

'Well . . .' Luke gathered his thoughts together. He'd rehearsed this interview carefully for the past two nights, mouthing the words he might use in his bedroom before he went to sleep. He forgot all the careful businesslike phrases, however, as soon as he started speaking of his longings.

'You both know how much I love gardening.'

They nodded.

'Well, I'd like to make it my life. No.' He frowned. 'That's not quite right. I *intend* to make it my life.' He looked at them and shrugged, holding out his big work-stained hands in a mute appeal. 'It's not that I'm not grateful for my place in the yard, Annie, not that I don't appreciate what you've done for me – for all of us – over the years. But somehow I can't see myself working in a junk yard for ever.'

'What do you want to do, then?' Frederick prompted.

'I want to get hold of a bit of land, *good* land, mind, with a southern aspect, not sour moorland stuff, and grow things. I thought – I thought I could grow plants to sell to folk. Fancy ferns and such for their parlours. And some of the new plants that naturalists are finding in other countries. And flowers, of course. Cut flowers to sell by the bunch. Roses. Delicate flowers for corsages. And eating stuff, too. Not taties and cabbage, but *different* vegetables, the sort your cook might like to buy if you didn't have Nat and the kitchen garden – asparagus, say, or tender young peas early in the season, all sorts of things. A market garden, but more – more special.'

It was the longest speech Annie had ever heard him make and when he started to falter, she nodded and smiled in encouragement.

Luke paused, then said softly, sharing a cherished dream: 'And if it all goes well, I'll get myself a hothouse eventually.' He sighed with longing at the mere thought. 'You can do so much more with a hothouse. Well, you've seen what Nat produces for you.'

He stared down at his hands, which were clutching one another in his lap, and gathered his strength for the final push. Then he looked from one to the other. 'I've been saving my money for years, but it's not enough. So I wondered if you—' He took a deep breath. *Don't be a coward,* he told himself. *They can only say no.* But it meant so much to him that he was afraid to finish, to voice the words that might bring a sharp refusal, that might take all hope away from him. When the silence lengthened again, he pushed the words out slowly. 'I wondered if you'd help me, lend me some money?'

'I didn't realise you cared that much about gardening,' Annie said, composed enough now to join in the conversation. 'Do you remember when we first moved into Netherleigh Cottage and I asked you to learn about it?'

Luke nodded, relaxing a little. 'I was that frightened – well, I was frightened about everything at first. It was all so grand after our house in Salem Street. I didn't know the first thing about plants, I was that ignorant. But Michael Benworth was a good teacher. I think he loved his gardening nearly as much as I do. I was sorry when he died.'

Annie drew in her breath sharply at that reminder of Frederick's mortality, for Michael Benworth had been about the same age as her husband was now and had just keeled over one day. But she would not let herself give in to her sorrow. Not again. She and Frederick had laid their souls bare. Now they must pack the emotions away again and live through whatever came, helping one another, concentrating on the good things in life. 'Mary says you put flowers on his grave sometimes,' she said, seeing her brother looking at her apprehensively. Did Luke think she'd refuse him, then?

He nodded. 'When I'm out tramping the moors I find things Michael would love, early wildflowers or catstails, so I share them with him.' He fell silent, staring down at his hands again, wondering what the two of them were thinking, not daring to hope – although they had not said no straight away, at least.

'Do you know enough about gardening to do all this?' Frederick asked, with the perceptiveness that had won him a fortune.

'Not yet.' Luke raised his face and his pale blue eyes shone with their own quiet beauty, still reflecting his dream. Clearly, he was picturing his garden in his own mind. 'And that's the other part of what I wanted to ask you. Could I come here and work with Nat Jervis for a year or two first? I'd – I'd need some wages. Not a lot. Just enough to pay my way at home.'

Frederick nodded. 'I see.' He hadn't expected Luke to be such a good planner, somehow. 'And then later, we could look for a piece of land.'

'No.'

They looked at him in surprise.

Luke blushed at the sheer brass of it, contradicting them when he was asking for help, but he had been making plans for years. 'No,' he repeated firmly. 'We'd need to get the land now, so that in my spare time I could set a few things going on it, fruit trees and such. They take time to mature, do you see, years some of them. And happen I could even earn a bit of money from it in my spare time. I shouldn't mind how hard I worked, not if I had my own piece of land.' He fell silent. Frederick made a non-committal noise, looking inquiringly at Annie, who nodded.

Luke was grimly determined to point out everything, the bad as well as the good. 'Dad says it wouldn't look good for me to work here, me being your brother-in-law, Frederick, but Tim Burbin's just left, so I wanted to come and ask you before Nat took on anyone else – well, he knows what I'd like, of course. I've talked about it to him a few times now.'

'What's so special about Nat?' Frederick asked, curious. He knew he had a skilled gardener, but was surprised at Luke's insistence on working with Nat.

'He knows more about – about *organising* plants than anyone else in Bilsden.'

'One of the things I enjoy most about being rich,' Frederick smiled warmly at Luke, 'is having the power to help people. Yes, Luke, of course we'll lend you the money. I don't even need to ask if your sister agrees, for we always think alike about such things.'

Luke sat there gaping at them, amazed at how easy it had been, when it had taken him a whole year to screw up his courage to ask for help.

'But I think we'll do more than have you working with Nat,' Frederick said thoughtfully. 'I think we'll send you to London, too, if we can. I must think whom I know – who'll have the influence to get you taken on in Kew Gardens for a season or two.'

'Kew Gardens!' Luke's voice was breathless with longing.

'Don't you agree?'

He nodded, then said in a thickened voice, 'You've fair taken my breath.' He knuckled away a tear, and then when it was followed by another one, he stood up. 'I can't – can't talk about it any more now. I'll come back tomorrow.' He hugged Annie convulsively, shook Frederick's hand and then rushed out of the room.

'You're a lovely man, Frederick Hallam,' Annie said softly.

'Well, it is a pleasure to help people. And especially now, for it shows me I still have some worth in this world. James would say that I'm getting soft in my old age and Mildred would be scandalised at the waste of the family money – she's already thinking about how to spend what I leave her.'

'No!'

'Oh, Annie, love, of course she is! James, too. Their mother married me for my money and she taught them to think money the most important thing in the world. As she did.' He frowned. 'Do you think Mildred sounds a bit – oh, I don't know – a bit anxious in her letters recently? As if she's worrying about something?'

Annie shrugged. It usually fell to her to write to Mildred, although Frederick occasionally penned a few lines at the end of a letter. She frowned, thinking back to the last communication. 'Yes. Now that you mention it, I do think she sounds less – *smug* than usual.'

He chuckled. 'She is smug, isn't she?' Then his smile faded. 'But there's something else worrying her. I can't put my finger on it. I'll have to ask her straight out next time I see her.' Both his grown-up children were smug, and as for the other one ... He tried not to think of Beatrice, for it reminded him of how he had failed as a father.

For James and Mildred came regularly to visit their father, and previously had invited him to stay with them for his grandchildren's birthdays. They were very conscious of Frederick's wealth and position. Annie could have done without those visits. Stiff formal occasions, with the children of such well-to-do parents so frilled and starched that they could not play like normal children. More than once, Tamsin had caused a rumpus at such gatherings and scandalised James's straight-laced wife, Judith.

Annie realised that Frederick had said something. 'Oh, I'm sorry. My mind was wandering. What did you say?'

'I said that my son and daughter might be fond of me, but they're very fond of money, too. And they know I've got a lot of it.'

'You don't seem upset by that.'

He sighed. 'Well, we've never been close. They've always been more Christine's children than mine. And that's partly my fault. I was too busy avoiding her and making money to get to know them. They'd never understand what I intend to do with the time that's left to me.'

Now his face had taken on the same blissful dreamy expression as Luke's. 'What?' Annie prompted.

'I'm going to help people, as many people as I can.' He gave his old pirate's grin. 'I'm as bad as your William, aren't I? And – most important of all to me – I'm going to do something for Bilsden.'

'For Bilsden?'

181

His face had lit up at the thought and he looked young again for a moment. 'Yes. I'm going to do something about the town centre, something to make it beautiful. It's the only memorial I shall want, love. A big square at the end of High Street, with a garden in the middle, and a fountain. I haven't quite decided on the design of it all, but I do have a few ideas.' He looked at her. 'That'll do me more good than sitting in front of the fire like an invalid.'

'And the mill?'

'I think I'll give Matt a stake in it, a small share to ensure his absolute loyalty. He's certainly earned it. He can go to the Exchange in Manchester for me, buy the cotton, sell the yarn. He loves all that and I've grown weary of it. I've given enough of my life to that mill.' He frowned for a minute. 'But we'll still need to keep an eye on things. Will you do that for me, Annie love? Will you act as my go-between with Matt?'

'What do I know about cotton?'

His old grin was back. 'Not much. But if I know you, you'll soon learn. And you're a shrewd businesswoman.'

She was still puzzled at this request, but if he wanted her to act on his behalf, then she would. She would do anything to make his life easier.

'One day, you'll need to be able to watch out for our children's interests,' he added, and saw the instant comprehension in her face. Yes, he thought, he would make sure she learned more about the Great God Cotton, which dominated people's lives in Bilsden, whether they worked directly in a cotton mill or not.

This was all part of the many plans he'd made while lying in bed, but he didn't intend to tell her any more about them yet. No, he might be failing, but he still had the time and the wit to arrange matters so that his Annie would not only be left well off, but would be equipped to manage her money. His eyes rested on her and he was still smiling. She could cope with anything, his Annie could.

14

March: Rebecca

*R*ebecca Gibson stood near the window of the Bilsden Ladies' Salon, looking down the street and enjoying a rare break in the rain. The clouds had cleared and the sun had suddenly brightened the whole world, shining on the puddles and making people think that spring really was on its way. She could see them smiling at one another as they did their shopping, stopping to chat for a moment and turning their faces up gratefully to the sun, instead of hurrying to get inside again out of the cold wind.

She peered down the street. Was that – yes, surely, it was that woman again, the one who sometimes came to stand and stare at the salon? She never came close enough for you to see her face, and in any case she was always muffled up in widow's weeds and veils. She just stood and stared at the salon and somehow you could feel the antagonism radiating from her. Who on earth was she?

Mary said that Rebecca was imagining things, but Rebecca knew she was right. Sometimes another woman would join the watcher and the two would move off. At other times, the widow would stand there alone for an hour or more, just staring. What was there about the salon that so fascinated her?

The clouds covered the sun again and Rebecca banished the stranger from her mind, turning her attention back to

the salon. She had a much better predictor of the changing
seasons than the weather – the clientele of the salon.
There had been a trail of ladies in and out all morning,
ordering their spring outfits, sitting and discussing the
latest fashions – how wide skirts would be this year;
whether they'd need to buy new cages for their crinolines,
to change the bell-shaped fullness into the latest pyramid
effect; whether to order a day and an evening bodice with
each skirt, since so much material in a skirt was ruinously
expensive; whether it was true, as someone had heard
from London, that some sleeves were now being made
tight to the wrist. If they no longer had the removable,
washable muslin engageantes, how would they ever keep
such sleeves clean ... On and on and on they went.
Somehow, today, she didn't feel in the slightest bit
interested.

Today, in between the showers, when the sun twinkled
at Rebecca so brightly through the windows, she had
trouble keeping her attention on her customers. More and
more Mary was leaving it to her to speak to them, because
she handled everything so tactfully, and the customers
seemed to enjoy dealing with her, for all her youth. And
usually she enjoyed it, too. But today she felt restless,
today she wanted to go out and stride across the moors,
holding up her face to the sunshine like the flowers did.
And of course she couldn't do that. She had her living to
earn. Clients to deal with. Designs to work on. Sewing to
do, for she still took a share of that.

She sighed and went to fiddle with the display of caps
and lace. The trouble was, it might not be sunny on
Sunday, the only day she was free – well, it was almost
certain not to be. She couldn't remember the last really
fine weekend. 'You're just being a fool, Rebecca Gibson,'
she said aloud. 'Get on with your work.' But at twenty-one,
you couldn't help feeling foolish sometimes, couldn't help
wanting to hand everything over to Mary, who was in her
mid-thirties and presumably untouched by the wild

feelings which sometimes threatened to overcome Rebecca's good sense and send her rushing off outside to feel the spring breezes on her face.

Another customer came in and Rebecca dealt with Mrs Marshley tactfully, as Annie had taught her, but firmly. It was a house rule that any clothes made in the salon must be in materials and styles flattering to their wearers. If a customer insisted on having something that was unflattering, then it was gently suggested that the lady go elsewhere, and such was the prestige of the salon in the town, such was its reputation for producing clothes that really flattered the wearer, that few did.

She heard a step behind her and turned to smile at Mary. 'Talk of the devil. I was just thinking about you.' Like all John's second brood of children Rebecca had had a hard childhood, and it had made her mature beyond her years. She had been working in the salon now for nearly ten years, since just after her mother died and they went to live with Annie. She and Mary shared the major tasks and often worked together on designs for their regular customers, knowing in advance what sort of things would be needed each change of season and preparing for it efficiently in the quiet times.

'I was coming down to see if you wanted to get your dinner now.' To Mary, as to Rebecca, the mid-day meal was 'dinner' and the evening meal, 'tea'.

'No. You go first. I'd just like to sit here quietly and think about the spring designs. Mrs Marshley wants a new outfit for Sunday best.' She frowned. 'I wonder if Annie would like to go up to London with me this year? I feel we're getting out of touch. Don't you ever fancy a trip to London?'

Mary Benworth shook her head. 'No. I'd go if I had to, I suppose, but I don't like big cities. Too many people, too much traffic. Even Manchester's too crowded for my liking, with so many vehicles that you can hardly find space to cross the street. It's a wonder the horses endure it so quietly. I feel sorry for the poor things. No, I'll stick to the magazines to show me what's popular, and rely on you and Annie to tell me more details after your trips.'

Rebecca pulled a face. 'It's not the same, looking in the magazines. You don't see what people are actually wearing.'

Mary smiled. 'Well, it's a good thing I've got you to tell me, then, isn't it? Anyway, I'll go and eat my dinner now, if you want. Since your Mark opened his chop house, I'm finding it easier to eat a hot dinner there and just make myself bits and pieces in the evening.'

Sunday proved to be another sunny day, even though there was a chill wind blowing, and Rebecca, desperate for some fresh air and exercise, tried to persuade one of her brothers to go for a walk with her on the tops. But Mark wanted to go back to the chop house and do his accounts while it was quiet, and Luke had arranged to go down to the 'Stute.

It was no use asking her younger sister Joanie to go out walking on the moors. Joanie's only idea of a walk was to saunter along High Street or round the park with her friends. And Rebecca had refused to go with her since the day they had met Maddie and her brother. She had also refused to go to the chapel dance, which Joanie had enjoyed enormously, though it had taken a bit of courage for Rebecca to stand up against her father's wishes there.

Rebecca didn't know what Joanie saw in Maddie or in her dull brother. In fact, she didn't like any of the young men in whom Joanie had expressed an interest. And that brought the same unwelcome thoughts to haunt Rebecca that had been haunting her for the past two years. Was she destined to remain a spinster? She'd like to find a husband one day, of course she would. However much Joanie taunted her with not liking the company of lads, Rebecca knew she was not that unnatural. But who was there in Bilsden for a person like her?

There were plenty of the rougher sort of people, people

like Harry Pickering, but working at the salon had spoiled her for them, though it didn't seem to have affected Joanie. Rebecca didn't want a husband who worked in the mill, or even one who worked in a shop or office. She wanted – oh, she didn't know what she wanted! But it was something special, a husband who would bother to talk to her about the broader world, a husband who was well educated, who didn't just treat her like a superior servant.

And that was stupid, because she wasn't well educated herself. Like her sister, she'd never really gone to school. It was Annie who had taught her to read and write, Annie who had lent her books and given her a love of reading. Kathy scolded Rebecca sometimes for sitting there with her head in a book, but the things she read took her right out of herself and she loved that. Frederick always gave her books for Christmas or birthdays. He was a wonderful brother-in-law, Frederick was. She wished she could meet someone like him, only younger, perhaps, and with dark hair . . . Oh, what was the use in wishing?

'I think I'll go for a walk up on the moors by myself, Kathy,' Rebecca said after fidgeting around the kitchen for another ten minutes. 'If I don't stretch my legs I'll go mad, after a week of sitting sewing or mincing around town in my hoops.'

'Nay, I don't think your dad would approve of that. Anyway, you won't have time before morning chapel.'

Rebecca had been contemplating doing something about that for a while. 'I don't think I'll go to chapel in the mornings any more. Twice on Sundays is too much, when it's my only free day. I'll just go to the evening service from now on.'

'You'll go in the morning as well, young lady!' said a voice behind her. 'It's not much to ask that you visit the Lord's house with your family on Sundays.' John walked into the room, looking both disapproving and hurt.

Rebecca steeled herself. 'Dad, that's not reasonable. It's my one day off. I work heavens hard all week. I think I

187

have a right to some time for myself.'

'You talk as if you don't like going,' he said sadly, the hurt showing clearly now and the rare anger fading as quickly as it had arisen.

'I don't like going twice. And you don't insist that Mark and Luke do that. Why me?'

He looked at his wife, who shook her head ruefully, then he opened his mouth and shut it again without speaking. His daughter had a point. He didn't nag the two elder lads to go twice, though he wished they would. After a long silence, he sighed and said, 'Well, you mun do as you think right, I suppose, now that you're a woman. We mun all follow our own consciences.'

Rebecca almost gave in then. Her dad didn't shout at her and he certainly didn't hit her, like other fathers did, but when he looked at her so sadly, she usually did what he felt to be right. But a stray sunbeam touched her hand even as she was drawing in her breath to agree and somehow that gave her the courage to refuse. 'Then I'll go out for a walk this morning, Dad, and come to evening service.'

'You're not going over the tops on your own!' said Kathy at once. She disliked the moors and the wide windy emptiness up there. 'I'm not having that. It's dangerous walking up there alone – especially for a pretty young woman like you.'

Rebecca smothered a sigh. 'I'll go and see if William wants to go for a walk, then. He often does.'

Kathy nodded reluctantly. 'But not on your own, mind.'

Rebecca didn't answer, just ran upstairs to get her things.

When she arrived at Ridge House, however, Annie told her that William had already gone out for a walk with Miss MacNaughton and the children.

'I'll see if I can catch them up, then.'

'They'll be on their way back by now.'

'Oh, Annie, if I don't get some fresh air in my lungs, I'll

suffocate, and you know how Kathy frets if I go out on my own!'

'You're usually in chapel on Sunday mornings.'

'I told Dad today that twice on Sunday was too much.'

Annie stared at her half-sister in surprise. Usually Rebecca was such a self-contained sort of person, never letting her feelings show, always in control of herself. Today she seemed to be bursting with repressed energy, and her dark smoky grey eyes betrayed her Gibson heritage – 'cheeky eyes' Frederick sometimes called them.

Annie could understand and sympathise with this need to get away. She sometimes went walking on the moors herself, though she hadn't been up there since her illness and didn't suppose she and Frederick would ever go for a really brisk walk together on the tops again. She willed away the sadness that thought brought. It was unfair to burden Rebecca with her own worries. 'Well, they took the Heythram track. You can *try* to catch them. And when I'm fully recovered, I'll go out walking with you sometimes, if you like?'

Rebecca bounced to her feet, hugged Annie, tossed her a quick, 'I'd love that. Thank you!' and was out of the house before anyone else could say her nay.

Annie watched her go enviously. She was well enough now to want to do things, but not well enough to lead her usual active life. 'They're all getting to a rebellious stage, the young ones are,' she said aloud. Why she should be so surprised by this she didn't know, but she was. She was used to thinking of her family as children, but most of them were grown up now – even William. I'm getting old, she thought, and got up to stare at herself in the mirror.

The reflection showed a grave woman, whose hair was as rich a colour as ever, with only the occasional thread of silver, not enough even to show. Her face was almost unlined and her figure still trim. No, she wasn't old. But Frederick was. And it had happened quite suddenly, taking her unawares. She sucked in a breath so sharp with anguish that she had to hold on to the mantelpiece to steady herself. No dwelling on it! she told herself firmly. Make the most of what you've got.

Straightening her shoulders, she went upstairs to the small studio where she worked on designs for the shop, or even an occasional watercolour landscape. And although she had no major gift for painting, yet she thought her pictures were pleasant enough. Her father had a few on the walls, pictures she had painted 'specially of places he loved, and he often commented on the pleasure they gave him. Tom had a few pictures, too.

She got out her paints and sighed. She would rather have been immersed in business. This was an idle way of filling your time, but at least you could pick it up or put it down at will. She didn't want to start anything that would take her away from Frederick when he wanted her company. Not now.

Up on the moors, Rebecca was enjoying herself. Here she could run and stride along without any fear of showing too much petticoat, or worse, as Edith Benderby had the previous week when her hooped skirt got caught in a high wind after chapel, showing her limbs right up to her garters. She giggled at the memory. Edith's legs were fat and white, but Edith's face had been a very bright red.

Edith should have worn knickerbockers under her petticoats as the salon was discreetly advising its customers to do nowadays. Knickerbockers, with their two separate loose-fitting legs attached to a waistband, leaving a space in the intimate body areas, could save a great deal of embarrassment for fashionable ladies.

There was no warmth in the sun, but its brightness made Rebecca feel more cheerful. She strode along the Heythram track, not in the least concerned about catching up with William and the children. When she got further up, she sat down for a few moments on a rock, staring across the undulating grey-green landscape. Ah, the air was so good here! In Bilsden, you sometimes felt you could taste the smoke from the mill chimneys and when the wind was in the wrong direction, Kathy complained about the smuts that blew on to her washing.

After a few minutes Rebecca felt the chill of the wind and started walking again, sure now that she wouldn't catch up with the others, sure that she'd have some time to herself. Still feeling rebellious, she turned off the main track along a barely defined path that would give her an extra mile or two of peace.

When she saw the figure on the path ahead of her ten minutes later, she hesitated, all Kathy's warnings coming back to her. But he was clearly a gentleman and seemed lost in thought, not waiting to attack anyone. She would have nodded and walked on past, but he raised his hand as if to lift his hat in greeting, then smiled as he realised that he was hatless. She smiled in sympathy. Obviously, he did not often walk hatless. Perhaps he also was escaping from the constrictions of genteel society.

'I beg your pardon, miss, but could you tell me the way back to Bilsden? I seem to have been walking in circles for the past hour and I'm not at all sure that I'm on the right track.'

Rebecca hesitated, still eyeing him cautiously, but she liked what she saw. He was tall and his clothes were top quality. You could always tell, somehow. He reminded her of someone, though she couldn't think who. He wasn't exactly good-looking, but there was a direct air to him that was attractive, and his eyes were very blue and clear as he studied her in return.

'I'm Rebecca Gibson,' she said, holding out her hand.

'Simon Darrington.' He shook her hand gravely.

'Darrington? *Lord* Darrington! Then you're lost on your own land.'

He looked rueful. 'Yes. Embarrassing, isn't it? I beg you won't tell anyone.'

'If you just follow this path, Your Lordship, it'll take you to the Heythram track. Turn right on to that and you'll come to the Bilsden road.'

'Thank you. Er – are you walking that way?'

Suddenly she felt a little flustered. 'Well, yes, I am.'

'Then may I join you, Miss Gibson? I know we haven't been introduced properly, but I have met your sister and brother-in-law, and quite frankly, I'd be glad of a little company.' He let his voice trail away, then grinned. 'And after all, I might get lost again.'

Kathy would have a fit to think of her walking back with Lord Darrington. Rebecca's lips curled into a smile at the thought.

'May I share the joke? Or are you laughing at me again for getting lost?'

She started walking and he fell into place beside her. 'I wouldn't be so impolite as to laugh at you to your face, Your Lordship,' she said demurely, but her eyes were still dancing.

'I'd rather you called me Simon. I get enough of "Your Lordship" at home.'

'It wouldn't be proper, Your Lordship.'

He gave an exaggerated sigh, then returned to his original query. 'Why were you smiling just then? May I know?'

'I was smiling at what my step-mother would say if she saw me now, walking with you. She doesn't approve of my walking alone on the moors, you see. She feels it's dangerous.'

'And what do you feel, Miss Gibson?'

It was out before she could think what she was saying. 'I feel that if I don't get some fresh air and peace every now and then, I'll stifle to death.'

He stopped walking for a moment to stare at her in surprise, then realised what he'd done and began moving again. 'I know exactly what you mean. To tell you the truth, it's the family retainers I'm escaping from. They're not used to having a Darrington in residence, so they fuss over me all day, from the minute I poke my nose outside my bedroom. Inside my bedroom, my man scolds me about maintaining my dignity. And my step-mother does the same thing, too, on the rare occasions I see her. She has very firm views on how a lord should behave.'

'And you don't agree with her?'

'Not always. I don't feel much like a lord, you see.'

She could not hide her astonishment at this.

'I never expected to inherit a title, you know. Or wanted to.' His sigh seemed to come from the depths of his soul.

She knew about that, about how his brother had committed suicide. Who didn't in Bilsden? 'Most people would envy you your position.'

'Do you?'

It was she who stopped walking for a moment, her head to one side as she thought about her answer. 'No. But I'm not most people. I'm no lady. I work for my living, and I enjoy it, too.'

He was intrigued. He had never met anyone so ladylike who admitted frankly that she worked for a living. 'May I ask what you do?'

'I work in my sister's dress salon in Bilsden.'

'Does Mrs Hallam own the salon?' He had seen it on the High Street, an elegant little place with a single item only displayed in the window in a soft drift of material. No London shop window could have looked more stylish.

'Yes. She started the business.'

'But I'd have thought—' He broke off, realising he was on the verge of being impolite.

Rebecca finished for him. 'You'd have thought she'd have no need to be involved with any business when she has a wealthy husband?'

'Well, yes.'

'Annie's got too much energy. She'd go mad with nothing to do but look after her house.'

'A remarkable woman.'

'Yes, and a wonderful sister. She taught me all I know.'

'So Mr Thomas Gibson is your brother as well?'

She nodded. 'Half-brother. He's Annie's full brother.'

Simon Darrington was silent, then he looked at her, sadness on his face. 'Tell me – do you hold what my brother did against me, as your brother Thomas does? He glares at me if he sees me in the street and turns in the other direction to avoid meeting me face to face.'

Her voice was soft. 'No, of course not. It was a dreadful accident, and all due to your brother's reckless behaviour, but he must have been upset by it to take his own life. And anyway, that has nothing to do with you. You weren't even in Bilsden at the time.'

'Thank you.' He had never got on with his brother and it upset him to be tarred with the same brush. He was neither dissolute nor a gambler. And Jonathon had taken his own life as much because of the size of his gambling debts as anything, though Simon wouldn't tell the Gibsons that. It was probably due to the ennui, as well, the ennui that Jonathon constantly complained of, the ennui that had driven him into one wild excess after another.

'Your brother-in-law has been equally generous,' he said, 'though I feel your sister still holds me in suspicion, like a wild beast that might suddenly spring on someone.'

'Give Annie time to get to know you. She's a very fair person.'

'I need to let everyone get to know me, I think. I've never spent much time in Bilsden. My father hated the place.'

'I've never spent much time anywhere else – except when Annie and I visit London to keep up with the fashions.'

He was surprised. 'Is your sister still so much involved in the work of the salon, then?'

Rebecca put one finger to her lips and made a soft shushing noise, her eyes dancing. 'She doesn't work there *officially*, but it's an open secret in the town that she still designs for us. She and I usually visit London twice a year to look at what's being worn.'

'And do you enjoy London?'

'Yes, I do. Bilsden is,' she shrugged, 'a bit small. Not much to surprise you here.' Except finding a peer of the realm lost on his own land!

They walked in silence for a while and stopped by mutual accord to catch their breath after a steep bit of track.

'Why did your step-mother let you come out alone today, then, if she's afraid of the moors?' he asked suddenly.

Rebecca rolled her eyes. 'She didn't. I was trying to catch up with my nephew William and the children. The trouble is,' she smiled, 'I took the longer way round and I didn't manage it.'

'I'm glad of that,' he said softly, his glance admiring.

She stared at him, then drew herself up. Her family would have recognised that expression immediately – Rebecca in her no-nonsense mood. 'If you think you're going to flirt with me, you're very much mistaken, Your Lordship. I'm not that sort of woman.'

He looked startled. 'You're very blunt, Miss Gibson.'

'It's usually easier.' She had discouraged several unwelcome suitors with her bluntness and was known for it in the salon workshop, too. Only with the customers did she bridle her tongue. 'Well, let's get going again, shall we?' Without waiting for an answer she set off briskly along the path and he had no choice but to follow.

'If I promise not to flirt, could we be just friends?' he asked a little later.

She looked sideways at him, not slowing her pace. 'That would be rather difficult, wouldn't it, given our respective positions? How would we even see one another? I'm not going to do anything that will damage my good name. Life's a lot easier for you men. No one cares if you flirt. Or have friends of the opposite sex. But women have to take care, especially young women like me. My good name is extremely important to me. So, no, I'm afraid we can't be friends.'

She did not realise that she was echoing her sister, that Annie, too, had once guarded her good name quite fiercely. Now, as Frederick's wife, she could relax a little, be somewhat unconventional – though not too much. Rebecca envied her that freedom.

When they got to the main track, she walked smartly along it, setting such a cracking pace that neither of them had the breath for conversation. Then, at the road, she stopped and gave him a dismissive nod of the head. 'Your way lies over there, Your Lordship.'

'Yes. I recognise the route the carriage takes.' He held out his hand. 'Goodbye, Miss Gibson. And thank you for rescuing me.'

'Goodbye, Lord Darrington.' She shook his hand very briefly and dropped it as if it were too hot to hold. She did not turn her head as she walked away, so did not see him stop to watch her stride down Ridge Hill.

'She's not exactly beautiful,' he murmured to himself, 'but what expressive eyes! A sort of twilight grey.' He smiled. 'And what a direct manner! I like it.' It was a relief after the restrained conversation of his step-mother, who would have thought it in appalling taste to say what she really thought about anything. Her ladyship always suited her views to her company.

He sighed as he walked slowly along. But Miss Gibson was right, really. There was no friendship possible between a respectable young woman like her and the local lord of the manor. However reluctantly he filled that role. However attracted he was to her. However lonely he was.

As he continued to stroll back towards the houseful of fussing servants, Simon decided suddenly that he would not go back to London with his step-mother for a visit, as she wanted. He loathed the social round and had no intention of looking for a wife among the graceful daughters of the nobility, who were all far too like his step-mother: pretty, well-mannered, but oh, so boring. No, he'd stay here as he'd originally planned and see if there was anything more he could do to get the estate into better condition. It had been shamefully neglected.

His decision had nothing to do with Miss Gibson, he told himself. Nothing to do with anyone but himself and the unwanted burden he had gained by inheriting the ancestral title and lands of the Darringtons.

'Damn you, Jonathon!' he muttered to himself, not for the first time. 'Why did you have to kill yourself? Couldn't you face up to anything in your life?' For his brother's gambling debts had crippled the estate and even his stepmother would have to moderate her spending from now on. 'I'll have to make it plain to her,' he said aloud, 'that there's nothing beyond her jointure. Though she can live in the town house for as long as she likes. I've had more than enough of London.'

Decision taken, he felt his mood lighten a little. There would be problems, he knew, for his step-mother was determined to find him a rich wife. But he was not his father, to let her lead him around by the nose. She would realise that eventually. And it was much harder to manage people at a distance. Yes, there were many reasons for staying on in Bilsden.

15

May: Tom and Rosie

'*I*'m – er – going down to London for a day or two next week,' Tom announced one Sunday, when all the family were gathered for tea at Netherleigh Cottage.

'What's brought that on?' John asked. To him and Kathy, a trip to London would have been purgatory and they regarded it as others would have regarded a voyage to Australia.

Tom had never been to London before, though he had long wanted to and he and Marianne had talked of it often. But as soon as the babies came, Marianne had lost interest in everything but them, so it had never happened.

The farthest Tom had been from home since his wife died was to Blackpool, and he had only gone there at Kathy's insistence that young David needed a few days of bracing seaside air after a slow recovery from the measles. Bracing! Tom had found it freezing and it had rained four days out of the seven they spent there. He had been bored to tears. Nor had the children seemed to enjoy themselves much.

He had, of course, stayed with his sister Lizzie, though he did not feel the same affinity towards her as he did for Annie. He never had. Lizzie had always been the odd one out of the three of them, and her love had been reserved for her step-sister May, daughter of John Gibson's second wife. The two of them had been inseparable from an early age right until May's death. But even if his feelings for Lizzie had been outright hatred, he couldn't have stayed anywhere else in Blackpool except at her house, or their father would have wanted to know why.

Lizzie had proved as sharp-spoken as ever, but respectable now, at least. She provided comfortable beds and set a good table, Tom had to grant her that. And William's orphaned half-brother, Jim, who lived with her, was a surly lad. He worked hard enough, but hadn't a civil word for anyone. No wonder he got on so well with Lizzie!

'Eh! What's brought on a trip to London?' John asked again.

Tom couldn't tell his family why he was going to London, so he shrugged. 'I just feel like a change.'

There was absolute silence as thirteen pairs of eyes studied him. He tried to keep his expression calm and confident, as if going to London were a minor thing, but it was hard to maintain his sang-froid. That was the trouble with large families. They always wanted to know every detail of what you were doing. And if one of them didn't ask prying questions, then another did. At the moment Tom hardly knew himself what he was doing, just that he had to see Rosie again. He looked around the room, tensed to fend off more comments and questions.

His own children already knew about his trip, so they just glanced up for a moment then carried on with what they were doing. Annie and Frederick looked interested and perhaps slightly surprised, and Tom saw Annie open her mouth, then shut it again, as if she'd thought better of whatever she was going to say.

Rebecca looked outright envious and he wondered if she'd try to persuade him to take her with him. She loved her trips to London, Rebecca did. If Tom had really been going to London just for a change, he'd have loved to have her with him, showing him round. But he was going to see Rosie, not the sights, and he wanted no audience for that.

Mark shifted his long legs, yawned and returned to staring into the fire. He looked half asleep. He'd been working all the hours he could stand upright lately, Tom knew, doing what he had long wanted to do, building up his own business, instead of working for his brother and sister. And good luck to him, too. Tom still put in long hours himself. It's hard work, not luck, that makes money, he always said to his children.

William was leaning back in another chair, lost in his own thoughts, as usual. He was obsessed with that work of his in Manchester. He looked very tired and only his mother's insistence made him take Sundays off. The young fool! thought Tom. How will he ever make a living for himself from something like that? He was amazed that meeting the practicalities of life head on had not changed William's mind about what he wanted to do; if anything, it seemed to have made him keener to help his fellows. All the family were amazed at that. But the lad was proving as stubborn as his mother, in his own way. A true Gibson, for all his name was Ashworth.

Luke ruffled young David's hair and remarked, 'Well, you three will miss your dad while he's away, won't you?'

'I will,' said Lucy. 'There'll be no one to have tea with after school.' She enjoyed playing the lady of the house, carefully pouring out cups of tea for her father and passing around plates of scones. The boys endured the formality of these sessions because of the good food on offer, and because they liked to be with their dad, but they agreed privately that good manners were a nuisance.

'Me an' your grandma will come to tea with you, then, one day. We allus enjoy having tea with you lot.' John smiled at his grandchildren. 'An' we'll bring our Samuel John and Benjamin with us.'

His own sons did not look as if this was their idea of a treat, but they just grimaced at one another across the room and said nothing. They both heartily disliked their cousin Lucy, who always insisted on joining in with the boys' games, instead of playing with her dolls. In fact, the two of them were not fond of girls at all, regarding them as a very inferior form of life.

David wriggled and tried to move away from the big hand of his Uncle Luke as it lay casually around his shoulders. Like his grown-up cousin William, he hated having his hair ruffled. He was far neater than his sister Lucy, whose hair was already in wild disorder and whose dress was already rumpled, showing one black stocking which had somehow acquired a hole. She was sitting comfortably on her grandfather's knee. Richard, their younger brother, was sprawled on the window seat, playing noughts and crosses with his young Uncle Benjamin, with whom he was on far better terms than with the twins.

'I think it'll be a good thing for you to have a change, Tom,' Annie said, when the silence went on for a bit too long. She nodded her approval to the family. 'It's about time our Tom looked after himself for once, isn't it, Dad? You work much too hard, Tom.'

'What's the matter, lad?' teased Frederick. 'Are you getting tired of making money?'

'I'll never be tired of that. But I do feel like—' Tom shrugged. 'Like getting away from Bilsden for a bit, seeing somewhere new.' Actually, he did not expect to enjoy himself in London, but Rosie had refused point blank to come up to Manchester to meet him, so he had no choice.

'But who will you go with?' worried John, who couldn't imagine doing anything on his own.

'Myself.' Tom made a mock bow to the room. 'I shall be a man on the town. I shall go to the theatre, do a bit of shopping to smarten myself up and dine out once or twice in posh places.'

Annie was looking at him thoughtfully. Theatres! Shopping! This was so unlike Tom that her suspicion that there was something behind this trip grew into a certainty. She exchanged glances with Frederick, who obviously had the same feeling.

As the others started arguing about the merits of visiting London, and what you could do there, John came down firmly in favour of staying in Bilsden, where you had your family. Blackpool was near enough for an occasional holiday. Manchester was there for an odd day's outing. What more did anyone need?

Tom endured the teasing and questions for a while, and when he could take it no longer, he stood up. 'I'll have to leave here early today, I'm afraid. I've got some accounts to finish.'

'Oh, Dad, me and Grandpa are just going to play backgammon!' Lucy wailed.

David and Richard chimed in with their own protests.

'I can take them home later,' Luke said, smiling gently. Since he had left the yard to work with Nat Jervis, he always seemed to be smiling. 'I can't leave it too late, though. Me and Nat have some seedlings to prick out this evening.'

'Nay, you'll miss chapel!' John protested.

Luke just shrugged. 'The other lads don't have the whole day off on Sundays, so how can I, Dad? It was chapel or come here for tea. So I came here. You don't have to go to chapel to say your prayers, you know.'

Kathy patted John's hand. One by one the grown-up children were abandoning the regular attendance at chapel that was so central to their father's life. Only last week, Rebecca had said she'd like to try the services at St Mark's, for a change, and had gone there with Annie and Frederick. Kathy knew it hurt John, but that was how life was. You couldn't control others, not once they were grown up, and even Rebecca was twenty-one now – nearly twenty-two. And still showing no signs of finding herself a lad.

Tom left as quickly as he could, letting his breath out in a low growl of relief as he strode down North Road and turned into Market Street. Telling the family had gone better than he had expected, though. He slowed down as he came to High Street, strolling along it towards the station. As always, he paused to admire the window displays in the Emporium, the goods showing to advantage behind the big panes of glass which had caused a sensation when he had them installed. Impelled by a restless uncertainty, he continued to stroll around town. He had no accounts to do. He'd just had enough of his family.

At one point he found himself in the Rows and made his way along to Salem Street. The houses there were kept in good repair because Frederick was a responsible landlord, but they were getting older, looking tired, with the bricks a little grimier each year and the slates sagging in places. It seemed strange to see faces he didn't know in the street he'd been born and grown up in, faces that stared at him in his well-cut suit and highly polished boots as if wondering what he was doing there. Well, what *was* he doing there?

The sun was still shining and he unbuttoned his pilot coat, then, on an impulse, took off his brimmer, the low-crowned, wide-brimmed hat he favoured. Let others wear top hats. He would have felt a fool in them. In fact, if he'd had his way, he'd not have worn a hat at all, but in his position it was expected.

He moved on from the Rows towards what had been Claters End, but there were new warehouses there now, clustered around The Shepherd's Rest. He stood outside the public house which had been one of his earliest businesses. He and Seth had a manager in there now, and the place brought in a steady profit, though not so much as when Seth was running it.

Tom remembered suddenly the days when Rosie had served there and had sung to the customers. He grinned. No one had charged half a guinea entrance then.

When he found himself in Hallam Park, given to the town in memory of Frederick's father, Owd Tom, he felt more comfortable among the families from the better parts of town, who were taking the air, self-conscious in their Sunday best. That realisation made him frown.

After a while, he stopped and sat down on one of the new wooden benches the Town Council had put in. His mind was filled with images of Rosie, and had been all day. Rosie laughing at him, teasing him, when they were both young; Rosie in bed making love with wild abandon. And it had been love on her side, he acknowledged that now. But not on his. He'd had his eyes on money-making schemes, and later, on the doctor's daughter, Marianne. Slender, blonde, ladylike, gentle in speech, gentle in bed. She'd seemed like a vision the first time he saw her in Annie's salon. She'd always seemed too good for him.

'Am I a fool?' he asked the air. But he got no answer, only a disapproving stare from an old lady who was making slow progress through the park on the arm of a young woman with bold eyes and a demure demeanour. Tom shuddered at the glance she gave him. He didn't like women with two faces, one for the world and one for the bedroom. And he didn't want anyone, except – he cut off that thought sharply. 'I am a bloody fool,' he said quietly. 'I don't even know if she'll trust me again.'

He earned himself another glare from the old lady for that, so he tipped his hat to her, gave her a cheeky wink that made her bridle and mutter to her companion, and strode out of the park. Enough of this blasted reminiscing! He'd go and work on that new idea he had for the Emporium.

Two days later, Tom left for London. He took the train into Manchester, and as he waited at the station there for the London train, he went over to look at the W.H. Smith newspaper and book stall, which carried more newspapers than he had ever seen in his life in one place. Frederick said there were stalls like this in stations all over England. Imagine a business as far-flung as that.

Looking at it again, Tom was struck by a sudden idea.

Perhaps he could have shops all over the place? Well, all over the north, anyway. He wasn't too fussed about the south. He frowned. He'd have to think about that. See if Frederick or Annie was interested in the idea. He wouldn't have enough capital of his own.

He purchased a copy of the *London Illustrated News* and then on impulse a copy of *Punch* to read on the journey – or at least to use as a barricade against conversation with his fellow passengers. Frederick adored *Punch* and had it delivered to the house. He chuckled over it regularly, but Tom couldn't be bothered with it, or any magazine. He usually had other things on his mind, like his businesses or his children. With a sigh he opened one of the magazines, not caring which, his eyes unfocused and his thoughts on his own predicament. He didn't want to talk to anyone. He just seemed to be in limbo at the moment, and would be until he had seen Rosie, talked to her, asked her—

The journey seemed to pass very slowly and even in the comfort of a first-class carriage, Tom was thoroughly chilled by the time the train arrived. He should have bought himself one of the hooded railway comforters Annie's workpeople made for the Emporium. No wonder they were nice steady sellers. These narrow compartments made it impossible for you even to stand up and move your limbs around without trampling on your fellow passengers. There ought to be a corridor along the edge of the train, connecting all the compartments, then you could go for a walk. But when he'd said that to one or two people, the ladies had shuddered. They preferred to have the carriages separate. That way, you could be sure with whom you would be travelling. If there were a corridor, anyone could walk into your compartment.

So he just had to sit there and endure the journey. And it was grim endurance as he waited for one of the halts, so that he could go and relieve himself at the station conveniences. Even the aloof-looking ladies sharing his carriage made a beeline for the Ladies' Room during the twenty-minute halt. He grinned as he wondered how they managed to relieve themselves at all in those skirts.

When he disembarked in London, he was irritable, absolutely itching for some exercise. He had never been one for sitting around.

For all his anxiety to see Rosie, he stood for a moment in the station to stare around him in amazement. The place was huge, even bigger than Hallam's Mill. You could put his own Prince of Wales Hotel in one corner of this great echoing cavern. The high ceiling was supported on solid iron pillars, across which lay a network of minor iron supports, like a row of giants' umbrellas, and everywhere you looked were gas lights, though they had not yet been lit.

And the people! So many of them. Those who had just arrived with him muttered in irritation as they had to detour to pass him, or detour again to pass a lady in a wide crinoline who was standing looking bewildered. Those waiting at the station for friends were craning their necks, trying to spot them over the heads of the crowd.

There were long queues at the ticket office and the station buffet. Porters wove their way expertly through the crowds, murmuring, 'If you please, sir!' or 'Excuse me, madam.' They carried on their trolleys the expensive leather luggage and dressing cases of the first-class passengers. Humbler people carried their own lumpy bundles and packages. Tom had his suitcase firmly in one hand and a small portmanteau in the other and had refused all offers of help.

Eventually he found his way to the cab rank, where vehicles were arriving and departing all the time. After only a short wait, his turn came and he gave the address of the small hotel Rosie had suggested to him, sitting back with a weary sigh. But he couldn't relax when London lay outside in all its variety. He found excitement welling in him as he peered out of the window and marvelled at the amount of traffic there was and the number of shops. London. At last. How long he'd waited to see the capital of the most important country in the world!

The hotel was quiet, the room small but comfortable and the proprietor eager to help a friend of Miss Lidoni's in any way. Tom stayed there long enough to unpack his evening clothes and ask that they be pressed, for he was invited to dine with Rosie. Evening dress, she'd said. Just to have a meal at home. Or was she intending to invite others? He hoped not.

Then he went out for a walk, strolling along with a more light-hearted feeling now that he was actually here at last. He watched the street vendors in amazement, having difficulty understanding what they were crying out. You could buy anything on the streets here. On an impulse he bought a buttonhole from a girl selling flowers and listened carefully to her instructions on how to look after the flower – only she pronounced it *flahr*. How strangely folk talked here! And how quickly, too.

When he asked directions, he had to ask for them to be repeated and the fellow stared at him as if he were an idiot.

Tom arrived at Rosie's house spot on time, and was immediately glad of his smart new outfit. A maid in a frilly white apron opened the door to him and upon learning his name, nodded and led him through to a drawing room. Even before he got there he realised with annoyance that Rosie had indeed invited others to dine with them. For heaven's sake, didn't she realise he wanted to talk to her, really talk?

For a moment he paused in the doorway, stunned anew by how beautiful she looked and how at home in this elegant setting. Her dark gleaming hair was parted in the centre, puffed out over her ears and then gathered at the back into a low chignon. A froth of lace and ribbon and flowers surmounted it. And her eyes had never looked so huge and bright as when she came towards him, hand outstretched.

'Mr Gibson! How delightful to see you again.'

'Kind of you to invite me, Rosie.' He glared at her. What was she doing calling him Mr Gibson?

She grinned at him for a moment, the old cheeky grin he had loved. 'Tom, then.'

She knew exactly how he was feeling. She must have planned the evening like this on purpose. He nearly walked out as anger flared in him, then took a deep breath and waited for her to introduce him to the others. No need to act the fool, Tom lad, he told himself. You're not seventeen now. This is her world, so just behave your bloody self.

With the calm confidence of an experienced hostess Rosie took him round the ten other people who had gathered there. That weasel, Stephen Harris, her manager, was one of them. He looked no happier to greet Tom than Tom was to see him again. *You try intercepting any messages from me to Rosie this time, my lad, and I'll punch you right in that soft pink woman's mouth of yours*, Tom thought savagely. The other guests were a blur of names and faces. He thought he'd managed to do the pretty with them, but he wouldn't have bet money on it. And he didn't really care.

He found himself sitting halfway down the table. His years of dining at Ridge House stood him in good stead with the array of cutlery and glassware that faced him. The food was excellent, all six courses, but he ate very little. The woman next to him was a fool, who ate enough for six and babbled on about the dear Queen, and the dear little Princes and Princesses, until he could have strangled her.

He tried to pretend an interest, and then changed the subject to say that he was looking forward to going for a walk beside London's famous river. He'd never seen the Thames. But she shuddered and confided in him in a discreetly lowered voice that the terrible odour from the river was surely the worst it had ever been this year and she would advise him to stay well away from it. In retaliation he bored her with a lecture about the price of cotton, a subject on which Frederick had spoken briefly the previous Sunday, and had the pleasure of seeing her eyes glaze over. And the added pleasure of seeing the amusement in Rosie's eyes.

After a meal whose lavishness amazed him – how could Rosie afford to entertain on this scale? – they all went into the drawing room, where the same accompanist was waiting by the piano. A suspicion began to form in Tom's mind then, but he said nothing, just took his place with the other guests as Rosie prepared to sing.

As usual, the beauty of her voice made him forget all his troubles and for the hour during which she performed, he sat there entranced, more at peace with himself than he had been for a good long while. From time to time he looked at her and once or twice she looked at him, seemed to be singing only for him. But that was probably just his imagination.

When it was over, she bowed her head and there was silence for a moment, then a round of hearty applause.

She simply stood there, smiling slightly, then said, 'Thank you!' and left the room.

People began to take their leave of one another and the maidservant brought in the ladies' shawls and mantles. Tom let them all go, Stephen Harris last of all, casting an unfriendly glance in his direction. When the fellow had left, Tom went and sat down again by the fire. The maid came in and hovered next to him. 'Sir, the entertainment is over.'

'Tell your mistress that I need to see her. And I'm not leaving until I do.'

She looked scandalised and muttered something under her breath, but left the room.

The coals had burned quite low while Rosie was singing and now there were only the quiet sound of the embers settling in the grate and a clock ticking. He looked up at it. A fussy gold thing. He took an instant dislike to it. Probably French, with all that gilt. He wouldn't have it in his front room. Give him a good solid English clock any day. As the door opened behind him, he turned his head, saw that it was Rosie and stood up.

'I wondered if you'd stay behind,' she said, with that husky tone to her voice that he loved.

'Why did you invite me here with that lot?' he demanded, anger still dominant.

'You invited yourself, Tom. Didn't give me much choice, either, did you? Didn't even ask if I was free. This evening was already planned.' She chuckled. 'But I didn't charge you, love. That lot paid handsomely to dine here and have a private concert.'

'I guessed as much.' He cleared his throat and sought in vain for something to say. Now that he had her to himself, he didn't quite know how to start.

She had taken off her jewels and put a lacy white shawl around her shoulders. She looked like his Rosie again, not an elegant stranger. As she walked across the room, the silken skirts whispered around her, another gentle noise in the quietness of the room. When she sat down opposite him and gestured to the other chair, he sat down again and leaned back, staring at her.

'You're beautiful, Rosie.' He hadn't meant to say that, but the words seemed to speak themselves.

She flushed. 'Am I?'

He nodded. 'Yes. You've got style, too.'

' "Town polish" Frederick Hallam called it when he sent me down to London. It helps.'

The quietness pooled around them, broken only by her soft yawn. 'You can't stay for long, Tom. I've got my reputation to think about. And anyway, I'm tired. I've just finished a whole series of public concerts.'

'I'm sure they were a great success.'

She nodded. 'Yes. They were, actually.'

He took a deep breath. 'I came down to London 'specially to see you, Rosie.'

'Yes. I guessed that.'

'I'm lonely.'

Her voice was sharp. 'And you thought I might jump back into your bed, did you? No, thank you, Tom! I'm very respectable nowadays.'

He sat up indignantly. 'I thought no such thing! I can get any number of women into my bed – or into my life, if I choose. You – well, you're different, Rosie.'

'Am I?'

'Of course you are!'

'How am I different, Tom?'

'Because you're a friend, an old friend. And because you're Rosie.'

Her eyes were filled with unshed tears. 'It wasn't enough being Rosie before. You left me like a shot as soon as your Marianne was old enough to wed.'

'Yes. I'm sorry if I hurt you. I was a selfish young devil in those days. I couldn't think of anyone else after I met her. She seemed – oh, I don't know. Like a dream. But now she's gone and I'm trying to – to learn to do better.' He stared down at the rug, rubbing absently at the ache in his forehead. It had been a long day. 'Can we – get to know one another again, Rosie? Just – see how we go on.'

She was silent for so long that his heart started to thud in slow thumping fear. Surely she hadn't met someone else? When he looked up to ask her that, she was frowning. 'I don't think that's wise. You hurt me before, Tom, hurt me badly. And you've never tried to see your son. That hurts him. Other lads have fathers and he doesn't.'

'Albert?' He'd forgotten the lad – well, not forgotten exactly, but pushed him to the back of his mind. 'Where is he?'

'Where should he be? Here, upstairs, asleep.'

Another silence. 'So there's a lot to forgive,' she said at last, 'and I'm probably a damned fool, but – oh, hell, you can take me walking tomorrow morning! Call for me at ten.'

'Thank you.'

Before he could say anything else, she stood up and rang the bell. When the maid came in, Rosie nodded pleasantly to Tom. 'There's a cab stand on the corner. You'll have no trouble getting back to the hotel.' Then she said to the girl, 'Show Mr Gibson out, please, Jenny,' and sat down again in front of the fire.

He had been wanting to take her in his arms, wanting it quite fiercely, but now he could do nothing except nod and walk out.

When the door closed behind Tom, Rosie lifted one hand to wipe away the tears that would slip down her cheeks. 'I am definitely the biggest fool unhung,' she said aloud. 'He'll only hurt me again. And I'm well past being anyone's mistress.' But behind the fear and the memory of the previous pain, there was a spark, just a small spark, of hope. And she had to give that spark a chance to burn more brightly. Maybe this time . . .

16

Bilsden: July

'*I* think,' Frederick said, as he and Annie strolled around the gardens of Ridge House, 'that I'd like to have a family portrait painted.'

Annie stopped dead. 'What? After all you've said about that portrait of you with Christine and the children!'

He pulled a rueful face. 'Yes. Stupid, isn't it? But then, that's a very bad portrait.'

She had to agree with him. The father in the painting had Frederick's features, but somehow he wasn't Frederick. 'You've surprised me,' she admitted.

'I've surprised myself. But I've come to realise that I'd like to leave something of myself behind for the children – and for the children's children, too. And I want all of us in it – you, me, William, Tamsin and Edgar.'

Tears came into her eyes. 'William, too?'

He smiled down at her. 'Of course. I regard your son as part of our joint family.'

She smiled at that, but still looked unconvinced. 'It would be much easier to get some more photographs taken.'

He pulled a face. 'Stiff figures posed near equally stiff plants? You don't look at all like the Annie I know in those photographs we had taken last year. Even Tamsin looks ordinary and subdued.'

'Bored and sulky, actually.'

He grinned. 'Yes. She does rather.' They walked on for a few moments, then he said, thinking aloud, 'No, what I want is a portrait by a really *good* painter, one who can catch your vivid personality and your strength, Tamsin's mischievous nature, Edgar's quiet reliability, William's sincerity and determination. And for that, I'm afraid we'll have to go to London.'

'Oh, Frederick, are you sure?' For he seemed to get tired more easily since he had had the 'flu – or maybe he'd just stopped trying to hide it. She didn't want him over-exerting himself, desperately didn't want to do anything that would shorten the time they had left together. She'd almost abandoned her businesses this year, hadn't taken Rebecca to London in the spring, as she usually did to look at the fashions, and could hardly rouse an interest even when Tom spoke of increased profits and new possibilities for investment. It was a good thing the children had Elizabeth to look after them, a good thing that she now felt like a permanent fixture in the Hallam household, because Annie spent most of her time with her husband these days.

Frederick did not reply immediately, but stood poking at the ground with his toe, then he gave her one of his loving smiles – she knew he never smiled at anyone else like that – and said, 'Yes, Annie. I'm very sure. I've been thinking about it for a while now.'

'Oh.' She was still not certain that she fancied the idea, but if he wanted it so much, then he should have his wish. He should have every wish she could possibly make come true. 'Well, perhaps we can find someone without going to London, or get someone to come here.'

He sighed and the sadness she hated to see was in his eyes again. 'He'll have to come here. I'm not fit enough to go gallivanting around the country. But first we need to find him, talk to him, see what he's already done. I don't want it to turn out like the portrait with Christine. I despise that damned thing.' He chuckled suddenly. 'And it cost me twenty hard-earned guineas, too. I've never liked throwing money away.' After another pause, he added, 'I think it'd be better if *you* went to London, love. You've got more energy than I have.' And it would do her good, too. She deserved a break.

'Me? What do I know about portrait painters?'

'You have enough sense in that lovely head of yours not to be taken in by a poor painter. Just ask to see some of the paintings the man's done. You'll learn a lot from that.'

'Oh, Frederick!' She bit off her protests. The last thing she wanted was to go away from him.

'Annie, I will not be coddled! And this is really important to me.'

She sighed. 'All right. I'll go. If you want it so much.'

'Take someone with you. Rebecca. Or Tom. Go to the theatre, go shopping. Have a bit of fun!' He lifted her chin with one fingertip and kissed her lips gently. 'And then come back and tell me all about it. I shall enjoy that.'

She nodded, linked her arm with his and they moved on.

A few minutes later they stopped their slow progress to chat to Luke, who was gently sprinkling the flowers in a border with one of the big watering cans, his face happy and his whole body absorbed in the work he loved so much.

'Don't stop what you're doing. I just wanted to tell you that I think I might have found you a bit of land.' Frederick smiled at his young brother-in-law. 'Perhaps you could come up to the house for tea today and we'll talk about it then?'

Luke beamed at them. 'I'll be there.' Nat wouldn't mind. Nat was happy to have found an acolyte with the same love of plants as he had, an acolyte who drank in and remembered everything he was told. And the other lads who worked in the gardens and stables didn't seem to mind Luke's anomalous position, either. Well, they'd been a bit stiff at first, but he'd made sure he more than pulled his weight and didn't try to avoid the more unpleasant jobs, like turning the manure heap, so they'd come round. Especially when they saw how good he was with plants.

'You never said you'd found somewhere for Luke,' Annie complained as she and Frederick moved on.

'Didn't I? I thought I had. It was Jonas Pennybody who found it, or rather, his son Hamish. That young man's turned out very well, hasn't he? A real chip off the old block. That family has been serving mine in legal matters since my father built his first mill. I hope they'll continue to serve my son, too.'

'Yes. Hamish did well to ensure that Elizabeth got her father's things. I was so glad for her.' Annie wasn't really interested in Hamish Pennybody. 'Where's the land you've found?'

'Just along the road from here, in the lea of Meadley Dell.'

'Isn't that Darrington land?'

'Yes. But not part of the main estate. Simon Darrington's selling off some of the odd parcels of land. I'd guess he's been left with a few debts. I might buy some more land myself.' He chuckled. 'Pennybody said Darrington's step-mother is horrified by what he's doing. It's not done to sell off your birthright apparently. She told Simon that they're only tradesmen's debts, not debts of honour, and that tradesmen charge such outrageous prices that they can perfectly well wait until it's convenient for him to pay.'

'I hate rich people who behave like that!' Annie had had to wait a long time before she was paid for the gown she had stayed up all night to make for her ladyship once, in an emergency. Since then, she had a rule that the salon did not make garments for anyone who had a debt for previous work outstanding.

Frederick wasn't really listening to her, just staring up at the drooping lacy foliage of a willow tree with a half-smile on his face. 'Beautiful, isn't it? Oh, and before I forget, I invited young Darrington to take tea with us one day. I met him in town a couple of days ago.' He frowned and waved one hand. 'When I went to see Matt at the mill.'

She didn't say anything, but it was four days ago that he'd gone to the mill, and the outing had exhausted him. He'd begun to make mistakes about details like that lately. 'When is Lord Darrington coming?'

'I find it hard to think of him as *Lord* Darrington. He's too young and friendly.' Frederick stopped looking at the tree and stood frowning down at the ground. 'Damned if I can remember when! Never mind. We're always ready for visitors, aren't we?'

'It'd be easier if I knew, then I could dress accordingly.' She gestured down at her simple gown. 'I only wear these sorts of things around the house and garden.' She saw the frown return and said hastily, 'But it doesn't matter. I'll send one of the grooms over with a note to check on the exact day.'

He nodded vaguely, his eyes on a beautiful rose bush whose pink blooms were at their lush perfumed best. He leaned forward to smell them, then broke off a perfect bud and presented it to her with a courtly bow.

Watching him, Annie thought that sometimes now he seemed to be in a world of his own. As they walked on, she tried not to show how much she was having to hold herself in check to keep to his pace. Every fine day they made this leisurely tour of the garden, and Frederick, employer of many, maker of fortunes, landlord and millowner, commented with pleasure on the progress of his favourite plants and bushes, or simply sat on one of the new wrought iron benches, staring at the small lake and the birds that came to drink there. And when Matt sent from the mill to enquire about something that needed doing, Frederick seemed hardly to care. Yesterday he'd even grumbled that it was a poor look-out when a man who employed so many people couldn't get a bit of peace for a few days.

Every evening, as she watched him retire to bed early

or fall asleep in his big chair in the library, she gave thanks for another day spent together.

When the tour was over, she glanced at the little fob watch pinned to her bodice. 'Shall we go back to the house? I feel like a cup of tea and you need to decide which architect you want to contact.'

Frederick perked up immediately. One of the main focuses of his life, apart from his family, was now the design and development of a fine square in front of the railway station. The only time he was at all like his old self was when he was talking about that. The only time he went into town willingly was when he went to speak to the Council, who listened with flattering deference to the man who was prepared to spend so much money on beautifying their town.

As they got back to the house, Frederick stopped on the steps for a final gaze across the acre or so of gardens. 'It's not that I'm losing my memory, Annie,' he said quietly. 'Never think that. It's just that things which used to seem important to me no longer seem to matter much. If young Darrington calls and finds you without your fine feathers, who cares? You're beautiful whatever you wear.'

As they walked along the hall to the library, he added thoughtfully, 'And I think we should have a portrait of you, as well. Just you. In all the splendour of your mature beauty.' He grinned, as he added, 'With the widest hoops you own and your very best jewels sparkling against your tender white breast. Will you stand for a portrait?'

'Alone?'

'Yes, love, just you.'

She pulled a face. 'I'll do it if you really want me to. But it seems silly when we can just as well have some photographs taken.' She always preferred to use modern inventions and ways. That was real progress, to her mind. The kitchen and bathrooms at Ridge House were the most up-to-date in town. They had gas lights in every room. Portraits in oils seemed an old-fashioned thing. They'd only hang on the wall gathering dust.

A hint of the old mischief was still lighting Frederick's eyes. 'We can have some photographs done as well, if you like. In fact, let's have some photographs taken of our whole family. The Hallams *and* the Gibsons. Every last one of us. Even your Lizzie, if she has the time. Here in the grounds in front of the lake. And a photograph of the servants, too. Just think how Mrs Jarred will love that!'

They were still chuckling at the idea of the housekeeper surrounded by her maids when there was a knock on the door and Winnie announced in tones of hushed awe, 'Lord Darrington, ma'am, sir.'

They looked at one another and burst out laughing.

Simon Darrington paused in the doorway, surprised at this reaction and uncertain of his welcome.

'Oh, I'm so sorry! What a way to greet a guest!' Annie hurried forward to greet him. 'But Frederick had forgotten which day he'd invited you to take tea with us and we were just this minute deciding to send a groom over to find out.'

'Oh. Should I – is it inconvenient to call today?'

Frederick moved forward to join her. 'My dear fellow, it's not at all inconvenient – so long as you don't mind a family tea, with my wife unhooped,' Annie dug him in the ribs. 'And myself,' he looked down at his feet, 'still in my walking-around-the-garden shoes.'

'I'd prefer it, actually. I've no taste for formality.'

And him a lord! Annie thought disbelievingly, as she gestured to one of the comfortable chairs which were grouped in the large bay window during the summer. 'Do sit down then, Your Lordship. I'll ring for tea.'

He took a chair, folding his long limbs loosely into it. 'Thank you, Mrs Hallam.' He stared around in open curiosity. 'This is a lovely room. In fact, it's a lovely house, solid and with balanced lines. A bit like the Hall externally. I hate the modern taste for Gothic elaboration.'

'I modelled this house on the Hall, actually,' Frederick

221

admitted. 'I've long admired your place. I tried to buy it once. It always looks so solid and sturdy against the moorland winds.'

'And always so full of the moorland breezes inside,' Simon said, grimacing. 'I think it must be the draughtiest house in all of Lancashire, and the roof leaks quite badly in places, too. One of my first priorities must be to make it weatherproof and to modernise it a little. The kitchen is quite medieval and we don't have any gas on the premises.'

'Do you intend to stay here long this visit?' Annie asked, in her polite hostess voice.

'I intend to make Bilsden my permanent home from now on.'

They both stared at him, not bothering to hide their surprise.

'Then you'll be the first Darrington to do so for over a hundred years,' Frederick commented. 'May one ask why?'

Simon hesitated, then decided on frankness. 'I've no taste for London society. I never wanted to inherit, you see. I wanted to become an architect – much to my stepmother's disgust. I spent some time in Italy, studying architecture there, and in Paris, too. I even studied under Featherborne – a much undervalued man, I believe, because his style does not suit the modern taste for elaboration. But he has a sound grasp of the practicalities and there's no one better for clean lines and balanced shapes.' He broke off. 'I'm sorry! I shouldn't bore you with such things.'

Annie leaned forward, her interest caught. When enthusiasm lit up his face, Lord Darrington seemed a young man just like any other. And also, with that frank open expression on his face, his resemblance to his dead brother diminished considerably. The last of her hostility towards him faded at that moment. 'You're not boring us, Your Lordship. I like to hear about real things and detest gossip about trivia. We'd both be interested to hear more about your Mr Featherborne.' She gestured to Frederick. 'You may have heard that my husband intends to remodel the town centre, to make an elegant square? In fact, we're more likely to bore you with our plans and ideas than you are to bore us.'

'We'll do more than talk about it,' Frederick promised. 'I want to get you involved. If you're going to be a *resident* lord of the manor, it'll be your bounden duty to take an interest in the town's doings. We're becoming quite progressive in Bilsden nowadays, you know.'

Simon beamed at him. 'It'll be a pleasure, not a duty, to help design a beautiful square.'

'Well, the two can sometimes coincide.'

Frederick glanced at Annie as he said that and she smiled back. Simon could not help staring, for he had never seen love for a spouse shown so clearly on anyone's face. His father had been proud of his second wife's beauty, but that was a different thing, love of a possession not a person.

Winnie, full of the importance of the occasion, staggered in with a tray loaded with the best china, followed by her junior, Hazel, with another tray full of food, enough to feed half a dozen people.

When the servants had left, Annie busied herself serving the two men, listening in admiration as Frederick drew Simon Darrington out to talk of his plans and wishes. She often wished she had Frederick's conversational skills, but knew she was too blunt and to the point.

'You'll be kept busy at the Hall, then, Darrington, if you intend to renovate and repair it.' Everyone in town knew that it had been let go to rack and ruin.

Simon's face clouded over. 'I'm afraid I'll have to take things slowly.' He sighed. 'I think it's common knowledge that both my brother and my father left debts, and I tell you in confidence that my step-mother's lifestyle has been ridiculously extravagant. It'll take me a while to – to sort things out. I shall be living quietly and doing what I can to the Hall with the help of the men on the estate, and with any local craftsmen I can afford to employ.'

'Connor's got some good people working for him.'

'Has he? I must call and see him, then.'

When their guest had gone, Annie looked at Frederick. 'This Darrington doesn't resemble his brother at all, does he?'

'No. He doesn't resemble any of the family. I like him. And I find what he has to say interesting. Fancy a Darrington daring to train for a profession! No wonder he was not the favoured son. His father preferred an idle reprobate like his brother. This man must be the first Darrington to do something useful since the ancestor who made the family fortune in the first place. I'd like to invite him here again, if you don't mind. Perhaps to dine with Connor and that clever little wife of his. If Darrington really is so short of money, and if he has some good ideas, perhaps we could even hire him to help design our square.'

'*Hire* the lord of the manor?'

'Stranger things have happened, my dear. And I do need someone to put things together for me.' Although Frederick had definite ideas about some of the details, he knew that he had no gift for forming those ideas into a coherent whole. He would have to employ a good architect for this, his final project. He had thought of approaching Edward Walters, who was perhaps the best-known architect in the Manchester district, but had been afraid that Walters would insist on architecture as elaborate as that of the Free Trade Hall, whose design had never pleased Frederick, whatever others thought of it.

Maybe this Featherborne fellow might be the one to approach, with Darrington to act as his deputy. Frederick decided that he would look into things, see what Featherborne had built. For he was utterly determined to leave his town centre looking prosperous and beautiful. It would be his memorial. The only one he wanted or needed.

* * *

The next week, Annie did as Frederick had asked and arranged a dinner party, only making the stipulation that the dinner was not to keep him up too late. 'Everyone knows you've been ill and won't be offended if you go to bed early.'

'My dear, I'll retire gracefully when the hall clock strikes ten,' he promised with a sigh, for he knew his own limitations, 'and leave you to deal with everyone. You can invite your brother as well. Tom will be happy to stand as host in my stead when I vanish.'

She was startled. 'Do you think he will agree to dine with a Darrington?'

'Don't tell him. He won't walk out on us once he's here.'

'Hmm. That'll put my numbers out, though – always supposing that William can find time to join us.'

'Well, invite your sister Rebecca as well, then. She's more than presentable, and it's about time she did something other than work in that salon of yours. She behaves like a spinster of forty, not an attractive young woman of twenty-two.'

'For all her youth, she half runs the place, you know,' Annie said. 'Mary's growing to rely on her too much. I can never seem to persuade her that she can cope perfectly well on her own. I feel guilty at how little I've been doing to help them lately.'

He gave her a sad smile and patted her hand. Silence stretched between them for a few minutes. No need to put it into words. They both knew why Annie was spending so little time on her businesses.

The following day Annie put on some of her more stylish clothes and walked into town while Frederick took his afternoon nap. She needed some exercise, though she'd rather be striding freely across the moors than walking out sedately like this, except that it worried Frederick if she went up on the tops on her own. She had never lived such a quiet sedentary life and it was hard at times to keep cheerful when she was itching to do something vigorous.

Rebecca was serving a customer and Annie listened in approval from the back room as Mrs Bossith was eventually ushered out, having placed an order for two new gowns, each with a spare bodice, and a mantle that would match them both.

At the sound of footsteps, Rebecca turned round, ready to serve someone else, but beamed when she saw who it was. 'Annie! I didn't realise you'd come in.'

The two sisters hugged. Rebecca was several inches taller than Annie, but somehow it was the latter who always dominated any room the two of them were in.

'I like that gown on you.' Rebecca held her at arm's length.

'I haven't come here to talk of gowns and fashion, love. I came out for a brisk walk while Frederick's having his nap, so I can only stay a short time. Can you get one of the apprentices to bring us some tea and leave Mary to cope with any customers?'

'Is something wrong?'

'No.' Annie saw the understanding in her sister's eyes and added softly, 'No more than usual. It's just – I wanted to ask you something.'

When they were sitting in the back room, sipping cups of tea, Annie looked across at her sister, struck by her severe appearance and brisk manners. 'What do you want to do with your life?'

Rebecca gaped. 'You've come here to talk about my future? There is something wrong! You're not – not going to sell the salon!'

'As if I'd even think of selling the salon without telling you first! No, there's nothing wrong. It's just – seeing you today, looking so elegant, well, I wondered if you had any plans and hopes for the rest of your life. I realised suddenly how little I knew about your feelings.'

Rebecca's face took on a shuttered expression. 'I plan to continue working here, if that's all right with you?'

'And is that enough for you? Surely you hope to get married one day?'

Rebecca started fiddling with the folds of her black skirt. She had been needing to talk to someone, and who better than Annie? 'Who to? The sort of lads Joanie seems happy to flirt with don't interest me, and nor does flirting. I've felt like a fish in the treetops the few times I've let her drag me out on one of her walks. I don't really like that Maddie she's friendly with, either. She's very vulgar. She laughs so loudly people turn round to stare at you in the street. But if I say anything, Joanie tells me I'm being snooty.'

'Well, there are other men around.'

Rebecca stared into the empty grate. 'Who?'

'The ones you meet at chapel?'

Rebecca pulled a face. 'No one's caught my eye. I'm a bit too fussy, I think.' She looked at Annie and confessed something that would have upset her father dreadfully. 'And I'm not all that religious, actually. I only go to chapel to please Dad. I much prefer the services at St Mark's. And I definitely couldn't marry someone like Dad, who goes on about the good Lord all the time and wants you to go to chapel twice on Sunday. Some folk are even worse than him. Some won't do anything except read the Bible and go to chapel on the Sabbath . . .' She broke off. 'Oh, you know what Dad's like.'

Annie nodded. 'Yes, I certainly do. I'm not what you'd call religious myself.' She sometimes wished she were. Maybe it'd help her get through this difficult time more easily. 'What I actually came here for today, though, was to invite you to have dinner with us on Thursday evening.'

'Oh? I don't think Dad likes to stay out late in the middle of the week.'

Annie shook her head. 'Not the family. Just you, Rebecca. A formal dinner party. Tom's coming as well. We'll send the carriage for the two of you and it can take you back again afterwards.' She grinned. 'And as I'm your employer, I'll give you permission to take the afternoon off to get ready and the next morning off to recover, if you like?'

For a moment Rebecca could only stare at her in surprise, then she smiled. 'Well, I'd love to come, Annie. Of course I would. But what shall I wear? I haven't anything grand enough for one of your dinner parties.' She knew because she had designed clothes for other women to wear at such functions.

'How about I design you a new gown? A present from your elder sister. The girls in the workroom here could finish one for you quickly now that the summer rush is dying down, if we don't make it too fancy.' She stretched out and took Rebecca's hand in hers, feeling the fingers work-roughened from the sewing. She'd had hands like that herself till she married Frederick. 'I hadn't really thought about you, love, about your life, your future. I've taken you and made you into something a bit different from Dad and Kathy and Joanie, haven't I?'

Rebecca answered that question obliquely. 'You always feel responsible for the rest of us, don't you?'

Annie looked surprised. 'Well – yes, I suppose so.'

'You've been a wonderful sister, a wonderful daughter, too. But what about your own needs and pleasures?'

Annie stared at her, then shrugged. 'I'm happy if those I love are safe and happy.' What a strange thing for Rebecca to say to her! She had what she wanted in life: Frederick. And when he was gone, she'd still have the two other things that mattered – family and money. Not for love of money, she amended mentally, but for the security it brought you.

It embarrassed her even to think about herself like this, so she changed the subject firmly. 'Let's get back to you, love. I should have realised that you'd need something more than chapel folk after working here, meeting the gentry all day – so I'll start inviting you out sometimes with me and Frederick from now on, if you'd like?'

Rebecca nodded. 'I would like it. If I'm not – not in the way?'

'No. Far from it. I'd really welcome some company sometimes.' Annie's smile faded for a minute. 'Now that Frederick is not as – as strong as he was, I've no one to go into Manchester shopping with, or simply to share a walk over the tops. I'm still full of energy, you see.' She sighed and her voice was husky with pain as she added, 'And he isn't.'

Rebecca nodded in understanding, but as the moment passed, she could not prevent her face from lighting up at the thought of a new evening gown – she had only the one, a white tarlatan, trimmed with a little lace and a few knots of ribbon. It had been made a couple of years ago especially for grand occasions with Frederick's family and was in a simple style, which her father infinitely preferred. It was well out of date now, to a discerning eye. Excitement bubbled up inside her, animating her normally solemn expression. 'Oh, Annie, I'd love that! I'd absolutely love it! And *not* a white dress, please, whatever Dad says.'

They both laughed at that. No, white was not the best colour for Rebecca. It was a colour for a young girl. Rebecca was a woman now, and with her dark hair, would look wonderful in rich colours.

'Well then, let's go and find you some luscious material for your first silk evening gown. Goodness knows you've made enough of them for others. It's about time you had one of your own.'

Annie stood back and scrutinised her half-sister as she had once scrutinised clients in the salon. She hadn't really taken in before how very elegant Rebecca had become. Joanie had no style and no real interest in her work, though she was a neat plain sewer. I should make more effort to do things without Frederick, Annie decided, and what better company could I have for that than my own sister? 'Didn't Tom have some rose-coloured silk in his new stock?' she wondered aloud.

Rebecca stared at her, happiness colouring her usually pale cheeks. 'Yes. Oh, yes.' She and Mary always went to study the new materials before they were put on sale and she knew exactly which one Annie was thinking of; knew, too, that it would suit her better than anything she had ever owned.

'Let's go and find it, then.' Annie led the way next door to Tom's Emporium.

The silk was a soft shade of cyclamen pink, which, when draped across her, added a warmth to Rebecca's pale skin without overwhelming her delicate complexion as a brighter shade might have. While the assistant was cutting and folding a twenty-five yard length, Annie moved around the Emporium, muttering to herself, but she could not find ribbons in the right shade, or lace of the type she wanted for a bertha to frame Rebecca's graceful white shoulders. She really must put more effort into buying haberdashery for the Emporium. The stock had been left to run down disgracefully.

'And you'll need some of the new hoops, to get the right pyramid shape,' Annie added, her own face glowing with excitement.

'I'm sorry, Mrs Hallam, but we've run out of hoops and we're waiting for another delivery,' the assistant said.

Annie rolled her eyes at Rebecca. 'We'll have to go into Manchester tomorrow, then. I want you to look perfect.'

'But I can't let you do all this for me!' Rebecca faltered, staring at the purchases, for her own ideas had been much more modest.

'Oh, please let me, Rebecca! I haven't enjoyed myself so much for ages!' Annie waited until the assistant had moved away to wrap the material and added, 'What's the use of having money if you can't spend it on your family? Frederick's always teasing me about being too frugal and not caring about jewels and extravagances. He'll be delighted about this, I promise you.'

Rebecca abandoned caution and hugged Annie, not

caring who saw her. 'You're a wonderful sister.'

Annie flushed and hastily changed the subject. She liked to help her family, but gratitude embarrassed her. 'And we'll need a shawl.' She turned back to the young woman serving them. 'Do you have a black silk shawl? They're very popular this year in London, I'm told.'

Again, the assistant could not oblige.

I really will have to take things in hand, Annie thought to herself as they walked back along the street to the salon. We don't want folk going into Manchester to buy things we could perfectly well sell here.

Rebecca turned to beam at her. 'It's beautiful material, but I don't know what Dad will say to all this finery.'

'We haven't got all the finery yet. We'll have to go into Manchester for that tomorrow. But I'll set things moving at the salon first, so that they can make a start on your gown.' She smiled. 'And leave Dad to me. I'll call in at the yard on the way home and prepare the ground with him.' Her father wouldn't grudge her this pleasure, once she explained that with Frederick not always able to escort her, she was going to need her sister's company. She knew that that would win Dad to their side immediately.

Only as she was striding up Ridge Hill again in a final burst of energy did Annie remember that she hadn't told Rebecca who the other guests would be. Oh, well, it wasn't that important. Rebecca had had enough practice at what William called 'company manners' when Frederick's family came to visit. She wouldn't be awed, even by a lord.

The following morning, Annie and Rebecca took the early train into Manchester with William. Neither of them saw a black-clad figure stop dead in the street as they got out of the carriage at the station, nor did they see the woman follow them cautiously into the station. A widow in her mourning weeds was a very common sight and as a thick veil completely concealed the face of the wearer, such figures were almost anonymous.

When they had bought their tickets to Manchester, the woman followed suit, waiting around a corner until they had got into the train, then getting into a compartment further back.

'You're looking very happy,' Annie told her son as they sat together staring out at the familiar views. 'I haven't really had a chance to talk to you lately. How are things going at that mission of yours?'

He beamed at her. 'Well. We have a few regular benefactors now, so we can do more.' Frederick was among them, but William was forbidden to tell his mother that. 'We're managing to do some real good, I think. I've got a couple of lads living there with Alan now, to make sure he looks after himself. When his grand-daughter sends him food, they take care of it, or he'd give it all away. He's a wonderful man.'

'Hmm.' Annie still resented the influence Mr Robins had on her son. But she couldn't deny that William was looking happy lately, happy and fulfilled. 'Well, make sure you don't do too much. When I have time, I'll come and visit you, but today I want to make the purchases and get back as quickly as I can.'

They said goodbye to William outside the station and took a cab to Deansgate, where, in Annie's opinion, the best shop in Manchester was situated. Unfortunately, the Bazaar did not have any suitable ribbon, though they did have a beautiful black silk shawl, whose price quite horrified Rebecca. The two sisters had to go into several other shops and warehouses before they found exactly what Annie wanted, not only ribbon in the requisite shade, but also artificial flowers in black silk.

When they came out of the last one, tired but triumphant, clutching their parcels, the pavements were crowded and everyone seemed to be in a hurry.

'Can you see a cab?' Annie asked Rebecca, who was several inches taller than her.

'No.' They stood on the pavement for a few moments,

then suddenly Rebecca called, 'There's one!' and waved to attract the driver's attention. He stopped his horse, but the man driving a dray behind him was shouting at him to stop blocking the way, so he gestured to a space further along the pavement where there would be room for him to draw up without blocking the traffic. Three other carts had been delayed when he stopped and their drivers were still shouting as they moved away.

Annie turned to move along the street to the cab, but someone bumped into her and she felt herself falling towards the roadway. One of the carts was very close. It reminded her of the time when Marianne had been killed and for a moment she could not move. Then Rebecca grabbed hold of her sleeve and pulled her to safety.

The driver swore at Annie as he drove past, but she was clutching Rebecca in relief, so she did not notice.

'Are you all right?' Rebecca still had hold of Annie's arm.

'Yes. Thank you for catching me.'

'Some people are so rude!' Rebecca said indignantly. 'That woman bumped right into you and nearly caused a bad accident, but she didn't even stop to apologise.'

Annie straightened up and took a deep breath. The narrow escape had made her feel a bit shaky. 'Never mind. These things happen. Good job it was only the pavement. I've never liked heights.' She checked that all her packages were still there. Sometimes people pushed you in order to snatch what you were carrying. But nothing had been taken. 'Come on! Let's get into the cab and go back to the station. I like to come here shopping, but I'll be glad to get home again now that we've found what we wanted. And anyway, I don't like to leave Frederick for too long.'

'Is he – getting worse?' Rebecca asked, as the cab rolled along towards the station as briskly as the traffic would permit.

Annie shrugged. 'He's not getting any better.'

As they walked into the station, she noticed the

admiring glances Rebecca was receiving from passers-by, and smiled approvingly. Her little sister had grown into a very attractive woman. It did not occur to her that some of the glances were for her, or that these were equally admiring. She had not looked at another man since she married Frederick and considered herself a staid old married lady, well beyond that sort of thing.

They had arrived just in time to catch a train, and spent the journey back discussing how best to trim the dress. Neither of them bothered to mention the incident of the fall, or thought much of it. As Annie had said, these things happened in crowded cities. So when she told Frederick about her morning out, it was only the shops and purchases she mentioned, and how beautiful Rebecca was growing, in a grave sort of way.

'Not as beautiful as her elder sister,' he teased.

Annie pulled a face at him. 'Heavens, Frederick, I'm nearly forty. I'm past bothering about that sort of thing.'

'Well, I'm not past admiring you, or being glad that I have a beautiful wife.' And she might scoff, but she was still a beautiful woman.

17

July: Ridge House

*T*he Thursday of the dinner party was a day of bright
sunshine which softened gradually into a long mellow
evening. Annie had left the windows of the drawing room
open, to Winnie's dismay. Why, they'd have moths
fluttering inside and all sorts of insects! Winnie didn't
approve of too much fresh air. If you were not careful, it
could give you chills, fresh air could, even in the summer.
She opened the window of her small attic bedroom every
morning to air it, of course she did, but she made sure it
was tightly shut again by mid-day.

William had agreed to join his parents and guests that
evening for dinner, but in spite of his promises, he had
come back late from Manchester and was still upstairs
changing his clothes when Annie went down to join
Frederick in the drawing room.

Further down Ridge Hill, Rebecca had just finished
getting ready. She had left the salon early, for once,
walking slowly home through the late-afternoon sun,
thoroughly enjoying this rare moment of daytime leisure.
As she walked along High Street, she felt as though
someone was staring at her, but when she turned round,
she saw no one but a woman in black walking slowly along
in the other direction. Was it the old woman who
sometimes stood staring at the salon? No. This one was

moving much more briskly. It was just her imagination, stirred up by all the excitement, no doubt.

She had left Joanie at the salon, sulking in the workroom. In fact, Joanie had been sulking all week, flinging things around the bedroom they shared and refusing to speak to Rebecca. Annie had never made Joanie a fine gown or invited *her* up to Ridge House to meet Frederick's grand friends. Though it was the gown that rankled most. Joanie was rather shy whenever she went to Ridge House, but she was very fond of finery, and the brighter the colours the better. She did not dare complain in front of her father, but made sure her sister knew how she felt about the unfairness of it all.

Kathy went upstairs to help Rebecca dress and to arrange her hair. 'I used to do our Annie's hair once,' she said as she patted the last gleaming strands into place and pinned a rose amid the pretty arrangement of lace and ribbon that nestled above the low chignon. 'It were when she were just starting at the salon an' she used to walk through town to work looking that pretty. But your hair is just as beautiful as hers, Rebecca love, and see how that style suits your face. You should take more care, you really should, instead of screwing your hair up in that tight bun.'

'It makes me look too young like this.' Rebecca stared into the mirror. It made her look vulnerable, too, with her neck so fragile beneath the mass of hair. It was more flattering, but she couldn't possibly face customers looking like this.

Luke had nipped down to Netherleigh Cottage that afternoon to bring his sister a corsage of tiny roses, freshly picked in the Ridge House gardens, and a few extra flowers to tuck into her hair. They were pure white, the roses, just unfurling their petals, and he had set a froth of green fern around them. Strange, Rebecca thought, as she raised them to her nostrils to enjoy their perfume, how his lumpy hands could treat plants so delicately and arrange them so well. The stems of the roses were sitting in a tiny glass phial of water which was concealed by a silver filigree holder with a brooch pin behind it.

'That's a present from Frederick,' Luke said, then was off back up the hill, whistling cheerfully.

When she was ready, Rebecca took a deep breath and left her bedroom. The two boys came out into the hall to stare in amazement, then Lally shepherded them back into the kitchen.

John stood in the hall and gaped at his daughter as she walked slowly down the stairs. 'Eh,' he said, his voice thick with emotion, 'love, you look a real beauty!' He came across to give her a careful kiss, leaning forward across the wide expanse of silken skirts, then he blew his nose vigorously and put his arm round his wife as they stood in the doorway watching Tom escort his sister out to Annie's carriage.

Tom and Rebecca were the first to arrive, for Annie had sent the carriage down to pick them up early, wanting a little time to tell Tom who was coming before Lord Darrington appeared in person.

'I can hire a cab,' he had protested. 'No need to call poor old Robert out.'

'And get Rebecca's skirts filthy in the straw on the floor? Certainly not! This is no gown for wearing in a common cab.' Annie was delighted with the way the silk had made up and wanted Rebecca to look her very best that night. Later, she'd think of other ways to persuade her sister to start enjoying herself a little. Later, she'd start introducing her to more people, a few eligible men, perhaps. She couldn't think of anyone suitable at the moment, but she'd bend her mind to it.

'You look wonderful,' Tom said as the carriage left Moor Close, and he patted Rebecca's tense hand encouragingly.

'I feel nervous.'

'Why? Grand folk are no different from us, you know. Just behave as you would at home and you'll be all right.'

'I'll never dare open my mouth.'

'Of course you will!'

As she entered Ridge House, Rebecca touched the roses at her breast to give herself confidence. She knew her face was slightly flushed, for she was feeling shy of appearing in public in this new guise. She felt strangely unlike herself in this gown, which was as beautiful as any she had helped make for others. Normally she wore dark clothes, with high necklines, and she put cotton pinafores over them when she was at home to protect them. Normally she walked briskly, spoke crisply. In this gown she felt as if she were floating and her voice softened unconsciously as she thanked Tom for helping her out of the carriage and arranged the shawl around her shoulders.

When they were shown into the drawing room, Frederick stood up to greet them, and stared in open admiration at Rebecca. She was tall and willowy, like an elegant young tree, as she moved carefully across the room in her wide swaying skirts. Her hair gleamed in the light from the gasoliers, with a low chignon nestling at the nape of her slender vulnerable neck. Her arms and neck were white and soft, with firm young flesh to tempt a man to touch them. He shook his head and banished such thoughts. His days for that sort of thing were gone, to his deep chagrin.

'My dear, you look exquisite!' He moved forward to clasp Rebecca's hand and hold it for a moment or two, patting it to emphasise his words. 'Exquisite.'

'The ladies of our family always do,' Tom said proudly. He grinned ruefully down at himself. 'They've got all the looks. Pity they didn't share a few of them with us male Gibsons.'

'Mark didn't do so badly for looks,' said Annie. She had noticed how the lasses looked at him, especially that uppity little piece who served in his chop house. She hoped that there was nothing going on between the two of them.

'Well, me and Luke aren't much to look at.' But Tom's voice held no rancour. His looks had never held him back from attracting the girls when he was young, and he'd married the wife he'd chosen, too. No. Looks were all right, but it was determination and hard work that got you what you wanted. He went across and sat in one of the very comfortable chairs. Every time he came here, he decided to get himself some really comfortable armchairs like these, but somehow he never got round to it. If he got new chairs, he'd have to get new curtains and wallpaper, and he just couldn't be bothered with all the fuss of decorating a whole room.

Frederick fumbled in his pocket and produced a delicate pearl pendant on a fine gold chain. 'Please do me the honour of accepting this small present, *Miss Gibson*,' he said, bowing with mock formality as he held it out.

Rebecca's eyes filled with tears as she examined it. 'Oh, Frederick! How good you and Annie are to us all!'

Annie saved the moment from becoming over-emotional by stepping forward to unclasp Kathy's simple jet beads from Rebecca's neck and fasten the pendant in their place. 'There.'

Rebecca fingered the pendant.

'It looks lovely!' Annie approved.

'You shouldn't have!' But Rebecca couldn't help gazing at her reflection in one of the gold-framed mirrors and smiling at what she saw as she draped the black silk shawl more becomingly.

'Right, then, sit down and stop admiring our Becky!' said Tom. 'Tell us who else is coming tonight.'

Frederick obliged. 'Daniel and Helen Connor. I'm afraid we'll bore you tonight, Rebecca, with talk of our plans for the new square – though I promise not to talk about it *all* evening. Daniel is the best builder in town, you see, and he has all the best craftsmen working for him. I'm not having anyone else do the work for me.'

'William will be joining us as well in a few minutes,'

239

added Annie, continuing the list. 'He's just getting ready. And – and Lord Darrington's coming.' She looked at Tom pleadingly as she spoke.

He bounced to his feet. 'You didn't tell me he was going to be here.' His voice was harsh and his lazy good humour had quite vanished.

Frederick came up to him and put an arm around his shoulders. 'Time to let bygones be bygones, Tom lad. This fellow has never done you any harm.'

'He's still a Darrington, isn't he?' Tom pulled away and went to stand by the window, staring out blindly at the darkness. For two pins he'd leave, and to hell with upsetting their bloody dinner arrangements. Then Marianne's gently smiling face appeared before him and he knew that even she would not approve of his ongoing hostility. He turned round and said coldly, 'I can't guarantee to be friendly towards a Darrington, but I'll promise to be civil, at least.'

Rebecca's start of surprise and sudden flush of colour at the mention of their noble guest went unnoticed. No one knew that she had met Simon Darrington on the tops, and she hoped he would say nothing tonight to betray that, or else Annie would question her afterwards as to why she'd not mentioned the encounter. A meeting at her sister's dinner party would not cause gossip in the town, nor would it lead to anything else. She'd make very sure of that. 'Let's be friends,' he'd said. Well, friendship wasn't possible between two people from such different backgrounds. She knew it, even if he didn't. But that hadn't stopped her thinking about him once or twice. His lordship was a very attractive man, with a lovely smile.

Helen and Daniel Connor arrived next and it was Annie's turn to tense up a little. She had once been engaged to Daniel, and could never forget her outrage when she found out that he was planning to sell her salon against her wishes as soon as they were married, and use the money to bolster his failing business. He'd behaved abominably when she broke it off, too, for all his charm when he met her nowadays, for he'd tried to blackmail her out of her money whether she married him or not.

But as Frederick had said years ago, Bilsden was too small a place to hold grudges. You could not help meeting everyone you knew at least once a week, whether you wanted to or not. And Helen, who had taken the outrageous step of asking Daniel to marry her after Annie rejected him, had been Annie's friend for a long time, and was her friend still.

Annie looked towards Tom and made a moue, and his angry expression relaxed into a shrug. Aye, he thought, looking at her. They all had to learn to forgive people. As Rosie had forgiven him. At least, he thought she had forgiven him, though she'd kept him at arm's length during his visit to London: walks and afternoon tea in a café, but no more evening engagements, no tête-à-têtes. Still, she had not forbidden him to visit her again. And he would.

Helen Connor moved across the room to greet her hostess, small and self-assured as ever. She would never be beautiful, but she always caught the eye nowadays, dressing for chic and using colours with great daring. The birth of two children had not changed either her figure or her lively personality.

Only while her father, the previous Parson of Bilsden, was alive had Helen had to subdue her feelings and impulses, and dress quietly. She had also had to keep her interest in painting quiet. But now, as Annie knew, Helen was again painting the sunny foreign landscapes she loved so much, either going alone to southern Europe, or, as she had done last year, taking Daniel with her, now that he could leave his building business to his brother Rory's careful management.

Daniel might have the flair and the understanding of building processes, but Rory was the one who saw to the details and ordered the materials and paid the men. It was thanks to Rory and Helen that the business was prospering. But it was Daniel's ideas and knowledge of the trade that generated custom.

The two women exchanged greetings and Annie allowed Daniel a brief shake of the hand before turning back to Helen. She would never forgive him completely for the way he had treated her. She knew that every time she saw him. And so did he, for he never made any attempt to talk to her alone.

William came downstairs to join them just as Simon Darrington arrived, so the bruising on her son's face escaped Annie's notice until she had greeted her last guest and started introducing him to the others.

'And this is my son, William,' she said, her voice softening as it always did when she introduced her first-born.

Reluctantly he turned around and everyone gasped.

Tom let out a shout of laughter. 'What does the other fellow look like, lad?'

William grinned at his uncle, but carefully, because his eye was swollen and his lip was sore and throbbing. 'Much worse, I promise you. Someone tried to rob the mission. They didn't succeed.'

'William Ashworth, I don't know what you'll get yourself into next!' Annie scolded, coming up to pull her son round to face the light squarely and tutting with concern and annoyance at the sight of his face. 'Have you washed those cuts carefully?'

'Yes, Mother.' He made a mockery of his response, and was relieved when everyone else laughed. His mother didn't even smile. She did not have much sense of humour where her children's welfare was concerned.

Frederick came up to take her arm. 'Leave scolding him until later, love. Your guests are much prettier to look at, anyway.'

There was another round of laughter. In the general noise, Simon moved across to Rebecca. 'So we do meet again, after all, Miss Gibson.'

She cast a hasty glance around. 'Shh! Please don't tell anyone. I – I didn't mention that I'd met you that day.'

'I've not mentioned it to anyone, but I haven't been able to forget that I met you,' he murmured, eyes warm upon her.

She gave him a look that was half pleading, half warning, just as Frederick came up. 'Let me introduce you two properly.' He put his arm around Rebecca's shoulders. 'My sister-in-law, the lovely Miss Rebecca Gibson. My guest and friend, Lord Darrington.'

'Simon Darrington,' the guest insisted, taking the hand Rebecca stretched reluctantly towards him and clasping it for a moment in his. 'I dislike my title. I'd be more than happy to be a plain mister.'

There was no mistaking the sincerity in his voice and Rebecca was intrigued. 'Why?'

'Because the title places a barrier between me and other people.' He let go of her hand, but his meaning was unmistakable and his admiration for her all too obvious in his expression.

Neither of them realised that Frederick hadn't missed the quick exchange between them as he moved to introduce them, hadn't missed, either, the length of time Simon held her hand, or the way Rebecca flushed delicately and seemed uncertain of herself. Better watch this, he thought. Nothing can come of a relationship between those two, and I'm not having that girl hurt.

He liked Rebecca; not only her looks – which, as a former connoisseur of women, he considered to be the sort that grew better with maturity – but also her no-nonsense approach to life and her frankness. And he admired the way she had worked so hard at the salon from a very young age. She seemed as needful of security as her half-sister, Annie, or her brother Mark. All John Gibson's second brood were scarred by their years of childhood poverty.

Seeing that everyone was seated, Annie rang for Winnie

243

to come and serve drinks. She did not notice the encounter between her sister and Simon Darrington, and Frederick did not mention it to her. He didn't want his wife to find something else to worry about. And he was not yet too old or infirm to keep an eye on things himself.

The dinner table was balanced in numbers, but with more gentlemen than ladies. That did not worry Annie, who usually enjoyed the conversation of gentlemen more than that of ladies, though some hostesses made a huge effort always to invite equal numbers of ladies and gentlemen to their social gatherings. Annie didn't, but for some reason, she felt it unlucky to have odd numbers. And it made the table look untidy, too.

Frederick had forgotten that his wife, flanked at one end of the table by Simon and Daniel, had arranged for Rebecca to sit next to their noble quest. His lips twitched in amusement at Rebecca's imperfectly concealed dismay. He moved to the head of the table, where he was flanked by Helen and Tom. No fear of any lack of conversation with those two. Indeed, everyone had noticed how much Tom's spirits seemed to have improved since his trip to London. It was Rosie he was going to see, Frederick was sure, but he hoped she wouldn't just tumble into Tom's arms. People valued things more when they were hard to obtain.

Helen kept her end of the table laughing and chattering about the infamous steamship, the *Great Eastern*, which she and Daniel had gone to view in the docks in London, curious to see what all the fuss was about.

'It'll never replace sail,' Daniel still insisted.

'Well, if I can use steam to power my mill machinery, and if steam can pull all those trains around the country, then there must be some way it can be applied to ships,' Frederick said. 'It's just teething troubles, I expect.'

'Hah! It didn't do so well when it was launched in January,' Tom said, for once in complete agreement with Daniel. 'There were – how many? – five sailors killed in the explosion?'

'It isn't as pretty as a clipper ship, either,' Helen said, with a grimace, 'but then, trains aren't very pretty, and they throw out smuts everywhere, yet we all use them quite happily nowadays.'

'Well, I'll wait to see what happens when they refit the *Great Eastern,*' said Tom, who didn't like the thought of long sea voyages, anyway. 'Maybe they'll do better next time. Or maybe they won't.'

'Didn't you go to see it when you were in London?' Helen asked.

'Er – no.'

'What did you do with yourself, then?'

'Oh, I met a few chaps, went to the theatre, you know the sort of thing.'

'What did you see at the theatre?' she pursued, driven by an imp of mischief.

He scowled at her. 'I don't remember. I was tired by then, after walking around all day studying the shops and looking at the sights.' He sought desperately for some way to change the subject.

Helen allowed him to do so, but looked at him thoughtfully and later told her husband that she wondered if Tom Gibson had found himself a mistress in London. 'It's about time. It's unhealthy to mourn for so long.'

'Wouldn't you mourn for me if I died on you?' he teased.

'For a year or so. Then I'd go out and find myself another husband.'

'Thank you very much.' He was not sure that she was joking. She often kept him guessing about things. This was one woman whom he'd not dared to betray, either. Apart from the fact that it was she who managed the money, she kept him very happy in bed. 'Thank you *very* much indeed!' he repeated, peeved.

'It's all right, Daniel, love. Only the good die young. And you're definitely not good. So you'll probably outlast me.'

He lowered his voice. 'I'll make you pay for that tonight, you wretch.'

245

She just gave him one of her enigmatic smiles. He was the sort of man you had to manage carefully. The money she had inherited from her aunt was carefully tied up in a trust, and with some cajoling and Rory's help she had managed to take and keep control of the building company's accounts, leaving them in Hamish Pennybody's hands when she was away. Daniel was a good builder and good at inspiring confidence in clients, with his handsome face and easy charm, but he was not a good businessman. And if she had allowed him any leeway, he'd have been a womaniser, too. So she didn't. But she did love him in her own way, especially his hard muscular body and roguish Irish smile. She'd never regretted proposing to him, or paying off his early debts.

After they'd left the table, Frederick got Daniel on one side and asked him if he knew of an architect called Featherborne.

'Featherborne,' said Daniel thoughtfully, swirling the last of his brandy around his glass. Then he raised one finger as the memory clicked into place and he nodded. 'Ah, yes. I remember now. No wonder the name seemed familiar. He built a place or two in Hertfordshire near a railway cutting I was working on. Nice houses. They sort of fitted into the landscape, if you know what I mean. Not fashionable, but pretty. I used to travel around a bit looking at the buildings.' Buildings had always fascinated him, though he'd got his start digging the railways, then moved on to doing the brickwork for railway tunnels and cuttings.

'I was wondering whether to consult Featherborne about the town centre,' Frederick said, testing the water further.

Daniel looked thoughtful. 'Ask him to come here and discuss it first. See how you take to him. Weigh up what sort of ideas he has. You don't need to decide anything until then.'

'Yes, I think I'll do that.'

'Who told you about him?'

'Darrington. Did you know he had trained as an architect?'

Daniel gave a snort of laughter. 'What, our noble lord?'

'Yes. Only he was the younger son then, and it was very much against his family's wishes, from what he says. Might be a good idea to involve him in planning the town centre. You *are* going to rebuild it all for me, aren't you?' It was the first time he had said so openly.

'If I'm asked.' Daniel did not allow himself to sound pleased, but a smile curved his lips and his eyes lit up. He had been hoping for this plum to drop in his lap.

'Oh, you'll be asked.' There was, Frederick thought to himself, no one else in Bilsden capable of undertaking such a project, or of getting it done so quickly, thanks to the quiet but efficient Rory.

18

September: Darrington Hall

*A*nnie sent the garden lad down to Netherleigh Cottage with a note asking Rebecca to go for a walk with her across the tops. Frederick had declined to accompany her to church and was spending the morning studying the preliminary suggestions that Rodney Featherborne had put forward after his first visit to Bilsden. Pencil sketches, a bit messy, some of them, with scribbled notes around the edges. She couldn't raise much interest in them. Indeed, she was surprised at how obsessed Frederick had become with this town centre plan, though she could see that one would like to leave something of oneself behind. Whenever she got to that thought, however, she always changed the subject mentally.

Rebecca arrived at Ridge House within minutes of the garden lad bringing word to Annie that Miss Gibson would love to come. 'I was dying for a walk!' she exclaimed, hugging her sister.

'I'm so glad. I'm bursting to get out into the fresh air.' Annie was dressed like her sister in sensible clothes, with a warm shawl instead of a mantle or pelisse, and no bonnet or hat. It would have scandalised some of the town's matrons, if they had seen her bare-headed like that.

Frederick grinned as he came to the door to see them off. 'You look just like the young woman I courted when you're dressed like that, Annie lass. You'll be going off to serve in the salon again if you keep turning the clock backwards like this.'

She beamed at him, glad to see him in such a good mood. She didn't care what she looked like. All she wanted was to get outside and work off some of the energy that was boiling up inside her.

Frederick stood in the doorway, watching them go, but as soon as they were at the end of the drive, the smile faded from his face. For Annie really did look as young as she had ten years ago and he looked so much older.

'Are you all right, sir?'

Winnie's solicitous voice brought him out of his reverie.

'What? Oh, yes, just lost in thought. I think I'll go for a stroll around the gardens.' He went off to change his shoes.

Poor gentleman! thought Winnie, staring after him. I don't care what Mrs Jarred says, I think he's looking his age. And *she* isn't. Not that Winnie had anything against Mrs Hallam. No, a kinder mistress you couldn't hope to find. But it was a shame, all the same. Life could be cruel, even if you were rich. She went back to her dusting, humming tunelessly as she worked.

Warmly wrapped, for a chill wind was blowing fitfully, threatening showers later, Frederick paced slowly along his favourite garden path. As he passed by some bushes, there was a rustling sound. He stopped. 'Who's there?'

Silence. He grasped his walking stick more firmly. Was someone trespassing? And if so, why? 'I know someone's there, so you might as well come out.'

The bushes rustled again and then parted to reveal his daughter, Beatrice, the one he had disowned ten years ago. But she had changed so greatly that he was too shocked to turn and walk away. She had always been heavily built, but now she was extremely thin and looked old beyond her years, with the sort of ageing that only sorrow and hardship could write upon a face.

'This is quite a surprise,' he said, trying not to show how shocked he was.

She nodded, staring at him with a calculating and rather hopeful look on her face.

'What are you doing here, Beatrice?'

'Looking around. Remembering happier days. I'm not allowed in through the front door now. *She* has made sure of that.'

'If you're going to insult Annie, there's nothing more to be said between us.' He turned as if to leave.

She reached out and grasped his arm. 'No, wait! Father, *please!*'

So thin was the hand that he waited, looking at her with a puzzled frown. Why was she wearing black? Surely Reginald couldn't have died without his hearing of it from his lawyers, for it would have affected the trust fund he had set up for her? Her bonnet was heavily veiled, though the veil was thrown back now. Her expression was – wild. There was no other word for it. 'And has Reginald come to Bilsden as well?'

'Reginald is in France – with his dear friend, his very dear friend.' She threw back her head and laughed, only it sounded more like the cry of a creature in anguish, and the sound touched his heart as words would not have done.

'Shall we sit down?' he said, taking a sudden decision to listen to her. 'I've been ill.'

'Yes, I heard. Very ill, from all accounts. She's wearing you out. You look years older.'

Her acid tongue had not softened, then, over the past decade. 'So do you,' he said quietly. 'And you don't look well, either.'

'It's nothing that good food and warm accommodation would not put right.'

He looked at her in amazement. 'Are you telling me you don't have enough to eat?'

'No, I don't. And haven't had for a while. I've been selling things, but I've not got much left to sell now. So I came to see you.' She turned to walk along the path with him and sit on the edge of the wooden bench beside him.

'But your dowry is protected. Barrence can't touch the capital.'

'He can use the income, though. And he does. All of it. Or so I'm told.'

Frederick was trying to take this in. 'So you're told? Do you mean he's left you?'

She nodded, hatred twisting her face into a gargoyle's mask. 'He was never really a husband, anyway.' She looked sideways and let out a harsh caw of laughter at the expression on her father's face. 'Reginald doesn't love *women*. Did you never guess that?'

It took a minute or two for Frederick to gather his wits together. This was the last thing he had expected to hear. 'You mean the marriage was never consummated?'

'Oh, no. I don't mean that. Reginald is far too clever for that.' She was rocking to and fro now, the words spiked with bitter anguish, her whole body vibrating with it. 'He hired someone to consummate the marriage for him, since he can't.'

'*What!*'

'But there's no way anyone could prove that, Father. I'm definitely not a virgin now. He wanted a son from me, you see. So it happened more than once. But Mabel and I saw to it that he didn't get a son. We got rid of the only child I conceived.'

Frederick stared at her. Surely this nightmare tale was the product of a fevered mind?

She seemed to read his thoughts. 'I'm not mad. I wish sometimes that I was. I'm telling you exactly what happened.'

'But why did you say nothing to me before?'

Another bray of laughter. 'We didn't part on the best of terms, if you remember. No wonder Reginald encouraged me to burn my boats!'

'I remember it all very clearly. You hurt William deeply – and your poor cousin Jane.'

She did not seem to have heard that remark. 'And anyway, I had my pride. As long as Reginald lived with me, gave the appearance of being my husband, I kept up the pretence of our marriage. Then – ' the breath she drew in was a groan and she was rocking more quickly now ' – then he left London. I was away. He used to allow me the money for little holidays, you see, so Mabel and I would go and stay at the seaside or at one of the spas. It was a relief to get away and there's a great comfort in walking along a beach, especially in stormy weather.'

She looked suddenly into the distance as if she could see horrors there. 'When we got back, we found he had sold the furniture, everything. My personal possessions were piled in the middle of the bedroom, and there was a note.'

Frederick looked at the worn, crumpled piece of paper she held out and took it reluctantly.

Beatrice

I've gone to live in Europe. Our life has been a travesty and I can take it no more. You're as barren in body as you are in soul. There are others who love me, with whom I wish to spend my life. The rent will run out at the end of the month and I've made no arrangements to support you. I need the money from the trust and you have a rich father, after all. Go and make your peace with him. He'll not see you starve.

Reginald

'I can't believe this!' Frederick read the note a second time, then gave her back the piece of paper.

She folded it carefully, smoothing it as if it were a precious possession. 'Neither could I at first. If it hadn't been for Mabel, I think I'd have killed myself.' She threw him a glance filled with hatred. 'You bought me a poor husband, Father. And paid very dearly for him.'

He didn't make the obvious comment that Reginald was the only one who had offered for her. 'I'll consult my lawyers. We must be able to break the trust.'

'Mabel and I have already consulted lawyers. Unfortunately, the wording of the trust documents allows Reginald to do this.' She turned a hard burning gaze upon him. 'I want to come back home, Father. Please. It's all I want now. *Please!* It's what my mother would ask of you if she were alive.'

The mere idea of that horrified him. Spend his last years with this bitter twisted person? Watch her make Annie's life a misery? Never. He shook his head. 'No.'

'You put *her* before everyone else!' she hissed.

He stood up, distaste etched on his features. Beatrice seemed to have learned nothing from her troubles. 'Where are you staying in Bilsden?'

'We have lodgings.'

'Where? I must be able to contact you. You *do* want me to help you financially, don't you?'

'What I really want, you're not prepared to give me.' She glanced along the path towards the house.

'No, I'm not. But Reginald was right. I'll not see you starve.' Though he would not allow her malice to spoil his wife's life either, nor would he allow her near his two young children. 'Tell me your address. I'll make sure you have some money.'

'We're staying in one of the River Rows. Imagine a daughter of yours reduced to such a hovel!' She gave him the address, which she had already written on a scrap of paper. 'Mabel said that was all you would do for me.'

'Mabel was right. Go back there. I'll make arrangements.' He looked at her very solemnly. 'I'll give you a respectable income, Beatrice, but only on condition that you stay away from Bilsden, and most of all, away from my wife and children.'

'Mabel thought you'd say that as well.'

'She was right again. And I mean it.' When Beatrice said nothing, he waited for a moment, ashamed of the revulsion she inspired in him, then prompted her: 'Well? Do you accept?'

'What choice do I have?' She did not bother to say goodbye, just stood up and walked away, openly this time.

He watched her go, tears in his eyes. When he went back into the house, Winnie took one look at him and said, 'Ooh, sir, you do look badly.'

'Yes. I must have got chilled. It's colder than it looks today. I think I'll go and sit in the library.'

'Shall I send in a tea-tray, sir? And some nice hot crumpets?'

He shook his head. 'No. What I need is a brandy.'

Then he went away to shut himself up with his unhappiness. He was relieved that Annie was out, for he could not have concealed his feelings from her. But given a little time, he would come to terms with things. Beatrice was not going to come between himself and Annie. Indeed, she was not going to come near any of his new family. He'd make utterly certain of that. London would be the best place for her. Or some quiet town in the south. But not the north, not if she wanted the money. Hamish Pennybody could make the arrangements. He was as discreet and reliable as his father, and young enough to do the necessary running around. It could not be left to a clerk.

'How are things at the salon?' Annie asked as the two sisters strode off towards the wilder moorland.

'Going as well as ever.' Rebecca grimaced. 'But I've felt so restless this week. I don't know what's got into me lately.'

'Me, too.' Annie hesitated, then said, 'With you, it's sheer youth, I should think. I wish you could meet a young man and—'

'We've been into all that. There's no one suitable. You know there isn't.' Rebecca stopped walking to grasp

255

Annie's arm. 'And don't you start introducing me to people, either.'

'But that's how it's done. In fact, that's all some of the other ladies seem to talk about.' Annie made occasional morning calls, because it was expected, but found them deadly boring, and didn't make half as many as she ought to have done. All the talk was of babies and children and marriages, with occasional excursions into the latest fashions and the servant problem. That last subject really tested Annie's self-control. She could have told them that they'd keep their servants longer if they treated them better. But even the ladies who had risen in the world with their husband's success spoke as if servants were an inferior species with no minds or needs of their own. It made Annie's blood boil sometimes.

Rebecca scowled at her. 'Well, that's not how it's going to be done with me. I'm quite resigned to remaining a spinster, thank you very much. After all, I don't need a man to provide for me. I can earn my own living.' She speeded up and took the lead as the track narrowed.

Annie grimaced at the straight back and swinging arms in front of her, but let the subject drop. Halfway up the hill they stopped for a breather, staring at the farm in the undulating valley to their right.

'I've always liked the look of that farm,' Annie said. 'The way it nestles in the shelter of the clough, and the little footbridge over the stream. When I was a child, Dad used to bring us children up for walks on the tops sometimes and I used to imagine we lived there.' She smiled. 'And now they've dammed the stream and made a little reservoir to supply the mills with water in dry weather.'

'It looks pretty.' Rebecca moved right to the edge to stare down at it.

Annie shivered. 'Come away. You're making my stomach go all funny.'

'Just standing here?'

Annie nodded. 'I've never liked heights. And standing

right on the edge like that . . . Ugh! I couldn't bear it.'

Rebecca obediently moved back.

'I've never even been down there,' Annie said as they walked along again. 'The people who live on the farm are not very friendly sorts. Upperfold, I think they call the place.'

'It must be very lonely there in the winter.'

'Sometimes I'd welcome a bit of loneliness,' Annie sighed. 'Or at least, I'd like it if Frederick and I could get away from everyone.'

Rebecca threw a covert glance sideways. 'Tamsin again?'

Annie shrugged.

'I thought Miss MacNaughton had control over her?'

'No one has full control over that child. Heaven help the man she marries.'

'What's she been doing now?'

'Slipping off to go to the mill when she should be doing her lessons. She's fascinated by the place. I set her to work there on Saturdays to use up her energy and it's only made her more eager than ever. Do you know what she said to me the other day?'

'What?'

' "I'm a cotton master's daughter, and I'm going to be the first woman cotton master." ' Annie rolled her eyes. 'Of all the unreal expectations! As if the other cotton masters would let a woman run things. Even Frederick laughed at the idea, which only made her scream at him.' She grimaced. 'Oh, let's not talk of Tamsin any more. I came up here to forget my worries, not dwell on them.'

When they got right up to Knowleby Peak, they saw a figure sitting on one of the rocks there and stopped by unspoken accord.

'Isn't that Simon Darrington?' Annie lowered her voice. Sounds carried a long distance in the clear bright air.

'Yes. I don't think he's seen us. Let's go the other way.'

'Whatever for?' Now she had got used to him, Annie

rather liked Simon and would enjoy stopping to chat to him.

Rebecca shrugged. 'Because he'll join us in our walk and I was enjoying having you to myself.'

Annie stared at her. Rebecca's voice sounded altogether too airy. They'd met Simon Darrington a couple of times on their walks and on each occasion he had indeed turned to walk along with them, saying he could go one way as easily as the other, since he was just walking idly for the pleasure of it. Rebecca had been stiff at first, but each time had relaxed and soon started to show every sign of enjoying his company.

Annie's eyes narrowed now as she looked from one figure to the other. Was it possible that her sister was attracted to Simon? No, surely not! Nothing could come of that. Rebecca was not so stupid.

At that moment the figure on the rise looked round, stood up immediately and waved to them. 'Hello, there!'

'It's too late now, Rebecca.' Annie waved back. 'He's seen us.'

'Yes.' She stood back and let Annie lead the way up the hill. Simon beamed at them and came to shake Annie's hand.

Rebecca was standing staring out across the slopes that led down towards Bilsden, and did not seem to notice the hand he held out towards her.

He turned his attention back to Annie. 'I was just feeling that I'd enjoy some company. May I join you in your walk, Mrs Hallam?'

'Of course.'

When they turned back towards Bilsden, he looked sideways at Rebecca and opened his mouth as if he wanted to say something. But he closed it upon the unspoken words and just gave her a long level look.

Why, he's as attracted to her as she is to him! Annie thought. Oh, no! She definitely did not like that. If Rebecca was trying to avoid Darrington's attentions, she was doing the right thing. You couldn't be too careful with your good name, as Annie had told Mark only the previous Sunday. For rumours about him and that sly piece who served at table in his chop house were beginning to circulate. But he'd only told her to mind her own business, as Rebecca probably would if anything were said. Annie closed her mouth upon words better unspoken, but that did not stop her watching the two of them.

As they grew closer to the Hall, the sky clouded over and a rough wind began to blow. The sky grew darker and darker, with one of the sudden changes common to that area, and large drops began to fall, at first in ones and twos, then in flurries, with the promise of a steady downpour to follow.

'You'd better take shelter at the Hall,' Simon shouted above the noise of the wind, 'and I'll send you home in my carriage.'

'Oh, I don't mind a bit of rain. Do you, Annie?' Rebecca nipped Annie's arm and frowned at her.

Annie looked up at the sky. 'Don't be so daft! There's going to be more than a *bit* of rain.' She tugged at her sister's hand. 'Come on! Let's run.'

The three of them arrived at the Hall just as the downpour started in earnest and stood in the porch, laughing and breathless, shaking the droplets from their clothing and, in the case of the two ladies at least, trying to tidy their wind-blown hair.

The elderly butler who opened the door looked extremely disapproving when he saw how dishevelled his master was and in what company. 'Your Lordship,' he said, bowing.

'Ah, Findler. I met Mrs Hallam and her sister on the moors and brought them home to take shelter from the rain. Have tea sent to the library, will you?' Simon looked at Annie. 'Unless you'd like to tidy yourselves up first, Mrs Hallam, Miss Gibson?'

'I think we'd better,' Annie said ruefully. Her hair had

tumbled from its pins and was spread over her shoulders, and Rebecca looked just as much a hoyden. Their shawls had kept the worst of the rain from their heads and shoulders, but were quite damp now, as were their lower skirts.

'Fetch Mrs Hopeby, Findler.'

'Certainly, My Lord.'

A silent and grimly disapproving housekeeper led Annie and Rebecca up to a chill bedroom and took some ancient hairbrushes from a drawer. 'I'll send up a jug of hot water and towels, ma'am.'

'I wonder if you could do something to dry our shawls as well?' asked Annie.

'Certainly, ma'am.' Mrs Hopeby picked them up rather gingerly.

'They're damp, not dirty!' snapped Annie, annoyed by this.

Mrs Hopeby gaped at this bluntness.

Without even thinking, Annie elevated her chin and stared her right in the eyes. The mannerisms she had learned from Annabelle Lewis still came in useful sometimes. 'Well?'

'I'll arrange for the water, ma'am.' Mrs Hopeby craned her head for a final glance back at them as she left the room, her expression suggesting extreme nervousness, as if she were not sure what she was dealing with.

'You'd think we were a pair of – of wild lions!' said Annie. She walked up and down the bedroom, too angry to feel the cold now. 'If one of *my* servants treated a guest like that, I'd have something to say, I most certainly would.'

Rebecca began to unpin her hair. 'It doesn't matter.'

'It does. I won't have it!' Annie started fumbling for her own remaining hair pins. 'I'll just have to twist my hair into a low knot. I haven't enough pins to do anything else.' She grimaced at her reflection in the mirror then shivered. 'You can smell the damp in this room! The whole house has been let go to rack and ruin. I'd be ashamed to show guests into a place like this.'

Rebecca picked up a hairbrush and grimaced at its worn bristles. 'It looks like something's been nibbling at this.'

'Rats probably.'

They both chuckled.

'Big rats,' Rebecca said, 'with burning red eyes. And the hairbrushes belong to a lady ghost who walks around after midnight, her hair all tangled, searching for her brushes.'

Annie laughed at the picture that conjured up and returned to the mirror. Standing beside Rebecca, she ran her fingers through her hair to take out the major tangles, then picked up a brush. 'Oh, well, beggars can't be choosers. And it's not midnight yet, so we should be quite safe. Come on! I'll do your hair and you can do mine.'

By the time the lukewarm water arrived, both ladies' hair was neat again and they were as presentable as was possible in the circumstances.

'If you will ring when you're ready, ma'am, someone will come to show you down,' the maid who'd brought the water said primly. She, too, was elderly and looked just as disapproving of the visitors as the housekeeper had.

Annie inclined her head in another regal gesture. 'Thank you.' She washed her hands and face, then studied the room with an expert eye while Rebecca followed suit. 'That woman doesn't know her job. If a room's not being used, there should be dust covers over the furniture and they should keep the curtains drawn to prevent this carpet from fading even more.'

'Well, they didn't know we were coming, did they?' Rebecca was more forgiving.

'They shouldn't need to know. If a room is in use, it should be dusted, at the very least, every single day. It wouldn't take more than a minute or two.' She trailed her finger across the surface of a small table. 'But it's days since anyone's touched this place.'

'I can't believe how worn everything is,' Rebecca said, joining her sister by the window and picking up the edge of the curtain to examine it. 'I thought it'd all be – well, very grand here.'

'Hah! The Darringtons haven't spent a farthing on this place for years. You can see that. All the money's gone on London and high living.'

Annie had no time for people like that. It was common knowledge in Bilsden that many of the cottages on the Darrington estate were in a shameful state of repair. And yet her ladyship spent money freely on new clothes and jewels. That, too, had been common knowledge, for several of the servants who looked after the family in London came from the Lancashire estate. 'Well, it's none of our business, I suppose. Are you ready, love? Right then, let's go. I'm not waiting here for another ten minutes while that housekeeper decides to answer the bell. Come on. We'll go downstairs.'

'Oh! Ought we to?'

'Pff!' Annie made a disgusted noise and gave her sister a push towards the door. 'Who's going to shoot us?' She looked at Rebecca and guessed what was going through her mind. 'Look, love, it's only a house, for all it's so big, and they're only servants. Below you in status, though they'd hate to admit that. Don't you *ever* let places like this frighten you, Rebecca Gibson! You're as good as anyone. And that includes Queen Victoria herself!'

This time, when Annie took hold of her sister's hand, Rebecca came with her. 'I wish I had your confidence.'

'It's not confidence.' Annie grinned. 'It's sheer impudence. I never did know my place.'

On the way downstairs, they stared up at gloomy paintings on the walls and pulled faces at each other over more frayed curtains and threadbare carpets. 'It's a shame, isn't it?' Annie whispered. 'I'd dust and mend myself rather than let things get so shabby.'

'So would I.' Rebecca pointed to a moulded plaster ceiling. 'Look how lovely that is. All it needs is a fresh coat of paint.'

When they got down to the hall, the butler popped his head out of a doorway at the rear and gaped at them, scandalised. He came hobbling out of the servants' quarters and over to the two ladies. 'If you had rung, ma'am, someone would have come to show you down.'

Annie raised one eyebrow. 'I'm not so stupid that I can't find my own way back down one flight of stairs and I knew you'd be somewhere near the entrance. Butlers always are, aren't they? Now, perhaps you can take us to his lordship.'

A loud crash of thunder made both Findler and Rebecca wince.

'It's a good thing we took shelter, isn't it?' said Annie, making her voice deliberately loud and cheerful. She knew her sister had always hated thunderstorms.

Rebecca nodded, but she looked apprehensive.

'This way, h'if you please, ma'am.' Findler moved across the hall at his normal slow stately rate, which didn't disguise the way he was twisted with arthritis, and then led the way down a corridor towards the rear of the house.

Like the Hallams, Simon Darrington had made the library his main sitting room. It was a big square room at one side of the house, and looked out across the moors, showing a storm-swept landscape and masses of dark clouds scudding across a grey sky. Even as the two visitors stood in the doorway, lightning streaked across the heavens and within seconds, thunder rolled behind it.

Rebecca gasped, jerked closer to Annie and clutched her sister's arm again.

Simon had stood up when they entered and could not but notice Rebecca's distress. 'Do come closer to the fire, Miss Gibson. You must be absolutely chilled.'

'Thank you.' She did as he bade and he gestured to a chair which had its back to the windows, pulling up another for Annie. 'Findler, could you please light the lamps?'

'Sir?'

'The light's very bad. And I think Miss Gibson would prefer to have the curtains drawn. Would you not?'

Rebecca threw him an embarrassed but grateful glance. 'I would. Thank you. I'm a – a bit nervous of thunderstorms.' Her mother had always screamed and taken the children to hide under the bedcovers when it thundered.

'I like storms, myself,' said Annie, going over to stand by one of the windows. 'What a magnificent view you get from here.'

Wind was howling across the moors, sending the rain down at an oblique angle and making the trees in the gardens around the Hall lash their branches and shed their yellowing leaves. Lightning flashed at regular intervals and thunder boomed, but the dark storm clouds were, to Annie's mind, magnificent. She was sorry when Findler brought in some old-fashioned oil lamps and came across to clear his throat and gesture to the curtains.

She moved away reluctantly.

'Could you please send word to Ridge House that Mrs Hallam and Miss Gibson have taken shelter here, Findler?' Simon said. 'Give my apologies to the groom for sending him out in weather like this, but Mr Hallam will be worried about his wife. Say I'll have them driven back,' he looked at Rebecca, who winced as the thunder boomed again, 'when the storm is over.'

Annie smiled her thanks for his consideration and went back to stand in front of the log fire, which made a magnificent display in the huge old-fashioned fireplace. 'Thank you, Your Lordship. Frederick will indeed be worrying about us.' She looked at her sister, who was sitting in a huddled heap on the chair with her eyes closed. Another boom of thunder made Rebecca twitch and shudder.

It was no use expecting any conversation from her, so Annie turned to their host. 'It's a good thing we met you on the moors.'

'Yes.' His voice was soft and the glance he threw at Rebecca was definitely warmer than it should have been. 'Did Mrs Hopeby see to your needs?'

'Yes.'

He seemed very quick to pick up her mood. 'But—?'

Annie twinkled at him. 'I wouldn't be so impolite as to criticise my host's hospitality.'

'I wish you would. I'm aware that the staff are not doing their jobs as they ought. I know they're old, but I think there's something else as well. As a man, I've not been trained to understand the running of a house and I'm dashed if I know how to sort it all out.'

'Both Findler and Mrs Hopeby seem very. . .' Annie hesitated.

Simon said it for her. 'Disapproving?'

'Of you, too?'

He nodded. 'Oh, yes. Very. They much preferred my reprobate brother, who treated them like slaves and never said thank you.' He could not prevent bitterness from creeping into his voice. He ran one hand through his hair, looking more boyish than ever, hesitated then began, 'I wonder—'

'Look, let's just say what we think and stop pausing delicately,' Annie suggested. 'I'm used to plain speaking, Your Lordship.'

By this time Rebecca was sitting up and listening to them, no longer as frightened now that the storm was shut outside and the room was golden with lamplight. She was startled by her sister's blunt words, but when she looked at Simon Darrington, he seemed amused, not offended.

'Good idea, Mrs Hallam. Well, what I was wondering was, could you possibly find the time to advise me what to do about this house? My step-mother has made it very plain that she does not intend to come here again. And even a mere man like myself cannot help noticing the dust. But if I mention it to Mrs Hopeby, she weeps and says she does her best with the staff she's got, and you can't get good trained staff in the country. I have no money for expensive renovations, but surely, if I hired a few more staff, we could make the place look more – more lived in?'

Annie's eyes lit up. She would welcome a challenge, something to keep her busy. She saw Rebecca looking dismayed. Well, her sister need not be involved. In fact, Annie would make sure she wasn't.

'I'd love to help you, Your Lordship.'

'Are you sure you don't mind?'

'I'd say so if I did.'

He came across to clasp her hand. 'Then I can only thank you from the bottom of my heart. And Mrs Hallam – *please*, do you think you could call me Simon, as your husband does? I really do hate all this lordship business.'

'Very well. *Simon.*' Annie looked around her with a brisk air. 'We can start as soon as you like. I'll need a list of the servants and a complete tour of the house. And I think *you* had better take me, not Mrs Hopeby, or I might say something which will shock her even more.'

'Now?' He was startled.

'Well, we could have a quick look. I'm here and the storm is still raging outside.'

'But aren't you tired after your walk?'

Annie laughed up at him. 'Not a bit of it. Are we, Rebecca?'

'No, indeed. We're not fine ladies, Your Lordship. In fact,' Rebecca added, to stress the differences between them, which he must be made to realise were insuperable, 'I work hard for my living. As did my sister before her marriage.'

But his eyes were filled with admiration, not scorn, as he looked across at her. 'I think you're both wonderful!'

Which was not the effect she had hoped for.

By the time they returned to Ridge House, Annie was bubbling with enthusiasm, ready to pour out her ideas to Frederick. He was in full control of his own tangled emotions by then and determined not to let Annie find out about Beatrice, in case her strong sense of family loyalty made her invite her step-daughter back to live with them. Watching his wife ruefully, he thought how vivid and beautiful she looked and how much she had needed further outlets for her abilities. It was not just her beauty that was so attractive; it was her personality and the sheer energy she seemed to give off. He could only hope that Lord Darrington would not be as taken by her as her useless husband still was.

But when Rebecca had gone home, Annie snuggled up to him and told him about Simon's admiration for her sister, which made Frederick feel a lot better.

'What can we do?' She was chewing at her thumb, a habit she had when worried.

'Nothing.' He put one fingertip on her lips as she opened her mouth to protest about this. 'You can't look after everyone, Annie.'

'I don't want to look after everyone, just my family.'

'You can't even look after them. They must grow up and live their own lives.' But he could see she was not convinced.

19

October: Ridge House

*T*he following Sunday was the day the whole family assembled to have their photograph taken. John Gibson and Kathy arrived first, stiff in their Sunday best and ill-at-ease with the idea of being photographed, although most people were getting quite used to it nowadays. Accompanying them, in various states of mind, from rebellion to boredom, were John's children by his second and third wives.

Mark, tall and rather scornful, thought it a waste of both time and money. Luke was beaming at everyone, his face ruddy after nearly a year's exposure to the elements. Happiness radiated from him all the time now and he seemed to have developed a new confidence, taking everything in his stride, even the prospect of a stay in London in the spring, to work in Kew Gardens and learn as much as he could.

Rebecca was elegant in a new dress of cotton batiste which she had made 'specially for the occasion, again in her favourite pink, this time a subtle dusky shade, with dark brown and pink ribbons forming a pleasing trim. Let other women wear several violent colours and contrasts. Rebecca was too like Annie to make that mistake. Today her full double-tiered skirt was worn with a jacket bodice and tight sleeves with mancherons; she had another matching bodice at home more suitable for evening wear, and enough material left for a new frill when this one got too worn from brushing against the ground. She'd put braid around the inside of the hem to protect it, but with such full skirts, accidents often happened, and mud could not be prevented from splashing upwards.

Joanie was also in a new dress, of bright green cotton muslin printed with blue flowers. There was far too much trimming on it, and pink ribbons were utterly the wrong choice, as Annie did not hesitate to tell her. After that, Joanie wore the sulky expression that they were seeing more and more on her face at family gatherings. Today, she reminded Annie suddenly of May, dead many years now, but who had been Joanie's half-sister.

John's two younger boys were also stiff at first. They had been strictly forbidden by both their father and their mother to get themselves dirty or untidy, and privately thought this whole affair a waste of time. But it made a change from their usual morning visit to chapel, and Luke had promised that afterwards he would show them around the heated glasshouse that was Nat Jervis's pride and joy. But not until the photographic session was over. Until then, they were to touch nothing, do nothing.

Samuel John, who enjoyed anything mechanical, was privately determined to question the photographer about his apparatus. Jonah Triffcott had set up a photographic studio just off the High Street the previous year and was very popular in the town with engaged couples and newly-weds. He also did outdoor portraits of larger groups as the weather permitted.

Edgar ran to meet the two boys when they arrived, grinning with pleasure, but when they would have wrestled and given each other mock punches as usual, Annie's voice reminded them of the need to keep tidy. 'Yes, Mother.' Edgar rolled his eyes at his young uncles and they grimaced at him – making sure Annie could not see them. No one liked to be on the receiving end of her sharp comments.

A sulky Tamsin followed Edgar. She had got into trouble with Miss MacNaughton again that morning for mimicking the slow Lancashire accent of her grandfather. However, in the pleasure of telling Samuel John and Benjamin about her new 'job' at the mill office, Tamsin soon forgot her sulks and became animated again.

Edgar, who was already longing to earn his pocket money the same way, became huffy and jealous every Saturday when a very self-important Tamsin was put into the care of the kitchenmaid to walk to the mill if it was fine, or driven there if the weather was inclement.

As Annie had said ruefully to Frederick, Tamsin regarded going to the mill as sheer pleasure, and the pocket money she earned for doing little jobs there was far less important to her than her growing understanding of the processes involved in cotton spinning. 'She should have been a boy, that one.'

He just smiled. 'She takes after you.'

Annie drew herself up. 'She does not! I was never sulky and naughty like that.'

'No, but you did become a businesswoman, and do better than most men. Do you really expect your daughter to behave like a meek little miss?' He was getting worried at the increasing ill-feeling between mother and daughter, actually, but could not see how to remedy that. Tamsin had such a wild wilful streak in her that she reminded him of his son Oliver, dead for over a decade now, poor lad. Oliver had left Frederick with a great many debts to pay and a young wife to support. Adelaide had recently remarried, this time to a widower in comfortable circumstances, so after fifteen years of supporting her and sometimes her spend-thrift brother, too, Frederick was at last free from that burden.

'The photographer's here already!' Edgar told his cousins. 'He says we can watch him set up his equipment if we promise faithfully not to touch anything.'

The three lads set off at once for the lawn in front of the house, followed by Tamsin.

271

Jonah Triffcott greeted them with a little lecture on what he was doing. He had discovered that the best way to make young lads behave at these sessions was to initiate them into the mysteries of photography. In any case, he was himself such an enthusiast about the new technology that he loved to share his knowledge. He had already given several talks down at the 'Stute, and a small photographic society had been formed there, of which he was President and to which he sold the necessary equipment.

The three boys and Tamsin stood in a circle around Jonah, who had waited three weeks for a fine Sunday so that he could take the photographs outside. Large groups like this one were not easy to deal with indoors. You just couldn't get enough light. The boys listened eagerly to all he had to tell them. Tamsin sighed and gave up trying to understand the technicalities, which did not interest her. She had followed the boys simply because she could not bear to be left out of anything. Miss MacNaughton stood nearby, keeping an eye on the group, and also listening with interest.

Within minutes, Mr Triffcott was telling them about Monsieur Daguerre, who had developed the photographic process and revealed it to the world as early as 1838.

'The year William was born,' said Tamsin.

Three faces turned round to glare at her and three mouths said, 'Shh!'

She stuck out her tongue at them.

'But nowadays, we have more modern knowledge,' continued Mr Triffcott, 'and we use the wet collodion process for our plates.' He fixed the group with a forbidding stare. 'Can you keep still for a minute and a half? If not, your face will be blurred on the photograph.'

Four heads nodded solemnly and Elizabeth MacNaughton smiled in understanding of the way he was laying the groundwork for several successful photographs. She had heard that it was a tedious process standing stock still while the photograph was being taken and had wondered how the children could be persuaded not to fidget.

A few minutes later Tom and his family arrived at Ridge House, having walked up the hill. While he joined the adults in an earnest discussion of who should sit where, his children found their way to the fascinated circle around the photographer, where the knowledge gained was repeated to them by Samuel John, with several corrections from Mr Triffcott.

Joanie also joined them, having quarrelled with her sister Rebecca and not wanting another lecture from Annie about her dress. When she saw Mr Triffcott's admiring gaze, she stayed with the group, pretending an interest she did not really feel. He was a nice young fellow. Not good-looking, but with fine sidewhiskers and a stylish way of dressing.

The servants were also in a state of great excitement. Indoors, the maids were making sure each other's hair and dresses were perfect, and outdoors, Nat Jervis and Robert, the tyrant of the stables, had lined up their men and boys for an inspection. No other family in Bilsden had had a photograph taken of its servants, and Mrs Hallam had promised to hang it in the servants' hall for all to see.

There was no one working in the gardens, so the hidden watcher was able to look her fill. Lips curling scornfully, Beatrice kept her rage in check. Did her father really think she would stay away from the only home she had ever known? One day, *she* would pay for what she had done, pay for it dearly. But not yet. These things needed careful planning.

Beatrice watched on, so lost in her hatred of Annie that there was no longer any rhyme or reason in her tangled thoughts and feelings. Her love for Reginald had turned to disgust. She didn't even *want* him back now! Her social ambitions had crumbled to nothing. All that was left was her hatred for Annie, and that was still burning brightly, a glowing fire at which she warmed herself, giving herself the energy to continue. She would find a way to pay that woman back for daring to take the place of Beatrice's cherished mother, for daring to turn the love of Beatrice's father away from his children.

She often dreamed of ways to kill the woman. Pushing Annie Gibson over a cliff was her favourite, or thrusting the usurper down into a big dark hole and burying her. Beatrice was drawn to cliffs and had often wondered what it would be like to jump off one. In her dreams, she did it frequently. She had failed once, when she tried to push Annie under a carriage in Manchester, but she would not fail again. Mabel said it was not worth the bother, but Mabel had grown very timid lately. Mabel had hated being poor again.

For the time being, however, Beatrice could do nothing, nothing but watch that woman's posturings, and let the lovely warm hatred smoulder gently within her. *Later,* she crooned to the dark feelings coiled inside her, *later. I promise you I'll do something.*

In the event, the photographic session went much better than Frederick had expected, and took only two hours, because Mr Triffcott had so fascinated the children that they kept still. Indeed, they stared so unblinkingly at the camera that William always said in after years that they all looked as solemn as fishes gaping up from the waters of a lake.

As usual, the photographs were processed on the spot in the small hooded pony cart that Mr Triffcott had fitted up to further his outside trade. Then they were displayed for everyone to see and marvel at. There was much stifled laughter and teasing from the children at the sight of each other frozen in stiff poses for posterity. When the photographs were pronounced successful, each was put into one of Mr Triffcott's elegant frames (small extra charge, workmanship guaranteed) and one was presented to each section of the family by Frederick.

John and Kathy sat clutching their glass-fronted photograph for the rest of the visit, staring at it again and again. They could hardly be persuaded to put it down.

'Eh,' said John as he was getting ready for bed that night, 'that's a real treasure to me, that photograph is. All my childer in it, except Lizzie. I do wish she could have been here with us.'

'Well, it's a long way for her to come and she doesn't like to leave the house empty, you know that,' Kathy soothed. 'And anyway, she's sent us a photograph of her and Jim, so that's all right. It can stand next to the other one on the mantelpiece. So we'll all be there together.'

He knuckled his eyes. 'You must think me a right sentimental old fool, lass.'

She hugged him tightly. 'Nay, I think you a wonderful man, John Gibson, with a wonderful family.'

Not until the session was over and everyone had gone inside did the hidden watcher stir from her concealment in the bushes and go back to her occasional lodgings in the River Rows. Her father had made her promise to keep away from Bilsden, but he was a fool and had no way of finding out what she was doing. She had found a woman happy to put them up whenever Beatrice's desire to see for herself what was happening at her old home grew too strong. And the best of it was that the woman was friendly with Peggy, upstairs maid at Ridge House, so she knew a lot about what went on there.

Mabel was waiting for her when she got back. 'Oh, Miss Beatrice, why did you have to come back here again? And just look at your dress, all covered with leaves.' She began fussing over her mistress, but could tell from the wild look in Beatrice's eyes that the mood was on her again. Mabel blamed that on Annie Gibson.

'I'm not letting her get away with it, Mabel,' Beatrice whispered. 'You should see how ill my father's looking. She's probably poisoning him.'

'No, no. She wouldn't do that.'

'She'd do anything. She—' Beatrice stopped in mid-sentence and stared into space, as sometimes happened.

275

Mabel waited a minute and interrupted. Sometimes it did no good, but this time Beatrice sucked in her breath sharply and let Mabel attend to her. 'Let me take your mantle, miss. There. And your poor hands are so chilled. Come and warm them by the fire. We'll take the first train back to London tomorrow. Nothing more we can do here.'

Beatrice smiled. 'Not now. But Mrs Dawes has promised to let me know next time that woman comes to London. She does sometimes, you know. I'll find some way to stop her, Mabel, some way to save my father. It's my sacred duty.'

That night Beatrice crooned to herself for a long time as she lay in bed, chuckling and muttering until even the long-suffering Mabel felt like screaming at her to shut up. But it would do no good if she did. Her poor mistress lived in a world of her own most of the time. But Mabel was there to look after her. Mabel was the only one who truly loved her now. And Mr Hallam had sent word that if Mabel stayed with his daughter, he would see she never wanted again. Mabel didn't want to jeopardise that security.

The following day, a groom brought a note for Frederick from Simon Darrington, inviting him and Annie to take luncheon at the Hall. Afterwards, if Mrs Hallam was agreeable, Simon would show her around the house more comprehensively than last time and they could make a start on sorting out the domestic situation.

Frederick handed the note to Annie. 'Do you want to do it?'

'Why not? So long as you feel up to it.'

'I'm not *quite* in my grave yet.'

'Sorry.' Annie devoted herself to the rest of her correspondence, while Frederick scribbled off a quick reply.

The Hall was looking its best in the sunshine. Frederick pulled the check string and stopped the carriage just inside the gates to stare at it. 'I've always loved this house,' he said softly. 'I used to come up here as a lad and stare through the gates. And when the gatekeeper chased me away, I used to pull faces at him, climb a tree further along and perch on the wall. Later, when I'd plenty of money, I tried to buy it. But they wouldn't sell their precious heritage. They preferred to let it crumble away.'

Simon came hurrying to the door himself to greet them and before luncheon had shown them over the ground floor.

The meal was simple and not well presented.

'You need a new cook as well,' said Annie, for it would have been foolish to pretend that the food was good. In spite of that, she tucked into the plain meat and vegetables with her usual hearty appetite while Frederick picked at his food, as he had taken to doing lately.

Afterwards Simon looked hesitantly at Annie. 'Do you feel up to a tour of the rest now?'

'Yes.' She looked at Frederick. 'Do you wish to join us?'

'No. I believe I'll sit in the library and look at those old prints you were telling me about, Simon, if it's not too much trouble to find them?'

'No trouble at all. I'd value your opinion on them. If they have any worth, I shall sell them. Better to have roofs that don't leak on my cottages than a few pieces of fancy paper in my library.'

Frederick and Annie exchanged glances but made no comment. They had not realised how very short of money their young friend was.

Simon then led Annie through a maze of bedrooms on the first and second floors of the house, some with little sitting rooms attached, most without. Nowhere was there a bathroom. Nor had gas been brought to the house. Candles stood ready in candelabra, and on a small table near the top of the stairs, lamps were set out, ready to be lit and placed in his lordship's rooms.

'Dreadfully old-fashioned, isn't it?' he murmured. 'There I am helping your husband to plan a fine new square in town, with gas lighting and elegant arcades of shops, then I come back here and live in draughty state like some sort of feudal lord.' His grimace said that it wasn't what he wanted, but they both knew that he had no choice but to do his duty.

Annie turned her attention back to practicalities. 'Do you intend to install a bathroom or two?'

'I certainly do. I believe Mr Connor is the man to arrange such things? But the repairs to the roof must come first.'

'Yes. Of course.'

'Until that's done, it's useless to modernise things, but surely we can take care of the rooms better?' For there was a damp, unused feel to most of them, with dust and cobwebs and smeary window panes.

When they had toured the whole two floors, he turned to go downstairs and Annie grasped his arm to hold him back. 'What about the servants' quarters?'

'I've never been up there. Mrs Hopeby assures me that everything's all right, apart from a leak or two.'

'You should really take a look for yourself.'

He stood hesitating. 'Well, I did go up to the attics when I first decided to settle here, but I didn't like to intrude in the servants' private rooms.'

Annie suddenly realised that he was nervous of entering the maids' domain. 'Ring for Mrs Hopeby now and ask her if we can look round the servants' quarters after we've had a cup of tea. That'll give her time to check that everything's in order first.'

Mrs Hopeby was scandalised at the mere idea of his lordship inspecting the female servants' quarters. 'I do assure you, m'lord, that there's no need to trouble yourself.'

His lordship's voice grew suddenly icy. 'The tea first, then we shall inspect the whole of the attics.'

If the main parts of the Hall were shabby, the attics were an utter disgrace. When they climbed the narrow stairs, they walked on strips of threadbare drugget, dangerous because of the holes. They'd have been better taking these up and staining the boards, Annie thought scornfully. The walls looked as if they had not been painted in decades and damp patches were very evident.

The maids all slept in one long narrow room, as scantily furnished as a barracks. The cook and housekeeper slept in single rooms that were more like prison cells. The butler slept at the other end of the attics, but the rest of the male servants were lodged above the stables.

During the whole tour Annie said nothing, just watched Mrs Hopeby eye his lordship and falter out apologies for things that were not always her fault.

Afterwards, they went down to the library again, to find Frederick snoozing in a chair, so they tiptoed out and took refuge in the small room where Simon ate his meals when he was on his own.

'It's dreadful, isn't it?' he said gloomily.

'You need to repair that roof before you can do anything.'

'That will depend on the cost, I'm afraid.'

Annie stared at him in amazement. 'Are things really as bad as that?'

'Every bit as bad. Far worse than I'd expected. And my step-mother is still living in a luxurious manner in the London house, a manner we can no longer afford.'

'Does she know about . . .' Annie did not know how to phrase it tactfully.

'She knows that I've had to pay off huge debts, but as her jointure is secured to the estate, and as I've managed to pay that and have allowed her to live in the London house, she thinks no further.' He sighed and ran one hand through his hair. 'Once she's out of mourning, I'm afraid her extravagances will increase again. Her allowance barely pays her dress bills now, and I can only be thankful that her mourning limits what she can do socially.'

'I didn't realise. Oh, Simon, how awful for you! And you

didn't even want to inherit, did you?'

'No. I most definitely did not. But it's my responsibility now.' He took a deep breath. 'Well, it's no use dwelling on that. We must see what we can do, both here and in the worst of the cottages.'

'Leave your servants to me.' Annie smiled at him. 'I'll be most tactful, I promise you. In fact, I think I'll bring my own housekeeper with me next time.' She needed an escort to ensure that there were no grounds for gossip, and certainly did not intend to bring Rebecca here again. She sighed at the thought. She wished she knew what to do with Rebecca. She didn't want her lovely sister remaining a spinster.

Frederick, when she poured out her worries, simply shook his head and said, as he had several times already, 'Annie, you cannot hold yourself responsible for every member of your family!'

She didn't argue, but didn't pay his words any attention either. She would never change her mind. They were *her* family, and who else was there to look after them all?

1859

20

Bilsden: February 1859

After a promising week of watery sunshine, the weather turned cold, and it seemed as if winter had regretted slackening its chilly grip and was taking hold again. Frederick stared out at the rain, sighing in frustration. He had a head cold, a very slight one, and Annie was treating him as if it were a congestion of the lungs.

He would have to do something about the way she fussed over him, and about her dependence upon his company. It was not that he wanted to spend less time with her – heavens, no! – but he loved her so much that when he died, he did not want to leave her sunk in grief like some widows, who never seemed to come to life again after they'd lost the husbands they depended on utterly. He had never, he decided with a wry twist of his lips, been so selfless before. But then, he had never been married to his Annie before.

There was a knock on the door and he called, 'Come!'

Winnie poked her head around it as only Winnie could, like a plump but nervous chicken who is unsure whether a fox is lurking inside the room. 'Dr Lewis is here, sir.'

What! Frederick was unaware that he had only formed the word with his mouth, not spoken it aloud, as he hurriedly added, 'Show him in.'

Jeremy came in and stopped when he saw his patient's expression. 'Annie sent a message that you were ill.'

'A very slight head cold.'

'Ah.'

Frederick gestured irritably. 'You might as well come in and sit down.' He raised his voice. 'Winnie!'

The head poked round the door again.

'Fetch us some tea, please!'

Frederick looked at Jeremy and grimaced. 'Annie's getting fussier than any mother hen.' He hesitated. 'But since you're here, I suppose you might as well give me a check over and listen to my heart with that damned tube of yours.'

'You mean my stethoscope. And it's not a "damned tube", but a wonderful tool for listening to what's going on inside someone.' Jeremy smiled. 'Though some of my patients seem to think the devil himself is lurking inside it and flinch away as if it's going to bite them.'

Afterwards, Jeremy had put his things away and stood staring down at the carpet. Frederick knew that the news was not good. 'Tell me!' he ordered harshly. 'It would be far worse not to know.'

Jeremy looked at him, with all the compassion in the world shining in his thin face. 'The irregularity in the heartbeat is more pronounced. And your heart is labouring somewhat.' His expression grew stern. 'I thought you were going to come to me if there were any changes? You must have noticed some breathlessness and have felt palpitations.'

Frederick shrugged. 'Yes, I noticed. So I stopped walking on hilly ground and going upstairs unnecessarily. If I had come to you, could you have done anything to help?'

Silence was his answer, then Jeremy growled in his throat: 'Look, Frederick, you really are doing too much. You should rest more. Let others run this Improvement Committee. You're not the only enthusiast now, for you've infected several others, Lord Darrington included. And I hear that the planning of the new square is coming along nicely.' His tone became coaxing. 'You can afford to let others do the rest of the work.'

Frederick was not to be cajoled. He shook his head. 'No. It's something I want to do, something I care deeply about.' Far more now than the mill and making money. He had more than enough money to leave his family secure and that was all he cared about. The business was mainly in Matt Peters's hands these days, and he had been given a small share in the company, which had utterly delighted him. With Annie often acting as go-between for her husband, Matt was teaching her a great deal about the cotton industry, as Frederick had hoped. 'I wasn't cut out to be an invalid, Jeremy. I'd rather go quickly while doing something worthwhile than linger on huddled in a bath chair, afraid to move or do things.'

Jeremy nodded. He would have felt the same. 'There are medicines which may help a little.'

'You advise me to take them?'

'Yes. I think you'd better.'

'Then I will. Apart from that, I shall continue to live as normal a life as I can.' As normal as life could ever be when a man who had enormously enjoyed congress with women all his adult days was unable to pleasure his beloved wife. That was the most bitter part of all for Frederick. He could face his own death. Everyone had to face that. But not to be able to show his love properly to a young and beautiful wife . . . that galled and humiliated him.

The same afternoon, when Annie came back from having luncheon with her friend Pauline Collett, Frederick took her into the library, which had become both his refuge and his prison.

She kissed him. 'Should you be up, love?'

'Of course I should. I told you this morning that it's only a slight head cold.' He drew her across to the fire. 'We need to have another little talk.'

Her heart jumped in terror. '*What did Jeremy say?*'

Frederick put a hand on her shoulder and swung her round to face him. 'That's not what we need to talk about. Why did you send for him? It's only a cold. You make things worse if you treat me like this, Annie.'

She stared back at him, her hands reaching out for one of his. She cradled it against her cheek as she spoke. 'I'd noticed that you were getting breathless at times. You wouldn't talk about it, or call Jeremy in yourself, so I took it upon myself to send for him.'

He steeled himself to loosen her grip and push her to arm's length, holding her there. 'You must never do that again, Annie. It upsets me. If I need the doctor, then I'll say so.'

'I won't do it again, if you'll promise to look after yourself properly.'

He sighed. 'We had this discussion last year. I thought we'd reached an agreement.'

She looked at him, blinking away the tears she had sworn not to shed. 'I can't help worrying. I could tell things were getting worse.'

'You *must* help it. Oh, Annie girl, you've never been the clinging type before. It's one of the things I've always loved about you. Don't start now, for heaven's sake, not when I need you to be strong and cheerful. When I die—'

She managed to hold back a sob, but could not prevent tears from filling her eyes. '*Don't*—' She took a deep breath and spoke more normally. 'Don't say things like that!'

He shook her gently, then said, 'Oh, Annie girl, how I love you!' He folded her in his arms and held her there for a while, rocking to and fro a little. Before he pushed her away, he said softly in her ear, 'It's time to go and find that portrait painter now, Annie. I've set in motion all the other things I really want to do. There's just that now. But you'll have to go to London and look around carefully for me.'

She made a noise of protest in her throat.

'You *must*, Annie, for I can't go myself now! I had hoped

– well, I was waiting to see if I improved a little, but I didn't and I tire too easily nowadays to travel. I still want a good family portrait painted, though, want it most desperately. I don't know why it's so important to me, but it is.' He let go of her and walked across to the window, to his usual position, staring out at the small lake, ruffled now by flurries of rain but with the earliest spring flowers, coaxed by Nat, making a colourful show around it. 'You should have gone while Luke was working in London, then he could have escorted you.'

She stiffened. 'I don't need escorting, as if I'm a child from the schoolroom, thank you very much!'

'Well, I'd rather you had someone with you. I shall worry if you're on your own.' He held up one hand to stop further protests and said coaxingly, 'Why don't you take Rebecca? She loves her trips to London.'

Annie shrugged. 'Very well. I always enjoy Rebecca's company. But I really don't know how to start looking for a painter, Frederick, or how to judge what makes a good portrait.'

She was prevaricating and they both knew it. 'The second part is not difficult,' he said mildly. 'If the people in the artist's other portraits look real, not like stiff china dolls prettied up, if his pictures please you generally, then that's enough on which to base your choice.'

She nodded.

'The first part is harder, I will admit.' He frowned. 'But I thought we could call in Helen Connor and ask her advice. She's a painter herself, so should at least be able to tell us where to start looking.' His gaze was drawn to Helen's glowing scene of Italy which he had purchased from Annie on the first day she opened her salon. She had used Helen's paintings to add a touch of style to her premises, and, being Annie, had sold them on commission at the same time. 'You overcharged me on that, you know,' he said, chuckling quietly. 'I only paid five guineas for the other one I bought from her.'

Annie stared at the painting and a reluctant smile replaced the sorrow in her face as she remembered that day, nearly thirteen years ago, when Frederick had brought his sulky younger daughter to patronise the salon. 'Do you ever wonder what happened to Beatrice?' The words were out before she could stop them.

His face became rigid. 'I try *not* to think of her.'

'She's still your daughter.'

'To my eternal shame.'

'But Mildred says she's vanished and that Barrence has gone abroad without her.'

He had not told Annie about Beatrice's visit and did not intend to do so, if he could help it. 'Mildred enjoys making a drama of things. Beatrice probably went abroad with him or joined him later. It's not likely that the grandson of an earl would have abandoned his wife and left her to starve, is it?'

His expression was so grim that he suddenly reminded Annie of what he'd been like in his younger days, a stern master who ran the mill fairly, but with a fist of iron.

'But—'

'I don't wish to talk about her, love. Ever. I infinitely prefer talking about paintings. And you *did* overcharge me,' he added teasingly, though it cost him an effort to smile.

Annie accepted the change of subject, knowing she'd get nowhere with her stubborn husband. Mildred had written her several agitated letters about the disappearance of Beatrice, but whenever Annie had tried to raise the matter, Frederick had refused point-blank to concern himself, or to believe that his eldest daughter's worries had any foundation. Annie smiled, and it was as much of an effort for her as for her husband. 'Well, you paid me what I asked for it, Frederick, so who was the fool? And Helen's a good landscape painter or you wouldn't have bought another painting from her.'

'Sometimes she seems to capture the light and the

warmth so that you can almost feel it. I always wanted to take you to Italy.' He would not think about that, either, so changed the subject back to finding a painter. 'I thought Simon might have some ideas as well. He moves in the sort of circles where people have portraits painted. We'll invite them both to tea tomorrow.'

The next afternoon Helen leaned back in her chair and looked at Frederick in surprise. 'A family portrait? What about that magnificent photograph of the whole family?' The size of the venture had caused quite a stir in the town and several families had followed the Hallams' example, to Mr Triffcott's gratification. Helen nodded her head towards the silver-framed photograph that took pride of place on a small table. 'Isn't that enough?'

'You know it isn't. A good portrait painter can catch the essence of a person in a way that the camera can't. By the time one has stood posing, not daring to move a muscle, for well over a minute, one loses all liveliness. Look at Tamsin. Did you ever see our imp of a daughter look so solemn?'

'No. I see what you mean.' Helen threw her friend an apologetic glance, for Annie had sent her a note, begging her to try to dissuade Frederick from this search for a portrait painter.

Simon Darrington, who had also joined them to see if he could help, leaned forward, his expression thoughtful. Since Annie had helped him to find a new housekeeper and reorganise his staff, he had become almost like a member of the family. Even John Gibson had been known to call him 'lad', though he usually apologised for the lapse afterwards. Only Tom and Rebecca were still rather stiff with him, though for very different reasons, he was sure. 'There are several portrait painters who are much sought after by society people. I doubt they'd be prepared to come up to Lancashire, though, when they can earn so much more in London.'

'Then we'll offer them double or treble their normal fees.'

Simon raised his eyebrows. 'You *are* determined.'

Frederick nodded. 'Utterly. Even if I have to pay someone to kidnap this wife of mine and drag her down to London to find me a painter.'

Annie pulled a face at him. 'Just because I don't want to go travelling right now.'

Helen looked thoughtful. 'Well, I can give you one or two names, and a letter of introduction to a friend of mine who runs a rather elegant establishment selling paintings near the Royal Academy.'

Simon nodded. 'I can give you some names, too. Architects' circles overlap with artists' sometimes. And my step-mother, of course, has many contacts.' He would get Lady Lavinia to provide a list of the most fashionable portrait painters but wouldn't tell her until afterwards who had requested them. She disapproved of him hob-nobbing with mill-owning families, wealthy or not, and would think the idea of one of them having a portrait painted pretentious. She talked a lot about people 'knowing their place', but in his opinion, 'places' were changing greatly along with the modern inventions, like railways and gas lighting and plumbing, which had changed life so dramatically for everyone.

'There you are, Annie girl!' Frederick leaned back, looking very smug and satisfied. 'You can't refuse me now.'

'I wish I could come with you, Annie,' Helen said wistfully.

'Couldn't you?'

She coloured. 'No. It doesn't show yet, but I'm expecting another child. And Daniel is being very silly, almost wrapping me up in cotton wool.' For she had lost a baby the previous year.

'Annie can take young Rebecca with her,' Frederick said. 'They go up to London sometimes to look at the latest fashions, so they can kill two birds with one stone this time. And you'd better go and see Mildred while you're at it, Annie. She takes a huff if anyone goes to London and fails to call upon her.'

Annie threw up her hands in mock protest. 'Oh, have it your own way, Frederick Hallam!'

'I usually do.' He grinned and turned back to his guests. 'So if you two could kindly make us lists of possible contacts and give us advice about the right sort of questions to ask, then we'll make arrangements for Annie's little holiday.'

Little holiday, indeed! Annie scowled at him, but he just smiled serenely back at her. Sometimes he could be very provoking.

When Tom heard about Annie and Rebecca's proposed trip, he made an opportunity to see Annie on her own. 'Dad says that you and Rebecca are going down to London for a few days. Is that true?'

She nodded. 'Frederick insists on having a family portrait painted, and I'm going to try to find a suitable artist.'

'Is he still on about that? You'd think those fancy photographs we had taken last year would be enough!'

'Well, they aren't. He wants a portrait as well. Oil paints. All of us, dressed in our Sunday best.'

'Well,' Tom looked at her sideways, 'we might as well go to London together, then.' It would stop people speculating about his next visit, at least.

'Are you going there again?' Annie stared at him. 'Tom, I've tried not to pry, but—'

He shifted uncomfortably. 'Well, I'll tell *you* the reason, and you can tell Frederick, but I don't want the rest of the family to know – not yet, anyway.'

'Know what?'

'That I'm seeing Rosie again.'

'*Rosie?*'

'Yes. You knew Frederick had helped her to train as a singer, didn't you?'

Annie nodded. She had been very jealous at the time, thinking that Frederick had found himself a mistress.

'Well, Rosie is a very successful singer, much sought after by society hostesses. She came north to give a concert in Manchester last year and I went to it. We went out for supper and talked for ages after the concert. I missed my train back here and had to spend the night in a hotel. Remember? Then, later in the year, I went to see her in London.' He hesitated and added, 'Her and young Albert.'

'Your son.' Annie nodded her understanding. 'What's he like?'

'He's a lively young devil. Trouble is, he looks rather like me, and when he was born he looked exactly like young Samuel John. It was a good thing Rosie went away from Bilsden, or folk would have been bound to notice.' He paused and then burst out, 'Annie, I never thought to love anyone again, but I've come to love Rosie. I was always fond of her, but now she's got *style* and – and there's just something special about her. I want to marry her. That's why I'm going down to London, to ask her.' He stared down at the carpet. 'Though I'm not sure she'll have me.'

'She'd be a fool to refuse.'

'I don't know. She earns a pretty good living for herself with her singing. Her concerts are very popular with the nobs. She might not want to marry a shopkeeper and bury herself in Bilsden again.'

'There's no need for anyone to bury themselves. There are several trains a day connecting Bilsden with the rest of the world. She'll have no trouble getting to and from her concerts from here.'

He looked shocked. 'I wouldn't want her to continue her singing. Well, not for money anyway, though I suppose the odd charity concert wouldn't hurt. I can give my wife every comfort.' He sat in silence, steepling his fingers, waiting for his sister to say something. As the minutes dragged on, anxiety began to churn inside him. Would

Annie accept Rosie? It seemed, somehow, that if she did, the rest of the family would follow suit. It would be an omen.

Annie gave him a long scrutiny, then took him by surprise by saying in a low voice, 'If you love her, and she loves you, that's all that matters to me, Tom, and I'll do anything I can to help you. Life's cruel. It takes things away from you. So if you can find some happiness with Rosie, then do so.'

He knew that she was thinking of Frederick, for they'd all seen how frail he was looking lately, how the slightest exertion made him pant for breath, however much he tried to hide it. It frightened Tom, to tell the truth, how quickly a fit active man could turn into a semi-invalid. It frightened him, too, to think how Annie would cope if the worst happened. No, *when* it happened. For there was little doubt in his mind that Frederick Hallam would not make old bones. His sister was deeply in love with her second husband. Would fate never leave her to be happy for long? Hadn't she suffered enough in life?

He went across and gave her a big hug, not saying anything, just trying to show her that he cared, for he was not the sort to put his deepest feelings into words.

And she hugged him back silently, convulsively, then pushed him away and scrubbed at her eyes. 'I've promised Frederick not to – to dwell on his health,' she said in a husky voice. 'And I'd like very much for you to go to London with me and Rebecca. If we have a gentleman to squire us around occasionally, perhaps we really can go to the theatre.'

He gave her a sheepish grin. 'Aye. It must have been obvious that I hadn't been on that first visit, when Helen was questioning me. She's a sharp one, she is. I thought you'd have taken her with you. The two of you used to gad about together.'

'She's expecting another child.'

'Ah.'

'And Daniel's fussing. Wants a son and heir, as well as the two little girls.'

Tom nodded. 'Most fellows do. There's nothing like having a strong healthy lad to pass your business to. I've got David and Richard, and I can tell you, somehow a son is different, however much I love Lucy. Well, ask your Frederick. He's got Edgar, and must feel differently about him than he does about Tamsin. I reckon Edgar will be the heir to that mill of his, because James isn't interested in it, is he?' Then he realised that Frederick might not live long enough to see Edgar take his place and fell silent again as he saw the pain on his sister's face.

Annie could not understand why a shiver ran down her spine at the mention of Edgar, for Tom was just speaking casually. It was superstitious to feel that he was tempting fate by saying such a thing. And anyway, there was nothing fragile about her Edgar, who was a sturdy lad. She smiled even to think of his earnest little face, then the smile faded as she wondered how the children would cope with what was to come. Tamsin was tough. She could cope with anything, though she adored her father, so perhaps not. But Edgar had the softest heart she'd ever met. Why, he wept at the sight of a dead bird in the gardens, and distress sometimes made him wheeze and pant for breath. She shook her head to dismiss such thoughts. Nothing was going to happen to Edgar. Or to Frederick for a long long time. She wouldn't *let* it.

In London, Annie, Rebecca and Tom were to stay at a small but elegant hotel which Simon Darrington had recommended to Frederick. Tom had stayed in a couple of different places on his other visits, but both of them had left him feeling uncomfortable, if truth be told. He hadn't realised how much of a northern accent he had, until he heard his own voice next to the soft cultured tones of the other guests. And he had not missed the amusement in the waiters' eyes as they took his order. He hoped Rosie wasn't comparing him unfavourably with all the posh folk she met – that damned manager of hers, for example. She now spoke as genteelly as anyone, but Tom was damned if he'd change how he spoke. He was a Lancashire businessman and proud of it, and anyway, it'd be plain silly to pretend otherwise. He was Honest Tom, not Lord La-di-da.

Annie had wanted to stay at the hotel they'd used when they came to see the Great Exhibition seven years previously, but Frederick, delighted that she was to have Tom's company as well, had insisted on their going somewhere more exclusive this time. He would pay the bill for everyone.

It began to seem to her that every decision about this trip had been taken out of her hands, and she alternated between irritation and a growing guilty excitement as she got ready for what Frederick persisted in referring to as her 'little holiday'.

He was right in one sense, she admitted to herself. She did need a break. But she wished – oh, what was the use in wishing? And if Tamsin and Edgar didn't stop clattering around and trying to help her, she'd scream! And Nora, her new maid, was sulking because she was not to go to London, too. Annie missed Laura, with her quiet efficiency, at times like this. Nora was all right, but Laura had become a friend, as some servants did.

'What shall we do first?' Rebecca asked when they'd all unpacked their clothes and assembled in Annie's sitting room.

'Well, there's not much time to do anything but have dinner and go to bed,' said Tom. 'I thought you two ladies could – er – eat at the hotel tonight. I've got someone to see.'

'You'd better tell Rebecca who it is,' Annie said dryly. 'You'll not be able to hide anything from her now.'

When Tom had made his confession and left, Rebecca said in tones of disgust, 'Men!'

'They're made differently from us, love,' Annie said. 'It doesn't mean as much to them as it would to us.'

'Well, as I'm never going to get married, I don't need to know all that, thank you very much,' Rebecca said hastily, face flushed. In John Gibson's house, what went on between a man and a woman was never mentioned, and she didn't want Annie to find out how very ignorant she was of the details.

Mary kept an iron hand on the girls in the workroom at the salon, and although there was the occasional teasing remark about young fellows, nothing specific had ever been said in Rebecca's hearing, not even behind Mary's back. Rebecca's being the owner's sister had always put a little distance between her and the others. It didn't seem to have made as much difference to Joanie, though, whose friends were as working-class as her workmates.

'Let's eat downstairs in the dining room tonight, Rebecca,' Annie decided. 'We've been sitting cooped up in a train compartment for hours. Goodness, isn't it a relief to get to a station and be able to get out and walk around for a while?'

'Not to mention using the ladies' room,' Rebecca added. 'I don't know how people with children manage on long journeys.'

'We'll eat in the dining room, then? I don't feel like being cooped up here all evening.'

'I agree. What shall I wear?'

'Your aqua grosgrain would do nicely.' Over the past few months she had been filling Rebecca's wardrobe with new clothes, and inviting her regularly to Ridge House, or to go shopping in Manchester. At first a little shy in company, Rebecca had grown used to formal dinners and tea parties, and was beginning to be more herself at them. She had a very practical nature, leavened with a good sense of the ridiculous and a blunt way of speaking that could cut right to the heart of any discussion. Annie felt a great kinship with her.

How Rebecca and Joanie could be sisters, Annie didn't know, for the two were so unlike. She'd tried inviting Joanie up to Ridge House as well, because she felt guilty about giving Rebecca all the attention, but Joanie had tossed her head and refused, saying she'd feel out of place among all those grand people, but wouldn't mind a new dress or two, thank you very much.

Even John was beginning to worry about the people Joanie had made friends with, but as he could never find anything specific to complain about in her best friend, except Maddie's loud voice and raucous laugh, he had no excuse for putting an end to the friendship. And John was nothing if not fair.

The hotel dining room was filled with quiet-spoken, elegantly dressed people. All the other groups included gentlemen, and when a few curious people turned their way, Annie simply raised her chin and gazed right back at them.

'They're staring at us,' whispered Rebecca.

'Stare back at them, then.'

But Rebecca couldn't pluck up the courage to do that and lowered her eyes as they were shown to their table.

The food was good, and both ladies had hearty appetites. As they were finishing the dessert, Annie heard a voice she recognised from across the room, and turned to see Simon Darrington standing in the doorway, waiting to be shown to a table. He was among a party of laughing people in evening dress, who included his step-mother.

He spotted Annie and beamed at her and Rebecca in delighted surprise, then bent his head to murmur in his step-mother's ear. Lady Darrington did not look best pleased, but changed her path to stop at their table and incline her head to Annie. 'Mrs Hallam. I had not thought to see you in London. Is Mr Hallam here, too?' This was what came of dining out in hotels. Why had she let Simon persuade her that it was modern and exciting? Her eyes narrowed. Was he interested in young Mrs Hallam? No, there was nothing lover-like about the two of them.

'My husband is not very well, so I've brought my sister with me.' Annie introduced Rebecca, who was so studiously avoiding looking at Simon that it was a wonder her ladyship didn't notice something amiss.

But her ladyship noticed little that was not connected with her own needs and desires, so having done her duty – though why Simon wanted to bother speaking to the Hallam woman, she could not understand, just as she had not been able to understand why he'd insisted on inviting them to the funeral – she wasted no more time on a mere mill-owner's wife. She drifted across to her own table, where she was soon to be seen giving rather a lot of attention to a plump gentleman with a balding head, who seemed equally taken by her.

When Annie and Rebecca started to leave, Simon got up and came across to speak to them again at the doorway. 'May I invite you and Miss Gibson to take tea with me at Gunter's tomorrow?' he asked.

'We're here in London with my brother Tom,' Annie said, 'and I'm not sure of his plans for tomorrow.'

'Still in pursuit of a portrait painter?'

'Yes.'

'Then I may be able to help you. *Do* say you'll have tea with me tomorrow, all of you!' His step-mother had summoned him to London to sort out her tangled financial affairs once again, and had taken the opportunity to introduce him to an heiress or two while she was at it, to his intense annoyance. Why she thought he would be attracted to such insipid misses he didn't know, and so he'd told her the previous evening, though it had led to another full-scale quarrel.

In the end, he had threatened to put the London house up for sale if she went on overspending, which would mean she'd either have to return to Lancashire, which she loathed, or find herself somewhere else to live, which she could not now afford – well, not the sort of place she would consider suitable, anyway.

Annie gave in to Simon's persuasion. 'Very well, then. We'd love to come.'

'I'll pick you up here in my step-mother's carriage at three-thirty, shall I?'

Annie frowned. That would look too particular and would surely be noticed by the hotel's customers and staff. 'No. We'll meet you there. I'm not sure what our plans are for the rest of the day.'

He could only bow and accept that. As he returned to his table, he saw his step-mother flirting outrageously with Sir Anselm and allowed himself a savage hope that she would ensnare the wily peer and his huge fortune, for that would at least relieve Simon of one responsibility which he found both onerous and unfair. A woman of her age should know how to keep to a budget and should not make such heavy demands on an already depleted estate. Indeed, a woman like her was one of the reasons the estate had become depleted in the first place. Her extravagances and his damned brother's gambling debts.

He was poor company the rest of the evening and left early on the excuse of an early business appointment the next day. His step-mother stayed on with Sir Anselm.

As she and her sister walked upstairs to their rooms, Annie could not help realising that Rebecca was not in the best of tempers. 'What's wrong?' She unlocked the door of her suite and gestured her sister inside.

Rebecca hesitated, then joined her.

'What's the matter, Rebecca? Something's obviously put you out.'

'It's Lord Darrington. He's followed me to London!'

'I think Simon's here at his mother's bidding, actually, and not very willingly, either.'

'Are you sure?'

'Why? Has he been – er – showing an interest in you?'

Rebecca realised that she'd betrayed something she'd not meant to mention. 'I don't know what to call it.' She flung herself into an overstuffed armchair, and jumped up quickly again to control the crinoline cage, which needed careful handling if it were not to rear up and display her underwear. 'Stupid things!' she muttered under her breath, manoeuvring it more carefully.

Annie's lips twitched. Self-contained Rebecca rarely got as visibly agitated as this. 'Tell me about it, love,' she urged, and sat back to listen to a tangled tale of walks on the moor when Simon Darrington kept popping up, which she already knew about, and chance encounters in town around lunchtime when Rebecca usually went out for a stroll, which she had not known about before.

'I'm not going to be made a fool of,' Rebecca added, with tears in her eyes.

'Do you want me to warn him off?'

'I'll do my own warning. But thanks for listening to me, Annie love.'

'I think you may be exaggerating a little.'

Rebecca knew she wasn't, but did not pursue the point. As she got ready for bed, she even admitted to herself that she could not do anything drastic just now. Annie needed Simon's help to find a painter. And anyway, Rebecca didn't want to spoil this visit to London.

She'd say something when they got back, though. The very next time he waylaid them on the moors she'd tell him to leave her alone. Perhaps she could provoke him into a quarrel? No – Rebecca's face softened into a smile without her being aware of it – Simon Darrington wasn't the quarrelsome type. If he'd been an ordinary fellow, not a lord, she might even have wanted to get to know him better. He was kind and intelligent and attractive, too, in a quiet way. But he wasn't an ordinary fellow. So that was that! It had to be.

21

London: March 1859

*T*om had written to let Rosie know he was coming, so when he arrived at her elegant terraced house on his first evening in London, he found her on her own, for once, with Albert sprawled at her feet, reading a book.

Prompted by a poke from a maternal toe, he stood up and went to shake hands with Tom. 'Good evening, Mr Gibson.'

'Good evening, young fellow.' Hell! Tom thought, the resemblance between him and his son grew more pronounced with every year. You couldn't miss it. It was like looking at himself in a mirror when he was young. In fact, Albert looked far more like him than David and Richard did. He realised he'd been staring and added, 'What are you doing with yourself?'

'Reading. And waiting for dinner.'

Albert's voice, like Rosie's now, was unaccented. But his hair was a crinkly brown just like Tom's and he was stocky in build. Looking at him, Tom decided that Richard, although nearly two years younger, was almost as tall. The Lewis ancestry, that.

'Well, don't I get a greeting, too?' Rosie was smiling and holding out her hand.

Tom shook it, holding on to it, his eyes devouring her, but she drew it away, behaving as if he were just a distant

301

acquaintance and frowning meaningfully towards Albert when Tom tried to take her hand again.

'Did you have a good journey, Mr Gibson?' she cooed, mischief glinting in her eyes.

He scowled. 'Tom, surely?' She never called him Tom in company, but usually did in private. 'Mr Gibson' made him feel old – it was his father's name – and made him feel less than a friend, too. As she intended it to, probably. 'It was as tedious as train journeys usually are.'

Albert was sitting listening. 'I like going on trains. My mother says I'd get bored if I went on tour with her, but I get bored here when she's not at home.'

Rosie ruffled her son's hair. 'Well, you'd get even more bored if you came with me, I promise you. It's nothing but waiting around in hotel rooms and being polite to people you don't know, then waiting around some more on railway stations.'

Tom took heart. She didn't sound as if she enjoyed it all that much.

The conversation limped on through dinner until, with the bluntness of children, Albert asked Tom if he, too, sang for a living.

That broke the ice. Rosie chuckled, Tom could not even hold a tune properly.

He grinned at her. She had often teased him about his voice, putting her hands to her ears and pulling faces when he even hummed. He turned to answer the lad and within minutes found himself explaining about junk, and the money to be made from it, then about the Emporium and the hotel. The lad asked very intelligent questions, too, for one so young. But in some ways, Albert seemed years older than Tom's other children. Perhaps it was because he clearly spent a lot of time with his mother and other adults.

Rosie had an inscrutable expression on her face as she watched her son talk to his father and listened with bitter-sweet pride as Tom's explanations provoked more intelligent questions from Albert.

When the meal was over, she dismissed her son to bed. He pulled a face, but kissed her cheek and shook hands with Tom.

'It was jolly interesting talking to you, sir. I hope you come again.' Then he trailed upstairs, reluctance showing in every slow step.

Rosie tugged at Tom's arm and he realised suddenly that he'd been standing staring after Albert. 'Well, Tom lad, shall we go and take a cognac together in my sitting room?'

He raised one eyebrow as he accepted the glass she had poured for him and watched her pour an equally large one for herself. 'Taken up drinking now, have you, Rosie girl?'

'Just the odd glass of cognac. I like the taste of it.' It was a lonely little ritual she had when she felt a bit down, as she could not help feeling sometimes. Until she came to London, she had always been surrounded by people, and even now, after all these years, she still missed the constant company.

She sat down, spreading her skirts carefully around her to avoid creasing them. Tom had watched Annie do the same thing dozens of times, but now it seemed to touch something inside him to see the gentle movements of Rosie's hands on the gleaming silk folds, hands that were now soft and white. He wished those hands were touching him instead.

He moved to sit opposite her near the crackling fire, wanting to see her face as he talked. 'Not afraid of gossip, entertaining a man like this?'

She shrugged. 'People can always find something to gossip about. But my maids won't say anything about this visit and I doubt anyone will see you leave.'

'That's not what you said the first time I came here.'

She shrugged again and gave him an inscrutable smile. 'Well, there you are. We women are notoriously fickle, are we not?'

He nodded and took a sip of cognac. Now that the

moment had come, he was suddenly nervous. What if she said no? He looked across at her, wondering what she was thinking.

She was staring into the fire and her expression seemed faintly unhappy.

He couldn't bear to hedge around. The careful words he had prepared vanished from his brain like snowflakes on a pond. 'I came down to London 'specially to ask if you'd marry me, Rosie love. Will you?'

She turned to look at him, then looked away again and was silent for a long time. She had known he would propose sooner or later. And she had decided to refuse him. Well, how could it possibly work? Refusing was the sensible thing to do. And now, suddenly, all her common sense had flown up the chimney like that smoke was doing, and she wanted to accept him instead. She swallowed and when she did look up and speak, her voice was husky. 'How can I, Tom?'

He stared at her. This was the last answer he had expected. 'What do you mean, how can you? What's to stop us? I'm a widower, you're unmarried.' He looked at her in sudden anxiety. 'You *are* still unmarried, aren't you?' His eyes flew to the wedding ring she wore.

'Of course I am, you fool.' She waved her hand at him. 'This is just for show, because of Albert.' Though her unmarried state was not for lack of being asked. Several men had tried to court her, Stephen Harris included, but she had wanted none of them. They were too dull, too respectable. They didn't have eyes full of mischief and smiles a mile wide. But Tom's eyes weren't full of mischief any more, either. They were mostly full of quiet sadness.

'Then there's nothing to stop us, Rosie.'

'Oh, isn't there?'

Somehow he didn't dare move across and take her in his arms. She looked too aloof. 'Aw, Rosie, don't refuse me,' he pleaded softly. 'We still get on just as well as ever we did.'

'Now that Marianne is dead, you mean? We got on very well before, too, until you decided to fall in love with her. Did you think I wasn't hurt by that? Did you think I didn't care when you wed her? Well, I did care, Tom Gibson, for all you'd made it plain that you'd never wed me.' She had still hoped, foolish girl that she was then. She was a bit wiser now. Too wise to throw herself at him again, but not wise enough to stop seeing him.

He didn't know what to say to that. He knew he'd discarded her like an old shoe, but Marianne had been a fever in his blood, the golden prize for all that hard work of making money, the symbol that he really had left the Rows behind him.

'Are you even over her now, Tom? You took her death badly. Will you ever really be over her?'

That he could answer and he looked straight into Rosie's eyes as he said, 'Yes, I'm over her. Mind, I don't think you ever stop loving someone, nor should you, but there comes a time when you know you have to get on with your own life.'

'When did that happen, Tom?'

'It started when you came to Bilsden and pulled me out of my misery. Why did you come, if you didn't care for me?'

'I didn't say I didn't care.' Now she was twisting the bogus wedding ring she wore, avoiding his eyes.

He thumped the overstuffed seat of the sofa, frustration spilling out in a rush of words. 'Then what the hell is all this about? What can there possibly be to stop us?' Before she could prevent him, he had jumped up and pulled her to her feet. 'Oh, Rosie!' But as he bent to kiss her, she twisted her head away from him and the kiss landed on her cheek.

She held him off with one small firm hand. 'Sit down, Tom! I want to talk, not kiss.' Which was a downright lie, because she wanted very much for him to kiss her properly, ached for it each night after he'd left her. But she wasn't going to admit that. And she knew if she let him kiss

305

her properly, even once, then her common sense would evaporate. There had only ever been Tom Gibson for her.

He flung himself on the sofa again. 'Bloody well talk, then! Tell me what's to stop us?'

'Albert.'

'What?'

'How are we going to explain Albert? He looks just like you. People in Bilsden will soon guess that he's your son. And that'll not only hurt him, but it'll hurt your other children, too.'

He hadn't really thought about Albert, beyond a vague hope that she would leave the boy in London, as she did now when she went on tour. But that was until he'd come here tonight and seen the fondness between her and the lad, before he'd seen yet again what a fine young fellow Albert was. The thought came unbidden into his mind: *the sort of lad any father would be proud of.* No, Rosie would never desert her son and that he could never ask her to do. And she was right about one thing. It would hurt all the children to have folk gossiping about Albert. But there had to be some way around that. There just had to!

'And there's my career, as well,' she said, when the silence had gone on for too long.

Now *that* he could answer. 'You won't need to earn your own living if you marry me. I'm well-heeled now, Rosie. I can support you in style.'

She bounced to her feet and stood facing him, hands on hips. 'Oh, can you? And you think that I'll just give it all up and stay home to do your housework?' Her refined accent slipped a little as anger took over. 'Well, you can bloody well think again, Tom Gibson. I've made a name for myself, and I like that. I love singing and I love earning my own money and I love being known. Do you really think I'm going to give it up and stay shut up in a house all day? Do you think I want to ask you for everything I need? I didn't realise you were quite so stupid.'

She strode across to the sideboard and filled her glass again, sloshing the fine cognac all over the polished surface in her agitation. 'Do you want another drink?'

He walked across to join her. 'I think I need one. But first – ' He set his empty glass down, took her glass out of her hand and pulled her into his arms, kissing her hungrily. And this time she didn't protest or try to push him away. This time she kissed him back with a hunger to match his own.

When his grip slackened, she leaned back into the cradle of his arms, looked at him and sighed. 'Oh, Tom, what a mess it all is!'

He didn't pretend there were no problems. 'We'll work something out.'

'Hah! You believe in miracles now, do you?' She pushed him away, picked up her glass, looked at the brandy in it and gave a snort of disgust. 'I don't know why I poured this. I don't really want it. I never have more than one glass.' She set it down and looked at him. 'I'm tired, Tom. I need to think. I was all set to refuse you. I should have stopped this before it started. I knew we should never have got together again.'

'But Rosie—'

'Go back to your hotel, love. I'll be busy tomorrow. I've got a concert in the evening. How long are you staying in London?'

'As long as it takes to sort this out.'

She just shook her head and rang the bell. 'Show Mr Gibson out, will you, please, Jenny?'

And he went, because he needed time to think, too, time to find a way to persuade her. There had to be a way, there just had to. He'd lost Marianne. Now that he'd found Rosie again, he wasn't going to lose her as well.

The next morning, since Annie, Rebecca and Tom were all early risers, they breakfasted before anyone else had even entered the hotel dining room and then went out to take the air. It was a fine day, though the sun had no warmth in it.

Tom hadn't slept much, but he wasn't going to tell his sisters that, and anyway, it was no use sitting alone in his room. His thoughts just kept beating at his skull until his head ached and throbbed. And threading through his thoughts were pictures of Rosie, elegant now in her spreading skirts and smooth, carefully arranged hair, with fine lace around her shoulders, gold in her ears and around her neck. Pictures of Rosie years ago mingled with them, not at all elegant then, with work-roughened hands and her long dark hair tumbling about her shoulders as she threw back her head and laughed. He didn't know which Rosie he loved most, or even if the old Rosie still existed.

Annie, Tom and Rebecca were soon walking along the gentle curve of Regent Street. It was not a fashionable time for shopping, of course, and employees were still washing down the shop windows and dusting the stock inside them. An old woman was sweeping up the rubbish in the gutter and putting it carefully into a sack which she dragged along the ground with hands twisted by age. Occasionally she'd look furtively around and slip something into the pocket of her sacking apron.

Maids hurried past them with hatboxes or shopping baskets. Errand boys ran along the pavements, and a couple of them had stopped for a minute behind a dray delivering goods to chat to one another, their eyes wary and alert, in case they were seen committing the crime of loitering. Horses clopped slowly along the street, wheels rumbled gently, without any sense of urgency, and two gentlemen on horseback cantered along, weaving in and out of the traffic, looking proud and disdainful, as if they owned the whole world.

'Why does it always seem to be sunny in London?' Rebecca wondered aloud.

'It rains here just as often as it rains anywhere else,' said

Tom, who was somewhat curt this morning.

'Well, it's not raining today.'

'It's cold enough,' he muttered. 'And it was raining yesterday.'

'The place changes every time I come here,' said Annie, wondering what Rosie had said last night to put Tom in such a bad mood. 'I think this street looked better with the colonnades, though. I can't understand why they pulled them down.'

'To make it look more modern, I suppose,' said Tom, squinting at the façades.

'Frederick would hate it now.'

Annie stopped to look at the windows of the Argyll Mourning Warehouse, opened only a few years previously. 'You know, we really ought to expand the mourning section of the Emporium, Tom. Not just clothes, but black-edged notepaper and little black-bound prayer books and things. Just look at all the things in those windows. We should come back here and make a list. There's Jay's General Mourning Warehouse just across the road, too.'

'And another place further down,' put in Rebecca. 'So there must be a lot of money to be made from mourning.'

Tom said nothing. His expression was so bleak that Annie put one hand on his arm. 'Does it bring it all back to you?' she asked gently.

In fact, a lad who had just run by had reminded him of young Albert. 'What? Oh, no. No, I'm over Marianne now. I was thinking about something else, I'm afraid. My mind was just wandering.'

They walked on. 'They're still selling lots of tartans,' said Annie, looking into another window. 'Amazing, isn't it? I thought that fad would have died by now.'

'With Her Majesty so devoted to Scotland?' scoffed Tom. 'No, we've even got tartan rugs in the Emporium and tartan cushions, as well as tartan travelling blankets. I wouldn't have a tartan rug in my house, personally, but some folk like to imitate the Queen.'

'I doubt she's got tartan rugs, either,' said Annie, pulling a face at the mere idea.

After they had walked slowly up and down the street, Annie looked at the time and suggested they return to the hotel. 'I arranged for notes to be taken to the artists on Helen's list, asking if they were free to accept a commission and could spare me a little time to discuss it. And for the messenger to wait for a reply.'

But back at the hotel, both replies regretted that the artists in question had as much work as they could cope with at present.

'We'll go out to that gallery Helen told me about, then,' Annie decided.

But once more, fate was against them. The owner of the gallery was not there that day, and the assistant seemed to know only about the pictures that were on sale. When he found they were not interested in making a purchase, he became even more unhelpful. 'We'll come back tomorrow,' said Annie and led the way out.

Rebecca had to nudge Tom to follow them, because he was standing in front of a seascape, lost in his own thoughts again.

'What's the matter with him today?' she whispered to Annie.

'I don't know, but I intend to find out. He looks like he's just lost a guinea and found a threepenny bit.' Struck by a sudden idea, she stopped dead. 'Look, Frederick wants me to call on Mildred. Let's go and get it over with today, then we can enjoy the rest of our holiday.' For she was enjoying it, to her own surprise, in spite of the setbacks. She was not made for a quiet life.

'You don't need me for that,' said Tom.

'Oh, yes, we do.' Annie grabbed his arm. 'You're not getting out of it.'

He groaned.

'I haven't called on her before,' said Rebecca. 'What's so bad about it?'

Annie chuckled. 'Wait till you see her house. You'll soon understand.' And she refused to tell Rebecca any more.

A skinny little maid showed them into the comfortable parlour of the Jemmings' commodious double-fronted villa and Mildred rose to greet them. In the past couple of years she had gone from plump to fat, and she looked older than her step-mother. 'My dear Annie! How delightful to see you. *Do* sit down. I didn't know you and Papa were coming to town.'

'Your father's still at home.' Annie did not enlarge upon that, and in any case, her hostess was rushing to fill the silence with a babble of words.

'Well, I'm still delighted to see you, of course. Mr Gibson and Miss Gibson, too. Goodness, it's quite a family outing, isn't it? But then, families should stick together, don't you think? And whatever Papa says, I shall *not* refuse to receive Beatrice.'

'Have you found her, then?'

Mildred beamed at them. 'Yes, indeed. Though it was she who came to us.' She lowered her voice. 'I'm afraid she and Reginald are no longer living together. He's gone abroad. But she's taken rooms nearby and I see her quite often. She *is* my only sister, after all.'

Annie made a non-committal noise in her throat, which seemed to suffice. Mildred continued to talk at them, flitting from one subject to another, but thank goodness, not referring to Beatrice again. 'And how are your younger children, Annie? Dear William came to see us once or twice when he was in London. Not as often as I would have liked, of course. Such a tall young man he is, now. Quite dominates a room.'

Looking around her, Annie hid a smile as she wondered how William had managed to thread his way through so many tables, chairs and footstools without tripping up or knocking something over.

They spent half an hour with Mildred, during which Rebecca watched in amazement as her hostess handed out tea and small cakes without pausing for more than a quick breath and without really listening to their answers to her questions. Rebecca also found time to stare round at the fussy room, with its wallpaper patterned in lozenge shapes, its striped curtains, and the myriad pictures and ornaments. Every surface was so laden with bric-à-brac that you wondered where it all came from.

When another caller turned up and allowed them to escape, they were all relieved.

'Goodness!' Annie said when they were sitting in a cab, driving back to the hotel. 'I've never seen her so – so—'

'Garrulous!' Tom finished. 'And how I kept quiet when she went on about that damned sister of hers, I don't know. If I ever see Madam Beatrice again, I shall be strongly tempted to wring her spiteful neck.' After that, he slumped down in the corner of the hackney cab and left his sisters to chat.

Back at the hotel, he said abruptly, 'I think I'll go and have a lie down.' He looked bowed down with worries.

Annie exchanged glances with Rebecca and they both took hold of his arms and dragged him into her sitting room. 'All right, Tom Gibson. You're not going back to your room until you tell us what the matter is with you today.'

'Nothing. I've just got a bit of a headache.'

'You don't get headaches.'

'Well, I have today. It must be the London air.'

'You might as well tell me, because I won't let you go until you do.' Annie frowned at him. 'Did Rosie turn you down?'

'Mind your own business!' He turned to leave, but Annie grabbed his arm.

'Tom?'

He shook his head, pushed her away roughly and strode out of the room.

Annie exchanged glances with Rebecca. 'She *must* have turned him down.'

312

'I wonder why?'

'Perhaps she doesn't love him like she used to.'

'If that's the case, why has she been allowing him to call on her? He's been to London a few times now,' Rebecca pointed out. To which Annie could offer no answer.

Later in the afternoon, Annie and Rebecca took a cab to Gunter's in Berkeley Square, to take tea with Simon Darrington. If Tom was still in his room, he wasn't answering their knocks.

Simon, who was already sitting waiting in a corner of the café, came striding across to greet them. 'How lovely to see you both! Do come and sit down. Can I persuade you to try one of Gunter's famous fruit ices?'

Annie shivered at the thought, for the sun had gone in and it was starting to look like rain. 'I'd rather have a warm drink, if you don't mind. Ices are for the summer, so far as I'm concerned.'

'Hot chocolate, then?'

'Lovely.'

Rebecca was looking around her with great interest. Although the London Season had not yet begun, there was a sprinkling of well-dressed customers, talking quietly in the drawling accents she had noticed before among the upper classes in London. 'I'd like an ice cream,' she said, remembering the Great Exhibition. 'I've heard that they make wonderful fruit ices here.' She could feel Simon's gaze upon her. His eyes showed admiration and perhaps something warmer. She flushed slightly and looked away from him.

Annie watched the pair of them with interest. I'll have to warn him off, she decided. I'm not having him fooling around with my sister. And I'll have to do something about Tom, too. He's got that unhappy look on his face again.

'How is your quest for a portrait painter going?' Simon asked Annie, realising that he was neglecting one of his guests.

She explained that the two painters Helen had

313

recommended were both fully occupied.

'Well, I've got one or two names from my mother, and I know a few other people who may have some ideas. I'd enjoy helping you to find someone.'

Annie was torn between not wanting to throw her sister and Simon together, and wanting to carry out Frederick's wishes. Her husband's need won. 'I'd be most grateful for your help. Frederick has got an absolute obsession about this and with his health as it is . . .' She did not need to finish the sentence.

'Then I shall put myself at your disposal for the next few days. Let me pick you up tomorrow – Mr Gibson, too, if he'd like to join us – and escort you to see the artists my mother's told me about.'

'Won't your mother need her carriage?'

'It's my carriage, actually, and she has friends who can take her around while I'm here.'

'You must have business of your own to attend to,' Rebecca protested, not wanting to spend several days in close company with him.

He smiled at her. 'I've been in London for a few days now and have sorted out most of the things that brought me here.'

Rebecca found herself smiling back before she knew what she was doing.

'And if you're doing nothing tonight, I thought you might like to accompany me to a concert. I have spare tickets and Rosa Lidoni is singing.'

Annie threw a doubtful glance at Rebecca, but she could not go without her sister, and she would definitely like to see what sort of a singer Rosie had turned into.

'There's a ticket for Mr Gibson, too, if he's free,' Simon added.

'I'll ask him.'

'Good. We'll have supper together afterwards.'

They found Tom back at the hotel, sitting in the lobby,

staring glumly out at the weather, for it had started to rain now. 'Who says it's always sunny in London?' he growled by way of a greeting.

Rebecca just shrugged. 'I think I'll go up and change.'

Annie nodded. 'I'll join you in a minute.' She turned to Tom. 'Are you busy tonight?'

He shook his head, scowling. 'I've been trying to get tickets for Rosie's concert, but it's sold out.'

'Well, Simon Darrington has got some tickets and he's invited us all to join him.'

'Oh.'

'Don't you want to go?'

'Of course I do. But I don't want to be obligated to a Darrington.'

'I can't believe you're still holding a grudge against him. Tom, he's nothing like his brother.'

'He's still a Darrington.'

She shook her head. 'Then I'll give him your apologies and say you have another engagement. I presume you won't object to that!' She turned and walked away. As if she hadn't enough on her plate, without Simon's obvious attraction to her sister, now she had to cope with Tom's surly behaviour! It had been a dreadful day. No luck with artists, the visit to Mildred . . . Did no one ever think of *her* feelings?

22

London: Concerts and Galleries

*E*very seat was taken in the small exclusive hall. Simon apologised for the fact that he'd only been able to obtain seats at the rear, but once the music started, that did not matter, for Rosie's voice carried perfectly across the hushed audience.

Annie sat there amazed. She had not expected Rosie Liddelow to change this much. The woman on the stage was elegant, confident, and her voice was like something out of a dream. Annie herself wasn't very musical, and would never normally have bothered to go to a concert, but you could not help but enjoy singing like this. It washed over you like a warm caress.

Beside her sat Rebecca, her eyes like stars, thoroughly enjoying the evening. She looked lovely in her pink silk, but it was the sheer joy emanating from her which drew men's eyes. Rebecca always enjoyed her trips to London, and this one was very special, in spite of Simon Darrington's presence. Annie frowned. Or perhaps because of it?

She could not help noticing that he spent more time watching Rebecca than he did watching Rosie. Tom, who had changed his mind about joining them that evening, had eyes for nothing but the singer. Annie felt suddenly very alone. No one to exchange glances and smiles with. Which only made her hold up her head more proudly.

The music brought tears to Tom's eyes and left him feeling somehow relaxed and refreshed. His expression was lighter as the concert ended, for the sight of Rosie had only reaffirmed his intentions. He *would* find a way to get what he wanted. He always did. Especially when it was something so very important.

'I can't believe how much she's changed,' Rebecca breathed after the applause had died down.

'I gather that you all know her?' Simon asked.

Tom was still lost in his own thoughts, so Annie answered. 'We all grew up together in the Rows, and Rosie got her first singing job in Tom's music room at The Shepherd's Rest. I personally owe her more than I can ever repay. When my son collapsed in town, ill, she was the one who recognised him and sent him home in a cab.' Without Rosie's prompt action, William might have died on that dreadful day when he had run away after Mabel told him who his real father was. Annie had never had a chance to thank her personally for that.

Simon smiled, with the air of one planning a treat. 'Then you'll be pleased to know that I've arranged for us to go backstage and meet her.' He was a little puzzled by the silence that greeted his words.

'That would be delightful,' Annie said, seeing that Tom was just scowling down at the ground and Rebecca was looking at him in concern. 'You've rather taken us by surprise. I didn't realise one could – er – do that.'

Too well-bred to ask about the undercurrents of emotion that were more than obvious, Simon offered Annie his arm and led the way across to the side of the stage, where the gentleman who had introduced Miss Lidoni to the audience was waiting for them.

When Stephen saw Tom among the group, his expression changed to dismay and hostility for a moment, then he pulled himself together and managed a tight smile. 'She'll see you for a few minutes only. The concerts are very tiring.'

Simon smiled. 'We won't keep her. But we'd love to tell her how much we enjoyed her singing. And my friends actually know her. They grew up together. Thank you for arranging this, Stephen, old fellow.'

'My pleasure, Simon.' But his expression said otherwise.

Rosie was waiting for them in her dressing room. When she saw Tom she let her surprise show for a minute, then pulled herself together.

'It was beautiful music, Miss Lidoni,' said Simon. 'Your voice is a gift. It's wonderful that you're willing to share it with us.'

Rosie gave him her cool professional smile, but her eyes kept sliding sideways towards Tom. He was looking downright miserable, the poor sod. Oh, hell! And she was feeling the same. Albert had been on at her today to invite Mr Gibson round again. He was much taken with Tom and had talked about him non-stop, right till the moment Rosie had claimed the need to lie down and rest before the concert.

Annie stepped into the breach. 'I've never managed to thank you personally, Miss – er – Lidoni.'

'My name's Rosie to old friends. And what have you to thank me for?'

'Rosie, then. And my name's Annie. I've wanted for a long time to thank you personally for sending my son home from The Shepherd's Rest when he was ill all those years ago. Dr Lewis said that without your prompt action that night, William might well have died.'

Rosie pulled a face. 'I only did what anyone would have done when they found a sick child.' She looked sideways at Rebecca, frowning as if she half-recognised her.

Tom stepped forward. 'This is my sister, Rebecca.'

'Heavens, love, you're making me feel old.' Rosie offered her hand to Rebecca. 'I remember you as a scrawny child.'

Everyone laughed and then, as Stephen looked meaningfully from the visitors to his watch, Simon said, 'Well, we promised not to keep you, Miss Lidoni, so we'll take our leave. Unless you'd like to join us for supper?'

Rosie looked at Tom. 'I don't think – oh, why not? It's not every day that you meet old friends like this.'

Stephen looked even more disapproving at that, but he said nothing.

When they squashed themselves into the Darrington carriage, Tom managed to sit beside Rosie and take hold of her hand beneath the ballooning folds of her skirt. 'I'm not taking no for an answer,' he said in a low voice. 'I'm not!'

She shook her head, but did not pull her hand away.

For the rest of the evening, Tom stayed by her side and although the two of them conversed with their companions, it was quite plain that their attention was mainly on one another.

As Annie was getting ready for bed, she stood there with a froth of frilled, lace-edged petticoat in one hand. 'I really enjoyed my outing,' she whispered, and a surge of guilt washed through her. She shouldn't be enjoying herself like this when her husband was trapped at home, not well enough to take her out to concerts himself.

Slowly she continued to undress, placing the clothes automatically into a tidy pile and leaving the cage crinoline to settle into a flat pattern of concentric wire circles and tapes in one corner. She climbed into the bed, and as she sank into the feather mattress, reached out without thinking as if to touch her husband. 'Oh, Frederick!' she sighed. 'If only you were here, too.'

What made her most guilty of all was that she didn't feel sorry she'd come. Frederick's illness tied her down so much. He was right, as he usually was. She had needed a break. Not a long one, of course, but a short break. Her life had been very circumscribed lately.

The following morning, the Darrington carriage arrived at the hotel at ten o'clock to take the ladies to the picture gallery again. Tom, of course, had arranged to see Rosie, so Annie and Rebecca were glad of Simon's company. People were not nearly so helpful to unescorted ladies as they were to gentlemen. It infuriated Annie sometimes, but there was nothing she could do about it. That was how things were.

The owner of the gallery, a Mr Sendling, was there this time and when he realised that one of the party at least was a member of the nobility, bestowed a flattering amount of attention upon them. But he was not of much help to them otherwise, and tried to sell them a painting or two rather than help them to find an artist.

In the end, Simon had to make it very plain that not only would he be offended if Mr Sendling did not give them the benefit of his advice, but that he would make sure his mother passed on word of this displeasure to her friends. Only then did Mr Sendling condescend to tell them about a young painter he knew of. 'It is just possible that the young man in question may be free to undertake your commission.' He looked down his nose as he added, 'His name is Tian Gilchrist, I believe, but he is not yet well established as a portrait artist. I don't think Correnaud should have put on a solo exhibition for him yet. It will give him ideas, make him fractious. Mature artists are so much more reliable.'

Simon frowned. Was Sendling recommending this young man or not? 'You don't like Mr Gilchrist's work?'

Sendling shrugged. 'It's quite good. His flesh tones are particularly realistic. But I don't always approve of his compositions. It's Mr Gilchrist's attitude I mistrust most of all, though. His manners are not, shall we say, very polished. He must learn to deal with the nobility, if he is to *take.*' Mr Sendling leaned closer. 'The young gentleman is Irish, too. Very Irish. And he hasn't even tried submitting one of his paintings to the Academy.'

'Then why is Correnaud putting on an exhibition?'

'Well, Correnaud likes his work, and Gilchrist is *beginning* to make a name for himself. But he may not suit

321

you. He paints portraits which are rather too honest, if I am to be frank. People generally prefer portraits to show them at their best. And his backgrounds are . . .' again a delicate wrinkling of the nose betrayed Mr Sendling's distaste '– unusual. As I said, he needs to learn to follow his clients' wishes.'

They left the gallery and went on to visit the two painters Lady Darrington had named, both of whom would have been delighted to oblige Mrs Hallam had the commission allowed them to remain in London. But no, with great regret, they just could not take the time to go to Lancashire. The way they said it, Manchester might have been the North Pole, and the people who lived there savages. While as for Bilsden, they seemed to doubt that such a place was part of civilisation.

'So we'd better try this Gilchrist,' Annie decided as they said farewell to Simon outside the hotel. 'Later this afternoon, perhaps, if that's convenient to you? Where did you say the gallery was?'

'In Pearsby Street.'

'Is that far?'

'No.' Simon frowned. 'And tonight I'll see if my mother can come up with some other names.' It was proving more difficult than he had expected to find a portrait painter for Frederick Hallam.

Neither of them noticed the woman standing just inside the hotel doorway, as if waiting for someone, a woman dressed in heavy black mourning apparel, a woman whose eyes glittered with hatred beneath the thick veil that covered her face. But the woman noticed them, or rather, she noticed Annie, and when she overheard their plans, a hiss of satisfaction left her lips. 'Yes,' she muttered, 'this might be just the opportunity to make sure you pay for what you've done to me, you bitch. But it'll need better planning than last time.'

When one of the waiters came to see if he could help her, she dabbed a handkerchief to her eyes, murmured something about 'Must have mistaken . . .' then turned and walked away slowly. When she was out of sight of the hotel, her footsteps speeded up and she began to talk to herself, oblivious to people's stares.

Later that day, Annie and Rebecca got ready to go out again. Tom had not yet returned, so presumably was spending the whole day with Rosie.

'Do you think she'll take him?' Rebecca asked as she and Annie were putting the finishing touches to each other's hair in Annie's room.

'I don't know. She's made a good life for herself here. She might not want to return to Bilsden.'

'I think Tom will find some way to persuade her.'

Annie nodded. 'I hope so.' But her thoughts were more on the failure of the morning's outing. She was starting to worry. What was she to do if she couldn't find a painter? A good painter. Frederick was utterly determined to have a portrait painted and she was just as determined that he should not be disappointed.

There was a knock on the door and a chambermaid informed them that Lord Darrington had arrived and was waiting for them downstairs.

'Come on,' said Annie. Then she grinned. 'Let's go and look at some paintings, for a change.'

Rebecca smiled. 'I'm enjoying myself, actually. Aren't you? It's all so different from Bilsden.' She clamped her lips shut as she nearly added how bored she sometimes got in the quiet times at the salon. She did not want Annie to find that out, because it would seem so ungrateful, after all her sister had done. But for twelve years, Rebecca had been shut inside that building on High Street and she was beginning to feel like a change. Sometimes, she felt as if she had not had a childhood at all, as if she'd always been either caring for her little brothers and sisters, for her mother, or working for Annie. That was why she enjoyed walking on the moors so much, or coming to London.

Annie shrugged. 'I'm enjoying myself in a way, yes, but I'm missing Frederick, too. And I'm getting a little worried about him. I'd expected to receive a letter from him today.' It was one of the reasons she'd insisted on coming back to the hotel for a rest.

Mr Gilchrist's exhibition was in a less fashionable part of town, though Annie did not bother to ask Simon exactly where they were, since he and Rebecca were deep in lively discussion about a book they had both read. Annie just sat looking out of the carriage window as grey street followed grey street. It wasn't raining today, but it wasn't sunny, either, and things looked dull, somehow.

Everywhere there were carriages and carts and crowds of people. She'd definitely not want to live in a big city. Bilsden suited her much better. She didn't know why Rebecca enjoyed coming to London so much. Annie looked sideways at her sister, whose whole face was animated. Goodness, Rebecca had become very pretty lately! They would have to make sure she met some suitable young men, whatever she said about not wanting Annie to try to arrange anything. Rebecca mustn't waste all her life in the salon, however well she performed her role there.

When they pulled up, they were in a respectable area, but it was not as fashionable as Regent Street. The people were less well-dressed, the shops smaller, even the carriages seemed less glossy. And there was a big hole in the road in front of the gallery, with a group of workmen digging it deeper.

Their driver rapped on the little window in the roof and opened it to call, 'I'm afraid I can't get any closer, M'Lord.'

'Yes, I can see that. They must be digging up the road to put in a new gas main.' Simon peered through the carriage window at the hole. 'Do you think we should come back another day, ladies? You're going to get your shoes and hems dirty walking through this.' His step-mother would not even have set foot outside the carriage in a muddy place like this.

But Annie and Rebecca both laughed at the idea that a little dirt would put them off, so he helped them out. 'Mind how you tread!' He frowned. The workmen seemed very careless with their tools, which were just lying around anyhow, and there was no barrier along the edge of the hole to prevent people falling into it after dark.

They all three stopped to look at the gallery. It was clear that the place had previously been a shop, and might become one again if the owner did not succeed in attracting the right sort of clientele. The smell of new paint inside could not be disguised, but a sweep of vivid orange material draped from ceiling to floor, with a huge urn at its foot containing a particularly lush fern, lent distinction to the entrance. Clever, that, thought Annie. We could do something like that at the salon. I must mention it to Rebecca later.

A gentleman who introduced himself as Miles Correnaud came hurrying forward to greet them and urge catalogues and price lists upon them, then moved away to flourish greetings and catalogues at another, larger group, who had followed them into the gallery.

Annie did not know what drew her eyes to the rear of the shop. Another gentleman was leaning against the wall, watching them. No, he was watching *her*. In fact, he was staring at her so openly that she was not sure whether 'gentleman' was the correct term for him. It was not polite to stare at a lady like that.

He smiled slightly as he saw her notice him, but still he continued to stare and this annoyed her, so she glared at him. He was making no pretence of even looking at the paintings, just lounging around in a corner. And what was someone like him doing in a gallery, anyway? He looked tall, not quite so tall as Frederick perhaps, but not far off six foot, and he had a very fresh complexion. He looked as if he should be outdoors, striding over the meadows or through some woods, anywhere but in a picture gallery.

She looked away and followed Simon and Rebecca to

the first painting. When she glanced towards the rear of the long room again, a couple of minutes later, the fellow was *still* staring at her. Even from here, she could see how bright a blue his eyes were and how rich a chestnut his hair. He inclined his head in a sort of nod, acknowledging her presence, and she turned her eyes away from him determinedly.

The other group of people walked past them, barely pausing at each painting and making scornful remarks about the choice of subject matter or the background. It seemed to be her day to encounter ill-mannered people. She turned back to the first painting again. Remembering Frederick's words, she studied it carefully and nodded in approval. The people in it did indeed look real, not like pretty dolls.

Simon and Rebecca were now discussing the second of the paintings. Annie moved closer to them and stared at it. An old woman sitting at a cottage door, dressed in her Sunday best, with her work-worn hands lying still in her lap. You almost expected her to get up and step out of the frame to bob a curtsey at you.

Making more loud scornful remarks, the other group began to move back up the gallery again.

Well, thought Annie, you lot didn't give the paintings much time. In fact, from what she could see, the two youngest members of the group were more interested in each other than their surroundings and the older ladies were immersed in a confidential conversation, hiding their whispering mouths behind their hands and rolling their eyes at one another expressively at particularly juicy bits of scandal. It was left to the elderly gentleman escorting them, who clearly considered himself something of a connoisseur, to pass judgement, and this he did most scornfully. From time to time the others endorsed his utterances with nods or an occasional 'Yes, indeed', which was all he seemed to need.

Annie was glad when they left, because they seemed to

spoil the whole atmosphere with their patronising ways. She moved slowly from one painting to another, sometimes with Simon and Rebecca, sometimes on her own. Each work featured people so real you could almost feel you'd met them somewhere, or were going to meet them one day. The backgrounds were well painted, and seemed somehow to reflect the people's characters or even to add to them. Annie couldn't have said why she felt that, but she did. She began to feel more hopeful. Perhaps they had found what they were looking for. But would the artist come to Bilsden to do the painting?

As they moved down the long narrow room towards the windows at the rear, the observer remained where he was, watching them, not even pretending to do anything else.

'I've a good mind to give that fellow a piece of my mind,' Simon muttered after a while. 'Who does he think he is, staring at us like that?'

'He's not staring at us,' Rebecca said thoughtfully. 'He's staring at you, Annie.'

'Is he annoying you, Mrs Hallam?' Simon asked.

'What? Oh, no. Don't pay any attention to him.'

Mr Correnaud came bustling up to them again. 'I hope you're enjoying our little exhibition.'

Simon nodded. 'Very much. This Gilchrist is a talented artist.'

Correnaud beamed at him. 'You're right. Very talented. I'm sure he's going to be famous one day. Buying a Gilchrist painting now is as much an investment as an art purchase.'

He and Simon promptly became involved in a discussion about whether art should be regarded as a commercial investment, Rebecca drifted away to look at another painting which had caught her eye and Annie found herself at the end of the room, face to face with the stranger. She drew back and would have turned to rejoin her friends, but he moved and deliberately stationed himself between her and them.

'You have the most beautiful hair I've ever seen,' he said, by way of opening a conversation.

She stiffened. 'That, sir, is none of your business!'

He grinned lazily. 'Not at the moment, I agree. But I'd like to make it my business. I'd like very much to paint you, with your hair loose about your shoulders, O bewitching lady.'

An unwelcome suspicion began to creep into her mind, for his voice was lightly burred with an Irish accent. She frowned at him. Surely he couldn't be the artist? Oh, no, she hoped not! He would have heard the other party's rude remarks. And besides, there was something rather disturbing about him. She had been aware of him the whole time she was walking down the room; not just aware of him studying her, but aware of his presence. Even now, she didn't quite know how to respond to him.

'I'm the artist, you know,' he said, confirming her suspicions. His eyes were softly teasing. 'Tian Gilchrist. Very much at your service.'

'We haven't been properly introduced!' she said coldly.

He raised his voice, but didn't take his eyes off her. 'Correnaud!'

The owner broke off in mid-sentence and turned round.

'Come and introduce me to the lady. Then perhaps she'll talk to me.'

Correnaud sighed, looked at Annie's disapproving expression and bobbed his head in a sort of apology to Simon. 'Tian, I told you to mind your manners! Madam, may I present to you the artist who has created all these wonderful paintings. Tian Gilchrist.'

Simon stepped forward and shook the hand Tian had been holding out to Annie, with a quizzical expression on his face, as if challenging her to shake it. 'Pleased to meet you, Gilchrist. I'm Darrington.'

'*Lord* Darrington!' Correnaud said, with a frown which was meant to reinforce his earlier injunctions to the artist to behave himself.

Tian immediately flourished an impudently exaggerated bow. 'I'm vastly honoured by your presence here, Your Lordship.'

Annie could not help chuckling and Tian turned his intense blue gaze back upon her. 'And now may I know the lady's name?'

It was Simon who spoke. 'This is Mrs Hallam, a neighbour of mine in Lancashire, and this is her sister, Miss Rebecca Gibson.'

Annie could not avoid taking Tian's hand then, though she held it for as short a time as was polite. It was too warm, that hand. And it grasped hers far too firmly. Like its owner, it was too impudent! But he was handsome. Goodness, how very handsome he was! The blue eyes were fringed with dark lashes. He had a generous mouth, too, with an attractively crooked twist to one corner when he smiled at her.

'Let me tell you about my paintings, Mrs Hallam.' He offered her his arm. There was nothing he had said which could be objected to and it was a normal courteous gesture for a gentleman to offer his arm to a lady, but she didn't want to take that arm, didn't want to touch him again. She could see Rebecca staring at her, see the puzzlement on Simon's face, and realised that if she didn't accept Mr Gilchrist's arm, it would cause an uncomfortable scene. So she took a deep breath and laid her hand lightly upon it, amazed at her own feelings.

He turned to lead her along the other wall of paintings, and as he talked about them, she forgot to feel uncomfortable and he forgot to flirt. He explained just why he had wanted to paint that person, and gave her details about the subjects' lives, as if he cared about them still.

'You seem to have got to know them all,' she commented.

He stopped and stared at the next painting. 'Yes. I paint a better portrait when I know something about the person. This fine old gentleman is spending his declining years tramping about the Irish countryside. He knows every little animal which creeps along the hedgerows, and every plant, too. In the spring, he picks flowers to sell to the ladies; in the winter he struggles to survive. He came to my house one stormy day to beg for food and shelter. It cost me a week of good meals and a makeshift bed in an outhouse to persuade him to sit for me. And then he wanted to wash and spruce himself up. I had the devil's own job persuading him to stay just as he was. By the end of the week he was getting restless, so I gave him a handful of change and wished him well.'

The next painting was of a little girl, sitting quietly on a stool, dreaming her dreams. It was delicately worked and quite beautiful.

'My youngest sister,' Tian Gilchrist breathed into Annie's ear. 'Sarry.'

Frederick would love that painting, Annie realised suddenly. Indeed, she loved it herself, instantly and unreasonably. 'How much is it?'

Tian shrugged. 'I've promised to leave talk of money to Correnaud.' He stared at her. 'Do you like it, then, Mrs Hallam?'

'Yes. Very much. But I'm buying it for my husband, who was unfortunately too ill to accompany me to London.'

'There is a husband, then?'

She could feel her face softening. 'Oh, yes. There's definitely a husband.'

'Pity!'

The word was spoken so softly that Annie wasn't sure she'd even heard it. As she turned to look at him suspiciously, Gilchrist stepped back to wave at the owner of the gallery. 'The lady likes this painting, Miles.'

Correnaud's face brightened and he came forward, beaming at Annie. 'Then move away and let me talk to her.' When Annie looked surprised, he added, 'Mr Gilchrist is a true artist and would give away his paintings to those who admired them, if I didn't keep him firmly in check.'

'I like them to find good homes with people who appreciate them, not have them bought because they're the right size to fill a gap on a parlour wall.' Gilchrist moved away to stand next to Rebecca, who wanted to ask him about another painting, but his eyes kept wandering back to Annie.

'How much is it?' she prompted, annoyed at how differently Mr Gilchrist was behaving with her sister. Utterly polite and cool. The picture of a gentleman. She dragged her eyes away from the two of them.

'Twenty guineas,' Correnaud said.

Simon came to stand at Annie's side. 'Too much! Far too much. He's an unknown still.'

'But look at the fine detail. And there's the frame as well. A moulded gilt frame like that costs a great deal.'

Annie looked across at Tian and gave way to a sudden mad impulse. 'I'll take it. Twenty guineas is perfectly all right with me.' She raised her voice and added, 'I have a space on my parlour wall that's just the right size for it and the colours will match my curtains.'

Tian threw back his head and laughed. 'Touché!' They might, for that very brief moment, have been all alone in the world. Then it passed, and Annie wondered guiltily if anyone else had noticed the rapport between them. She hoped not. She did not understand why it made her feel guilty, but it did.

She followed Mr Correnaud to a small desk half-hidden behind another piece of draped material and produced her purse. After she had counted out the guineas, she stood back and let Simon deal with the practicalities of arranging transport of the painting to Bilsden. After a moment or two, she and Rebecca began to walk slowly along towards the front door, where Gilchrist was now lounging. He watched them all the way. Well, let him watch! Much good might it do him!

'Are you going to ask him to paint the portrait?' Rebecca whispered.

'I don't know. I find him a little – disturbing.'

Rebecca nodded. 'Yes. I know what you mean. And his eyes have hardly left you from the moment you came in here.'

'He said he wanted to paint my hair,' Annie whispered back. 'What a thing to say to a complete stranger!'

'I suppose artists are a bit different from normal people.'

Annie could not resist asking, 'What was he talking to you about?'

'He was asking about Frederick. I told him how happily you were married, and do you know what he said?' Rebecca's voice was indignant. 'He said, "What a pity!" '

Annie nodded and pressed Rebecca's hand, making a faint shushing noise. She didn't want Gilchrist to overhear them discussing him, didn't want him to think she was interested in him in any way. Though she did wonder how he came to be an artist. He seemed so much more like a country gentleman. You could imagine him striding across the meadows with the wind in his hair, not bending over an easel for hours fiddling with the details of a painting. And how difficult it was to remain cool and calm, with his eyes lingering on her like that.

Simon came up to join them. 'All business concluded now, Annie?'

She knew what he was hinting at. 'For the moment.'

He seemed surprised that she had said nothing about the portrait when this artist was clearly very skilful, but he did not comment, just followed the two ladies to the door.

Annie stopped for a better look at the single painting in the window, which again had a soft drape of material behind it, cream satin this time. She wondered whether this display method was the artist's taste or Correnaud's. It was certainly very effective. This picture showed two little boys playing in the mud of the village pond, with an irate mother, who must just have noticed them, standing staring across the green in horror. Annie's lips curled in amusement just looking at it. She knew exactly what that mother was about to say to her sons.

The workmen had abandoned their digging to congregate down the street around a brazier. Simon was helping Rebecca across the narrow muddy pathway beside the hole in the roadway. He always treated ladies as if they were too fragile to find their own way. This irritated Annie, so she set off following them on her own, trying to conquer her dislike of being on the edge of a hole. She despised her own weakness about heights and usually managed to conceal it from others.

As Simon turned to come back for her, his mouth suddenly opened in shock and he yelled, 'Look out!'

Annie stopped dead, but not in time to prevent a heavy hand from pushing her towards the hole. She could not seem to find her balance, and teetered on the edge, looking down in horror to see a pickaxe with its sharp end pointing upwards, as well as the edge of a spade protruding upwards from a pile of muddy earth. She heard herself crying out, felt herself start to fall. She knew she was going to be speared on the pickaxe. Death was staring her in the face.

23

London: Accidents and Encounters

Everything whirled around Annie as her feet slipped in the mud and she felt herself sliding inexorably towards the edge of the hole, then a hand grabbed her flailing arm and dragged her back towards the pavement. Pain shot through her as her body was twisted round. She had little control over her movements and stumbled to her knees in a muddy mess of skirts and flattened crinoline cage. Her legs were dangling over the edge of the hole and she cried out as she could gain no purchase to pull herself to safety. But that strong hand did not let go and she sobbed in relief as she felt herself being slowly dragged away from the edge, away from the hungry steel gleam of the pickaxe's sharp edge.

As both feet touched solid ground again, she stumbled forward against somebody, clutching at her saviour convulsively, drawing in ragged breaths that threatened to change into sobs. She had been staring down at death, or at the very least serious injury. She still could not believe she was safe. Shuddering and gulping at the air, she continued to cling to her rescuer. All she could think was that she had not fallen down the hole, not been impaled on those sharp edges. She was alive. Her shoulder was hurting, but she was still alive.

Around her there was a babble of voices, and her

rescuer startled her by shouting, 'Keep back! Give her air!'

As people continued to press closer, he muttered a curse and swept her up in his arms, cradling her against his chest and making soothing noises against her hair.

Reaction had set in and she couldn't seem to distinguish the words he was saying, but the sound of his voice was immensely comforting and she huddled even closer to him. She could feel him carrying her, but her eyes were closed and she didn't want to open them, not yet, not until she could control the sobs that still threatened to throw her into hysteria.

Her rescuer climbed some stairs and then laid her down on a sofa. She was still shaking and kept hold of his jacket sleeve. She couldn't seem to think straight. She only knew that she wanted someone to hold her. She had never been so close to death before. When he would have pulled away, she moaned in her throat and clutched at him again.

A hand stroked her hair. A voice ordered someone to, 'Get the brandy! It's over there by the window.' Then the voice came closer again and he sat down, wrapping his arms around her and murmuring, 'It's all right, darlin', it's all right.'

He seemed to know how deep her need was just to be held and she was grateful to him. In the safety of his arms, she began to regain control of herself. Slowly the room came into focus around her and she blinked at it. 'I th-thought I was going to d-die.'

'Well, you didn't. I wouldn't have let you. Don't think about it now. Don't think about it at all. It's over.'

How could she think of anything else? She could still see the sharp steel gleaming in the fitful sunshine, still feel herself powerless to do anything but fall, fall, fall towards it.

He raised her to a sitting position, which hurt dreadfully, and she could not help crying out. He put an arm around her shoulders to support her and held a glass to her lips. His soft voice urged her to drink, so she swallowed obediently, then choked and coughed.

'Only live people can choke like that,' the voice murmured in her ear and it made her utter a sound between a sob and a laugh. She opened her eyes again and looked up, really looked up, at her rescuer. She was in Tian Gilchrist's strong arms. She would have moved away, should have moved away, but her limbs felt as limp as pieces of unspun cotton. A movement at her other side made her turn her head slightly, and she saw Rebecca kneeling by the sofa. But her sister looked blurred and wavery, and the light from the window hurt her eyes, so Annie closed them again.

'I'm sorry,' she muttered. 'I'll be all right in a minute.'

'Take another little sip, Mrs Hallam.'

'I don't l-like brandy.'

Tian chuckled. 'Just one more for me, there's a darlin'.'

The glass was at her lips again, and it was too much trouble to argue, so she did as he asked. This time she let a little of the spirit run into her mouth, and the warmth of it was indeed comforting. She sighed and looked up at him. 'I thought I was going to die.'

'Yes, love, but you didn't.' He handed the glass to Rebecca and pushed Annie gently to arm's length, with one hand on each shoulder. 'How's your shoulder feeling?'

'What?' Annie made an effort to move away from his hands and cried out, suddenly becoming aware that her shoulder was hurting dreadfully. When she tried to move it, someone stabbed fiery knives into her. She looked down at it, feeling stupid. 'Oh.' She moved her arm very cautiously and gave an involuntary mew of pain.

'I'm afraid I twisted your shoulder when I pulled you back from the edge of the hole. I had to catch hold of you quickly, d'you see?'

He was feeling the shoulder now, his big firm hands warm through the material of her jacket, and then suddenly he pressed down. She gasped and bit off a shriek. A red blur of pain danced around her for a moment,

337

but his arms were there again and his soft soothing voice.

'That's my girl. Your shoulder was dislocated. I had to put it back in place. If I'd told you, you'd have tensed up and it'd have hurt more. It'll get better now. A few days and you won't know anything was ever wrong with it.'

The shoulder still hurt, but he continued to massage it very gently and that seemed to help. She just lay there like a doll and let him do what he would, feeling quite safe with him. She closed her eyes for a moment and when she opened them again, the sun was shining through the window, haloing his head, and he was beautiful. The world was beautiful. She was alive.

It took her a minute to realise that he had stopped massaging her shoulder. She looked up at him and tried to smile. 'Thank you for saving me.'

He just stared down at her with his blue, blue eyes and there was puzzlement in them, puzzlement and something else. 'It was a privilege,' he said softly, and reached out to run one fingertip down her cheek.

She blinked at him, then he moved back along the sofa seat and she remembered that they were not alone. But when he stood up, she felt bereft, wanting the comfort, the reassurance, of his touch. Don't be a fool, she told herself. You're safe now. He turned to speak to someone else, but she was still watching him, still feeling the featherlight touch of his fingertip on her cheek.

'Your sister's shoulder should be all right now, Miss Gibson. It'll be a bit sore for a day or two, but that's all. No, I don't think we need to call in a doctor. I've dealt with this sort of thing before at home, with people who'd been thrown from horses, so I knew exactly what to do. Mrs Hallam should sit here quietly for a while and not try to move. I'll go down and get Miles to send out for some tea.'

Rebecca came to kneel in front of Annie and hold one of her hands. 'Are you all right, love?'

Annie nodded. It was a huge effort to say, 'I feel strange, a bit distant, but yes, I'm all right.'

When Tian got to the bottom of the stairs, he saw Simon coming back through the door, frowning. He strode along the gallery to ask quietly, 'Did you find the woman?'

Simon shook his head and he, too, spoke softly. 'No. She escaped. I think she'd paid some urchins to get in my way. A couple of them were extremely unhelpful.'

Tian growled under his breath. 'Whoever she was, that woman pushed Mrs Hallam deliberately. I saw her get ready to do it through the window, but I was too far away to stop her – and then, when I ran outside, I was too busy catching Mrs Hallam to go after her.'

Miles Correnaud came to hover next to them, looking nearly as pale as Annie. 'You saved Mrs Hallam's life, Tian,' he said.

'Yes, you probably did,' Simon agreed, his expression very serious. 'Someone had propped up the pick, you know, so that it couldn't slip sideways when she fell on it. And the spade.'

Tian did not like to think of those sharp pieces of steel piercing Annie Hallam's soft flesh. 'Well, I certainly saved her from injury, but it's a bit of an awesome responsibility, saving a life, isn't it?' he said, trying to make a joke of it, but could not manage even a faint smile. He kept seeing the terror on Annie's face, seeing the sharpness of the steel edges, feeling the way she had trembled and clutched at him afterwards. His usually generous lips were set in two thin straight lines and there were frown lines creasing his forehead. 'I'll just go out and speak to the men myself, I think. I want to see if I can find out anything more.'

Simon shook his head. 'Mr Correnaud and I have already spoken to them. They know nothing.'

Tian grinned. 'I think they might be persuaded to say a little more to me.' The grin widened. 'I'm not a lordship an' if I speak broadly,' his Irish accent suddenly became much more pronounced, 'they might not even think of me as a gentleman at all. Sure, an' didn't I make a sketch of one of them yesterday? And wasn't he tickled pink by it?' He started to stride out of the gallery, then turned to toss a couple of orders at them. 'Don't let her leave yet, Lord Darrington. She's still in shock. Miles, get some tea sent in, will you? And put plenty of sugar in hers.'

Simon nodded agreement and went up the stairs.

Miles bustled off to order in some tea, glad to have something to do. After this incident, he thought gloomily, Mrs Hallam would probably ask for her money back or tell her friends not to visit his gallery. And who could blame her?

By the time Tian Gilchrist came back upstairs, Annie was feeling more herself, but annoyed that she was still so shaky. Rebecca sat on one side of her, patting her hand from time to time, and that helped, but secretly Annie wished she still had Tian's broad chest to lean against. Or that Frederick were here to hold her. Tears rose to her eyes at the thought of her husband.

'You mustn't tell Frederick!' she said suddenly.

'Who's Frederick?' Tian demanded, kneeling down in front of her and reaching up to brush a strand of hair from her forehead.

'My husband.'

'Of course he should be told. He'll want to know.'

Annie shook her head. 'No. No, he shouldn't. He has a weak heart. The shock would be bad for him. I don't want him worried about anything.'

Tian took her hands in his. Without thinking he used her first name, as her sister had, and hurriedly corrected it, though it was hard to think of her except as 'Annie', somehow. 'Annie – Mrs Hallam, your husband *must* be told.' He hesitated, but she had to know, had to realise that she might still be in danger. 'The woman pushed you deliberately. I saw her do it myself. And – I think she was trying to kill you. The workmen swear they didn't leave their tools propped upright like that. They were very sure on that point and I think they were telling the truth. They said somebody must have moved them. There were lads playing around, and some of them deliberately got in Darrington's way when he tried to chase your attacker.'

Annie stared at him in horror. She had assumed that it was just an accident, that the tools had been carelessly left upright and that the woman who had bumped into her had run away in fright, scared at what she had inadvertently done. 'Are you sure?' she whispered.

He nodded. 'Yes. Very sure. So you see, you can't just ignore this. If someone wants you dead, they might try again.'

Memories of another day, a busy street in Manchester and a sudden inexplicable stumble in front of a horse omnibus, suddenly came back to Annie. She drew in a shuddering breath, opened her mouth to tell Tian about it, then changed her mind. If she did, Simon, who was standing nearby, would certainly tell Frederick. And why was she thinking about him as 'Tian'? He was Mr Gilchrist, a stranger, even if he had saved her life.

But Rebecca had been with Annie that day. 'You nearly fell in front of an omnibus in Manchester,' she blurted out before Annie could stop her, clutching Simon Darrington's arm without thinking in the shock of the realisation. 'Someone bumped into you that day, too. And – and it was a woman in mourning that time, as well.' Her eyes were wide with horror. She was unaware that Simon was now holding her hand.

Ice seemed to trickle down Annie's spine and everything went distant again. How could anyone want her dead? You'd have to hate someone with a passion to try to kill them. Did someone really hate her so much? Why? And if they'd tried twice, would they try again? And perhaps succeed this time?

'What happened in Manchester?' Simon prompted.

Rebecca explained in more detail. They'd thought nothing of it at the time, but now . . . When she stopped talking, she realised she was clutching his hand, flushed bright red and let go of it.

Annie just sat frozen in horror, shaking her head in answer to their questions. 'I don't know, I tell you. I can't think of anyone who could possibly—' She was feeling physically sick now. But she was clear on one thing. 'And it makes no difference. I still don't want Frederick told.'

'But he's your husband!' Tian protested. 'It's his duty to protect you. He'll *want* to know.'

'He's also a sick man. He has a weak heart. The shock and worry of it all could kill him. That's more important to me than anything.'

There was silence in the room. Annie could hear the silence as clearly as any noise. Somewhere, a million miles away, a clock was ticking. Somewhere, a million miles beyond that, people were walking and talking in the street, horses were trotting, carriage wheels rumbling. But in the room the silence seemed to creep around them on tiptoe.

'Is Frederick really that ill?' Simon Darrington asked.

Annie nodded. 'I'm afraid so. That's why I've had to come to London for him.'

'I'm sorry. I didn't realise.'

She blinked away a sudden tear. 'No. He doesn't want a fuss made. He wants to carry on as usual.'

Tian was looking puzzled. 'He sent you to London to buy some paintings?' It seemed a strange thing for a sick man to do.

Annie shook her head. 'No, of course not. He sent me to find a good artist. Frederick wants a portrait of our family painted.' She was recovering now and refused to let the tears fall. Tian – Mr Gilchrist – and all of them would think her a weak fool. 'My husband's very set on it.' She looked up at Tian. 'I was going to come back here tomorrow to ask you if you could come to Bilsden and do the portrait for us? We'll pay you well for the inconvenience. Frederick is absolutely set on the idea.'

He was intrigued by that and not a little suspicious. 'Why me?'

'Because I like your paintings. I was going away to think

about it, though. It's not something you decide in a minute.'

'What do you like about them?' He did not intend to accept charity, just because he had saved her from a dreadful accident. Her answer was immediate, and if she was lying, then she was the best actress in the world.

'They seem so real. Frederick said he didn't want any pictures of us looking like pretty dolls, dressed up for the occasion.'

'Well, you certainly won't get that from me. I'm not a fashionable painter,' he warned her.

She shrugged and winced as the shoulder twinged. 'We're not high society people. My husband is a mill-owner. I used to run my own dress salon. But when you have photographs taken, everyone looks so stiff. Frederick doesn't want that.'

'Then I'll come with pleasure.' He had wanted to paint her vivid face and glorious hair from the first moment he set eyes on her.

She looked at him and, once again, they seemed to be all alone in the shabby little room. 'You don't even know what we're offering to pay,' she protested, recovered enough now to disapprove of this unbusinesslike approach.

'It doesn't really matter. I'd like to paint you.' A wry smile creased his lips as he touched a curl that had escaped and was lying on her shoulder. 'Like Mr Titian, I have a weakness for red hair.' He let the curl drop. 'It's the hardest colour to paint, especially as I'd like to paint you, with the sunlight shining on it.'

Simon and Rebecca exchanged glances.

Annie tried to set matters on a less personal footing. 'It's a family portrait we're wanting, not a picture of me.'

Tian smiled. 'I do good family portraits. But you'll have to talk to Miles about the money and the other arrangements. I'm not really interested in that side of things, so long as I have enough to eat and to buy my painting materials.' He stood up and moved away from her, turning to address Simon. 'I think perhaps you should go back to the hotel now, Lord Darrington. Mrs Hallam really ought to rest.'

'Don't talk about me as if I'm too stupid to make my own decisions!' she snapped.

Rebecca beamed at her. That sharp comment showed that Annie really was recovering, even if she did still look pale.

Simon nodded. 'I'll go down and check that the carriage is ready to go.' Unspoken behind his words was the determination to check that there were no suspicious people lurking near the entrance to the little gallery, either.

Tian turned back to Annie. 'Tell me where you're staying and I'll call tomorrow to see how you are.'

She still found his gaze too blue and too direct. 'That won't be necessary.'

'I'll call anyway.'

They locked eyes, and after a moment she told him. After all, she did need to talk to him about the portrait, but most of all, she needed to get his promise not to tell Frederick that someone had tried to kill her.

It seemed a very long journey back to the hotel. Annie's shoulder was hurting now, a dull throbbing pain. She stared down at the mud on her skirt, and when she noticed that her hands had a tendency to shake every time she remembered the accident, clasped them together firmly in her lap. She could feel Rebecca watching her and once she raised her eyes to smile at her sister, though the smile wouldn't stick to her face. 'I'm all right now, really I am.'

'I know,' said Rebecca, in a tone of voice which meant she knew how Annie was really feeling.

'And don't speak to me soothingly!'

When they got inside the hotel, Annie found it an enormous effort to walk up the stairs, and Simon must have noticed, because he came forward and moved to her uninjured side, putting his arm around her. And his touch didn't disturb her in the slightest. Not like Tian Gilchrist's touch had. That, too, annoyed her immensely.

'You will get dinner sent up to your room tonight, Mrs Hallam, won't you?' he said, as they reached the door.

She nodded. She couldn't imagine wanting any food. Then she realised why he was saying that and added tartly, 'Yes, of course. And I'll lock my door, too. I'm not utterly stupid! Or perhaps it'd be better if I hid under the bed?'

Behind her, Rebecca rolled her eyes at Simon and jerked her head to indicate that he should leave. She mouthed the words, 'Wait for me!' and he nodded agreement.

When Rebecca had helped Annie to undress and seen her settled in the bed, with a hot water pig provided by an obliging chambermaid, she locked the door and went back down to the foyer, where, to her relief, Simon was waiting for her. She had forgotten about the impropriety of a young woman's meeting a young man on her own, and if someone had reminded her, would have made a very blunt response. This was too important. Her sister's life might be at stake.

They sat together on a sofa. 'What are we going to do?' she asked immediately.

He shook his head. 'I don't know. Frederick really ought to be told.'

Rebecca shook her head. 'No. Annie's right about that. He's not well. And there's nothing he can do about it, after all. This happened in London, not Bilsden.'

'It happened in Manchester, too,' he reminded her.

She drew in a shaky breath. 'I can't believe it. I can't believe that *anyone* would hate Annie that much. She's such a wonderful person. When my mother died, she took us all in, gave us jobs, taught us so much—' Her voice broke and she felt his hand clasping hers, warm and comforting.

After a moment, she said slowly, 'We needn't tell Frederick the details, but I'll have a word with the

345

housekeeper myself and explain what's happened.' Even if Annie found out and was furious, it was more important to keep her sister safe. 'I'll ask Mrs Jarred to warn the indoor staff to be on the watch for – intruders. And I'll ask Luke to speak to the outdoor staff. He's working part of the time at Ridge House, still. They'll all keep their eyes open. They're very fond of my sister.'

'They might say something to Mr Hallam.'

'We'll just have to risk that.'

He nodded, but reluctantly. If it had been up to him he'd have told Frederick Hallam what had happened the minute they got back.

A lady came into the foyer, paused at the sight of Simon and turned as if to come over to him. Then she saw that he was with a young woman and her mouth opened in surprise. From the way the two of them had their heads together, they were on very good terms and were so immersed in their conversation that they had not noticed her, or anyone else. And he was holding her hand! In public! The lady stared. The young person seemed to be a lady, by her dress at least if not her behaviour. But no young lady of any breeding would meet a young man clandestinely like this.

The onlooker frowned. Who was this person? Certainly no one from polite society, for she knew everyone who was worth knowing. The frown turned into an angry expression. If her own daughter had not been good enough for Simon Darrington, then this unknown female was certainly not to be encouraged. Her very good friend Lavinia Darrington would want to know about this. She left quietly, taking care not to call attention to herself. And she drove straight round to her dear friend's house.

Simon and Rebecca did not even notice her.

When Tom returned to the hotel that afternoon, there was a message from Rebecca waiting for him at the reception desk and another pushed under the door of his room. On no account was he to disturb Annie. He was to see Rebecca immediately he got in, whatever the hour. It was urgent. *Very* (underlined several times) urgent.

This dramatic note was so unlike Rebecca that Tom ran up the stairs and was knocking softly at the door to his sister's room within seconds of reading it.

She opened the door and sighed with relief when she saw who it was. Glancing along the corridor towards Annie's room, she put a finger to her lips and pulled him inside.

'What's the matter?'

She told him what had happened.

He stood gaping at her. 'I can't believe this.'

'Unfortunately, it's true.'

'Our Annie? Who would want *her* dead?'

Rebecca shrugged. 'I don't know. But if it hadn't been for Mr Gilchrist . . .' She could not finish the sentence.

'It's like one of those bloody stupid novels, with wicked counts and castle dungeons!' he declared. His housekeeper, Megan, was much addicted to such reading and had regaled him with the gist of several of the more exciting tales. But that was imaginary stuff. What had happened to Annie was real. 'I can't believe it,' he repeated indignantly.

'I've just *told* you!' Rebecca was beginning to grow irritated. 'It happened. S— Lord Darrington was there. He'll bear me out.'

'If anyone is trying to hurt our Annie, I'll strangle them myself!' he declared.

'*If* you can find out who it is.'

Tom shook his head. His mind seemed to be going round in circles. It was all so shocking. 'But who can it be? I mean, Annie's not the sort to make enemies. The only one who—' He broke off, then said slowly, 'Surely even that spiteful cat Beatrice wouldn't try to murder anyone?'

'Beatrice?' Rebecca stared at him, then shook her head. 'Oh, no, it can't be her. Mildred said Beatrice was living in London now.'

'Well, there you are.'

'Tom, there was an incident in Manchester as well.'

'What?'

Rebecca explained.

He sat there frowning. 'Beatrice could have come up to Manchester . . .'

'And just happened to be there on a day when Annie and I took a sudden fancy to go shopping?' Rebecca asked scornfully.

'I suppose it is a bit improbable.'

'It certainly is.'

And there they had to leave it.

The next morning, Annie looked very wan, but made it plain that she intended to behave normally. 'I've thought what to say to Frederick,' she began over breakfast. 'We'll say that I had a nasty fall, and that Mr Gilchrist saved me from a worse one.' She pulled a face. 'I have a dreadful bruise on my shoulder. I can't hide that, for he'll see it himself.'

'What can I do to help?' asked Tom.

'Take me home,' she said simply. 'I'm worried about Frederick. I haven't received a letter. Something must be wrong.'

'What about a portrait painter? That's why you came to London in the first place.'

'I've found one.' On reflection, she would rather *not* have hired Tian Gilchrist and now regretted her impulsive offer. She had thought about it, and about him, during the long hours of a wakeful night. He was a very disturbing man. She could not deny that there was something, some attraction, that had flared between them. And that was stupid, for she loved Frederick dearly and anyway, she was a few years older than Tian.

She just couldn't understand it. He was the last person she would have chosen to be attracted to. She had found out the hard way that Irishmen were not to be trusted.

They were charming to your face and then they cheated on you behind your back. Hadn't she learned her lesson with Danny Connor?

And she was a happily married woman. She shouldn't be feeling like this about another man. She was quite horrified by the way her body had reacted to Tian Gilchrist. But she'd pondered on that, too, during the night. It had been a long time since she and Frederick had made love. That must be why she'd responded like that. She was a healthy woman. Frederick said it was normal for women to enjoy the marital act, and she'd certainly heard her father and mother, then her father and Emily, enjoying it many times when she lived in Salem Street. So it didn't *mean* anything.

But she did not intend to do anything about her feelings; or even, if she could help it, to let Mr Gilchrist see again how he affected her. She would be calm and cool with him, very cool. She was, after all, about to become his employer. She might have offered him the job of doing the portrait on impulse, but there would be nothing impulsive about her behaviour from now on. Nothing. What mattered most was Frederick.

And as for the idea that someone was trying to kill her – a night's consideration had shown her that it was, it must be, ridiculous. She had no enemies. None at all. It was just an unfortunate coincidence that she had stumbled that time in Manchester, and that when the woman had bumped into her the previous day, the pickaxe had been left lying carelessly upright. Of course the workmen had not admitted they were at fault to Tian. They would have been fools to do so and risk getting themselves into trouble.

'We'll go home tomorrow,' she decided aloud, not realising how pale she was looking or for how long she had been silent. 'And, Tom, if you need to stay here to talk to Rosie, well, Rebecca and I can perfectly well travel home together. We've done that many times before.'

He wanted to stay longer. There was a lot still to be sorted out. A lot! Nothing had really been decided yet. Rosie was still insisting that it was impossible for them to marry, because of Albert. But she would understand if Tom went back earlier than he had intended this time. He was not going to allow his sisters to travel on their own, just in case there really was someone trying to hurt Annie. He would come down to London again in a month or so, and in the meantime, he'd write to Rosie. Every day.

He looked at his sister. 'Don't be silly. Of course I'm going back with you tomorrow.'

Annie looked at him and smiled, a wan wobbly sort of smile. 'Thanks, Tom. And could you see Mr Gilchrist for me today? Perhaps you could go to the gallery to make the business arrangements and tell him I'm all right?' Then Tian needn't come to the hotel.

'Of course.'

She let her head roll back against the chair, sighing. She felt very tired today after her broken night. Her shoulder was still hurting and she could not get the memory of the fall out of her mind. Every time she dozed off, she felt herself slipping into the hole again. And then jerked fully awake to the feel of Tian's strong hands gripping her.

Drat the man! Why did the best portrait painter have to be so young and attractive? Why did all this have to happen to her? Hadn't she got enough problems?

24

Bilsden: Frederick

*T*he next afternoon, Tom set off for the gallery to sort out the business arrangements for his sister, but went first to call on Rosie.

Annie, bored silly by a morning spent lounging around her room, bullied Rebecca into helping her dress her hair properly, for it hurt to raise her injured arm. If they went down to take a pot of tea in the elegant guests' sitting room off the foyer, they could at least watch people coming and going.

'I hate doing nothing!' she fumed, as Rebecca put her shawl around her shoulders and fussed with the frills of lace and ribbon that served her as a cap. Unthinkable to go out in public without something on the head.

'That looks lovely,' Rebecca said. 'But you're still very pale. Are you sure, Annie—'

'Look, I'll go mad if I have to stay in this room for another minute!' snapped Annie. 'And I'll go even madder if you don't stop hovering over me and treating me like a half-witted invalid!'

'Then stop behaving like a half-wit!' Rebecca snapped back. She had had more than enough of Annie's bad temper this morning. 'You know very well that we're only trying to protect you, but first you scolded Tom, and now you're snapping at me.'

'But I'm not *ill*! I'm just tired. And now I've had time to think about it, I don't believe anyone is trying to kill me. It was just a coincidence, that's all.' She snatched up her handkerchief and stuffed it through the slit in her skirt into her hanging pocket, muttering, 'The only good thing about these stupid crinolines is that you've got room for a decent-sized pocket under them. There! I'm ready.' Heavily sarcastic, she added, '*Now* can we go downstairs?'

Rebecca put her own shawl around her shoulders. 'I don't know what's got into you today, Annie Hallam. You're like a – a whole nest of wasps.'

Annie caught sight of her own scowling face in a mirror and that of her sister, who looked equally angry. She took a deep breath, then sighed again. 'Sorry, love.'

Rebecca pulled a face at her in the mirror. 'It's me who should be apologising. I shouldn't be snapping at you, after—'

Annie interrupted hurriedly. If one more person expressed pity for her, she'd scream. 'Do me good to be snapped at. Oh, come on! Let's get out of here.'

Downstairs, Annie sat with a cup of tea at her left hand, because it still hurt to move her right arm. She wasn't drinking the tea, though, just fidgeting with the fringe of her shawl and watching the people around them. And Rebecca was equally silent, for she had her own troubled thoughts.

When Simon Darrington walked into the foyer, Annie was relieved to see him, but Rebecca did not know whether she was glad to see Simon or not. The man at the reception desk pointed towards the sitting room and Simon strode across.

'Oh, heaven help us!' Annie exclaimed. 'He looks angry, too.'

She and Rebecca looked at one another and burst out laughing.

Simon had stopped in the doorway, thinking how beautiful they both were in their own way. But it was

Rebecca who attracted him. He could not, he admitted to himself, have coped with a woman like Annie Hallam. Too forceful, too independent. Not that Rebecca was a clinging vine, but there was something softer about her, something infinitely more appealing, to his mind.

And whatever his step-mother said, Rebecca was perfectly respectable. He and Lady Lavinia had quarrelled bitterly over her this very morning. Someone had told his step-mother that he had been sitting in the hotel holding hands with a 'young female person'. He had been furious that his step-mother was trying to interfere, but it had really made him think when she told him he was leaving himself open to be trapped into marriage by a mere nobody – she hadn't even wanted to know who Rebecca was, had just ordered him to break off the liaison, as if she had the right to tell a thirty-year-old man how to run his life. Why, the last thing Rebecca was doing was trying to trap him into marriage. In fact, she usually tried to avoid him!

He did not want to avoid her, but did he want to go so far as marrying her? He had not really thought that through. He only knew that he enjoyed her company enormously and was physically attracted to her. And that the thought of never seeing her again made him feel cold and very lonely inside. Even lonelier than he usually was at the Hall, where he wandered around the empty rooms sometimes, longing to hear a human voice that was not a deferential servant's.

He had been thinking about the possibility of marriage all morning, ever since his quarrel with his step-mother. Rebecca had once told him there could never be anything between them, and it would certainly be an unequal match. But maybe, just maybe, they could be happy anyway. His step-mother considered that it was his duty to marry money, and would no doubt expect a share of it. But he remembered how unhappy his own parents had been, living almost separate lives, and how much happier his father had been with the second wife whom he had truly wanted to marry, even if she had cared mainly for his position and money.

Simon banished such thoughts as he entered the sitting room. This was not the time for soul-searching. He smiled down at the two women, seated like flowers amid their wide silken skirts. 'Can anyone share the joke?'

It was Annie who enlightened him. 'I've been a bit bad-tempered today.'

'A *bit*!' snorted Rebecca, and they both laughed again.

'Very well, I admit it, a lot bad-tempered. We had just been exchanging a few sharp words, then you came in and you looked angry, too.'

He smiled. 'I was. Until I saw you two laughing.'

Annie gestured to a comfortable chair opposite her. 'Do sit down! And don't you think it's about time you started calling me by my first name? After all, you call my husband Frederick.'

'It's against the rules of polite behaviour to address a married lady to whom one is not related by her first name,' he teased.

Annie blew a soft scornful noise at him. 'I'm not a high society lady, and the more I see of them, the less I'd like to be one, so bother their rules.' She gestured around them, where some very quiet and proper conversations were being pursued. 'This lot look as if they've swallowed a plank, they're so stiff.'

He could not stop himself from chuckling at that, which made people stare at him. And that made him laugh even harder.

'What's been making you angry, Lord Darrington?' Rebecca asked, when he'd calmed down.

'Call him Simon,' Annie corrected. 'And you're Rebecca.'

'Simon, then.' But Rebecca flushed hotly as she said the word. That was how she thought of him secretly, but it still seemed wrong to use his first name in public.

'It was my step-mother who made me angry. As usual.'

He leaned back in his chair and accepted a cup of tea from Rebecca, admiring her firm white hands with their roughened fingertips. He hated soft droopy hands. But he did not go into detail about Lady Darrington's complaints of his improper behaviour with some unknown young woman: 'It's too bad, Simon, it really is. You're Lord Darrington now and should behave accordingly. Keep your fancy pieces for less public places.' It had absolutely enraged him to hear her describe Rebecca as a 'fancy piece'. Rebecca, of all people!

He pulled a wry face and looked at Annie. 'I don't think I fit into high society, either. As my step-mother has just been pointing out.'

'Was that what made you angry?'

'Yes. She has very fixed views of what one should and should not do. I've just been accused of vulgarity.'

'Good. Let's sit here and be vulgar together in our little corner,' said Annie promptly.

'Agreed.'

A little later, Annie looked up just as Tian Gilchrist entered the foyer. *Oh, no!* For a moment, she thought she had spoken the words aloud, then she realised with relief that she had just thought them. She didn't want anyone to realise how much he disturbed her.

Simon and Rebecca, who were arguing animatedly about the gardens of Darrington Hall, which needed just as much attention as the inside of the house, didn't notice him. Rebecca had been helping Luke occasionally lately with his piece of land and had found to her surprise that she, too, enjoyed growing things, especially flowers.

Annie watched Tian nod his thanks to the man at the reception desk, then turn and saunter across towards her, smiling as he caught sight of her. 'Mr Gilchrist.' She held out her hand coolly, the difference between her recent behaviour and her reception of the newcomer so surprising to Rebecca and Simon that they both stared at her.

'My brother must have missed you at the gallery.' She deliberately did not ask him to sit down. 'He went there to discuss business with you on my behalf.'

Tian looked down at her, eyes narrowed, and then those blue eyes began to twinkle, as if he had guessed what she was doing. He took her hand, holding it for a moment too long, then shook hands with the other two and sat down without being invited.

Annie bit her lip. 'Don't you think you'd better go back to the gallery and try to catch my brother?' she asked pointedly.

'No. I never discuss business matters. Miles will do what's necessary. Besides, I came here to see how *you* were.' He put his head on one side and studied her blatantly. 'You're still looking a bit pale.'

Annie glared at him.

'And cross.'

They could all hear Annie's breath hiss at that.

Rebecca hastily intervened. 'Would you like a cup of tea, Mr Gilchrist?'

'I'd love one. I'm a great one for taking cups of tea with friends.' He raised one eyebrow at Annie, as if challenging her to refuse him the tea.

She stared at him for a minute, then looked down at her hands, clenched tightly in her lap.

'Sell any more paintings, old fellow?' Simon asked.

Tian nodded. 'Actually, we did.' Mischief crinkled his face. 'You seem to have brought me luck, Mrs Hallam.'

'I'm glad.' Her voice was chilly.

Rebecca and Simon, puzzled, tried desperately to fill the silences, but everything they said, Tian managed to turn so that he was addressing only Annie. And she replied mainly in monosyllables.

After a few minutes of this, she stood up. 'I think I'll go and have a rest now. I'm – er – feeling tired.'

'Liar!' murmured Tian, for her ears only.

'But you said that your room was driving you mad!'

Rebecca protested. She got to her feet, clearly reluctant to break up the party. 'I'll come up with you.'

'Don't you think I can manage to find the way on my own?' Acid etched Annie's words and made Tian smile even more broadly.

Rebecca's face took on an obstinate expression. 'I'm coming.' She went upstairs, but only stayed long enough to check that Annie was safe in her room and had locked the door behind her, then went down again to rejoin the others. 'My sister,' she said, as she sat down again, 'can be the most infuriating woman on earth.'

'Your sister,' said Tian, 'is one of the most beautiful women on this earth. I shall enjoy painting her. And teasing her.' When he grinned knowingly, Rebecca and Simon exchanged glances. 'I think I'll go now and see if I can catch her brother.' He nodded and sauntered off, leaving them staring after him.

'You don't think he –' began Rebecca, then looked at Simon and flushed. She had been going to say '– is interested in her'. Instead she continued, 'I'd better go.'

'Stay here and talk to me for a while.'

'We've already discussed this. I don't want my reputation damaging.'

He was already pushing a chair behind her so that she had either to sit down or make a fuss. He bent over her. 'We're in a public room in a hotel, Rebecca, not walking tête-à-tête on the moors. Surely there's nothing wrong with that?'

In fact, so far as he was concerned, everything was right about it. Even this short time with her had made him decide that he wanted to get to know her better, much better. Without committing himself to marriage quite yet. Just – get to know her first, see if they really were as well suited as he thought they might be.

And for once, Rebecca, the sensible one of the family, gave way to temptation. She spent a blissful two hours talking quietly to Simon, until Tom came back and interrupted them.

* * *

The next day on the train, Annie, Rebecca and Tom were disinclined to chat, all three wrapped up in their own thoughts. By the time they pulled into Bilsden, Annie was even ready to confess that she was tired.

'Now remember,' she added, 'nothing is to be said that will worry Frederick.'

'Just so long as you tell him you've had an accident.'

'I wouldn't if it weren't for my shoulder,' she muttered. 'I hate people fussing over me.'

The station cab took Rebecca and Annie up to Ridge House, for Rebecca had refused to go home until they had both seen Frederick and she had made sure that Annie told him about her fall, at least. She also intended to see Mrs Jarred at the same time and warn her that someone might be trying to harm her mistress. But she didn't tell her sister that.

To Annie's horror, they saw the doctor just coming out of the gates, battered leather medical bag in hand. Clearly a professional visit.

She pulled on the checkstring and banged on the window. 'Jeremy! Jeremy!' Before the horse had time to stop, she had thrown open the cab door to yell again, 'Jeremy!'

He turned and came to join them. 'Annie! I'm so glad you're back. But you can't have received my letter yet, surely?'

Her heart sank and a chill ran through her. 'What letter? What's wrong?'

He looked up at the cab driver, who was listening with great interest. 'I'll come back up to the house with you.' He swung into the cab.

'You can check Annie's shoulder at the same time,' Rebecca said immediately. 'She had a bad fall in London.'

Annie scowled at her, then, as the horse clopped slowly along the well-raked gravel driveway, she had to ask, 'Is Frederick—' She did not know how to finish her question.

'Frederick's had a small problem, but he's all right.' It hurt Jeremy to see how upset Annie was looking. She was also looking very washed out. It must have been a bad fall indeed to give her that bruised look around the eyes.

When they got inside, Annie brushed off the housekeeper's enquiries about London and led the way into her own parlour, leaving Mrs Jarred standing open-mouthed in the hallway. It was not like the mistress to be so rude.

'Tell me!' Annie commanded, once the door was shut.

'It's not serious, Annie,' Jeremy said. 'A small heart attack. Very small. Frederick is to rest in bed for a few days, and he behaved very sensibly when it happened.'

'I must go up to him.'

'What about your shoulder?'

But she was out of the room, running up the stairs.

Rebecca took the opportunity to explain to Jeremy about the shoulder, and after hesitating, also told him that they suspected someone was trying to hurt Annie. Then she went out to tell Mrs Jarred to be on the watch for possible intruders, leaving that lady gaping after her in disbelief.

While Rebecca was waiting for Annie to come downstairs again, she caught sight of Luke through the window and rushed outside to have a word with him, too, and ask him to tell the other outside staff. After that, feeling she had done all she could, she asked Winnie to summon the carriage to take her and her luggage home. She was, she admitted to herself, exhausted. And she, too, had her worries.

Upstairs, Annie had flung open the door of the bedroom and rushed inside. Frederick, sitting propped up on pillows, opened his arms wide and she flung herself into them.

'What have you been doing with yourself now?' she scolded softly.

'Nothing much.'

She scanned his face, reaching up to brush a strand of hair from his forehead and wincing as her shoulder hurt.

'I might ask the same question. What's the matter with your shoulder, love? I didn't expect you home for another week.'

'I had a fall in London. I hurt my shoulder.'

'Badly? We must ask Jeremy to look at it.'

She was about to refuse, then realised that Jeremy's coming up to see her would prevent too close an enquiry into what had happened. 'He's in the house still,' she admitted. 'I asked him to come back with me.'

'To talk about me or to look at you?' he asked.

'Both, of course.'

Frederick pulled the bell and Jimson was there within a minute. 'Ask Dr Lewis to come back up, would you?'

Jeremy inspected Annie's shoulder, then nodded. 'Whoever it was who put it back knew what he was doing.'

Annie blushed furiously. 'It was an artist. I was just coming out of a gallery when it happened.' She saw Frederick staring in amazement at her red face and heaved a sigh. 'You might as well know that I clung to him like a leech afterwards. I feel embarrassed every time I think of it.'

'Shock.' Jeremy nodded. 'Perfectly natural.'

'Not for me, it isn't!'

Frederick hid a smile. 'You always did hate showing any weakness, Annie girl. Now tell us exactly how it happened.'

She might have known he wouldn't be satisfied unless he knew all the details. 'I was coming out of the art gallery – I've bought you such a beautiful painting, Frederick – and they were digging up the road outside. It was muddy. I slipped.' She hesitated, then saw that her husband was still looking at her suspiciously and let out an angry huff. 'If you must know, there was a pickaxe standing upright in the hole. If I'd fallen on to it—' She shuddered. She'd woken two or three times each night since and relived that moment again. 'Mr Gilchrist, the artist I was telling you about, was standing nearby. He managed to catch me. That's how I hurt my shoulder.'

Jeremy was watching Frederick carefully, but he merely held out his arms to Annie again.

'Then I owe this Mr Gilchrist a great debt.'

She nodded. 'Well, it'll be easy enough to pay him back. He's just starting out as an artist and I've hired him to do our portrait. I was going to anyway. Tom went back to the gallery the next day and made the arrangements for me.' She realised that she had not once asked her brother what exactly he had arranged, and added ruefully, 'I must have been more shocked than I realised, for I haven't even asked Tom when Mr Gilchrist is coming.'

There was a noise at the door and Edgar rushed inside, hotly pursued by Tamsin. Elizabeth stood just outside. It was an unconventional household in many ways, but she did not feel she should go uninvited into her employer's bedroom while he was lying in bed.

'You might as well come in, Elizabeth,' Frederick called. 'Everyone else has and I'm very respectably clad.'

Jeremy had caught Edgar and prevented him from throwing himself at his mother. 'Just a minute, young fellow. Your mother's hurt her shoulder.'

Tamsin and Edgar both gaped at her. They were used to their father's being ill now, but not their mother.

'I had a fall in London,' Annie said. 'I'll be all right in a day or two. It's like when you bruise your knees, love.'

She's holding something back, Frederick decided, watching her. Presumably for my own good. But we'll see about that. He exchanged smiles with Elizabeth as the children bombarded their mother with information about what they'd been doing in her absence and asked her if she'd bought them any presents in London. Hmm. He would have to wait till they were in bed tonight, then he would have it out of her.

But Annie was so tired that night that she was asleep

almost before her head touched the pillow, and by the next morning a problem had arisen, a Gibson family problem, and bad shoulder or not, she went rushing off down the hill to Netherleigh Cottage, in response to a note from her father, to see how she could help.

25

Bilsden: Mark

*T*he trouble had started several days previously. Mark was checking everything, as he usually did, before locking up the chop house for the night, when Nelly came back into the kitchen. She must have been waiting outside until the others left.

He groaned inside himself at the sight of her. His early fascination with her body had soon dissipated and now he was desperately trying to work out how to get rid of her. 'Not tonight, love. I'm tired out.'

'I need to talk to you, Mark.'

He looked at her. She had lost her usual sparkle. In fact, now he came to think of it, she'd been looking peaky for a few days. 'Can't it wait till tomorrow?'

'No. It can't.'

'Very well. Let's go into the eating room.' It was less intimate than his office. He led the way and gestured to a chair. 'Well?'

'No hug, Mark? No kiss?' Her voice was bitter.

'Nelly, I'm tired out. Just tell me what the matter is and let's both get home to our beds. Do you need some money?'

'Not exactly.' She took a deep breath and said, 'I need to tell you that – that I'm expecting a child. *Your* child.'

It was the stuff of his worst nightmares. Black bile rose

363

in his throat and for a moment he wanted to pick her up and strangle her. He forced himself to sit motionless, fists clenched, until the sudden urge had passed. 'How do I know it's mine?'

She scowled at him. 'When would I have had the chance to go with another fellow? When I'm not working here, I'm at home, an' you know what it's like there. The only chance I've had is when you an' me have stayed behind after everyone's gone, for our bit of fun.' She gave a scornful snort of laughter. 'Let alone I don't fancy another fellow, when would my father let me out alone?'

He bowed his head. She was probably right. They only let her go home alone because they thought she was with her cousin. But she had not been a virgin when he took her that time, nothing like, so she must have ways of eluding her own family.

Her voice became coaxing. 'Aw, Mark, don't be like that! You know how much I love you. It's not the end of the world.'

Love! She didn't know the meaning of the word. Love was what Annie felt for Frederick and he for her. Love was what Mark one day hoped to find for himself. All he'd known with Nelly had been lust, and he suspected that lust was all she would ever know.

He raised his head to stare at her, and so calculating was his gaze, so full of scorn and even outright hatred, that her mouth fell open in shock, moist and pink, like a cat's. A cat permanently on heat, this one, though.

He felt sick to his guts, for he saw in her the ruin of all his bright hopes. She hadn't said it yet, but she would in a minute. She would expect him to marry her. And if he did, his whole life would be spoiled. For not only did he not love her in the slightest, but already her ways had begun to irritate him. She wasn't particularly clean. She was so ill-educated and full of stupid prejudices that her shrill chatter grated on his nerves. All her conversation was gossip about the people around her, or talk of the finery she'd like to wear. A month shut up in a house with her and he'd strangle her.

And yet, if it was his child, how could he turn his back on her? He'd been raised to put family first. His father would be horrified if his son refused to marry the mother of his child, however it had been got. Gibsons always looked after their own.

'I'll give you some money, see you and the child right,' he said at last. 'But I'm not marrying you, Nelly.'

Tears sprang into her eyes.

He gritted his teeth and refused to let her obvious pain move him. He could not, would not, marry a woman like her.

'That's not what I want, Mark,' she said in a stifled voice. 'You know how much I love you.'

He shook his head. 'No, you don't, Nelly.' His voice sounded like that of a stranger, even to himself. 'What you love is the money I earn. Well, you can have some of it. I'll look after you properly, provide for you and the child. But I won't marry you.'

She scrambled up and threw herself on him. 'Mark, you don't mean that! My father will kill me if I come home with a big belly and no husband. Mark, please! I'll make you a good wife, never look at another fellow.'

He stood up and pushed her away so violently that she fell. And he didn't move to help her as she lay there on the floor, sobbing, because he didn't even want to touch her now.

'No,' he said, very quietly and firmly. 'I won't marry you, Nelly. Not under any circumstances.'

She got up, then, and wiped her tears away with her sleeve, and when she spoke her voice had lost any trace of softness. 'I'll give you until tomorrow to change your mind, Mr Mark Bloody Gibson. An' then I'll go an' tell your father. *He's* a holy Joe like my father. He won't let his precious son abandon the mother of his grandchild.'

She was right, too. How the hell did she know that?

He didn't let his anxiety show in his face. 'I'm twenty-five, Nelly. My father can't make me marry you. No one can.'

Her face was downright ugly as she spat at him, 'We'll see about that!' and then rushed out of the room, sobbing loudly.

He could only stand there, frozen in horror. He would have to persuade her, pay her off with some of his precious savings. If he gave her enough money, surely, surely she would leave him alone? She was always greedy for money and trinkets. Show her a few guineas, promise her more, regularly, a little house, and she'd stop insisting on marriage. She must.

But as he walked home through the dark streets, he could not persuade himself that Nelly would change her mind. Marriage to him would be like a dream come true to a woman like her. He felt sick inside himself about what had happened. He'd known. Oh, yes, he'd known from the start that no good could come of a relationship with Nelly Burns.

'The Gibson curse,' he said aloud as he turned into Moor Close. They all had it, the men of his family. Well, perhaps not Luke, but his father and Tom certainly did. And lustiness wasn't always a gift from a good fairy. More like a devil's curse, at times.

As he lay wakeful in his bed, listening to Luke's peaceful breathing, he debated whether to ask his Uncle Tom's advice. But then he remembered that Tom was in London. And Frederick Hallam, who might have helped, was not a well man. Should he tell his father himself, then? No. He shuddered at the mere thought. Nelly had been right about that. John Gibson would insist on marriage. He must try to keep it all from his father.

Marriage to Nelly Burns. Again and again, the thought floated through Mark's brain. No, he could not, he just could not, tie himself to her for life. He glared into the darkness. And he wouldn't do it, either, no matter what anyone said.

* * *

The next day Nelly turned up to work as usual and her white angry face followed his every move around the chop house.

'I'd like to speak to you after we close,' he said once, when they were alone together in the passage.

She scanned his face. 'Changed your mind?' Then she shook her head without waiting for his answer. ''Course you 'aven't. A *Gibson* wouldn't want to marry a girl like me, would he?'

Mark flushed. She had read his thoughts exactly.

'Well, you owe me marriage, Mark Gibson, *owe* me. Because that's what decent fellows do when they get a girl into trouble.'

'Decent girls, maybe, not you,' he threw back at her. 'You weren't a virgin when you came to me. You enjoyed it as much as I did, and knew as much as I did. You're not a decent girl, Nelly Burns.'

She gasped and tears came into her eyes. 'You 'ad no need t'say that. I really loved you, Mark.' But now she felt more as if she hated him.

He bowed his head and would have apologised, but another of the waitresses came through into the corridor just then and eyed them both curiously, so he turned and went back into the eating room at the front to sit at the cash desk as he did every night. Usually he enjoyed seeing the happy faces of his customers, enjoyed the solid feel of the money they paid him. He knew that the food he gave them was good, if plain. It was a goldmine, this place. And Nelly knew it. Oh, yes, she knew it well.

She didn't stay behind after work, and Mark didn't know whether to be glad or sorry about that. And she didn't come in next day. He hoped desperately that she had lost the child. Women did sometimes. Oh, God, let her lose it!

But she was back the next day, with a bruise on her cheek and red-rimmed eyes. 'I need to talk to you, Mark. It's urgent,' she whispered, as they passed one another.

367

'Very well. After work.' Her unhappy face made him add, 'I told you I'd look after you. I'm not trying to get out of that.'

'Hah!'

Someone came past them. 'Thank you, Mr Gibson,' said Nelly, and moved on, her lips clamped tightly together.

After the noisy chop house had emptied and the big warm kitchen been cleared up, Mark stood waiting at the back door to lock up, saying goodbye to his staff.

Nelly was the last. She stood in the kitchen doorway, as if about to leave, then stepped back inside as the footsteps of the others died away. She stared at him, her expression totally hostile now. 'We'll go an' talk in the front room again, I suppose?'

'Yes. Put the latch on the door.' He turned and walked through the kitchen area, choosing a small table in the centre of the eating room. He watched her come in. She looked sad and pale, tired too. It had been a busy evening. Guilt swept through him. 'I do intend to look after you, Nelly,' he repeated.

She slumped in her seat. 'That's not what I want. Mark, *please* change your mind.'

'No. I won't marry you. We're not suited. We'd make each other unhappy.'

She looked over his shoulder and shrugged, raising her voice. 'He hasn't changed his mind,' she said tiredly to someone else.

He turned quickly, to see three fellows push through the doorway. They were large and they looked angry. They walked across to the table. One sat down next to Nelly. The others remained standing behind Mark.

She waved a hand. 'These are my brothers. Bill an' Don an' Bart.'

Mark stared across the table at Bill, who was obviously the eldest of the trio. Fear was fluttering within him. He knew they were going to beat him up, knew it deep in his bones. And nothing would stop it happening, because he wasn't going to agree to marry Nelly, he wasn't, whatever they said or did.

Bill leaned forward. 'Nelly tells me you're the father of her child, *Mr* Gibson.'

'Yes. So it seems.'

'An' that you refuse to marry her.'

'Yes. But I'm not refusing to support her and the child.'

Bill shook his head very slowly. 'But you 'ave refused to marry our Nelly?'

'Yes.'

'I think you should change your mind, *Mr* Gibson.'

Mark shook his head. 'We'd make each other miserable within the month. We're not suited.'

'You were suited enough to tumble her on t'floor o' that storeroom back there.'

Mark stared at him. '*She* came to me.'

There was a hiss of anger from the two men behind him, but Bill gestured to them to keep quiet. 'Easy enough to accuse her. But if you think that gives you t'right to abandon her now, you can think again.'

'I told you. I'm *not* abandoning her. I'll pay for their keep. Nelly and the child will never want.'

'She'll want a good name,' Bill growled. 'Our good name'll be tarnished.'

The two men standing behind Mark took a step nearer. He could feel them breathing quickly, as if they were angry. Fear began to throb in his belly. He could handle himself in a fight, but not when he was one against three, and three such large men, too. Funny, that, with Nelly so small.

As they dragged him out of his chair and held his arms behind his back, Nelly looked up at them, tears in her eyes. 'Don't hurt 'im.'

'Go home now, Nelly,' Bill said, and when she didn't move, he pulled her on to her feet and pushed her out into the kitchen. He turned back to Mark. 'Last chance.'

Mark shook his head.

The pain was so sudden and sharp that he cried out. He struggled to defend himself, but the hands holding his arms were stronger than he was and the fist kept coming at him, again and again. First at his face, then at his belly, and his chest. His eye was half-closed, his lip was split and for all his struggles, the few times he got his arms free, the three men caught hold of them again.

In the distance a woman was sobbing.

'Stupid bitch! I told her to leave,' said Bill, putting his face close to Mark's. 'Can you hear her, Mr Bloody Gibson? She won't go home like we told her. She says she loves you.' He spat right into Mark's face.

Through his bleeding lips, Mark repeated, 'Well, I don't love her.'

'You don't have to love her, you just have to marry her. You're the father.' A pause, then, 'Well? Changed your mind yet?'

Mark hung there in a blur of pain and shook his head. 'No.' For a dreadful moment, he thought Bill was going to kick him in the balls. Then a black mist started to come between him and the world.

The last thing he heard before he lost consciousness was Bill's voice: 'Right, then. Bring him along, lads.'

When Mark came to, he was lying tumbled in a handcart and felt so sick that he could not control his stomach.

'Ah, shit!' said a voice. 'He's puked all over the cart.'

They stopped jolting over the cobblestones and Mark sighed in relief.

'Make sure he isn't choking in it.'

A rough hand pulled Mark's head higher, then the jolting started again. Where were they taking him? Were they going to kill him? It wasn't unknown for bodies to be tipped into the river. He tried to move, but a heavy hand pushed him back and a voice growled, 'Lie still, you stupid sod!'

Next time the cart stopped, Mark saw to his horror that

they were outside Netherleigh Cottage. No! He didn't want his family to see him like this, didn't want his dad brought into this. He tried to speak, but the sickness was still waiting in his stomach and he closed his mouth again, gulping.

Someone banged on the door and John Gibson came to open it.

'We've got your son here,' Bill said. 'An' we have something to tell you. I think we'd better come inside for that.'

At first, John thought that they'd found Mark lying beaten up somewhere and started to tell them how grateful he was to them for bringing his son home.

Bill soon put him straight on that matter.

Kathy came to the top of the stairs and when she saw Mark being carried in, went back to fling a shawl over her nightgown and rush down to tend him.

Don and Bart dumped Mark unceremoniously on the rag rug in front of the kitchen range.

John pulled Kathy over to him and placed himself in front of her protectively.

'Nay, we don't beat up women,' Bill said. 'It's only selfish sods like your son.'

'Why?'

'He's got our sister in the family way, an' he's refusing to marry her.'

Kathy gasped.

John stood frozen for a moment. 'Let my wife tend him an' we'll talk. Kathy?'

The men nodded, stood back and let her go and bend over Mark.

There was a sound at the door and Luke came in. He stopped with a gasp and looked quickly around. 'What's happened to our Mark, Dad?'

Bill stared at him. 'Here's another Gibson lad who's prob'ly too fine to speak to us. Go back to bed, sonny, an' let us talk to your daddy.'

Luke ignored the jibe and went to stand shoulder to shoulder with his father.

John looked up to see the rest of the family standing in the doorway. 'Get back to bed!' he said curtly in that tone of voice which none of his children ever disobeyed. 'Rebecca, you can stay an' help your mother.'

'Our Rebecca's tired. An' she doesn't like the sight of blood. I'll be more help,' said Joanie. She gave her sister a shove. 'Go on! Back to bed.'

As Joanie came into the room, she looked at Bart with a half-smile, as if she knew him, then went over to help Kathy get Mark out of his soiled clothes. His body was covered in bruises, so that both women exclaimed aloud and the glance Joanie threw at Bart now was less friendly.

He shuffled his feet uncomfortably and avoided her eyes.

As she cleaned Mark up, Kathy kept glancing at the three men in terror. Were they going to hit her John next? If they did, she'd claw their eyes out. She would. He was her very life, John was.

After a few moments, Bill clicked his tongue in annoyance. 'We aren't goin' to touch anyone else, missus. We only have a quarrel with that cheatin' coward on the floor there.'

'Let's sit down and talk, then,' John suggested and went to his usual place at the head of the kitchen table. Sitting there gave him confidence and he felt better when the leader of the three men sat down, too. 'Who are you?'

Joanie bobbed up to point from one to the other. 'This is Bill Burns, an' Don an' Bart. They're brothers.'

'Our sister Nelly works in your Mark's chop house,' Bill added. 'He's fathered a child on her, an' all we asked was that he marry her. These things happen. We all know that. An' we all know the remedy.'

It was Bart who spoke next, and the look he threw at Mark, now slumped in a chair near the fire, was filled with hatred. 'Only he's too grand to marry our Nelly, that one.

We gave him a chance to change his mind, but he refused. An' he kept on refusing.'

John turned to his son. 'Is that right, lad?'

Mark nodded. His words came out of his swollen mouth sounding muffled. 'Yes. I offered to look after her an' the child, but I'm not marrying her.'

'Nay, lad!' There was condemnation in John's gentle voice.

Even Kathy looked at him in disapproval. 'Eh, Mark, you can't leave her to face things on her own.'

'Nor you can't let your child be born a bastard,' added John.

'I wasn't the first with her,' said Mark. 'Not by a long chalk, I reckon.'

'Was she your first?' Bill threw back at him.

Mark didn't answer. He was looking at his father. 'I can't marry her, Dad. We wouldn't suit.'

Bart thumped the table. 'You mean our Nelly isn't good enough for you! Good enough to roger, but not to wed.'

Mark looked at him tiredly. 'All right, that's what I mean.'

Luke edged forward to stand between the three men and his brother.

'You'll have to marry her, our Mark,' Joanie piped up. 'The Burns family's the same as the Gibsons. They all stick together, too. They'll not let you off.'

John looked at his three unwelcome visitors. 'We can do nothing at the moment. Will you leave this with me?'

Bill stared at him. 'We shan't change us minds.'

John stared back. 'I'm in agreement with you on one thing. Not the way you've chosen to try to persuade my son, no, never that. But if a man fathers a child,' he threw a disapproving glance at his son, 'then he should give it his name.'

The brothers looked at Bill, who nodded and led the way out. 'We'll be back for our answer tomorrow night, then,' one of them shouted from the hall. 'We'll not be put off.'

Kathy rushed straight into the haven of John's arms and he patted her on the shoulder, staring disapprovingly at Mark, who sighed and closed his eyes. 'I won't wed her,' he repeated. 'I just couldn't, Dad. I don't even like her.'

26

For Better, For Worse

The next morning, Peggy brought a note in with the tea-tray. 'Master Samuel John brought this up for the mistress,' she said. 'He's waiting downstairs for an answer.'

Annie recognised the rounded child-like handwriting. 'It's from my father!' She cast a worried glance at Frederick, then nodded dismissal to Peggy. 'Just wait outside a minute, will you? I'll want you to give him a reply.' When the door had closed behind the maid, she tore the note open, read it and frowned as she handed it to Frederick.

'Something's wrong?'

She nodded. 'Yes. Dad wants me to go down there straight away. There's trouble. I'll have to do as he wants, love.' She raised her voice. 'Peggy!'

The door opened. 'Yes, ma'am?'

'Tell my brother I'll come down to Netherleigh Cottage as soon as I'm dressed.'

Peggy goggled at her. 'Yes, ma'am. Shall I tell Robert to get the carriage ready?'

Annie shook her head. 'No. I'll be just as quick walking.' Though that would put Robert in a bad mood for the day. He seemed to take it as a personal affront if she went anywhere on foot. But that couldn't be helped.

375

As the door closed behind Peggy, Annie threw off the covers and got out of bed, wincing as she moved her shoulder incautiously.

'Do you want me to come with you?' Frederick asked.

She shook her head. 'No, of course not. You're not nearly well enough to go out yet.' And anyway, she wanted to protect him from worry if she could. Her father's laboriously scribbled note gave nothing away, but it was not like him to send Samuel John up to the house at this hour of the morning, not at all like him to summon her so peremptorily.

Completely forgetting her own problems, she dressed quickly, not ringing for her maid, not bothering about fashion, but putting on one of the simple walking dresses she used for tramping over the moors. It had rained in the night, but the sun was coming out now and she would have enjoyed the brisk exercise were it not for her anxiety.

She knocked on the front door of Netherleigh Cottage and pushed it open. 'It's me, Annie!' she called and went inside.

'We're in here,' her father's voice answered from the parlour.

That was unusual enough to make her feel even more worried. Her father and his family did not sit in the front parlour, except when they were receiving guests. She strode across the hall and went into the large front room which she had loved so much when she lived here. 'What's the m—?' Her voice trailed to nothing as she saw Mark lying on the sofa. Her handsome brother had his face all battered and one eye was closed and puffy. 'What's happened?'

Mark pushed himself up to a sitting position. 'I want to speak to Annie on my own, Dad.'

Kathy tugged at John's arm and he hesitated, then the two of them left the room.

'Don't go without a word, lass,' John said as he passed Annie.

There was silence, while Mark swallowed hard and tried to think how to tell her. There was no easy way. 'I've messed things up,' he blurted out in the end.

'At the chop house?'

He shook his head. 'No. That's doing well.' His laugh was a jangle of discordant sound in his throat.

Annie plumped to the floor next to the sofa and patted his hand. 'Tell me, then, love.'

So he faltered out the sorry tale.

She sat silent for a long time when he had finished. 'You have a duty to the child, as well as to Nelly,' she said finally, sick at heart that her brother had indeed, as he had said, 'messed things up'. And so very thoroughly, too.

'I'm not trying to escape my responsibilities, Annie, but I won't marry her. I won't.'

His eyes flashed with such determination in his poor bruised face that she didn't try to remonstrate with him, although she knew her father would expect her to.

'They can kill me and I still won't marry her,' he added, his voice rising, his whole body taut as a bowstring.

'But, Mark, she's expecting your child. What else can you do?'

He shuddered. 'Not you as well, Annie? I thought *you* would understand. You were keen to get on, too, when you were young, and you didn't let anything stop you.'

'And I was also in the same position as Nelly once,' she said, memories flooding back of her own despair at the age of seventeen. 'That was why I had to marry Charlie.' She took hold of his hand and tried to explain. 'It's quite terrifying for a girl, Mark. She's on her own. She knows everyone will scorn her, and in her belly there's something growing, something she can't hide. Nelly will be frightened of everything – her parents, being sent to the poor house. Sometimes families just push the girls out into the street when they get into that sort of trouble. And even if they don't, even if her people let her stay on at home, there'll be the neighbours, who will look at her scornfully and call her names as she passes.'

Mark shook his head. 'It makes no difference. If I gave her enough money, she could go somewhere else, pretend to be a widow. I'm not refusing to support her and the child, Annie. But not marriage, not with *her*!'

'If you think so badly of her, why did you—'

He groaned and avoided her eyes. 'The Gibson curse. I didn't persuade her into it, you know. I resisted for a long while, but Nelly pushed herself at me, time after time, until I couldn't resist any longer. And I wasn't the first with her, not by any means.'

Annie didn't pretend not to understand. 'No. The Gibson men never can resist,' she said with a snort. 'Dad was as bad. And Tom. But he had Rosie. And she didn't have any babies.' Not until after Tom had married Marianne, anyway.

'I thought,' Mark said tentatively, 'if you were here with me, I could talk to her brothers again, get them to listen to what I'm offering.' It was hiding behind a woman's skirts and it made him feel like the lowest type of coward, but you couldn't fight three burly fellows at once, and nothing would make him change his mind. Nothing. He was *not* going to marry Nelly Burns. 'They wouldn't start a fight if you were here, Annie. Maybe we could all – you know, talk, work something out.'

She looked at him. He was exhausted. And hurting. Near despair. But so stubborn. He seemed years older today than he had the last time she had seen him. In fact, she had never seen him like this, never truly recognised him as an equal adult before. 'Well, you know your own mind best, love. I'll speak to Tom, see what we can arrange.'

He sagged back in relief. 'Thank you. I'm a bit – a bit knocked about today. I can't seem to think very clearly. All that keeps going round my head is that I couldn't bear to be married to Nelly Burns. I don't even like her. I'd already stopped seeing her before this happened, you know.'

Annie hesitated, then leaned over to give him a careful hug. 'Oh, Mark!' Then she bit off further words and went through into the kitchen.

John and Kathy were sitting waiting for her.

'How is he?' Kathy asked softly.

'Upset, but determined not to marry her. It's a mess, isn't it?' Annie went to sit with them at the table.

'He mun marry her,' John said. 'He mun think of the child, not himself, now.'

Kathy sighed and got up to pour Annie a cup of tea. Her John was so fixed in his ideas about this. She'd never seen him so angry, or so determined. He and Mark had had a right shouting match this morning.

Annie waited. There always seemed to be a pot brewing at Netherleigh Cottage. Nothing was ever settled there without a cup of tea.

'I know of the family,' Kathy said as she set a cup down in front of Annie. 'Well, a bit about them, not a lot.'

'Tell me,' Annie encouraged. It would help to know what they were facing. She seemed to have lost touch with the ordinary folk in Bilsden lately.

'The mother's a poor downtrodden creature. I see her at the market sometimes. She hardly raises her eyes and her voice is that quiet you can hardly hear what she says. And I've seen the lass around, too. She's a pretty lass, but a bit common-looking. An' when her father's not there, she speaks right pertly to her mother. I don't like that in her.' She didn't like the thought of the girl marrying Mark, either, but she was too loyal to John to say so. 'But when the father's around, the girl hardly says a word. He's a proper tyrant, he is. Bible crazy. The whole family is. They'll insist on marriage. Well, you saw what her brothers did to our Mark when he refused.'

Annie fiddled with her cup. 'Mark said she pushed herself at him.'

John shook his head stubbornly. 'That doesn't matter now. There's a child to think on.'

And from that standpoint Annie could not move him, not a fraction. 'Have you told Tom?' she asked in the end, sipping her tea for something to do, but not really tasting it.

They shook their heads. 'The lad wanted to talk to you first,' said Kathy. 'He thinks a lot of you, our Mark does.'

'I were sure you'd tell him to wed her.' John looked at his daughter disapprovingly. '*You* know what it's like for a lass.'

'It's his own life, Dad. And he seems very determined about this. What shall we do if he can't be brought to marry her?'

John looked down, then looked up at her with tears in his eyes. 'What I shall do is tell him he's no son of mine. And ask him to leave my house.'

'Nay, John!' Kathy protested. 'You can't do that!'

'I can. I must.'

Annie was shocked to the core. 'You really mean that, Dad?'

'I do. Some things are – they're just the right thing to do. Whatever the cost. You have to look after your childer.' He would have given his life without hesitation to save any of his children.

'Even if you dislike the mother? Even if she's – not worth much?'

'Even so. You take someone for better, for worse.'

She could tell from his expression that he was remembering his feckless second wife, Emily. After the silence had gone on for too long, Annie sighed and changed the subject slightly. 'Mark wants me to talk to her brothers. Can I arrange a meeting for this evening? Here?'

John's expression was rigid. 'You can if it's to plan a wedding, not if it's to try and buy off that poor lass.'

Kathy put her hand on his arm. 'Oh, John, don't be like that. He's your son!'

He looked at his wife, his mouth a tight line of determination. 'Yes, and I brought him up to do better nor that. I mean what I say, love. I shan't change my mind about it.'

Annie recognised that look in his face. She'd seen it in her own mirror often enough. We're a stubborn lot, us Gibsons, she thought. 'Then we'll arrange the meeting for somewhere else,' she said aloud.

'You're in agreement with him?' John asked sadly.

Annie shook her head. 'No. Well, not exactly. I can see both sides. I remember—' She broke off. No use going back over all that. 'I want to talk to her myself. And her family. See what she's like. Then I'll decide what I think.'

She walked back up the hill through a light drizzle, not bothering to cover her head with the shawl she'd flung around herself in her hurry to find out what was wrong. She was unaware that people were staring at her or that she was gazing fixedly ahead like someone who had seen a ghost.

Sometimes she wished, and at the moment she wished it quite desperately, that she was not the one everyone turned to when they were in trouble. She loved her family dearly, but she seemed never to have been free from responsibility. One thing after another. The nearest she ever came to freedom was when she was out walking on the moors. But always, when she got back home, there were burdens to pick up, responsibilities to face, decisions to be made. Could you go on being strong for ever? She didn't know. But she did know that she was getting very, very tired.

She suddenly remembered Tian Gilchrist, the relaxed way he had moved, the easy smile on his face, and a feeling of envy stabbed at her. Then she grew angry with herself for remembering him at all. But she could not help thinking wistfully as she turned into her own gates that she would like to feel as relaxed as that, just for a little while. She had never known what it was like to be carefree. At ten she had become mother to Tom and Lizzie, and kept house for her father. At twelve she had been sent into service by her new step-mother to earn her own way in the world. At eighteen she had become a mother herself, with a slow-witted husband also depending on her. And when her father's second wife died, she had brought him and his family to live with her and looked after them, too.

The urgency of such demands had eased when she married Frederick, but by that time she had not wanted to lay down her burdens, not wanted to depend on him, or on anybody, ever again. So she had insisted on keeping up her business interests, for William's sake, to make an inheritance for him. And now she had to look after Frederick, see that he did not overdo things, make his final years happy. After which she would be on her own again.

But what was the use of wishing for the moon? You did the best you could with what life dealt you. That was the only choice you had. Because wishing didn't make troubles go away, didn't make your path through life smooth and easy.

Frederick advised Annie to hold the meeting at Tom's house. 'Do you want me to come with you? I should be helping you in this. I hate being so useless!'

She clasped his hand. 'When you're better again, you'll help me in a lot of things. At the moment, it's a help just to have someone to talk to. I was so glad to be coming home to your good sense.' Which was the truth.

He squeezed her hand, a little appeased, but not completely. 'Send that note off to Tom, then, and we'll have a council of war here in my bedroom.' He even managed a smile. He had promised himself never to betray the resentment he sometimes felt, never to spoil their last few years together by regretting something he could not change.

Her face brightened. 'Oh, yes! That'll be the best thing to do. Oh, Frederick love, you always make me feel better, somehow.'

And that, he felt, as he watched her ring for her maid

and walk into the dressing room to change, was something at least.

Tom came up to Ridge House immediately he got Annie's note. 'What's up?' he asked as he walked into her little parlour.

'Aren't you going to sit down?' When he flung himself into a chair, she explained about Mark.

For a moment Tom was silent, then he cursed softly and leaned back, his hand shading his eyes. When he opened them, he stared at Annie, a surprised look on his face. 'I think I agree with Dad.'

She raised her eyebrows. 'Oh?'

He nodded. 'Yes.'

'I'd have thought you'd be on Mark's side.'

'I would, once. Now – well, I've seen how hard it's been for Rosie, raising young Albert on her own. And it's still hard, even when I want to marry her. The lad's bound to suffer whatever we do. He looks too much like me. And if Mark doesn't marry this girl, he'll be setting up another child for grief and trouble.' He realised suddenly that Annie had omitted one vital piece of information. 'Who is she, anyway, this girl?'

'Nelly Burns.'

Tom cursed again and thumped his clenched fist several times on the arm of his chair. 'Oh, hell! Bible Burns's daughter. He had to pick that one, didn't he? Burns will be content with nothing less than marriage, Annie love. There's no way he'll change his mind.'

She did not need telling that. 'That's fairly obvious. Her brothers have already beaten up Mark for refusing.'

'What? Is he all right? If they've—'

'He's badly bruised and Kathy thinks he's got a cracked rib. That's all.'

'It'll be her father who comes hammering on the door of Netherleigh Cottage next, and if he doesn't get what he wants, he'll disown the poor lass and trumpet her shame all over town, which will make us Gibsons look bad. He'd enjoy getting back at the Gibsons, that old bigot would.'

She was surprised. 'Does he have a grudge against us?'

Tom nodded. 'Sort of. Well, he feels jealous, anyway. I've run up against him a few times in the past couple of years. He came here from Oldham. They call him "Bible Burns" because he's a temperance man and a strict Sabbatarian, but that doesn't stop him being a very sharp businessman. Strange, isn't it? He pays the lowest prices for what he buys, to poor folk as need every farthing, and yet he boasts that the only book in his house is the Bible and that he lives by its word. He's been the leading light in founding that new chapel down Henny Lane. Redemption House, they call it.'

'Oh. That one.' It made the Methodists look lax and sinful, that place, and those who went there were sour-faced people in dark clothes.

Tom nodded. 'Yes. That one.'

There was silence for a few moments and he started drumming his fingers on his thigh, trying to piece together some bits of information in his mind. 'I've heard something about the girl, too. I think they've had trouble with her before. Hushed it up. Now's their chance to get rid of her *and* marry her to money into the bargain.

'Did I mention that old Burns has a tripe shop down near the market? The sons work for him. That Bill has been out trying to push into our rounds and buy food direct from our farmers. He's threatened some of them, too. There's a nice Christian approach for you! I had a few words with him about that last year. Made sure he understood that two can start threatening folk.'

After a minute, Tom added with a grin, 'I bet the father collects Nelly's wages every week. They'd never let her have any money of her own. The mother has none. She buys on her husband's accounts, or else the odd sixpenn'orth of stuff at the market.' He saw that this was all news to her. 'Surely you've heard of the family, Annie?'

'If I have, I didn't take much notice. I'm out of touch with the folk in the Rows now.' Once she would have known everyone, but the town had grown so much bigger that she just couldn't keep up. And she'd been somewhat preoccupied with other things lately.

Tom was looking thoughtful. 'Well, I've still got my finger in a few pies in the Rows. I'll see what I can find out about Bible Burns and his dear sons. I'm not having them beating up my brother again, for whatever reason.'

'And Frederick's suggestion?'

'That we hold the meeting at my place?' He grinned. 'Nothing I'd like better.' The grin faded. 'I'd better go and have a talk to our Mark first hadn't I? Find out exactly what's been happening.'

'All right. Go up and see Frederick before you leave, though, will you? He's fretting because he can't do anything to help. Ask his advice about something, if you can. It'll make him feel better.'

'How is he? Really?'

She just shook her head blindly, tears filling her eyes. 'Failing. Slowly. You've seen the changes.'

Tom nodded, gave her a long hug, then went towards the door. 'We'll find a way to sort things out, love.'

But Annie wondered about that. Some things you just couldn't sort out. Not satisfactorily, anyway.

27

Solutions and Resolutions

$\mathcal{E}$arly that evening, Annie picked Mark up in the carriage and drove him to Tom's house. Mark winced as he got inside, and by the light of the single carriage lamp his face looked awful, black and blue, and very puffy still.

'How are you feeling?' She pulled the rug over him and pushed the hot brick his way. It was a damp chilly night.

'All right, considering.' He stared glumly down at his lap.

'Have you – changed your mind about anything, love?'

He stared at her, his eyes dark and somehow wild-looking. 'You mean about marrying Nelly Burns? No, I haven't. Dad's not speaking to me. He says I know in my soul what's right and must do my duty by the girl. Only *he* wouldn't have to live with her and her silly neighing laugh, or hear the stupid spiteful things she says about folk who've done her no harm.'

Tom let them into the house himself, and even though he had seen Mark that afternoon, whistled at the sight of his face. 'They certainly did a good job on you, lad.'

'Mmm. There were three of them. I could have held my own with one, but not three. And they took me by surprise. I hadn't expected the attack.'

Inside the hallway two men were waiting, hard-faced muscular men who usually helped keep order at The

Shepherd's Rest. Tom jerked his head at them and grinned at Annie. 'I'm not having any fights in my house. But if the Burns boys do insist on causing trouble, then I'm making sure we have the numbers to win.'

He looked suddenly like the old Tom, Annie thought, the tough lad who knew every street corner in the Rows. Heavens, what a long time ago that all seemed now!

The three of them went into the parlour and sat waiting, mostly in silence.

At eight o'clock exactly there was the sound of boots on the cobbles of the street and men's voices, then someone knocked on the door.

One of Tom's men went to open it.

A harsh voice said, 'We've come to see Mester Gibson.'

The parlour door opened, and four men filed inside, the three younger ones sporting the odd bruise, but nowhere near as many as Mark. The old man leading them had white hair and staring eyes. He was carrying a Bible in his hand. 'There he is, the defiler of innocents!' he brayed as soon as his eyes fell upon Mark.

Tom's voice cut in, sharp and cold, 'Sit down, Burns. If you're here to discuss the situation, that is. Otherwise get out. You can save that sort of canting talk for your chapel.'

One of the brothers took a step forward, bunching his fists.

Annie watched Tom go right up and stand toe to toe with him, undeterred by the fact that Bill Burns was several inches taller than him.

'One sign of trouble and you're out of here, the lot of you.' Tom smiled, a confident smile but not a nice one. 'I've got my children sleeping upstairs and I'm not having them upset. I've also got some of my men in the house in case we have to throw you out. Three to one wasn't fair odds against our Mark. I've evened them up this time.'

The father made a gesture. The son grunted and took a step backwards. But the anger was still there on his face, and the promise that given half a chance, he'd do something about it.

'We're here to demand justice!' Mr Burns declared, and his finger shot out to stab towards Mark. 'That fornicator must pay the penalty for his sins! He must stand up in chapel and repent, then he must make an honest woman of my daughter.'

Mark glared across the room at him. 'I'm not setting one foot in that chapel of yours, let alone repenting in public, and I'm *not*—'

Annie intervened hastily. 'We're here to discuss the situation, Mr Burns, and then afterwards we'll decide what to do.'

He glared at her. 'Woman, "Study to be quiet, and to do your own business", and leave your menfolk to deal with this sinful wretch!'

She glared back at him. She could not believe what she was hearing. That sounded like a quote from the Bible, but it was not one she'd ever pay any attention to.

Tom winked at her and took over. 'My sister's part of the family, and as such she has a right to speak. Are you saying now that families shouldn't stick together?'

'I'm saying it's for us menfolk to settle such things. Women have neither the sense nor the moral fibre. They're the weaker vessels, as the blessed Peter himself said, and are here to be guided by their natural masters.'

'Well, I'm no weak vessel,' Annie declared, staring right back at him, 'and you either deal with me as well, or you can get out of here now.' It was a long time since anyone had dared to speak to her like this, and the man's arrogance made anger sizzle through her.

Tom hid a grin. Burns had picked on the wrong one to browbeat with their Annie!

Mr Burns swelled visibly with rage, opened his mouth and then shut it again, pointedly turning his shoulder to Annie and addressing himself to Tom and Mark. But he couldn't prevent her from speaking, or the others from bringing her into the discussion, and it seemed to throw him off his stride a little.

' "Sinner, repent!" ' he threw at Mark. 'What have you to say for yourself today, Mark Gibson? Have you acknowledged your sin, realised your duty?'

Mark was stony-faced. 'I've acknowledged my *fault*, and I'm prepared to support Nelly and the child, but I'm not going to marry her.'

The three brothers growled in their throats. Bill clenched his fists and took a step forward.

'Watch it, you!' snapped Tom. 'We're here to talk, and that's all.'

For a moment all hung in the balance, then Mr Burns jerked his head and Bill stepped back again.

'Mark, what are you offering Nelly exactly?' Tom continued.

'I'm prepared to find her a house, here or in another town if she prefers that, and give her fifteen shillings a week. When the baby gets older, I'll make sure it gets a good education and a decent start in life.'

Mr Burns raised his eyes. 'O Lord, look down upon this sinner! Bring him to redemption! Let him—'

'Does that mean you won't even consider Mark's offer?' Tom interrupted ruthlessly, tired of this canting.

'Our Nelly will lose her good name,' Bill said, ignoring his father's scowl. 'We set store on our family name. She'll still be unwed, and the child will be a bastard. So your offer isn't good enough, Mark Gibson. There's only one thing we want, your name, an' we're going to make sure we get it.'

'Well, I've told you all I'm prepared to do,' Mark insisted wearily. His head was throbbing and he could see anger in every line of these men's bodies, but he was unshaken in his determination not to marry their sister.

'Perhaps,' Tom suggested, 'you should go away and think about it. Come back tomorrow.'

Mr Burns shook his head. 'It needs no thinking about.

Right is right, and we're demanding justice for our girl.'

'Perhaps we could find someone else to marry her,' Annie suggested. 'With a house and income, there must be men who'd be willing.'

'What sort of man would take defiled goods?' demanded Mr Burns. 'And anyway, it's a Gibson who did it, and a Gibson who must pay the price.'

Annie was beginning to feel glad that Mark did not want to marry into this family. She shuddered at the thought of being related to them, of having to acknowledge them, even invite them to her house. She resolved to speak to the girl herself, see if Nelly would be more amenable than her father. 'I think you're pushing our Mark too much, Mr Burns. You'll need to give him time to think about things.' She shook her head as Mark opened his mouth to reiterate his position and he closed it again with the words unspoken.

Burns cast a scornful glance at Annie. 'Woman, a righteous man would need no time to think about his duty.'

'But an unrighteous man might need time to repent,' Tom suggested craftily, with a wink at Mark.

'I'd like to meet your daughter, Mr Burns,' Annie said. 'Talk to her myself. Could she and her mother perhaps come up to Ridge House and take tea with me?' She could see him considering that and nodding slowly.

'Yes,' he nodded, 'yes, that is women's business. I shall send them to you tomorrow.'

'At four o'clock.' Annie didn't want them meeting any of the ladies who sometimes called on her earlier in the day.

Mr Burns inclined his head.

'So are we all decided that we'll think about things?' Tom pressed his hand on Mark's shoulder to keep him quiet.

'My position will not change,' Mr Burns said, and scowled at Mark. 'I had thought that a son of John Gibson would have known the Lord's ways, but I can see that I'm mistaken.' He seemed pleased to find fault with John Gibson.

'My mistakes are my own, not my father's.' Mark wasn't having anyone insulting his father.

Mr Burns brandished his Bible at him. ' "Be sure your sins will find you out." *Numbers*, chapter thirty-two, verse twenty-three.'

Mark just stared stonily back.

' "Be strong and quit yourselves like men," ' Mr Burns tossed at him, speaking more loudly still, as if Mark were half deaf. '*Samuel I*, chapter four, verse nine.'

'This way, Mr Burns,' said Tom.

'My wife and daughter will call on you tomorrow afternoon, Mrs Hallam.' The father was not too outraged to finalise arrangements with Annie as he was moving towards the door.

His loud voice floated back to them down the hallway, still bugling out his demands. 'I shall be back tomorrow for my answer, Thomas Gibson. There is no need to wait longer. Your brother's duty is clear. But time and wiser counsel might just prevail upon a sinful soul. If not, we shall see what else can be done to persuade him.' On the doorstep he paused to add, in quite another tone of voice, 'I do not rule out taking legal action for breach of promise.'

Annie sat down in a chair and exhaled loudly. 'I can see why you don't want him for your father-in-law, Mark love, but just think what poor Nelly must be suffering at the moment.'

'And must I suffer all my life for one mistake?'

'Sometimes you have no choice.' She thought of her years married to a slow-witted man, the boredom that had sometimes driven her near to screaming point, for all that Charlie had been a gentle kindly soul. But she had never shown how she felt to him, or, she hoped, to anyone else.

'Well, I won't do it.'

When Tom rejoined them, he was shaking his head. 'He'll not budge, Mark lad.'

'Nor will I.'

'But, Mark—'

'You won't change my mind, no matter what you say or do! I will not give my name to that woman!'

Later that evening Mark went to the chop house, ignoring Kathy's pleas that he was not well enough. 'I've got the day's takings to count up,' he insisted. 'I'm not leaving that to anyone else. Maud can run the kitchens and Bet can run the eating room, but I want to be there to get the money safely hidden.'

His father said nothing, just looked at him sternly, and as he left the house, Mark dashed away a tear. He had never thought to be so at odds with his father. Never.

Kathy, torn between the two of them, could think of nothing to say and wept into her cooking. Lally came and gave her a quick hug, but John seemed lost in his own thoughts.

Mark went into the chop house by the back door, ignoring the shocked comments that his staff made when they saw his battered face. He felt sick and slightly light-headed after his walk down the hill, but no less full of determination to hold to his decision.

'Nelly isn't in tonight,' Maud announced. 'Her brother came to tell us she wasn't well.' Her knowing glance said that she had a fair idea of what was going on. 'So I brought old Wilf in to help out.'

Mark nodded. 'That's good. See that he keeps his hands clean, though.'

Out of habit, he made a quick check of the kitchen, to make sure everything was clean and tidy, then he went into his storeroom-cum-office. He closed the door and sagged against it for a minute, until the dizziness had passed, before locking it. As he made his way to the little desk in the corner, he was hurting as much from the knowledge that this was his last time here as from the physical pain of his wounds. He stroked the desk before he sat down. It had been his pride and joy. A beautifully made article. A gift from Annie. He would miss it. He would miss his chop house. And his family. He closed off that thought, for he could not bear to linger on it. His decision was made.

He pulled out his watch and stared at it. Yes, there was time enough. Then he set to work. First of all, he pulled out of his desk a scrap of newspaper with an advertisement that had caught his fancy. He flattened it out and stared at it. 'Well, I've got no choice now,' he said aloud, but his voice sounded bleak and unhappy, even in his own ears. What might have been a rosy daydream to beguile an idle moment was now the only solution he could see, and it had suddenly become far less tempting as an idea. He began to make his arrangements as methodically as he did everything else, stopping once or twice to rub his aching forehead, but that was all.

A little later, he called in Maud and Bet to witness his signature on one of the documents, but hid the writing at the top from them with a piece of paper. Fingers tapping impatiently, he watched first Maud, then Bet, laboriously trace out their own signatures.

'Now, I'm going to be counting on you two to look after things here for me.'

'Won't you be here?' Maud ventured, amazed.

He shook his head, swallowing a hard lump of pain. 'No. I have to go away for a time. This paper that you've signed is for Mr Gibson – my brother Tom, mind, not my father – to tell him about things, so that he can keep the chop house going.'

'Phew!' Maud let out her breath in relief. 'I thought for a minute you was going to tell us you'd sold the place, or you was closing it down, Mr Gibson.'

Mark shook his head. 'Not likely. It's a good little business, this one is, and you two do your jobs well. I'm sure you'll be able to help Mr Gibson keep things running.' He had another idea. 'And I'll tell him to give you a rise. A shilling a week each more, because you'll be doing more work from now on. He'll have to wait and see how things go, of course, but if you keep the business running well – and mind, you're always to keep things clean – then I'm sure he'll increase your money again later.'

Both women, who were widows in their forties, beamed at him. He'd chosen them very carefully when he first opened the place, and had not been disappointed in them, for they were good workers and utterly honest. 'Thank you for all you've done,' he said and could not say more, for his throat suddenly felt too full of emotion.

Maud threw her arms round him and gave him a smacking kiss on each cheek. 'I wouldn't marry her, either,' she whispered.

He stiffened, then gave her a lop-sided grin. 'How did you know?'

'She were talking yesterday, boasting of how her father would make you marry her. Boasting of how she were going to get rid of some of us once she became Mrs Gibson.'

This information only strengthened Mark's determination. 'Well, don't tell anyone else I'm leaving Bilsden, will you, Maud, or I'll be in even more trouble? Let someone else tell you the news tomorrow.'

'Where are you going, though, Mr Gibson?' Bet asked.

He shook his head. 'It's better if I don't tell you.'

'Well, don't stay away too long.'

The two women's words of support were the only comfort he carried with him as he went through his business papers, taking a few of them, leaving most for Tom. His last act was to open the secret place where he kept his reserve money and take most of it out. He would have to buy a good money belt to keep it in, he decided as he rolled some of the softly chinking coins in a piece of rag and stowed the roll under his shirt, round his waist. He put the rest into the battered leather suitcase he'd bought at a pawnshop on the way here, which he'd hidden outside until the staff left.

When he got back to Netherleigh Cottage, everyone

was in bed, as he'd hoped, so he took the suitcase inside with him. He peeped into the kitchen, where one gaslight was still burning low, but no one was there. He went through and woke his brother Luke, with whom he shared the room at the back of the ground floor. 'I'm leaving, Luke.'

Luke sat bolt upright. '*What?*'

'Shh!' Mark sighed, and sat down on Luke's bed. 'I'm going away. I'm not marrying Nelly Burns and I reckon it'll be easiest for the rest of you if I just vanish. I'm going to catch the early milk train to Manchester. No one will be around to stop me at that hour.'

'Well, I don't think you should marry her if you're that set against it,' Luke said in his soft slow voice, 'but I don't like to see you going. An' I shall miss you.'

Mark's shoulders sagged. 'And I'll miss you, Luke lad.'

There was silence for a moment, then Luke asked hesitantly, 'Have you ... um ... left some money for her?'

Mark nodded and handed over a thick envelope. 'I want you to give this to Tom tomorrow, but not till late afternoon. It explains what I want him to do. And will you tell him and Annie how—' his voice broke on the last word, 'how sorry I am to have caused all this trouble?' He passed over a second envelope, very slim this one. 'Give Dad this.'

Luke swung out of bed.

'You won't stop me!' Mark said quickly.

'I won't try. But I can walk to the station with you and help you with your bags. You're in no fit state to go lugging a heavy case across town.'

Mark felt too near tears to answer, so he just nodded his head. Then he began to pack the new suitcase and the one that was kept on top of his wardrobe, the one he had used to go to London, the one his parents used to go to Blackpool.

As they were creeping through the kitchen, a sleepy voice called down the stairs, 'Who's that?'

Luke put a hand on Mark's arm and answered. 'Me,

Dad. I can't sleep. I reckon I'll go and walk round the garden for a bit. I don't want to wake our Mark with my fidgeting.'

'All right, lad.'

It was not unknown for Luke to get up in the night and wander around, especially since he'd started working on his piece of land. As he'd said to Kathy, the ideas and dreams just teemed in his head some days, and he couldn't sleep, no matter how tired he was.

The two young men let themselves quietly out of the house and tiptoed along the street. They didn't say much as they walked to the station, but once they got there, Luke asked gruffly, 'Are you sure you're all right for money?' He put his hand in his pocket. 'I've got my savings here.'

Mark shook his head. 'Keep them. You need them. But thanks. And you don't need to worry, because I've taken what I had at the chop house, and I had quite a bit saved.'

As the train pulled into the station, the two brothers embraced, then Mark got into a compartment. His face was wet with tears, but there was no one to see this shameful unmanly emotion in the chill shabby compartment. Not many passengers rode the milk trains. He raised one hand to wave, but understood perfectly well why Luke turned abruptly and walked out of the station even before the train had left.

Mark dashed the tears from his eyes and told himself to set his thoughts firmly on the future. He'd messed up his life once, but he didn't intend to do it again.

Just as the train was starting to move, someone flung open the door of the compartment and clambered in.

Mark looked up, annoyed at having his privacy disturbed, then stared at the newcomer in dismay. 'William!'

'Mark!' William had never called his mother's half-brothers 'uncle' because they were more like brothers to him. 'Why on earth are you going to Manchester at this time of the morning?'

'I'm . . .' he swallowed hard, then admitted the truth
' . . . I'm running away.'

William gazed steadily at him. 'I heard about the girl.'

'I won't marry her.'

'No.'

'My father's disowned me.' It hurt to say that.

'That was wrong of him,' said William, laying one hand
on Mark's.

'Do you think I'm wrong?'

'I've learned not to judge people. How can I possibly
know what drives another person to act?' William's gaze
was very clear and direct. 'But I do think Grandad was
wrong to disown you.'

Mark sighed. 'Maybe he'll find it in his heart to forgive
me one day.'

'I'm sure he will.'

They sat in silence, but a little later, Mark said, 'I don't
want to go, you know, but I reckon it'll be best for
everyone. And before you ask, I've left her and the child
well provided for. I never intended to leave her to fend for
herself.'

William nodded approval. 'That's good.' He squeezed
the cold hand beside his, then clasped his hands in his lap.
'Do you want to tell me about your plans?'

'If you'll promise to say nothing, not even to your
mother.'

William nodded. 'I promise.' His clear gaze rested on
Mark and as the tale unfolded, he asked just once, 'Are you
sure?'

Mark could only nod.

'Well, I think I can help you a little, then, if you'll let me?'

Mark could not speak. Telling the tale again had
brought him close to tears. As he listened to William's
suggestion, he sighed with relief. He was not, he knew, in
a fit state to make proper plans for his future yet. Already
he was feeling light-headed and chilled.

'Thank God I met you,' he managed huskily, as William

helped him off the train in Manchester.

'The Lord will have some purpose in it,' William agreed tranquilly. 'Here, give me those suitcases. We'll go and find a cab, for once.' Usually he walked across town, but Mark was in no state to walk anywhere. He looked near to collapse.

28

The Gibsons

The Gibsons did not find out until the following afternoon that Mark had run away. Luke got up before dawn, after a mainly sleepless night, and, as he did occasionally when he went to snatch an hour on his own land, ate his breakfast at one of Tom's street stalls in the Rows, which were open from very early until very late. He was gone from Netherleigh Cottage, striding away through the half-light of the false dawn, before even Lally had woken up.

By early afternoon, Tom was getting annoyed that Mark hadn't come to see him to discuss the next move. He stormed over to the chop house, to find Bet cleaning the scrubbed wooden table tops after the midday trade. 'Where's Mark?' he demanded.

'I don't know, sir.' Which was true in one sense. 'He hasn't come in today.'

Tom stared at her, feeling unease start to trickle down his spine. 'Is he often this late?'

She shook her head, glanced around and kept her voice to a whisper. 'No. He's usually the first here. I told the others he wasn't well.'

Tom stood stock still. Mark wouldn't have—? No, he wasn't the sort to do away with himself. Surely not? Tom went into the kitchen. 'Has anyone seen Mr Gibson?' he asked loudly.

Maud frowned into the soup she was stirring and abruptly gave the ladle to her assistant. 'See that that doesn't stick.' She turned to Tom. 'Can we go into the office, sir?'

Hope flooded through him. She must know something.

Maud opened the locked door with her own key, then let Tom through and closed it carefully. She stood leaning against it, wondering how much to say. 'I'm worried about him, sir.'

Tom's heart sank again. 'Tell me, Maud.' He'd known Maud Bedsby for years. Unlike Annie, he still knew, or knew of, most people in the Rows, for many of his smaller businesses were still situated there or depended on trade in the area. He gestured to one of the hard wooden chairs. 'Take the weight off your feet and tell me.'

She sat down, clasped her hands together in her lap and sighed. 'I don't know whether I'm doing the right thing telling you, sir. He said to keep quiet, Mr Gibson did, to let *you* tell us that he'd gone away. But my heart's fair bleeding for him, it is that. I even burned my onions this morning!'

He waited as she fell silent, then as she continued to stare down at her hands, he admitted, 'I'm worried about him, too.'

She nodded, as if making up her mind. 'That Nelly, she's no good, sir. A right spiteful piece, she is. Oh, she can work hard when she wants to, especially when Mr Gibson is around, but she doesn't mind blaming others for her own mistakes and she's forever spreading nasty gossip. I told Mr Gibson to let her go, but, well, he had other ideas on his mind by then.' She sighed.

When the new silence went on for too long, Tom prompted softly, 'Go on, lass.'

'Well, sir, last night Mr Mark called me an' Bet in here an' asked us to sign a piece of paper to say we'd seen him sign it first, which we did. He covered up the writing at the top, but he told us . . .' again she paused 'he told us the

402

paper was for you, to tell you what to do with things, after he'd gone.'

'*Gone!*'

She nodded, biting her lip.

Tom sat there, with the word 'gone' echoing in his head. What a fool he was! He should have guessed this might happen. He should have stayed with Mark. He shouldn't have left the lad on his own. Guilt flooded through him. 'Do you know where he's gone?'

She shook her head. 'No.'

'Do you know where the piece of paper is now?'

Again she shook her head. 'No. All I know is he said you'd keep an eye on the chop house and me an' Bet were to run it for him. And we were to get a bit more money. But much as I need the extra shilling, I'd rather have Mr Gibson back where he belongs, I would that.'

'You don't think he'd – harm himself?'

She looked at him, her eyes brimming with tears. 'I don't think so, sir. But you never quite know how trouble can take people, do you?'

Tom looked at her honest open expression. Mark had chosen well with Maud. She'd been a bonny lass once, but widowhood and care had set lines on her face and her hair was mostly grey now. 'Can you keep things going here, then, Maud, as my brother wanted? At least till we find out where we are.'

'Yes, sir. But,' she hesitated, 'I'm going to need some money. Not much. Mr Gibson liked to pay cash for everything. He got a few discounts that way. He says every farthing counts in business, and I can see that he's right.'

Tom dug into his pocket. 'How much?'

While Tom was speaking to Maud, Annie was entertaining Mrs Burns and Nelly to tea. She'd fretted, unable to settle to anything, for an hour before they arrived, then she had stood behind the curtain to watch the two of them walk up the drive. They were escorted partway by Mr Burns.

Meekly, heads bowed, dressed in unfashionable gowns in dark colours, they walked along on either side of him.

When he stopped moving, they stopped, and when he began to harangue them, waggling his finger in their faces, they nodded compliance.

Once Mr Burns had stalked out of the gates, however, the girl perked up, and stopped again to stare around her and smile. Not a nice smile. Annie sought for a word to describe it and the only one she could think of was 'gloating'. Then the mother tugged at her daughter's sleeve and they moved out of Annie's sight towards the front door.

When Winnie showed the two of them in, Annie went forward to meet them. Somehow she could not summon up a smile. 'How do you do?'

'Mrs Hallam.' Mrs Burns took the hand offered her for a very brief moment and whispered some sort of greeting. She obviously felt ill-at-ease here, but Nelly was still smiling and looking around her. She appeared to be calculating the worth of every single item in the room.

I definitely don't like her, Annie thought. She's pretty enough, in a coarse sort of way, but they're the sort of looks that fade early. And I'm sure she's a sly piece. Aloud she said calmly, 'Do sit down, Mrs Burns. No, over here by the fire. It's a chilly day, isn't it?'

Nelly sauntered over to Annie's own chair without being invited.

'That's my chair. Sit here, if you please, Miss Burns!' Annie snapped, in the sort of voice she would have used with a sloppy maidservant. She pointed to a hard upright chair between herself and Mrs Burns.

Nelly began to pout, but did as she was told.

Annie turned to the mother, for whom, if truth be told, she felt rather sorry. 'Would you like a cup of tea, Mrs Burns?'

'My mam's allus ready for a cup,' Nelly volunteered.

Mrs Burns nodded.

Annie gave the girl another cutting look that made her wriggle in her seat, then rang the bell. Winnie already knew to bring in a tea-tray when she rang. 'I believe I was speaking to your mother. Kindly be quiet until you're spoken to, miss!' Her tone changed as she turned to the mother again. 'You don't look well, Mrs Burns. Do draw your chair closer to the fire.'

For the first time Mrs Burns really looked at her hostess. 'He's set on marriage,' she said in a dry tired voice. 'He'll accept nothing less. It doesn't matter what you say or offer.'

'And Mark's just as determined not to marry your daughter, I'm afraid.'

'My dad'll *make* him wed me,' Nelly said confidently.

Annie looked at her scornfully. 'And would you want to marry him in those circumstances?'

Nelly gave a slow smile and patted her belly. 'I know how to bring him round.'

Annie turned back to the mother. 'Do you know what Mark has offered, Mrs Burns? I think you should at least know that.' She explained. Clearly they hadn't been told this.

'That's not much!' Nelly declared, pouting again. 'Not from a rich family like yours.'

'It's more than you deserve, in my opinion!' snapped Annie.

Nelly gave an aggrieved sigh.

'It's no use,' Mrs Burns said tiredly. 'It doesn't matter what Mr Gibson offers. My husband is set on them getting wed.'

'Any road, I shall have more money than that once I wed him,' the daughter said, once again eyeing the furniture with a calculating eye.

Annie sat and dispensed tea, but could not get Mrs Burns to say anything, except to reiterate that *he* would only accept marriage. Nor could she keep the girl quiet. She knew by now exactly why Mark was refusing to marry

Nelly and she agreed with him. She just wished he'd had more sense than to get entangled with her in the first place.

When the two of them had left, Annie sat on, staring into the fire, her heart aching for Mark. Now that she had met the minx, she was sure that this had all been planned from the start, by the girl at least. Then she realised how long she'd been sitting there. Frederick would be waiting to hear how things had gone. She went along to the library to tell him what had happened.

'I peeped at them as well,' he said, grinning. 'If appearances are anything to go by, I didn't take to the girl.'

'She doesn't improve on acquaintance.'

'They can't actually force Mark to marry her,' he said, trying to comfort Annie.

'No, but they can make Dad's life a misery, and they can blacken our name, which might harm the Gibson businesses.'

'Only for a short time.' He pulled her to him for a hug. 'My lovely girl, you can't protect your family from everything. This mess is Mark's responsibility, not yours.'

She just sighed against his chest and stood there, feeling comforted by his arms around her and his love for her.

There was a sudden banging on the front door and they heard Winnie patter across the hall to open it, tutting to herself as the knocking started again. 'Eh, Mr Tom, what's up?' she demanded. 'I was—'

'Where's my sister?'

'In the library with the master. But—'

Footsteps, then the library door was flung open and banged shut behind Tom. 'Mark's run away,' he announced, leaning against it.

Annie took an involuntary step towards him. 'What!'

Frederick sat down on a sofa and pulled her with him. 'You might as well come over here and sit down, too, Tom lad.'

He flung himself on to another sofa. 'Our Mark's run away,' he repeated, thumping the nearest cushion. 'When he didn't come round to see me, I went to the chop house and spoke to Maud. He asked her and Bet to witness his signature on a piece of paper last night, and told her that I'd be keeping an eye on the place from now on, but that they'd be in charge of running things.'

'Oh, no!' Annie clasped Frederick's hand for comfort.

'So I went up to Netherleigh Cottage,' Tom went on. 'Me an' Kathy searched his room. He's taken a fair lot of his stuff with him.'

'Didn't they realise what he was doing?' Annie wondered.

'No. She didn't hear him packing and when Mark didn't come in to breakfast this morning, she thought he was just keeping out of his father's way. He sometimes gets breakfast at the chop house. But it seems that Luke was up and about during the night, as he often is. It was he who answered when Dad called down to see who it was. So I bet Luke knew what Mark was doing.'

'Mark would have told him anyway,' Annie said. 'They're very close, those two, and always have been. Have you seen Luke?'

Tom shook his head. 'No. I can't find him anywhere. Not at his piece of land, not at the junk yard. So I thought he might have come here.'

'I don't think so. But we'll ask Nat.' She jumped up to ring the bell.

But once again they drew a blank. Nat Jervis hadn't seen Luke all day.

'What the hell do we do now?' Tom demanded.

'There's nothing much you can do,' said Frederick. 'And when I think about it, I reckon Mark's probably done the best thing, given the circumstances.'

Annie's mouth dropped open in surprise.

'What I'd advise is that you see the Burns family tonight, Tom, and tell them what's happened. Say you'll pay off the girl on Mark's behalf, for the family's sake, but only on condition that they keep quiet about it all. Tell Burns the money will stop the minute he opens his mouth. They'll make a fuss, but they'll be glad to accept it in the end, because she'll start showing soon. It's my guess they'll find someone else to marry her, so you must promise to keep up the payments even after marriage. Pity, but there you are. One always pays for one's sins.'

Annie stared at him, then let out a long slow breath and began to nod her head.

Tom began to chuckle. 'You're right, Frederick lad. It's all we can do. And by, I shall really enjoy telling that Burns lot tonight!'

As Annie walked him to the door, she said thoughtfully, 'I should think Luke will turn up at your place tonight as well, Tom.'

'He'd better.'

John Gibson was devastated when he realised that Mark had run away from home. 'I were wrong,' he said again and again. 'I should've forgiven him. I say the Lord's prayer night and morning, and still I didn't heed what it says. "Forgive us our trespasses, as we forgive them that trespass against us." Eh, lass, I were too puffed up with my own pride.'

'You did what you thought right,' Kathy consoled him. 'And it's just as prideful to think you can be right every time.'

But he shook his head at her, and as the days passed nothing that she said or did could take away his sorrow and grief. He had failed his son in the lad's hour of need. What sort of father was he?

As he had expected, Tom enjoyed the confrontation with Bible Burns and his sons. However, he took the precaution of hiring a few fighting men again, just in case.

'Well?' demanded Mr Burns, black-bound Bible very prominent. 'Where is the sinner?'

'You're out of luck.' Tom grinned. 'Mark's run off.'

For once even Mr Burns was at a loss for words, then he looked around, as if he expected Mark to be hiding under the table. 'Where's he gone to?'

'He didn't say, only that he'd not be back for a few years.'

'You must find him. You must *make* him come back.'

Tom shook his head. 'I wouldn't know where to begin looking. An' I'll swear that on your Bible, if you want.'

The Bible was immediately thrust in his face and he duly repeated his statement, with his hand laid upon its black leather binding, his eyes dancing with amusement.

Burns stood frowning. 'Someone in his family must know where he's gone. Someone must have hidden him.'

'I'm his family, and I *don't* know.'

There was silence for a moment in the room, then Mr Burns said slowly, 'Then this will cause his father great grief.'

It was with difficulty that Tom restrained himself from punching his self-righteous visitor in the nose, for this was clearly meant as a threat. 'It'll cause *you* more grief.'

Bill stepped forward, one hand on his father's shoulder. 'What do you mean by that? Why should it cause us more grief this way?'

'I mean, you'll have to support Nelly and the child yourselves now.'

Mr Burns came out of his grief rapidly. 'Money was offered to support the lass and her child.'

Tom looked him straight in the eyes. 'You'll not get a farthing off us if you start telling everyone what's happened. I'm very fond of my father, and if you're hoping to get at him and blacken the Gibson name through this, you'll not get paid a farthing.'

The eyes staring back at him were filled with fury, then Mr Burns dropped his gaze. 'I shall want your offer in writing. And I shall still search for that fornicator before I accept it.'

Tom went over to the table and picked up a piece of

paper. 'It's here. I didn't want there to be any doubts about the conditions attached.' He pressed it into his visitor's hands, then went over to stand with one hand on the mantelpiece, staring into the fire. Where was Mark now? Was he cold? Hungry? Would he ever come back? Then he shook himself mentally. Of course Mark would come back. He'd said so in his letter, hadn't he? And Mark was a smart fellow. He'd look after himself.

Mr Burns studied the paper very carefully, reading it through, then starting at the beginning and reading it again, his mouth moving as he formed the words silently. While he did so, his sons studied Tom, and their expressions were not friendly. He just grinned at them. The clock ticked on and Tom began to drum his fingers on the mantelpiece, impatient to get this over with.

'What if she marries?' Mr Burns tapped the paper. 'It says nowt about that.'

'Because it makes no difference. The money is to support the child. Oh, an' I nearly forgot. We'll require regular proof that the child is being well cared for. Or else the money stops.' The child would be half Gibson, after all.

'We shall search for your Mark before we sign this.'

'Search away. And tell me if you find him, because I'd like to know where he's gone, too. But you still won't be able to persuade him to marry her. He can't stand the sight of her.'

Bart and Don had to restrain Bill from punching Tom there and then.

When the outraged Burns family had left Tom's house, a figure slipped into the kitchen, making Megan call out in shock.

Tom went running out to see what was wrong and stopped dead in the doorway. 'Well! I was beginning to think you'd run away too!'

Luke shook his head. 'I'm sorry to have startled you, Megan, but I didn't want to bump into the Burns family.'

'You'd better come through, then.' Tom held open the door to the hallway and followed his half-brother into the parlour. 'Well? Where's our Mark?'

'He's run away.'

'We've bloody realised that! Where's he gone?'

Luke stared into the fire. 'I can guess, but I don't know for sure.'

'Guess away, then.'

'Australia.'

'*What!*'

Luke raised his eyes. 'He cut a piece out of the newspaper a while ago. It told you how to go about emigrating, said they needed decent folk to run trades and businesses. He allus did want to travel, Mark did. He's not like me.'

'Are you sure of that?'

Luke shook his head. 'No, I told you. It's only a guess. But I reckon I'm right.'

The ticking of the clock was the loudest noise in the cosy room for the next minute, then Luke fumbled in his pocket and held out a thick envelope. 'He left this for you.'

Tom tore it open and scanned the neatly written sheets of paper inside. Only a blot near the signature betrayed Mark's feelings. 'He says he'll get in touch with us in a year or two. *Year or two!* Doesn't he know Dad'll be fretting himself silly until he finds out where the lad's gone? Doesn't he know we'll all be worrying?'

'He knows,' Luke said quietly. 'But it was all he could think of to protect you. He said if he stayed, Mr Burns would find some way to make him wed Nelly, or else to get at Dad.'

Tom began to curse softly and fluently, then looked across at Luke and wiped a tear from one eye. 'I don't like to think of him going so far away on his own.'

'No. I don't, either. I'd have gone with him, only,' he looked at Tom helplessly, 'I've got my land. I can't leave it now.'

'It's not your fault, lad.'

Luke just shook his head. Last night when he had got back, the bedroom had seemed so empty. He would miss Mark more than anyone else, he knew that.

Tom tapped the papers. 'I'd better study this lot and see what needs to be done. I'll make sure he has a good sound business to come back to.' Unspoken were the words 'if he comes back'. 'Will you go up the hill and tell our Annie?'

'Yes.'

'Tell her Burns is thinking about our offer. Tell her Frederick was right.'

Tom saw Luke out, then went back to sit in front of the fire. It was a long time before he moved. Then he took the bundle of papers and began to peruse them carefully, nodding from time to time. 'I will look after things for you,' he promised the absent Mark. 'I'll make sure you've more to come back to than you left.'

And if Mark didn't come back in a year or two, he'd send someone across the sea to fetch him. He would that. No Gibson was going to be driven away from Bilsden. But, hell, they'd all miss the lad.

It took the Burns family only a day to find out that Mark had left Bilsden on the milk train and had not been seen since. Under their questioning, with the three large Burns brothers standing over her, Maud admitted that her employer had made her sign a paper and had left her and Bet in charge of the chop house.

And all this time, Nelly stayed locked in her bedroom, confidence slowly giving way to despair.

In the end, Mr Burns signed the paper on behalf of his daughter. Within the month, Nelly had been married off to a distant relative who could not believe his luck at getting such a rich wife, even if he did have to pay her father two shillings a week for the privilege out of the child's money. Since he was fond of children, Timothy Hill didn't see any problems with fathering Nelly's child.

But he would, he said slowly, as he signed Mr Burns's piece of paper, make very sure that Nelly was a faithful hardworking wife. Yes, he and his mother would take care of that, for obviously his mother would be living with them, now that his father was dead. She was a good strong woman, his mother was. She'd help Nelly back to the path of righteousness.

29

April to August 1859

To Annie's relief it would be four months before Tian Gilchrist was free to come to Bilsden to make a start on the portraits, due to some family commitments. That would give her time to prepare herself, she decided, though she was not really sure for what she was preparing. She explained to the children about the family portrait and asked William if he would make himself available to pose when Mr Gilchrist came.

William frowned. 'It's a frivolous thing to do. And we're very busy at the mission.' The warmer weather seemed to be bringing an outbreak of fevers and belly upsets that were decimating the weaker inhabitants of the Manchester slums.

'The portrait is Frederick's dearest wish.' She had no need to explain the importance of that. Her son nodded slowly. He seemed fully a man now, and a man fulfilled and happy at that. She moved forward to give him a hug. 'I know you're doing important things at the mission, William, but Frederick deserves our support, too.'

He smiled down at her. That was the first time she had acknowledged the value of what he was doing. He gave her a rib-cracking hug back, and then, eyes alight with mischief, swung her off her feet and twirled her round.

'William, stop! William, you idiot! Stop that!'

415

'Very well.' He put her down, dodged a mock slap and pulled out his watch. The frown came back. 'I must go now, though.'

'You spend more time with your Mr Robins than you do with your own family,' she complained.

'Mr Robins is failing in health. I feel honoured to be working with him, learning from him.'

'He's ill?'

William shook his head. 'No, just old and getting very frail. He's nearly eighty, after all. I must make the most of my time with him.'

His mother often grew impatient with his praise of the man who had, she seemed to think, tricked him into helping at the mission, but William knew that he would have found something similar to do, with or without Alan Robins. He hadn't been able to persuade her of that, so it had more often been his step-father and grandfather to whom he had confided his plans, and he knew this made his mother more annoyed still. But today – today she had sounded almost approving, even accepting.

He would love to talk to her about his long-term plans. Frederick and John always listened with interest, approved, made suggestions and even contributions to the upkeep of the little 'city mission'. They could see, if Annie could not, how he was growing, maturing. He really was. He could feel it.

So when his grandfather invited him to stand up at the chapel and speak about his work, he accepted the invitation. He still felt too young to preach, too young to tell others what to do with their lives, but the realisation was growing upon him that he would one day be called to the ministry and that he would follow that call joyously. Soon he must start playing a more active part in the Methodist church if he were to take that step. Though what his mother would say about it all, he did not like to think.

Still, it would be years before anything came of it. Time for her to grow used to the idea. He still had to prove himself in so many ways. Methodist ministers did not go to university and then look for sponsors with livings to bestow, as did the priests of the Established Church. Methodist ministers came up through the ranks, preaching and proving above all that they had been called. Then they went to a centre, like the one in Didsbury, to spend a year or two training formally before acting as relief preachers on one of the circuits until they gained a more permanent posting.

William intended to go and talk to someone in Didsbury about his hopes and plans, as well as to Saul Hinchcliffe, his old teacher, who had himself once been a Methodist minister. There was no rush. William still had a lot to learn about his fellow men and women. And he intended to work with Alan for as long as he could.

It gradually came to him that he might not feel so shy about standing up as a lay preacher if he did it first somewhere other than Bilsden. He was sure the Lord would forgive this small weakness in him. He knew there was a chapel about twenty minutes' walk from the mission. He might start going there occasionally on Sundays, even taking some of the people he was helping with him. He had long ago come to the conclusion that in such an imperfect world you had to save bodies as well as souls, though the latter were the more important in the end, of course. Now, he felt, was his time to prepare for that great task, the saving of men's souls.

When the time came, he would consult his step-father about how best to break the news to his mother that he felt himself destined for the ministry. But not quite yet.

Frederick's greatest interest continued to be the development of a proper town centre for Bilsden. He had already finalised the plans for it with Mr Featherborne, who had worked mostly from a distance, using Simon Darrington as a locally based assistant, and had only two or three times visited Bilsden. It had surprised Frederick and Annie how much the young lord of the manor seemed to be enjoying himself, how much enthusiasm he was showing for the task at hand. He was more than earning the money Frederick was paying him, and had once naively confided that this was the first real money he had ever earned.

Now, through Matt Peters and Hamish Pennybody, Frederick was starting to make arrangements to move the shopkeepers out from the end of High Street nearest the station, the end where the buildings and the narrow streets of shabby workshops and warehouses behind them would be demolished. New shops would be put up to match The Prince of Wales hotel and the station, but with a much wider space between them and the station, and there would be two small arcades leading off the square.

It was Frederick, not the Town Council, who took it upon himself to compensate people for the trouble this was causing them, promising them first pick of his new shops, and finding them temporary premises at much reduced rents in a large warehouse which he had partitioned into shop and storage areas. The block of buildings with Tom's Emporium and the Bilsden Ladies' Salon in it was not to be changed much, except for some minor alterations to the façade to give the building a similar appearance to the new terraces of shops which were to border the square.

The Council hired Rory O'Connor to start the major demolitions that would widen the end of the street and make it into a square, and he was also instructed to make a fountain and small garden at its centre. That was to be done quite quickly, and temporary paved pathways set around it, because no one wanted the centre of their town to look like a mudheap while the new buildings were going up. What would people think of Bilsden when they got off the train if they found themselves faced with nothing but sludge and chaos?

Rory's brother Daniel Connor had changed his name to make it less Irish, but Rory himself remained defiantly an

O'Connor. He was of medium height only, with black curly hair, and looked so much like his mother, Bridie, that when she met Rory in the street one day, Annie felt guilty about not visiting her old friend and neighbour more often. What a long time ago it seemed since they'd all lived in Salem Street!

She therefore took the children and their governess with her one afternoon and they all spent some happy hours at the O'Connor farm, which had been reduced in size by the railway and was now used mainly to house convalescent children. Mick was beginning to show his age and he was glad that he no longer had to earn his living by farming. He had his clever daughter-in-law Helen to thank for the idea of setting up a convalescent home for children, which was easier work for someone his age. But he kept a few animals, partly for the fresh milk and eggs, and partly because the children enjoyed playing with them.

Elizabeth MacNaughton tactfully left Annie to gossip with Bridie, and turned a blind eye as Tamsin and Edgar got themselves gloriously dirty playing with two little girls and a slightly older boy, who had all been pale and listless when they arrived, but were now rosy and nearly ready to return to their families.

Even Annie was in a relaxed mood as they drove home, just laughing at the filthy condition of her children's clothes and enjoying the sunshine on the open carriage.

'The square is going to look wonderful,' Frederick said that night as he and Annie got ready for bed. He had been enormously cheerful all week, having recovered enough now to organise things, even if he could not do much of the to-ing and fro-ing himself.

Annie smiled to see him so happy. As far as she was concerned, he could have knocked the whole town down and rebuilt it, if it made him feel better. 'What are you going to call the square?'

'I don't know. The Councillors insist that they must have

the choosing of the name, but they've graciously invited me to submit ideas. What do you think of Victoria Square?'

She pulled a face. 'Everywhere you go things are being called after the Queen. Let's think of something different for a change.'

'Station Square?'

'Oh, no! That's ugly. And not Market Square or Bilsden Square or Manchester Square, either.'

'I haven't suggested those names,' he protested, climbing into bed.

'No, but others have. People are always asking me what it's going to be called. As if I know! I'm getting fed up of it.' It was not until she had put out the gaslight and climbed into bed that the idea came to her. She gasped aloud at the rightness of it.

'What's the matter?'

'What? Oh, just a touch of cramp. I'll wiggle my toes for a minute and it'll go away.' She beamed into the darkness, but did not enlighten him.

The next day she made the excuse of visiting the salon with some of her sketches and left Frederick happily going through some designs for fountains, which had just arrived from a stonemason in Manchester who was starting to specialise in fountains as well as the usual headstones for graves.

In town, Annie did not go to the salon, but turned off High Street and walked along the little side street which led to the new Council Offices. They had started in one old house in Pound Street a few years previously and now occupied two adjacent houses.

She turned to look behind her as she walked along, feeling as though someone were staring at her, but there was no one to be seen, only an old woman hobbling slowly along High Street. I'm getting very fanciful since that accident in London, she thought with annoyance, always imagining things. Why would anyone follow me around?

She still felt that the London accident was the work of a deranged person and the Manchester accident was just that. An accident. No one could possibly have any reason to wish her dead.

In the Council Offices, she was greeted with a flattering amount of attention by the young man at the counter near the entrance. Sometimes she wished she were not so well known in the town, but today she hoped to use her influence as Frederick Hallam's wife.

When she asked to see Mr Yatesby, who was in charge of planning, he overheard and came rushing out of his little office along the corridor. 'Mrs Hallam! My dear lady. Your husband should have sent me a message. I'd have come up to the house to see him.' He ushered her into his office and dusted off a chair with his handkerchief before gesturing to it. 'Please do me the honour of sitting down.'

She did as he asked, settling her full skirts around her. She had dressed very elegantly today, wanting to impress. 'I've come to ask your help, Mr Yatesby. And I don't want my husband to know I've been here.'

He blinked in surprise and a certain wariness crept into his expression. 'Oh?'

'Yes. I was wondering – has any decision been made about naming the new square?'

He shook his head. 'No. The Council has done nothing but argue about it, actually. But I think they'll end up calling it Victoria Square, because that's the least contentious name.'

'Mmm. Well, I wonder if I could suggest another name and ask you to approach the Council quietly with my idea?' She cocked her head on one side and smiled at him. 'I felt sure you'd be the best person to speak to first. You know how everything is done.' He did, too, for he'd been one of the first employees to be hired when the new Town Council was formed.

He went a little pink. 'Oh, well, I'm right flattered you should say that, and I can assure you, Mrs Hallam, that if there's anything I can do to help you and Mr Hallam, anything at all, you have only to ask. A very civic-minded gentleman, Mr Hallam, and we could wish there were more like him in our little town.'

She leaned forward with a conspiratorial air. 'What I was wondering was whether you, that is the Town Council, would consider naming the square after my husband?'

His mouth fell open, then he smiled and nodded. 'Eeh, that's a champion idea,' he said. 'Hallam Square. Oh, yes! Couldn't think of a better name. And he deserves it, too.'

She steeled herself to say it. She always hated admitting it. 'My husband is not a well man, you see. It would mean a great deal to him to leave a memorial behind him.'

Mr Yatesby stared at her. 'Oh, dear. Oh, dear, dear, *dear*! Are things really that bad with him?'

She nodded. 'I'm afraid so. It's not – the danger is not immediate, but his heart has been weakened. Dr Lewis says he must be careful. And he's not likely to make old bones.' She sucked in a deep breath, smoothing the back of one gloved hand until she was in control of her emotions again.

Mr Yatesby looked down and fiddled with his pencil to give her time to recover, then, seeing the distress she was trying to control, he leaned forward and patted her hand, forgetting his usual awe of her. 'I'll do what I can, I promise you, Mrs Hallam. Personally, I think it's a wonderful idea.'

'Thank you.' She stayed to ask about his wife and children, then took her leave, well satisfied.

But the next month, when the Council met, they did not regard Annie's suggestion with approval. Some said that the Hallams had had too much influence on the town already and that it was about time someone else got a look in. After all, there already was a Hallam Park, though admittedly that was named after Owd Tom, Frederick Hallam's father. No one called it the Thomas Hallam Park, of course. That was too much of a mouthful. The argument was lively. Other Councillors remained firmly in favour of honouring the Queen, to show her what loyal subjects she had in Bilsden.

Afterwards, Mr Yatesby wrote a regretful note to explain the impasse, assuring Annie that he would need to work on it a little, but that he had not given up hope of *achieving our purpose* (underlined twice in purple ink).

She was very angry and since she could not talk to Frederick about it, she went and had tea with Tom at the Emporium.

'Ungrateful devils!' he said. 'Leave it to me.'

'But you're not on the Council!'

He gave a tight smile. 'Of course not! I've got my businesses to run. But I have a couple of friends who are on the Council. In fact, I helped them get elected, so they owe me a favour or two. It'll take time to change a few minds, but since the square isn't finished, there's no great hurry, is there?'

'Not so long as Frederick keeps in good health.' And indeed, he seemed to have taken on a new lease of life lately, though he still got breathless when he climbed stairs or hills and admitted occasionally to pains in the chest.

She looked at Tom thoughtfully. It seemed to her that he'd been very quiet since the trip to London. 'Now, tell me about you and Rosie. What did she say in her last letter? Have you persuaded her to marry you yet?' She watched in surprise as his expression grew gloomy.

'Tom? Is something wrong? Why didn't you say before?'

'What good would that do? And anyway, you've enough to worry you.'

'Tell me!'

He scowled down at his teacup. 'Rosie won't give up her singing.'

Was that all? Annie relaxed. 'I should think not!'

He stared at her somewhat indignantly. 'What do you mean by that? I don't like the idea of my wife traipsing all over the country singing, so that anyone who can afford half a guinea can gawp at her! I don't want her to do it!'

'But, Tom, Rosie has such a wonderful voice. You can't expect her to hide it. Why, it's cruel even to think of stopping her singing.'

'She'll have no *need* to go out and earn money once she's married to me,' he repeated stubbornly.

'Her wanting to go on singing has nothing to do with earning money and well you know it, Tom Gibson. Honestly, you men want us women to be *doormats*. Look at that poor Mrs Burns. Daren't open her mouth when she's with her husband. He probably tells her when to breathe in and when to breathe out!'

'You don't understand!'

She tossed her head at him. 'I most certainly do! I had the same problem myself with Frederick.'

'Yes, but you hide your interest in the salon and in the Emporium. It's done discreetly. No one can give concerts discreetly.'

'My involvement in the salon is an open secret in the town and well you know it.'

He got up to stand with his back to her, staring down into the fire. 'It's not only that, love. There's the lad as well. She wants to bring Albert to Bilsden with her.'

'Well, of course she does! Would you leave Lucy and the others behind if you married again, or moved to another town?'

Tom turned to face her, his eyes looking positively haunted. 'Albert looks exactly like me. And like Samuel John, too. Folk might wink their eye at your taking an interest in the salon, and they might accept Rosie's singing, too, but they wouldn't be so complaisant about me flaunting my bastard son everywhere, now would they? And what would that do to the other three? Especially as Albert's nearly the same age as Lucy and David.'

'Oh. That does cause a bit of a problem. Does he look very like you?'

'Yes.' There was pride as well as pain in his voice as he

added, 'Spitting image. And as smart a lad as anyone could wish for.'

The only respite Annie got from all her own and her family's worries was when she went walking on the moors with Rebecca. It had become quite a habit with the two of them to take advantage of every fine day, and they would tramp for miles, sometimes talking, sometimes just enjoying the scenery.

Annie now knew all about Simon Darrington's attempts at courtship which had been renewed since they all returned from London. She knew, too, that Rebecca was not so indifferent as she tried to make out. But she agreed that it would be unwise to pursue matters. However, this was made more difficult by Simon's habit of joining them on their walks. They could hardly tell him to go away, and anyway, they both enjoyed his company.

A favourite destination was Knowleby Peak, a piece of high ground, where the rock jutted up as if some giant had pushed it from below. At one side the rock was much steeper, forming a small cliff that local lads loved to climb and local mothers loved to worry about. Annie never went near the edge, but she did enjoy the view.

Most days the Peak was deserted, except for an old woman they sometimes saw on their walks, taking the air slowly, leaning on a much younger woman's arm. The first time they met her, Annie was a bit puzzled. Was this the old woman she had seen once or twice in town, the one who had seemed to be watching her? No, it couldn't be. This old dame could barely put one foot in front of the other. The young woman bobbed a respectful greeting and volunteered the information that her gran *would* come out walking on days like this, when there was more than enough work needing doing at the farm.

The old woman, whose face was half obscured by an old-fashioned sunbonnet, mumbled something and dragged her grand-daughter away.

'See what I mean?' the young woman called over her shoulder. 'She's right determined about it. Won't take no for an answer.'

After that, they saw the strange couple several times, but never close enough to speak to. The old woman seemed particularly fond of sitting right on the edge of the cliff, sitting rocking to and fro and mumbling to herself.

'You're very cross with everyone lately, Mother!' Tamsin observed on the day Tian Gilchrist was due to arrive. 'Is something wrong?'

'No, of course not!' Annie looked at her daughter in exasperation. That young lady was getting too observant for her own good. 'I'm just trying to get everything in order so that we can all pose for the portrait.'

'I want to wear my best dress for it. Or a new dress. This one is getting too small for me.' Tamsin peered at herself in the nearest mirror, holding her dress up against her face. 'You were right about the cream material looking better with my hair than white, though. Why can't I have cream pinnies, too?'

'No reason. We'll buy some cream material for the next ones. And I'll show you how to sew them yourself.'

Tamsin pulled a face. She did not like needlework. Then she went back to gazing in the mirror.

The girl had a complacent expression on her face as she posed this way and that, and certainly, Annie thought, the child had a lot to be complacent about. Tamsin seemed to get prettier every year, and where Annie's hair had been uncompromisingly red at that age, and had only turned darker later, Tamsin's was a rich auburn already. Annie had been as scraggy as a scarecrow at that age – well, no wonder, with all the work she had had to do – but Tamsin had soft rounded limbs and looked what she was, a rich man's beloved daughter.

She continued to study herself in the mirror.

'When you admire yourself like that, you get a sickly

expression on your face, which is definitely *not* attractive,' Annie observed tartly. Frederick indulged the child so much that she often felt the need to bring her daughter down to earth.

Edgar went to stand next to his sister and stare at his own reflection beside hers in the mirror. 'I'm nearly as tall as you now,' he said. 'When we grow up, I'll be much taller. And next year, Father says I can go and earn my spending money in the mill office like you do.'

'You won't know where anything is,' Tamsin said loftily.

'I will if you show me.'

'I might not want to.'

Tears came into his eyes and he just gazed at her in the mirror.

Annie stifled an impulse to shake the girl.

When Tamsin felt that Edgar had been humbled enough, she condescended to say, 'Oh, well, I suppose I'll have to. I can't have my brother doing silly things there, can I?'

Contrary to Annie's expectations, Tamsin loved 'working' at the mill, and the way Matt and the operatives petted her was enough to turn anyone's head, though Annie made sure the child had real, if minor, responsibilities there: filling inkwells, ruling up pieces of paper for the rough accounts (she was not yet neat enough to touch the permanent accounts books) and running errands around the mill, among other things. But at least Elizabeth MacNaughton had been able to improve Tamsin's behaviour and attitude. Elizabeth was a real treasure, more of a friend than a governess now. Annie didn't know what she'd have done without her.

'There's the carriage!' squealed Tamsin, turning towards the front door.

Annie caught hold of her arm. 'Where do you think you're going, young lady?'

'To see the artist.'

'You'll stay beside me and behave yourself.'

Frederick, who had come to the doorway of the library, added his mite. 'Mr Gilchrist is not a raree show, you know, Tamsin. He's just a man who's very clever at painting.' As Annie had expected, Frederick adored the painting of Tian's little sister, and it now graced a wall in the library. Unlike Annie, he was looking forward very much to making the acquaintance of Mr Gilchrist, but she hoped he had not guessed her feelings of reluctance.

She turned towards the door as Winnie reached for the handle. She could cope with this, she said to herself for the umpteenth time. She could cope with anything, if she had to.

30

Tian Gilchrist

*T*he man who walked in through the front door seemed taller and more imposing than Annie had remembered. He paused for a moment to take stock, as people do when entering a new place.

'Goodness,' said Frederick's voice in her ear. 'You didn't tell me how handsome he was.'

'Irish handsome,' she whispered back. 'It doesn't impress me.'

'The Irish are not all like Daniel Connor, love.'

She just shrugged and made a little sniffing sound, and he tried not to smile. Since her troubles with Daniel, Annie was always suspicious of Irishmen.

As Winnie took Mr Gilchrist's hat and the coat he had been carrying because the weather was so hot today, Frederick walked forward, hand held out. 'Welcome to Ridge House, Mr Gilchrist. I'm Frederick Hallam.'

Tian beamed at him and clasped the hand. 'I'm delighted to meet you at last, Mr Hallam. Delighted.'

Annie had to swallow hard against a sudden pain. Next to a vibrant and energetic young male, Frederick looked older and – faded, somehow. The contrast was cruel. She forced a smile to her face, however, and moved forward, keeping her arms around the shoulders of her children. 'Mr Gilchrist.'

She would have nodded and left it at that, but he strode forward, hand outstretched, so she had to let go of the children and take hold of it. She looked up to see luxuriant sidewhiskers framing a rosy suntanned face. Even the hair on Tian's head seemed to have more bounce in it than other people's hair. He must have spent half the summer in the open air. Goodness, how blue his eyes were against that tan! And how curly his chestnut hair, if a trifle long for Bilsden taste, for it reached nearly to his shirt collar.

'How's the shoulder?' he asked with a mischievous grin.

'What? Oh, the shoulder. It's fine now. Our doctor said you did a very good job of putting it back.'

He nodded. 'I've had some practice.' He tore his eyes away from her lovely face to smile down at the miniature version of her. 'You don't have to tell me that this young lady is your daughter, Mrs Hallam.'

Annie inclined her head. 'Tamsin. And this is my younger son, Edgar.'

Both children wriggled in pleased embarrassment as Tian solemnly held out his hand to each in turn. They were not used to more than a glance from strange adults, most of whom truly believed that a quiet child was a good child.

Tamsin stared up at Mr Gilchrist's face and gave a nod, as if in approval. 'I'm going to wear my best cream dress for the painting,' she announced. She had talked of little else for days.

'And lovely you'll look in it, too, darlin'. And what about you, young fellow? What do you want to wear?'

Edgar gave him the solemn assessing stare that was so much a part of his personality, then shook his head. 'I don't know. It'll depend on what you put in the background, won't it?'

Annie looked at him in surprise. Edgar hated to wear anything whose colours displeased him, but such an artistically perceptive comment from someone so young had surprised her.

'You're quite right,' Tian said, nodding. 'And I haven't

even begun to consider backgrounds yet. I'll have to get to know you all first, won't I? See what sort of a background really suits you.'

Watching them, Frederick felt left out. He had to admit to a twist of jealousy. Mr Gilchrist looked fit and healthy, as did Annie. And the two of them looked so *right* together. If only – No! He resolutely pushed away that thought. What use was it wishing for the impossible? If you could not change something, then you had to accept it gracefully, as he was trying to do. That was the most he could achieve now. If he did not manage that, then it would sour what time was left for him and his beloved girl.

'Well, Mr Gilchrist,' he said, moving forward to put an arm possessively around Annie's shoulders, 'shall we let Winnie show you up to your room?' He nodded to the waiting maid. 'And then perhaps you'd like to join us outside on the lawn for tea?'

The summer had been so glorious, the rain so infrequent, that the family had made a habit of this alfresco gathering on fine afternoons. Of course, if the river got any lower, the mills would not have enough water for their steam engines. The Bil was usually a very reliable river, taking its source from the hills and welling from the foot of Knowleby Peak, whether it had rained recently or not. But when the water got really low, the mill-owners had the small reservoir that Owd Tom had insisted they build to fall back on. They could always open the sluice gates and increase the flow... He realised from Annie's worried expression that his mind was wandering again and turned his attention resolutely back to his guest.

Tian was waiting with an understanding expression, as if he understood Frederick's need to ponder something. 'I'd love to join you all for tea on the lawn. I shan't be long, Mr Hallam, for I can see the sunshine lighting up one of the prettiest gardens I've ever seen. It's calling out to be explored.'

He was as good as his word. Five minutes later he came

outside, pausing for a moment in the front doorway to gaze with appreciation at Nat Jervis's creation. The sun was glinting on the lake. The roses at each side of the entrance were perfuming the air, for Nat favoured the sweet-smelling ones above all others. Gardens were not just for looking at, as he often told his underlings. They were for smelling and for providing good fresh food for The Family (he always said the words as if they had capital letters) and for those who served them, too. For the servants ate well in this household.

The family in question was sitting around a table in the shade of a huge chestnut tree. The dappled sunlight was flickering on their faces and a light breeze was teasing the twist of lace and ribbons that Annie was wearing in lieu of a cap. If Mr Gilchrist had not been there, she would have been bareheaded, but she had decided on dignity and conformity while he was with them.

'Do take a seat, Mr Gilchrist.' She pointed to an empty chair at the opposite end of the oval garden table from her. 'And may I introduce Miss MacNaughton, our governess?'

'I'm delighted to meet you.' Tian treated the governess to one of his glowing smiles.

Elizabeth, as Annie did not fail to notice during the next few minutes, was not unaffected by Tian's good looks and charm. The man was probably a flirt, as Daniel Connor had been, she thought sourly, then decided that she was being unfair. She didn't know that he was a flirt. She didn't know very much about him at all.

There was no lack of conversation, for if it was Frederick who mostly led them from one subject to another, Tian also played an active part.

'I've never seen a cotton town before,' he said at one stage. 'The smoke was obvious before the train arrived in Bilsden. And yet up here on the hill, the air seems clean and tangy.' He raised his head and sniffed it. 'Are there some good walks across those moors of yours?'

Frederick nodded. 'Wonderful walks. My wife and I

often used to go for long tramps. Now, she goes with her sister. The two of them are indefatigable walkers.'

'You don't ride, Mrs Hallam?'

Annie shook her head. 'No. Not many people in Bilsden do. We're not gentry.'

Frederick's lips twitched. His wife had very definite views about the gentry, whom she considered idle creatures, and would have scorned any resemblance to them. And yet, she was a lady in every sense that mattered: caring for those dependent upon her, loyal to her family, gracious to those in need, and always dressing with grace and style.

Tian's eyes strayed to where a dip in the ground gave a vista across the surrounding garden walls to the moors. 'Such stark beauty,' he murmured. 'I'm itching to paint them already. The play of light over the rolling landscape is fascinating. Perhaps I may join you in a walk one day, Mrs Hallam?'

It took a huge effort for Annie to say, 'Yes, of course.'

'If you go out on your own, Gilchrist, don't stray from the well-marked tracks until you know your way,' Frederick warned. 'The moors can be dangerous as well as beautiful. People get lost and there are places where the rock falls away into miniature cliffs. Nothing huge, but steep enough to hurt you, maybe even kill you, if you fell over one.'

Tian nodded gravely.

By the time tea was over, Annie had changed her mind about her ability to cope with a long visit from Mr Gilchrist. His presence seemed to charge the air and even the children were hanging upon his words. Worst of all, there was no doubt that his eyes kept lingering warmly upon her. She would just have to make sure, make *absolutely* sure, that she was not left alone with him.

The next day, Tian was glowing from exercise by the time he joined the family at the breakfast table. 'I had a half-

hour's walk along the wide track that heads uphill,' he
announced. 'I was still twitchy after sitting around in that
train yesterday.' He looked down at himself ruefully. 'I'm a
country boy at heart, I think. London stifles me sometimes.
But these moors of yours are grand, they are indeed. Such
rolling lines and subtle colours. I wonder the English don't
value the scenery here more.' Clearly he did not consider
himself English.

He smiled wryly as he thought about his family, who
could definitely be considered both 'gentry' and 'idle rich'.
They had been very scornful of his latest commission to
paint a mill-owner's family portrait. Indeed, they still felt
uncomfortable with his earning a living by painting.

'Those people are aping their betters,' his father had
scoffed. 'I don't know why you don't stay here and breed
horses instead of dabbling around with paints. There's
enough land to spare here for that.' Tian had not bothered
to argue. It did no good. His father would never change
what he was, any more than Tian could bear to deny his
talent or live the idle life they expected of him. To him that
would have been sponging off his eldest brother, Paul. And
the Gilchrist money was not so plentiful that he would feel
easy doing that.

Later, when the children had left – very reluctantly – to
return to the schoolroom, Frederick looked at Tian. 'Well,
my friend, how do you wish to set about painting our
portrait?'

'I'd like to spend a day or two sketching you all and
getting to know you as a family. Then we'll discuss
background and composition.' He grimaced. 'I hope you
don't want a formal group, with stiff children in their best
clothes? That's not my style, as Mrs Hallam must have told
you.'

Frederick shook his head. 'No, we don't want that at all.'
Mischief lit his face for a moment. 'In fact, before you start,
I'll get Annie to show you the family portrait my first wife
insisted upon. It's up in the attic. It's a terrible piece of

434

work. Now the painting Annie bought of your little sister is just perfect. Complete harmony between subject and setting. How old is she now?'

'Fifteen. And thinks herself a woman grown.'

'How could you bear to part with that delightful portrait?' Frederick asked without thinking. 'Oh, I'm sorry. That was a tactless question.'

Tian just grinned. 'It's not the only one I've done of Sarry. I have others just as good. I find her easy to paint. And I'm glad to see that this one has found itself a good home. I have to earn my living, after all. I'm the youngest son of five, so there's little to come to me from my father.'

'Five sons!' Annie spoke before she thought.

He turned to her, his face warm. 'Yes. And four daughters, too. Sarry is the youngest. My eldest sister is married with children of her own. We Gilchrists are taking over the whole county, so we are.' His Irish accent was not pronounced, more a music behind the words, but every now and then he slipped into a phrase that reminded Annie of Bridie. And Daniel.

'Who do you want to start with?' Frederick asked.

'You.' Tian's reply was immediate.

'Is there a reason for that?'

He nodded. 'Yes. You're the paterfamilias. It may be that the group should centre on you. Certainly your family hangs upon your words.'

Annie blinked at him, then nodded reluctantly. It was true. When Frederick was there, they did all revolve around him without realising it. How perceptive of Mr Gilchrist!

'Even Miss Tamsin is quiet when she's with you, though I'd guess she's a handful, that one. She reminds me very much of my second-eldest sister, Caitlin.' He rolled his eyes. 'If she hadn't met a handsome young American gentleman who married her and whisked her off across the world in search of adventure, I think she would have burst with mischief. Ripe for a hanging, my grandfather always used to say.'

'I'll leave you two together, then,' said Annie, standing up. 'I have things to do.'

Tian was on his feet instantly to hold the door open for her. 'This afternoon, if I may, I'll sketch you, Mrs Hallam? In the garden, I think. And please, don't cover that wonderful hair.' He turned to Frederick. 'Would you not agree that we should leave that hair loose in the portrait?'

Frederick studied Annie, his head on one side, and nodded slowly. 'Yes. I think you're right.'

'But if it's a family portrait, it won't look respectable for me to sit with my hair loose like a young unmarried girl,' Annie protested.

The two men did not hide the fact that they were still studying her.

'Well, I've always preferred you without those caps and bonnets,' Frederick said at last. 'And the portrait is for us, not for the worthy ladies of Bilsden.'

Annie swallowed more protests and left them to it. What had she got herself into? She should just have told Frederick that she couldn't find a painter in London. But then she shook her head. She could never have done that, especially after she'd brought back the painting of Tian – Mr Gilchrist's – young sister. And why she kept thinking of him as 'Tian' she did not know. The man got under your skin. All that Irish charm. And he'd be here for weeks, probably. It was too much!

'Where in the garden do you want me to sit for you?' Annie asked after luncheon, which she and Frederick usually took together, without the children, but which today had been graced by the presence of Mr Gilchrist.

'I've changed my mind about that. Out on the moors would be better, with your hair blowing in the breeze. There's something a little wild in you that reminds me of them.'

She ignored that comment. 'I'm not going out on the moors with my hair loose like a – like a hoyden!' She scowled at them both and added darkly, 'Or worse!' then turned her attention to Tian. 'Nor would it be proper for me to be out there on the moors alone with you.'

'In the garden, then, for today.' He looked at her, puzzled by the vehemence of her tone, then turned to Frederick. 'But I'd rather you were not with us, sir, if you don't mind? For if you are, Mrs Hallam will be listening to you and watching you, and I think it'll come out better if I catch her with her own thoughts.'

Frederick smiled, but there was bitterness in his face as well. He knew very well that Annie was embarrassed by this need to pose for Mr Gilchrist. Now that he had seen them together, he guessed that it was because she found the fellow attractive, but it was also perhaps because the man had seen her with her defences down when he'd saved her from that fall in London. What else could it be? 'I have to go into town anyway this afternoon. We're finalising the design of the fountain for the new square.'

Annie immediately forgot Tian. 'Don't overdo things, love.'

'Don't fuss, love,' he mocked back in the same tone of voice.

Tian just watched them both, a little frown on his forehead.

After ten minutes of sketching, he threw down his pad on to the little wrought iron table. 'It won't do.'

Annie twitched her shoulders to loosen them up. Amazing how quickly you got stiff, sitting posing. 'What won't do?'

'You won't.'

She raised her eyebrows. 'Oh?'

'You're as stiff and suspicious as a virgin on a feast day,' he said.

'*Mr Gilchrist!*' She was shocked by his simile; not the words – she'd heard far worse in the Rows – but the fact that he'd say them to her.

He stared at her. 'Well, that got you off your high horse

for a moment, and put a bit of feeling into your face. What's the matter, Mrs Hallam? *You* chose me to do this portrait. Are you now regretting that I've come? Or have I offended you in some way? If I have, I can assure you that it's quite unconsciously.'

She could feel herself blushing. 'No, of course not. How could you have offended me?'

He was looking at her closely, his expression so open and puzzled that the blush on her face deepened.

'I just feel – silly, posing like this,' she said, as the silence lengthened.

'And uncomfortable with me,' he insisted. 'We can all of us feel it. If we can't change that, you'll have to find yourself another painter.'

'*No!*' She looked at him, then her shoulders sagged. 'No,' she said in more moderate tones. 'This portrait means a lot to Frederick.'

'But not to you?'

She bowed her head, fiddling with her wedding ring. 'Well, perhaps not in the same way.'

'You're worried about him, aren't you?'

She nodded.

'He doesn't look particularly ill.'

'It's his heart. It's not working as it should.'

'Ah.'

'What do you mean, "Ah"?'

'Well, a weak heart is unpredictable. My aunt suffered from a weak heart for many years. In fact, she outlived her husband and was killed in a riding accident at the age of seventy.' He paused, then said slowly, 'That's not really it, though, is it?'

'What do you mean?' She didn't meet his eyes.

'You know exactly what I mean, Annie Hallam. There is an attraction between the two of us and you're trying to deny that it exists, even to yourself, I do believe.' Most married ladies were not averse to a little mild flirtation. But Annie was not most married ladies.

She could not think what to say to that.

'But I can see that you love your husband dearly,' Tian's soft voice continued. 'Indeed, I've taken a fancy to the man myself. He's a great gentleman, mill-owner or not.'

She looked up, her eyes filled with tears. 'Yes, he's a wonderful person.'

Without speaking, he passed her a handkerchief.

The silence lengthened between them as she mopped her eyes, then mopped them again.

When it had gone on for too long, he said thoughtfully, 'Well, I can promise you that you won't be bothered by any unwanted attentions from me while I'm here, if that'll help?'

She gazed at him and managed a small smile. 'Yes. It will help.'

'I'm not denying the attraction's there, mind.'

'No.' She picked up his sketch pad and studied it. He was right. She did look stiff and angry. For some reason she believed his promise, and that did make her feel more comfortable. But she had had enough of discussing such personal matters. 'Shall we start again, Mr Gilchrist?'

'Yes, Mrs Hallam. Now look over there and think about – about Tamsin.' He shouted with laughter. 'My mistake. She must be a real Miss Mischief to put that expression on your face! Think about the garden, how pretty it is. How sweet the roses smell.'

After a while he said softly, 'Yes, that's more like it.'

But she was lost in thought and didn't hear him.

31

Knowleby Peak

*O*ver the next few days, Tian made himself at home in Ridge House. He was surprisingly unobtrusive when he wanted to be. He took Tamsin out on to the lawn and drew her, giving her one of the sketches which particularly pleased her to keep for herself.

When he was with Edgar, the two of them never stopped talking, for Edgar wanted to know all the technicalities of what Mr Gilchrist was doing. In the end, Tian gave him some paper and a soft pencil, and told him to draw the lake.

The sketch he later showed Annie and Frederick of Edgar engrossed in his drawing was so good that Frederick at once claimed it. 'I'll have it framed. You've caught the very essence of our Edgar.'

'If you'll allow me free rein in your workshops, I'll frame it for you myself.'

'*You* will?' Annie stared at him in surprise.

'I will so. I prefer to do that myself.' He gestured to the painting of his sister on the wall. 'I did that. And all the frames you saw in London. I enjoy working with wood, actually.'

'You have an artist's eye in everything, then,' she allowed.

'I'll probably need to go into town to get the wood properly cut. Perhaps you can tell me who's the best cabinet maker?'

'Lloyd Palmer,' Annie and Frederick said together, without hesitation.

When Tian had gone, striding away down the drive, whistling cheerfully, Frederick smiled at Annie. 'You did well, choosing him, my love.'

She was not so sure.

That Sunday, when Annie and Rebecca went for a walk, Tian asked if he could join them, and then inevitably they met Simon Darrington on the way up to Knowleby Peak. It was the prettiest walk around, but they met him here nearly every time they came out and Annie was beginning to get suspicious.

She soon found herself in the lead, partnered by Tian. She frowned at him, but he just grinned.

'Not my doing. I think his lordship is more than a little interested in your sister.'

'And she in him. But it won't do. There's too great a difference between them.'

'Love doesn't always follow a sensible path.' He stared into the distance and his smile faded into a tight, shuttered expression.

'Well, my sister is an eminently practical young woman and she's more sense than to—' But just at that moment, Rebecca tripped, Simon caught her arm to prevent her from falling, and as they looked at one another, their feelings were all too obvious to the two onlookers.

Annie made a little sound of disapproval, but said no more.

Knowleby Peak was their favourite walk because of the sweeping views from the top, where the ground fell away sharply. But the natural platform was wide enough for Annie not to feel afraid. From it, they could look down on to the stream that was the main contributor to the River Bil, though a lot of other streams joined it further down.

They passed the old woman and her grand-daughter again, as they often did. Simon and Rebecca were still lagging behind, so it was to Annie that the young woman said, 'Good morning, ma'am.' She turned to Tian and her eyes were openly admiring. 'Good morning, sir.' As always there was something a bit cheeky in her tone, though her words were respectful enough.

As she usually did, the old woman had turned away at the sight of them and was already hobbling down a side track.

'She dunt like strangers,' the grand-daughter said, chuckled and went running after her.

'And I don't like that young woman,' Tian observed. 'She has something sly in her face, as if she knew a secret or two.'

'She's always polite enough.'

He snorted. 'Her words may be polite, but her expression isn't. But we're not here to talk about her. Just look at that view. I love it more every time we come here.' He led the way to the highest vantage point.

They stood together, gazing at the clough where the farm lay next to the reservoir, and beyond it, the broad sweep of rolling moorland. There was no need to speak. Tian's pleasure in this place was obvious in his face and it had always been one of Annie's favourite spots.

'I'd like to come up here and paint this view one day before I leave,' he said quietly, as they turned to greet Rebecca and Simon. 'If you'll let me stay on a day or two longer after I finish the portrait?'

'I'm sure that'll be no trouble. In fact, my husband will probably want to buy the picture. He used to love coming here.' How cruel that Frederick could never come again!

The others joined them and Annie thought her sister was looking a bit flushed, but it could have been just the exertion of the climb.

On the way back, Rebecca stayed close to Annie and the two men soon fell behind, deep in a discussion of estate management. Listening to their conversation, Annie could not help realising how much Tian loved his family estate.

She wondered how he felt at being a fifth son, at knowing he could never inherit. Was that why he'd taken to painting and wandering around Britain?

Later in the afternoon, the whole family went down to Netherleigh Cottage for tea, Tian included, because Frederick had not felt it right to leave him out of the gathering when even Elizabeth was included nowadays. The garden lad took a message to John Gibson and brought back a warm invitation to bring the artist with them.

Annie was not surprised to see how well Tian fitted in. The man seemed to have the gift of making himself liked, she thought, eyes narrowed. He was soon explaining to John exactly how a picture was framed, and what sort of wood he preferred to use. He and Luke went on a tour of the back garden, where Luke's roses were just as showy as those at Ridge House, and even Luke's dog, who accompanied them as they strolled around his master's smaller domain, fawned upon Tian.

Kathy, too, succumbed to her visitor's charm, though she was usually shy with strangers. She let him help her carry things to and from the kitchen and pressed another piece of cake upon him, behaving as if he were a favourite nephew, though she was probably younger than he was. But in all things, she seemed to ally herself with her husband's generation.

In the bustle, with so many people talking to one another, Annie had no difficulty managing a quiet word with John. 'Are you all right, Dad?' He was looking a bit downhearted, she thought.

'There's nowt wrong with my health,' he allowed.

'But?'

He looked blindly out of the window. 'But I saw a young fellow in town yesterday as had such a look of our Mark that it fair tore my heart.'

'He'll be all right, wherever he is. He's a capable fellow, our Mark.'

'I'd feel better if I knew that for certain, if I could write to him and ask him to forgive me for my harshness towards him.'

She clasped his hand for a moment. 'He won't hold that against you, Dad.'

'I hold it against myself.' He looked her straight in the face. 'Never judge your children too harshly, Annie lass. I know William isn't doing what you'd want him to do, but he's a fine young man, for all that, a son anyone could be proud of.'

She nodded. 'I know. But I can't help worrying about him, and what he'll do with the rest of his life. He'll have a living to make.'

'Mayhap he won't want to make a lot of money. The lad's eyes are set on other riches.'

She could say nothing to that. Her father's serene faith always made her feel a bit uncomfortable, for she was not sure what she believed in.

Tom, too, was looking a bit gloomy. But then, he hadn't looked really happy all summer. 'Me an' Rosie just seem to quarrel lately,' he admitted, when Annie questioned him.

'You should get married and be done with it.'

'That's what I said. I even said she could go on with her singing. But that made her more angry still, and she told me she'd not have any man telling her what she could and could not do, thank you very much. Even a husband.' He shook his head and stared down at the carpet. 'I think she's most worried of all about how our marrying would affect young Albert.' He was silent for a moment, then he looked at her and shrugged. 'Oh, I'm sick of talking about it. Let's change the subject. I like that painter chap of yours.'

They both looked across the room to where Tian was holding a lively conversation with Joanie, who was, for once, smiling not sulking. John always insisted that Joanie attend the family tea parties, but given her own choice she'd have been off with her friends.

'He's a charmer, all right.' Annie scowled at Tian.

Tom shook his head. 'No. He's not a charmer, he's charming. And that's quite different. He's just an open friendly fellow, that one is, not at all like Daniel Connor.'

She did not trust herself to respond. Tom was quick to pick up nuances of meaning. They knew each other too well, she and Tom did.

The portrait started taking shape. Tian worked quite slowly, sketching the outline of a group several times before he was satisfied with the composition. In the end it was decided that they were to be sitting outside under the big tree, with the little lake as background. Tamsin would be sitting on the grass, hugging her knees, and Edgar would be sprawled beside her. Annie and Frederick were to be on chairs, both of them talking to William, standing by the tea table.

'Yes,' said Frederick slowly, as the sketch was explained to him. 'Yes, I see what you mean. I think it'll come out well.'

So Tian made a wooden frame and stretched a large piece of canvas over it, with Edgar in eager attendance, then he sketched in the group very faintly, before starting on the background. 'I shan't finish this background properly until the figures are right,' he told Edgar. 'But I want to get the basic colours in to be sure the harmony of one with the other is right. That's my way, mind. There's other ways to do things. You have to find what suits you.'

'Can I watch?'

'If you wish.'

'Oh, I do!'

With Nat Jervis prophesying rain for the following weekend, Annie decided that she and Rebecca would go for a walk on the Thursday afternoon. Perhaps, just for once, they could get away on their own.

But when she mentioned it at breakfast, Tian immediately said, 'I'd love to come with you, if I may? I need quite desperately to stretch my legs.' He'd been shut up in one of the spare bedrooms all the previous day, working on the central figure of Frederick. Tamsin and Edgar's figures were already finished, but Tian refused to show the painting to anyone except Edgar at this stage, and Frederick thought they should humour him on that. Even the maids were forbidden to go into that room to dust.

Annie did not look best pleased. 'If you want.' She would rather have gone with Rebecca alone. She wanted to talk to her sister, find out what was happening between her and Simon. She was sure something had happened, for Rebecca had been so quiet lately, with worry lines creasing her forehead whenever she lost herself in her thoughts.

'Where exactly are you going this time?' Frederick asked.

Annie shrugged. 'We'll probably take the north route to Knowleby Peak. It's a little steeper than the other. Mr Gilchrist hasn't been that way before.'

Tian nodded, sensing her reluctance to have him but not letting it stop him. 'I'll tramp along behind you, so that you ladies can chat freely,' he promised with a grin. 'But I'm still not used to the paths up there, so when I go out on my own I have to stick to the main tracks. Sometimes I can't tell a sheep trail from a path that leads somewhere. And yet the smaller tracks are very tempting, as are the distant vistas.'

He was right to be careful, Annie knew. It could be confusing up on the moors. Not many people went up to Knowleby Peak so the paths were not well marked. It was too far for most townsfolk, and farmfolk didn't waste their energy on idle walks. They had enough walking in their working day.

'I'll send a message down to the salon, then, to Rebecca,' Annie said. Mary was used to taking over now, since Rebecca went out regularly with her sister.

'You might as well send a message to the Hall as well,' Frederick said, grinning. 'I hear Simon's got the gatekeeper primed to send him word when you lot set out.'

'Who told you that?' demanded Annie.

'Nat. He has a nephew who works at the Hall.'

Annie's forehead wrinkled. 'I don't think Rebecca would like that. She's been trying to avoid Simon Darrington lately.'

'Well, I'd bet money that his lordship will join you.'

Tian grinned. 'You'd find no takers. It's a certainty.'

As he watched them set off, Frederick smiled, but with some difficulty. How he wished he was going with them! Then his thoughts brightened. No need to stay moping at home. He'd have Robert drive him into town to look at the new fountain. It wasn't playing all the time yet, because there was so much work going on still in the square, but if he sent a message down to Bill Yatesby first, maybe they'd switch it on for him. They had to do that regularly, after all, to prime the pump, and a man was entitled to a few weaknesses.

By the time he left, he was feeling much better. After he'd looked at the square, he might go on to take a look in at the mill. Matt Peters always seemed glad to see him, and Frederick didn't think that was feigned. Matt wasn't a leader of men, though he was a very able second-in-command. He liked to check what he was doing, either directly with Frederick or through Annie, who also went into the mill regularly nowadays, though she pulled a face at the fluff-laden atmosphere there on working days. As did Edgar, who said it made his chest feel funny. Tamsin didn't even seem to notice the fluff and was most scornful of her brother.

It was one of those sunny days when occasional clouds obscured the sun and sent shadows chasing one another across the land. Nat had assured them that it wouldn't rain until the following day, so they had planned to stay out for several hours. They took some food with them, just a few sandwiches wrapped in napkins and some newly picked apples. Tian volunteered to carry everything in his artist's knapsack, which held the sketching materials he was never without. They could eat the food on Knowleby Peak lookout and find a clear stream to wash it down later.

Inevitably, Simon turned up, striding along to join them with a beaming smile. Frederick was right, Annie thought, this was more than a chance encounter.

Rebecca was quite short with him, but he soon coaxed her into a better humour.

Annie sighed. Today, she couldn't seem to find her usual peace of mind up on the moors. If it didn't worry Frederick so much, she'd sneak away on her own sometimes. But he clearly preferred her to have not only her sister, but a gentleman accompanying her on these walks. Today Tian's presence disturbed her more than usual, too, for some reason, and she was very conscious of him striding along behind her. He had kept his promise about not upsetting her and now treated her almost like a sister, so she couldn't understand why she felt like this today.

Once she caught his eye and for a moment it seemed as if something leaped from one to the other. She had to make quite an effort to turn her own eyes away and that made her cross with herself.

Just as they got to the lookout, a cloud obscured the sun and the immediate surroundings turned dark, although the sun was shining still across the other side of the clough below. They all sat down to rest, for it was a steep walk up the last part of the hill.

Annie wrapped her arms around her knees and stared away into the distance, not feeling like talking.

Tian got out his sketching materials.

Rebecca sat down quietly for a few minutes, then got up and began to pace about restlessly. Simon joined her and laid one hand on her arm.

'I'd like to talk to you, Rebecca. Alone.'

She stood stock still, staring up at him. 'I don't know—'
He took hold of her hand. 'Please. It's important.'

So it had come, Rebecca thought. And she would have
to find the strength to say no to him. For although she had
lain awake night after night, knowing she loved him, her
common sense told her that it would not work, that they
would only wind up hurting each other if she tried to fit
into his world. That was, always supposing he meant
marriage and did not want her to become his mistress?
Even as that thought was born, she dismissed it. No,
Simon would not treat her like that.

Without speaking she let him lead her along the stony
path that traced the edge of the clough. About fifty yards
along it, they came upon the old woman, without her
grand-daughter this time. She was sitting on a rock,
muttering to herself, and when she saw them, turned her
back to them as she always did, with a grunt of annoyance.

'She shouldn't be out on her own,' Rebecca said,
frowning.

Simon didn't even hear her. He walked in silence until
they were a couple of hundred yards further on, then he
stopped. 'You know what I want to ask you, Rebecca.'

'Please don't.'

'Why not?' He took both her hands and held her at
arm's length. 'Rebecca, you know, you must know, how
much I love you. And I can tell that you're not indifferent
to me.'

When she would have spoken, he let go of one of her
hands to touch his fingertips to her lips. 'Shh. Let me
speak.'

She closed her mouth and looked at him. All the love
she had been trying to suppress welled up inside her. Life
was cruel. It made you fall in love with the wrong sort of
person.

'Rebecca, please say you'll marry me?'

She closed her eyes and began to open her mouth.

'No, let me finish! I know there are difficulties. But

they're difficulties other people make. There are no difficulties between you and me. I love you and I want to make you happy in every way I can. I want to marry you, have children, live a long life together. And I don't care about society. I never have. I don't care if I never see London again, never attend another ball or house party or grand dinner. I was quite happy to be the younger son. And if the estate is going to come between us, then I'll be quite happy to give it away.'

There was no mistaking his sincerity. She drew a long shuddering breath. 'Oh, Simon, how can I say yes? Even if you don't care for the differences between us, your family will. How can you hurt them so?'

He gave a scornful snort of laughter. 'Hurt them? What I do will hurt no one. There's only my step-mother now and a few stray cousins and aunts. They don't matter to me and I really don't matter to them, except as nominal head of the family. And even that matters less, now that there's no money to be had from me.'

She looked at him in puzzlement. How could he say there was no money when he had a great estate? When he was Simon, Lord Darrington?

A wry smile twisted his lips. 'Did you think I was rich, Rebecca? I'm not. In fact, I'm hard put to look after the estate, and I think I must soon sell some more of my land if I'm to finish repairing the Hall. All I can offer you is a draughty old house on the edge of the moors – although we have got the roof more or less watertight now. And enough money to manage on if we don't live extravagantly.'

Tears were sparkling in her eyes. 'It'd still be wrong for me to say yes.'

'Why?' He drew her towards him. 'Ah, Rebecca, let me show you how I feel.'

As his head bent towards her, she knew that now was the time to pull away, to stop it, but she couldn't move. His eyes were warm on hers, the love shining clearly in them. His lips felt so right. His body was hard against hers. With a sigh she gave up the struggle and wrapped her arms around his neck, returning his kiss shyly but ardently.

'Say yes,' he whispered. 'Oh, Rebecca, I don't think I can bear it if you turn me down.'

She stared at him, her dark eyes troubled. 'I'll – think about it,' she compromised. 'Maybe I'll talk to Dad.' For she had already talked to Annie, who had not even thought Simon Darrington would want to marry a Gibson, a girl who had been born in Salem Street, like Annie herself. But so far, Rebecca had said nothing to her father, partly because he had been so upset when Mark left. He would normally have realised something was amiss, but lately he'd been too wrapped up in his own guilt to notice that she, too, was troubled. And Kathy had been too worried about her John, for thoughts of Rebecca to burden her.

'I'll speak to your father, too,' Simon said firmly. 'And I'll discuss this with your sister.' His hand hovered beside her cheek for a moment, then he brushed a stray lock of hair aside, in a gesture that was just as intimate as an embrace. 'Perhaps if I get her on our side, you'll stop protesting.'

They walked back in silence, stopping once or twice just to stare at one another. They might have been walking along an underground tunnel for all they noticed of the magnificent views to their right. In the distance they could see Annie, sitting on her own. Tian had moved further along and was sketching furiously, lost in his work.

'That old woman's going across to talk to Annie,' Rebecca said, puzzled. 'That's funny. She usually avoids us. Who is she, Simon?'

'How should I know?'

'But isn't she one of your tenants? She's often up here when we are. I thought she was part of the family at the farm. One of the girls from there sometimes comes with her and I'm sure she said the old woman was her grandmother.'

Simon shook his head. He had come to know his tenants during the past year, not only the families but their relationships to one another and to the district. 'The grandmother died a few years ago. There's only the father, the son and the daughter living at Upperfold now.'

Rebecca felt anxiety surge through her. The old woman was nearly up to Annie now, and was moving in a cautious way, as if she did not want to be heard. Every line of her body spoke of intent, but intent to do what? And she did not seem to be moving like an old woman now, surely? 'Then who is she? She couldn't be—'

'She's going to push Annie!' Simon let go of Rebecca's hand and began to run, yelling and shouting and waving his hands, desperately willing her to look round.

32

On The Edge

Tian looked up when he heard Simon shouting, but Annie was still lost in her thoughts. What Tian saw made him also jump to his feet and start running.

As Rebecca and Simon ran, they watched helplessly as the old woman reached Annie, catching her unawares and pushing her towards the cliff edge. Annie cried out in shock and began to struggle, but the two women were so close to the edge that she had little space to do anything.

The old woman was shrieking now, her words too shrill and high to be heard above the wind which had been rising steadily. Only Annie could hear them.

Tian was pounding along, calling out desperately, but he was still quite a distance away when Annie shouted in panic as her feet found no purchase and the two figures tumbled to the ground on the very lip of the steep drop.

Rebecca ran as hard as she could after Simon, breath pumping into her lungs, legs feeling too heavy. 'Annie! Annie, hold on!' she sobbed, too breathless even to cry out now.

As Annie felt herself slipping over the edge, she clutched at her assailant. 'Stop! Stop! What are you doing?'

The old-fashioned sunbonnet slipped and revealed a face that was all too familiar.

For a minute Annie froze in shock. 'Beatrice!' Only the

hold she had on Beatrice's skirts kept her from falling. Beatrice tried to prise her hands loose, but Annie clung on with all her strength. She could not move the other woman back from the edge, though, for Beatrice had always been bigger than she was. And although she was gaunt now, a mere bundle of bones, she seemed full of wild strength.

'You're going to die,' she shrieked. 'Die! And leave my father in peace. You deserve to die.' And she burst into a peal of wild laughter.

'No! Beatrice, stop!' Annie's feet were scrabbling against a small fold in the rock, just over the lip of the sloping edge, and for a moment she thought she had found something to help her resist. Then Beatrice jerked her and with a wild shriek, tugged her right over the edge.

But the rock face was not sheer here, so they bounced and rolled downwards in a series of jerks that brought them to a temporary halt on a sort of ledge. The fall had torn Annie from Beatrice's clutches and instinctively she drew herself backwards, trying to crawl away from her assailant along the ledge.

For a moment, Beatrice lay there, winded, then she shook her head, as if to clear it, and lunged for Annie again.

With a desperate roll, Annie moved aside and pressed herself against the rocky wall behind her, not noticing that she grazed one hand quite badly or that she banged her temple and grazed that, too. There was just enough space for Beatrice to miss her. One of Beatrice's hands scrabbled at Annie's clothing, and she shrieked in triumph, but the material was thin and already torn by the fall. A strip of skirt shredded off with a soft tearing sound. Beatrice screamed in fury and continued to roll forward.

Everything seemed to slow down as the hatred in Beatrice's expression turned to surprise, then to shock as she realised what was happening. Terror etched itself quickly on to the gaunt face, the face that looked far older than her years, the face whose every line seemed graven by unhappiness.

Beatrice's voice choked off in mid-scream, followed by a sort of whistling noise, and then, from far away, there came a dull thump. After that there was silence. Even the wind seemed to Annie to stop blowing, the birds to stop calling, and the insects to stop buzzing. The silence echoed in her ears more loudly than Beatrice's scream had. And she had to shut her eyes to stop everything whirling her off the ledge.

The first thing Annie heard when the world stopped spinning around her and the silence blurred into sound again was someone calling her name. It was a moment before she could respond, because her mouth seemed so dry.

'She's alive,' the voice above her said. 'I saw her move her hand.'

'Annie!'

That was Rebecca's voice. Annie blinked and then shuddered as she realised where she was. On a ledge, with only a foot between her and a steep drop. And Beatrice had gone over that drop, fallen to her death. She must be dead. It was a long way down.

'Annie, are you all right?'

Tian's voice. Annie could not move, could not frame a reply. All she could do was try desperately to move backwards, to get away from the edge that seemed to be tugging at her. But there was only jagged rock behind her, pressing into her. She could not get any further back. She was unaware that she had sobbed aloud as she discovered that.

'Annie!'

That was Tian's voice, she thought, but he seemed to be such a long way away that she did not bother to answer.

'Annie, can you hear me?'

His voice was a little louder now. Perhaps if she shouted he would hear her. But her shout came out only in a dry rasping whisper as she said, 'Yes. I can hear you.'

'Annie love, don't move. I'm going to climb down to you

457

and help you back up. It's not so steep above you.'

She shuddered violently. What was he talking about? She could not move, not an inch. If she did, she'd follow Beatrice over the edge.

'Annie? Did you hear me?'

'Yes.' The word was cut off abruptly as nausea threatened, but Annie gulped back the bile. She must not move, must not do anything but lie here as still and quiet as an animal in a trap.

Small pieces of rock began to bounce down the cliff, most of them missing her. One or two pattered against her skirts and one hit her hand, but she did not move, just concentrated on breathing as evenly as possible, on not panicking, on not stirring an inch.

The noise came nearer, but she did not dare lift her head.

Then there was a soft thumping sound as feet made contact with the ledge beyond her and Tian's soft voice said, 'I'm here, Annie love. Right beside you.'

She raised her head very slightly and caught a glimpse of him before the world swam into dizzy confusion around her again. She gasped and shut her eyes quickly.

But he could not let her lie there. 'Annie, we have to get you to your feet. We have to get you back up to the top.'

'*I can't move. I can't!*' Even to herself, it didn't sound like her own voice. She wished he would go away and leave her alone, but he kept talking to her, asking her to do the impossible. '*I can't!*' she repeated, and her voice was shriller than usual. '*Leave me alone!*'

'The ledge is quite wide here and I'm strong enough to hold you safe. Trust me, Annie.'

'No! No, I won't move.' She did not open her eyes again. She knew if she saw that edge, saw the long drop, saw Beatrice's body below her on the rocks, she would panic.

'Do you not trust me?'

There was a long silence while she tried to consider this annoying question. Eventually, she decided that she did. 'Yes.' After a moment, she added, 'But I don't trust me.

Tian, I can't move. I just can't!' The words choked to a stop in her throat and her stomach heaved again. 'If I move, I'll be sick.'

'You can't stay there for ever, Annie.'

Silence.

'Let me help you. Trust me.'

Silence.

He had a sudden inspiration. 'Simon's gone for help, but Frederick will be worried sick when he hears about this. We have to get you home to him as quickly as possible.'

She whispered, 'Frederick!' and managed to open her eyes again.

Tian's voice was warm with encouragement. 'There's my girl. Think of Frederick. You need to get back to him.'

'How?' She could not prevent herself from trembling now. 'I d-don't think I can stand up, and even if I did, how would I keep my balance? I feel dizzy even lying here.'

'There's no need to worry about that. I can hold you safe once you're up. I promise you I can. I'm a strong man and you're a small woman.' He noted a lightening in her expression as he spoke, not a smile, but a lightening, as if a cloud was beginning to pass across the sun. 'Think of Frederick,' he repeated, for this seemed to be a magic talisman with her.

She swallowed back the fear and nausea. 'Yes. Frederick. He mustn't worry. H-how shall we do it?'

He considered her. There was enough space for her to stand up on her own, but he knew instinctively that she would not be able to do that. He knelt down and stretched out his hand. If she stretched out hers, he would be able to touch her fingers. 'Reach out just a little bit, Annie, and I'll take hold of your hand. Then we'll decide what to do next.' Once he had her hand, even if she fell, he could take her weight, keep her safe. *Oh, Lord,* he prayed, *please let me keep her safe!* It was the first time he had prayed for years. And he had never, ever prayed so fervently, or cared so much about anything.

Annie's shoulders were hunched tightly. If there had been the space, she might have curled into a ball, as people sometimes did when threatened. But slowly she forced herself to stretch out and touch him. First her fingertips, then her whole hand. He took hold of it slowly but firmly, afraid she would jerk back and throw him off balance. She gave a gasp of relief and clutched that big warm hand convulsively.

'There,' he coaxed. 'That's the first step taken. That's my girl. Now, let's see if I can pull you up to a sitting position. Shut your eyes and don't think of where we are. Think of Frederick. We need to get you back to him as quickly as possible.'

Actually, Tian had warned Simon not to send word to Ridge House, only to bring out some horses from the Hall, so that Tian could ride back with Annie in front of him. He was sure she'd be in no state to walk. But he didn't say that now. He could see how the thought of Frederick was giving her the courage to overcome her terror. Yes, he thought, the love between those two is as strong as anything I've seen. And a bitter pang shot through him.

Her hand trembled in his, but Annie allowed him to pull her up to a sitting position. She didn't close her eyes, just looked at his face, seeming to draw strength from his smile, from his soft words of encouragement. He doubted that she'd remember a word he'd said, but he could see that the sound of his voice helped her, so he kept on talking, saying the first thing that came to mind, telling her about his favourite walk as a child.

And then she was sitting upright and a little colour was returning to her face.

'There,' he said with satisfaction. 'Now rest a minute and then we'll get you to stand up.'

'I'd rather not r-rest. Just let's – let's carry on.' If she stopped moving, she'd never find the courage to start again.

'All right.' He braced himself and with one tug pulled

her quickly to her feet, so quickly that she gasped in fear, but by that time he had her safe in his arms, and even if she panicked, he knew that he was strong enough to hold her.

But she didn't panic. She just leaned against him, breathing deeply and raggedly, burying her face against him. Only a minute she stood quiescent, then she said in a harsh whisper, as if afraid to say it aloud, 'Go on! Don't stop. Let's – let's get back up while I still can.'

'You'll need to keep your eyes open for this part, Annie love. I can carry you if I have to, but it'll be far safer if you let me guide you up.' As he was speaking, he was pulling off his belt and fastening it around her wrist, thanking providence that the leather was soft enough to cling to her. 'See! Whatever happens, I'll be able to hold you. Now, you go first and take your time—'

She shook her head. 'No. You go first. It'll be better if I can see you ahead of me, see where you tread.' The sight of him would keep her moving. If she had to stare at the bare rock, she would freeze again.

He stared at her searchingly, then nodded.

And that was how they did it, step by slow step, with his soft voice offering support and encouragement every inch of the way, and the watcher above keeping absolutely silent. Annie didn't understand a single word he said. What helped most, what she really concentrated on, was the thought of Frederick. That gave her the courage to move her leaden feet, to hold herself upright in this vast and terrifying space.

All of a sudden, it seemed, Tian was pulling her up the last of the short stony slope and moving her quickly away from the edge, his arm around her waist, his eyes searching her face anxiously, in case she was near to fainting.

But she didn't faint. She just stood there, with her knees feeling as rigid as steel and a shudder going through her from head to foot. Then Rebecca's arm came around her from the other side, and between her two taller companions, Annie started walking again, walking and breathing the wonderful air and feeling the sunshine on her face.

Tears were falling down Rebecca's face, but Tian shook his head and made a shushing gesture when she would have spoken.

When they reached the level place where they had been picnicking, they stopped and Tian moved away, leaving Rebecca to support Annie, who was still clinging to her sister's hand.

Annie surprised them by speaking first, her words sounding slurred and tumbling over one another. 'I'll be all right in a minute. I will. We must get back. Back home. I don't want Frederick to worry and—'

Tian's voice interrupted her. 'Frederick doesn't know. I told Simon not to send word to him till we had you safe.'

Annie stiffened, then sagged back against Rebecca in relief. 'He doesn't know? You're sure of that?'

'Yes. Will you forgive me for lying to you?' he asked. 'I know how much you love him and I thought – I thought if anything would help you up that slope, the idea of your husband would.'

'It did.' She could admit it now. As she raised her eyes to him, she even managed a faint smile. 'You saved my life again, Tian Gilchrist. Thank you.'

Her eyes were, he thought, the most beautiful he had ever seen, the green very intense today and the pupils still dilated from shock. He wished, wished quite desperately, that he was the object of such love, for the thought of her husband had worked miracles on a woman dangerously near hysteria.

'Would you like to sit down for a while?' he asked.

She stood considering it, then shook her head. 'No. I think it'd be better if I keep moving. I want,' she swallowed hard, 'I want to be the one to tell Frederick about his daughter.'

Tian and Rebecca stared at her in astonishment. 'His daughter?'

'That old woman was *Beatrice*?' Rebecca exclaimed.

Annie nodded. 'Yes.' She saw the incomprehension on Tian's face and felt he deserved an explanation. 'My husband's youngest daughter by his first wife has always hated me. She tried to harm me once through my son, William. She hurt us all then and Frederick disowned her. Now I realise it must have been she who pushed me in London.'

'But why?'

Annie shivered as she saw again Beatrice's twisted face. 'She looked quite mad. She'd grown haggard and – just looked beyond reason.' She started moving. 'I don't want to talk about her. Let's just walk. Will you – send someone to fetch her body?'

'Yes, of course.'

'You don't think she might be alive?'

'No. There's no chance of that.'

In silence they made their way across the moor. When Simon came galloping towards them, leading a second horse, he shouted out, 'Annie! You're safe. Thank God!' and slid off his horse to take her hands and examine her bruised and bleeding face. 'Did that woman hurt you?'

Annie shook her head. 'No. Not really.' Not physically.

Tian picked up the second horse's reins and swung himself into the saddle. 'Pass her up to me, Darrington. She needs to get home.'

Annie opened her mouth to protest, but by that time Simon had swung her up and Tian had pulled her in front of him. He settled her there, one arm around her, and clicked his tongue to the horse. Behind them, Simon got up on the other horse and pulled Rebecca up behind him.

Tian had Annie cradled in his arms as he guided the horse across the moor. *The only time she'll ever lie willingly in my arms*, he thought bitterly. For now he had seen how very deep her love for Frederick Hallam was, he knew he had to leave, and as soon as he could.

When they arrived at Ridge House, Winnie came to the

front door and stood gaping at her mistress, who was as pale as chalk, with her clothes all torn, and a bloody hand and brow.

'Is Mr Hallam home?' Annie asked urgently.

'He just came in, ma'am.'

Annie pushed past Winnie and ran across the hall. At the library door she paused, took a deep breath and said firmly, 'I'm all right, Frederick. Just a small accident. I'm all right.'

He stood up, his heart pumping erratically, but as he saw that she was indeed all right, his heart steadied and he opened his arms. She ran across to fling herself into them, then pulled him down beside her on a sofa. 'Just hold me for a moment,' she begged. 'I need you to hold me.'

He did as she asked. Something had happened, but she was all right, so he could cope with whatever it was.

'I need to tell you—' she began.

Frederick's hand smoothed back the tangles of curls and he kissed her cheek. 'I'm listening, my love.'

Tian stood for a moment at the doorway, envying them their closeness, then he shut the doors on them and turned to Winnie. 'I think someone should prepare a bath for Mrs Hallam. She's had an accident. But she's all right. Let her tell your master about it, but send some tea in to them, perhaps.'

Then he walked slowly up to his own room to change from the filthy torn clothes into something more suitable for tea. Tea! he thought savagely. What I need now is some whiskey. What I need now is to get roaring drunk!

But he couldn't do that, not until he had finished the portrait and left. All he could do was act as if she was just an acquaintance. All he could do was watch the love that flared so brightly between her and Frederick Hallam. Watch and keep his own love to himself.

Tian thumped the bed as he paced to and fro like a caged tiger, then thumped it again. He had never been in love before. His family had joked about that. And now that he had fallen at last, he had fallen hard. But Annie was another man's wife. And she loved her husband as much as Tian loved her.

He walked across to look at his face in the mirror. The face of a gentleman and an artist, his mother always said. Well, he hoped the gentleman would stay in control until he left and not betray the feelings that were ravaging the artist's soul.

33

October: The Portrait

Before the weather could turn cold, Frederick commanded Mr Triffcott to come and take some more photographs of the family.

'But we're having the portrait painted!' Annie protested.

'It's not the same, love. I want to have photographs taken every year, to keep a record of the children.' He walked across to stand with his hand on the mantelpiece, looking at the previous year's photographs. 'Think how they've changed since these were taken.'

'Mr Gilchrist will be offended, I'm sure.'

'No, he won't. He knows that photographs are quite different from paintings.'

'He's nearly finished now.'

'He still has the portrait of you to paint.'

'Oh, Frederick, do we have to?' She would feel such a fool posing for Tian. Since the rescue, he had kept his distance from her and she had been glad about that.

'I very much want to have a portrait of you in your prime, my love.'

She stifled a sigh. 'Only for you would I make such a fool of myself, Frederick Hallam. And the scratches on my face haven't healed yet.'

'He needn't paint them in.'

'They'll show in the photographs.'

'We can get some face paint from Manchester, the sort that actors use.'

She gaped at him. 'Paint my face!' Only loose women painted their faces.

He chuckled. 'In a good cause, my love. In a good cause.'

She scowled at him. Since what she always referred to as 'the accident' he had seemed stronger somehow, and more determined to get his own way.

Nat Jervis had gone to retrieve Beatrice's body and it had lain in the church for two nights, before being buried. The local magistrate did not see any need for further investigation of the accident, with Lord Darrington himself being present and able to tell them exactly what had happened. Such a shame Mrs Barrence had endangered them all by her hysterics! He commended Mr Gilchrist's quick action, which had saved Mrs Hallam's life.

The tale Simon and Frederick had concocted was accepted by everyone.

Frederick had attended his daughter's funeral and seen her buried in the family mausoleum. He had told James the truth and had also coped with Mildred, who had come up from London for the funeral in response to his telegram. She stopped weeping to stare at him in horror as he told her exactly what had happened. He wanted no one blaming Annie.

He had even spoken to Mabel, who had come with Mildred, and been quite frantic to tend to her mistress's body herself.

'I tried to keep her safe, sir. I tried,' she sobbed. 'But when Mr Barrence treated her like that, it turned her poor brain, quite turned it.'

'Did you know she intended to harm my wife?' he asked sternly, for this he could never forgive.

Mabel shook her head. Of course she had known, but it would do her no good to tell him that. 'No. I thought she was trying to – to make friends with you again, sir. To persuade you to let her live in Bilsden. She used to say that she longed for the moors, that London stifled her. And when she came back from her little trips, she was always quieter for a time. So I thought no harm. Let the poor soul do what she wants.'

So Mabel was allowed to dress her mistress in the wedding gown that Beatrice had worn for her mockery of a marriage, and which had lain in the attics at Ridge House ever since. Mabel followed the cortège to the church, too, sitting weeping in a carriage all on her own immediately behind those of the family. She was furious that Annie Gibson had not attended, though of course she hid her feelings. But she did not want any talk to mar her poor mistress's good name.

Afterwards, Frederick provided money for Mabel to live on. She seemed uninterested in his generosity, however, and just kept saying, 'I'll never find another mistress like her. Never.'

He was utterly amazed that anyone could have loved his daughter so much.

It was quite a scandal in the town that only the family attended the funeral, for many people would have liked to demonstrate their respect for Frederick Hallam and also show that they were friends of the great man. But he was adamant about that. As he was about Annie not attending.

'It would be a mockery, my love,' he insisted. 'I shall follow her to the grave, but only to allay gossip. And for her mother's sake.'

'She had gone mad. She didn't know what she was doing.'

'She was always vicious. She always knew how to hurt people.'

Tom was not at the funeral. He had come to see Annie the day after the accident, to check for himself that she was all right, as all her family had done. While they sat talking, he said abruptly, 'I'm going to London tomorrow. I'm not taking no for an answer this time. Life's too short. You've got to seize your happiness while you can.'

As he was leaving, he surprised her by giving her a cracking hug and kissing her. 'I keep thinking – what if that damned woman had succeeded?' he muttered. 'I don't think I could have borne to lose you, too.'

She hugged him back, knowing the tragedy had brought back memories of Marianne's sudden death.

In London, he went straight to Rosie's house. When his luggage was carried inside, she came running down the stairs.

'What the hell are you doing with that, Tom Gibson? Take it away! You can't stay here.'

'I can and I will. We're getting married tomorrow.' He seized her hand and pulled her into the library, to the maid's scandalised delight.

'Tom Gibson, let go of me.'

He held her at arm's length for a moment, his face very sober. 'I'll never let go of you from now on, Rosie Liddelow. Not while there's breath in my body.' Then he folded her in his arms and told her about Annie.

When he had finished and they were sitting together on the couch, she leaned against him and sighed. 'It makes you think, doesn't it?'

'It certainly does.' He felt inside his pocket and waved a piece of paper in front of her.

'What's that?'

'Read it.'

She did, then sat very still for a moment, before looking up at him. 'How long have you had a special marriage licence, Tom?'

'For a couple of months. I thought,' he gave her a tender smile, 'if I could persuade you to say yes, I'd better get you wed before you could change your mind again.'

'You cheeky devil!'

'Well? Are you going to make an honest man of me?' he demanded, and before she could say anything, pulled her towards him and started kissing her.

When he let her go she was gasping for breath.

He just looked at her. 'We are getting married?'

And she could hold out no longer. 'Yes.'

'I suppose it's a bit late to arrange things today.'

'It certainly is.'

'Then tomorrow. I'm not waiting any longer.'

There was still a troubled frown on her brow. 'And Albert?'

'Albert is our son. I'd rather not publicise that fact. It'll do none of us any good. But he's our son and he's coming with us to live in Bilsden. And I'll treat him no differently from my other children, I promise you.'

The day after Beatrice's funeral, just as Annie and Frederick were sitting down to dinner, there was a loud knocking on the front door.

'Who can that be?' Frederick demanded, not pleased at the thought of visitors. From the loudness of the knocking, there was some problem. He'd had enough of problems. He just wanted some peace and quiet.

Tom's voice came from the hallway. 'We'll announce ourselves, Winnie.'

But several pairs of footsteps came towards the dining room, not one. Frederick and Annie exchanged puzzled glances and stood up. Tamsin looked at Edgar, and they got up, too, not at all averse to a bit of excitement.

When the door opened, it was Annie who spoke. 'Rosie!'

Tom grinned at them all. 'May I introduce my new wife? Rosie Gibson—' But he didn't have time to finish his sentence, for Annie had run towards him, beaming, to hug first him, then Rosie. Behind them stood four children.

Frederick followed suit, embracing Rosie and welcoming her to the family, then as he stepped back, Tamsin's voice came very loudly, 'Who's that boy with my cousins?'

'This is my son, Albert,' Rosie said. 'You must be

Tamsin. And Edgar, too. I've heard about you both.'

Tamsin scowled across at the boy, who returned her scowl. Albert was pleased that his mother had married Mr Gibson, of course he was, but he was not as pleased to find himself with two step-brothers and a step-sister – he had already had sharp words with Lucy – and now here was another uppity girl staring at him as if he was a black beetle who'd just crawled from under a piece of furniture.

'What relation does that make him to us?' demanded Tamsin.

'Step-cousin,' Elizabeth said quietly, from behind her.

'Huh! I've got enough cousins already, thank you very much.' Tamsin glared across at David, with whom she was not on very good terms lately, since he would keep trying to boss her around.

'Mind your manners, young lady!' snapped Annie.

Edgar stepped forward. 'Well, I'm pleased to meet you, Albert,' he said, ever the peace-maker. He offered his hand and another comment. 'Don't mind Tamsin. She's been in a bad mood all day because she doesn't like the photographs we had taken. They make her look too much like a little girl.'

Tamsin was about to give him a shove when Elizabeth hauled her off. Frederick could not hold back his laughter, as his eyes met Tian's across the table.

Tom joined in with a roar of mirth that made Tamsin bridle. Tom had never felt so happy in his whole life. He put his arm round Rosie's shoulders and beamed at her, then his eyes met Annie's across the group and she nodded approval to him, before turning back to smile at Frederick.

'More bloody Gibsons,' Tom said exuberantly. 'More and more of us.'

Rosie dug her elbow in his ribs and the children giggled in shocked delight.

* * *

Two days later, Tian asked to speak to Frederick after breakfast. 'I've finished the portrait,' he said abruptly, once they were alone, 'and now I'd like to leave.'

'You were going to do another portrait, one of Annie on her own.'

'I think it'd be better if I left now.'

The two men looked at one another, then Tian spread his hands in a helpless gesture. 'I'm afraid I've fallen in love with your wife, Frederick Hallam. She has eyes for no one but you, of course. Still, I think it would be wiser if I left now.' He looked down, then raised his eyes to add, 'If I did not respect you greatly, sir, I would be tempted to stay and try to win her for myself. And if she did not love you so very much. The thought of your anxiety was the only thing that made her overcome her fear on that ledge, you know. I've never seen anything so brave as the way she forced herself to climb to the top. And with your name on her lips all the way.'

Frederick was looking at him with sympathy, not knowing quite what to say. He did not need telling that Annie loved him.

Another pause, then Tian added: 'If I had met her first, I think she would have considered me. There is a feeling between us that one cannot mistake.' Then he gave a wry smile. 'But I didn't meet her first.'

Frederick nodded. This, then, explained the tension between Annie and Tian Gilchrist. 'Shall I come and see the portrait now?'

Tian became once again the artist. 'If you would. I'd greatly value your opinion of it.'

Frederick stood in front of the canvas for a long time before he spoke, then he said, 'It's wonderful.'

Tian smiled wryly. 'Yes. My best work ever.'

'Especially Annie. You've caught her exactly.'

'Mmm.'

'Shall you wait to frame it for us?'

Tian shook his head. 'No. But I've spoken to Mr Palmer.

He knows what to do. The sooner I leave Bilsden, the better for us all.'

Frederick looked at him with compassion. 'Thank you for finishing the portrait. I shall treasure it.'

Tian hesitated. 'There is just one thing. I'd like to speak to Annie alone before I go. If I give you my word as a gentleman that I'll do no more than say farewell, will you permit this?'

'Of course.' Frederick held out his hand. 'I can hardly blame you for finding her so attractive. To me, she is the most beautiful woman on this earth. I'll send her up to inspect the portrait.'

Tian nodded. 'Thank you.' He stood looking at his painting as he waited. Yes, his portrait of Annie was definitely the best thing he had ever done.

She hesitated in the doorway. 'Frederick said it was finished.' She had wanted him to come up with her, but he said he didn't want to climb the stairs again.

'What do you think?' Tian asked, his eyes not leaving her face.

She studied the portrait and her mouth fell open in a hushed 'Oh!' of surprise. 'It's beautiful. You've caught us all so cleverly.' Even William, standing behind his parents, was so real that he looked ready to step out of the frame.

'I'm glad you like it.'

'I love it.'

'I'm leaving now,' he said abruptly.

'Oh.'

'I've told your husband that I can't do your portrait. And I asked him if I could say goodbye to you privately.'

She stiffened and took a step backwards.

He made no move towards her. 'I told him I'd fallen in love with you.'

She drew in her breath, as if someone had jabbed a needle into her. 'I don't think I should—'

'You're quite safe with me, Annie.' He thrust his hands into his pockets and said with heavy irony, 'I was bred a gentleman, for all I earn my living as an artist, and I know how much you love your husband. I just wanted to say – if you ever need anything, if I can ever help you in any way, this address will find me.' He held out a card.

She moved forward to take it, reluctant to go nearer to him. 'I can't think how I would—'

'No. You don't think you'll ever need me. You have more than enough people in your lovely family to help you in need. Still, it'll make me feel better if you'll keep the card.'

She stared down at it. 'You'll get over me, Tian, find someone else.'

'Trite words, Annie. I doubt it greatly. I've reached the grand old age of thirty-four without falling for any other woman.' His voice grew soft with sadness. 'No, there will be no one else.'

He reached out and shook her hand gently, holding it in his for one precious moment. 'Go and fetch your children now. Show them the painting. I'm going to pack.' And once he was away from Bilsden, he was going to find himself a bottle of whiskey and lose himself in it. For a time, anyway.

Naturally, the whole Gibson clan was invited up to inspect the portrait, now propped carefully on an easel in the library until Mr Palmer could produce his frame, when it would be hung on the wall.

After they had all oohed and aahed over it, John tugged at Annie's sleeve. 'Could I have a word with you and Frederick, love? In private?'

She nodded and led the way into the morning room.

John seemed ill at ease. 'I don't rightly know how to say this.'

Frederick looked at him with concern. 'Is something wrong?'

'Not wrong exactly. But – I were so taken aback, I didn't know what to say to him. He must have thought me a right gormless lump!'

Annie pulled him down on to the chair beside her. 'Who

must?' Though she had a fair idea.

'Lord Darrington. He's asked me if he can wed our Rebecca! A lord born and bred. He says he loves her and she loves him, but she says though she loves him, she can't think it's right to wed him. Eh, it's a proper tangle, it is that!' John rubbed his forehead, reached automatically for his pipe, as he always did in times of trouble, then recollected where he was. The pipe was still at home in his other jacket.

'I knew they were in love,' Annie admitted. 'But I didn't think he'd offer her marriage.'

'He'll not offer her owt else while I'm there to look after her!' John snapped, in affront.

'He wouldn't have, anyway,' Frederick said. 'Not if he loves her, as I think he does. What I wasn't sure of was whether she loved him.'

'What exactly does Rebecca say?'

'She says she doesn't know what's the right thing to do, but she'll do nothing against my will. That's what's worriting me. It's not like our Becky to leave things up to others to decide. I never saw a lass as knew her own mind better.' He nodded to Annie. 'Except for you, love.'

'I don't know what to say,' Annie confessed. 'His is such a different world. If he falls out of love with her, she'll be so miserable. And his family will hate the marriage.'

John nodded.

Frederick looked from one to the other. 'Well, I think that if she really loves him, she should marry him and to hell with his family. He's a nice lad. I'd be happy to call him brother-in-law.'

John looked at him anxiously. 'You really think so?'

'I really do.' He took hold of Annie's hand. 'There is nothing in life more wonderful than to share a loving relationship.'

The love on both their faces made tears come into John's eyes. 'You're right,' he said thickly. 'I think the world of my Kathy.'

'So tell Rebecca to follow her heart—' Frederick was beginning, when the door opened.

Rebecca peeped in. 'I thought you'd be in here. Has Dad told you?'

Annie went over to take her by the hand. 'He's told us you're to wed Simon. We couldn't be more pleased about it.'

Rebecca gasped and turned so white that Annie and Frederick exchanged worried glances. 'I thought you'd tell me not to marry him,' she faltered. 'With the differences between us—'

'With the love between you, you can bridge the differences,' Frederick said firmly. 'Dare you do it, Rebecca Gibson?'

She stared at him and suddenly beamed around. 'Can I borrow your carriage?'

'Yes.'

'Where are you going, lass?' John asked.

'To see Simon.' She was already running down the hall and a moment later they saw her flying across to the stables.

John fumbled again for the missing pipe. 'To think of it! My lass wed to a lord.'

'Your lass wed to the man she loves,' corrected Frederick, putting his arm around his own beloved and giving her a quick hug.

34

May, 1860

The day the new square was to be opened and named dawned fine and with a balminess to the air more usually associated with full summer. Frederick watched as Annie and Rebecca came down the stairs towards him. How beautiful his wife looked! How beautiful they both were!

Annie's gown was of a light green silk, with five small flounces around the hem, each trimmed in narrow ivory lace. On her head was a small bonnet whose fine rice straw was nearly covered in ruched silk and lace. Around her shoulders was draped a patterned Paisley shawl in matching tones of green and ivory, and on her hands were ivory leather gloves. In one hand she carried a darker green sunshade with an ivory lace frill.

Rebecca was in a printed silk muslin, with a flounced skirt, and a light lacy shawl. She too was carrying a dainty parasol. But her face was so radiant with happiness that it was irrelevant what she was wearing. She had been ecstatic ever since she'd accepted Simon's offer of marriage.

Frederick stepped forward to greet his wife as she came down the last few stairs. 'Will you be warm enough with only a shawl, my dear?'

'Nat assures me that it's going to stay fine.'

He smiled. 'Oh, well, if Nat says so—' A tug on his frock

coat made him turn round, to see his daughter beaming up at him. Tamsin was wearing a full-skirted dress in cream muslin, short enough to show the broderie anglaise frills at the bottom of her pantaloons. Around her waist was a sash in her favourite green.

'Don't I look fine, Father?' she demanded.

'You look beautiful, darling.' He looked beyond her. 'And Edgar is very fine, too.'

Tamsin dismissed Edgar and his new sailor suit with a shrug of her shoulders. 'Aunt Rebecca looks lovely, too.'

They all turned and Rebecca flushed slightly under their combined gaze.

Frederick moved forward. 'My dear, he will not be able to look away from you.'

The happiness of the past few months had lent Rebecca an extra confidence that had been lacking before. Since the announcement of her engagement, she had spent much less time at the salon, although she had refused to leave Mary to cope on her own until they could find someone to replace Rebecca and deal with the customers. That replacement was now found, so Rebecca was staying with Annie and Frederick until the wedding, which was to take place from Ridge House in June.

A knock on the front door sent Winnie pattering across to open it and then curtsey awkwardly, but smile as she did so. All the servants liked Miss Rebecca's young man, lord or not, and Winnie often mentioned him with off-handed pride to her friend Margaret at church. It was not everyone who served a lord regularly, or had one call her by name.

Simon came in, but although he greeted his host and hostess politely, his eyes kept straying to Rebecca.

'He's gone all soppy again,' Edgar muttered to Tamsin.

'I think it's lovely, and when I grow up, I want all the men to look at me like that.'

He made a derisive noise and gave her a shove. Less and less was he allowing her to dominate him. Elizabeth intervened before the scuffle could develop into a real argument and finery be damaged.

Frederick, Annie, Rebecca and Simon drove into town in the Darrington carriage, with its top open for the first time that year. It was not as modern as Frederick's, but the crest on the door was very impressive. The children rode behind in the Hallam carriage with their governess and stopped on the way down the hill to pick up their grandparents. The rest of the Gibsons were walking into town.

They left the carriages behind The Prince of Wales, where Tom and Rosie were waiting for them with the four children, then they all strolled towards the new square. On the way they passed a man jealously guarding one of the new name signs, which was covered in thick sacking.

'A florin if you tell us what it says,' Tom called out to him.

The man shook his head. 'It's as much as my job's worth, sir.'

'I don't know what's got into that Town Council,' Annie muttered crossly. She could say no good of them since they had rejected her idea of naming the square after Frederick. He had, after all, paid for most of the improvements. He *deserved* to have his name on the square. She scowled back at Tom. He had let her down, too, for he had not managed to persuade his friends on the Council to do a single thing.

Tom shrugged and smiled back at her, knowing what she was thinking, then leaned sideways to listen to Rosie, with a fond smile on his face.

'They've certainly guarded the new name most carefully,' said Frederick, who was more concerned with the square than its name. It had come out better than he had ever expected and filled him with great satisfaction. He stopped to gaze at the scene. As many townsfolk as could cram into the square were standing around the edges, the fountain was creating miniature rainbow arcs in the centre, and the members of Michael Bagley's brass band, now in its tenth year of existence, were self-consciously formed up in rows, clad in their new maroon uniforms, ready to perform.

Mr Yatesby appeared before their group. 'If you'll come this way, Your Lordship, Mr Hallam, we have seats for you and your party on the stand.' When John and Kathy would have hung back, Mr Yatesby called out, 'We have seats for you and your wife as well, John,' and Simon went back to offer his arm to Kathy, who had still not lost all her awe of him.

When everyone was seated, with the children in the back row, very self-conscious, Royd Wilkins, Mayor this year, stood up and nodded to Michael Bagley. A roll on the drums sent a wave of shushing sounds across the square and within a minute or two, everyone was silent.

Mr Wilkins stepped to the edge of the platform and cleared his throat. 'Fellow townsfolk,' he called in the loud voice that Frederick swore was the reason he had been elected Mayor, 'I welcome you all here on this h'auspicious day. First I shall call upon the Bilsden Town Band to play for us.'

By the end of the third tune, all the children were fidgeting visibly, and even Frederick's smile was a trifle glassy. Fortunately, Mr Wilkins was not a devotee of music and he had refused to countenance more than three tunes.

Again the Mayor stood up, this time with one hand clutching the gold chain of office, of which he was so proud. 'We now come to the main part of this ceremony,' he boomed, 'the naming of our square. We have all seen our town centre change over the last year or so, and for the better, I think. And we all know that we have to thank Mr Frederick Hallam for the idea of this square, and for a good part of the money that paid for the h'improvements, too.'

He waved one hand towards an embarrassed Frederick.

'I think you will all agree with me that Mr Frederick Hallam is a shining example of civic virtue and Bilsden is fortunate to have him as its leading citizen and benefactor. Not only does he provide jobs and houses for many of our people, he also uses his profits for the good of our little community.'

Frederick muttered something under his breath. Annie looked at him proudly, hope beginning to rise in her.

There was a scattering of applause and voices calling 'Hear! Hear!' from around the square, then a voice at the back yelled out, 'Get on with it, fatty!' and Mr Wilkins sucked in a loud breath of anger.

Frederick spluttered, but managed to control the laughter that threatened to erupt. Annie coughed discreetly into her handkerchief, and John Gibson grinned broadly. Royd Wilkins had grown fatter each year and even his brand new suit seemed to be too small for his prominent belly.

'My fellow citizens, we on the Council have taken great care in choosing a name, seeking one which will reflect the feelings of our ratepayers. After long and h'earnest discussions, we were unanimous on the name we should give our square, and also on the desire to keep it secret until this day.'

Around the corners of the square, four men on ladders began to loosen the cords that held the pieces of sacking over the signs.

'Before we unveil the names, I just wish to say—'

A groan rippled round the square and the same voice yelled again, 'We'll be dead before you get to the point, Wilkins!'

The Mayor sucked in his breath, annoyed, then as groups of young men converged on the signs, laughing and tugging at the cords and hessian, he cut short his speech and got to the important part, rattling off the rest at top speed.

'The name we have chosen will, I'm sure, meet with

483

everyone's approval, so it is with great pleasure that I call
upon Lord Darrington to tell us the name and give the
signal for the unveiling.'

Simon stepped forward, accepted a pair of silver
scissors and ceremonially cut the ribbons that led from the
platform to each corner of the square. 'I name this square,'
he paused and inclined his head towards Frederick,
'Hallam Square.' The rest of his words were lost in a great
roar of approval from the crowd.

The men whipped away the sacking and people surged
towards each corner, trying to read the name for
themselves. Gilt lettering against dark green. There it was
for all to see: HALLAM SQUARE.

'The cunning devils!' Tom said softly.

'Hurrah!' yelled all the Gibson and Hallam children.

'Eh, that's champion, that is,' said John, squeezing
Kathy's hand.

Annie turned to Frederick, tears of joy in her eyes, and
saw that he was too moved to speak for a moment or two.
He fumbled for a handkerchief and she pressed her own
into his hand. 'Oh, love, I'm so proud of you, so very
proud.'

For a moment, Rebecca was by herself at the edge of
the platform, watching the sunlight dance on a cheering
crowd, smiling as the band played a fanfare that was
mostly lost in the great buzz of noise. How wonderful it all
was! she thought. How much Frederick deserved this
honour! Her eyes went inevitably towards Simon, who was
smiling across at her. Not long to wait now.

After blowing his nose, trying to speak and failing,
Frederick at last managed to control his feelings. 'I didn't
expect this,' he said huskily to Annie.

'You deserve it, love.'

For a moment, they stared into one another's eyes, their
hands clasped, and no one interrupted them.

Then Mr Wilkins cleared his throat and Annie realised
that he was waiting for Frederick to stand up and make

a speech. She let go of her husband's hand and watched proudly as he walked to the edge of the platform and stood there, tall and distinguished, his silver hair shining in the sun, happiness absolutely radiating from him.

'I can think of nothing which could have pleased me more,' he said, when at last the crowd had shushed itself into silence. 'Bilsden is my home. I'm proud to have been born here, to have grown up here and to have contributed to the development of one of the finest towns in all Lancashire. It isn't the mills which have made Bilsden, you know.' He paused to dab unashamedly at his eyes.

'What is it, then?' yelled the wit from the back of the crowd.

'It's the people,' he said simply. 'All of us.' He gestured with his arms, as if embracing them.

They cheered him, then, long and loud, after which there was a clattering sound from behind The Prince of Wales and a group of young men appeared, dragging the unharnessed Hallam carriage themselves. At their insistence, Frederick left the platform and got into it, holding out his hand for Annie to join him, then the young men dragged it off towards Hallam Park, where a couple of oxen were being roasted and where picnic areas and sideshows had been set up.

'This is,' Frederick confessed as he and Annie endured a very jerky ride with their inexperienced steeds, 'the second happiest day of my life.'

'Second happiest?' she queried, green eyes glinting at him in the sunlight.

'Yes. The happiest was the day you married me.'

More tears gathered in her eyes. 'I love you, Frederick Hallam.'

He gave her a hug, then the laughing young men pulled him from the carriage and chaired him up in their linked hands to the dignitaries' table near the bandstand. Annie followed on the arm of the Superintendent of Parks, her heart overflowing with joy. It was, she thought, the very best day of her life.

'Hallam Square,' she repeated softly to herself, mouthing the words with immense satisfaction.

ANNA JACOBS

RIDGE HILL

It's 1848 and preparations are underway for Annie Gibson's wedding to Bilsden's wealthy mill owner, Frederick Hallam. But not everyone is as pleased as they are.

Frederick's daughter, Beatrice, is horrified at the prospect of a new attractive stepmother arriving at the house on Ridge Hill. Even Annie's own family feels threatened. The only person who seems pleased is Tom, Annie's brother.

Soon, however, real troubles begin to pile up for the Gibsons. Tom's happiness is jeopardised by the news that he is a father to a child he never knew about. Annie's son, William, is devastated to find out that his real father is not the man who brought him up. And even Annie's joy cannot last. Because someone has uncovered the secrets she has fought so hard to keep hidden.

HODDER AND STOUGHTON PAPERBACKS